Soul of Solace

Soul of Solace

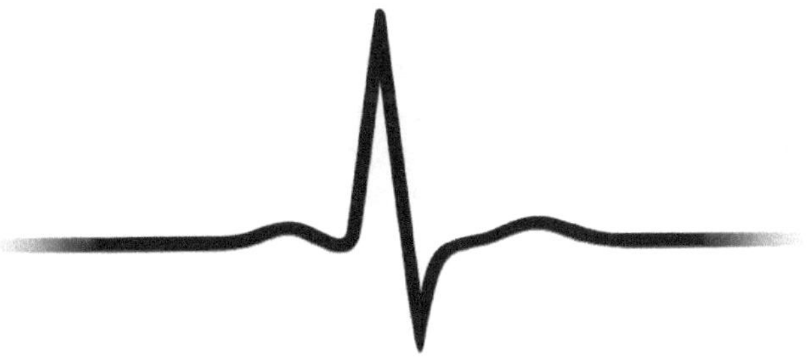

Alden Drake

ISBN: 979-8-9903841-0-1 (eBook)
ISBN: 979-8-9903841-1-8 (paperback)

The story, all names, characters, and incidents portrayed in this production are fictitious. No identification with actual persons (living or deceased), places, buildings, and products is intended or should be inferred.

Book Cover and Illustrations by Alden Drake
Edited by Barbara Magic

First paperback edition 2025

www.aldendrake-author.com

Table of Contents

Content Warnings

◊ Graphic Depictions of Violence
◊ Sexual Themes
◊ Discussion of Sexual Violence
◊ Sexual Abuse
◊ Voluntary Sex Work
◊ Gore
◊ Torture
◊ Murder
◊ Slavery and Imprisonment
◊ Domestic Abuse
◊ Child Abuse
◊ Psychological Torture/Abuse
◊ Traumagenic Mental Health Issues
◊ Vampirism

Chapter 1

Athaeÿn

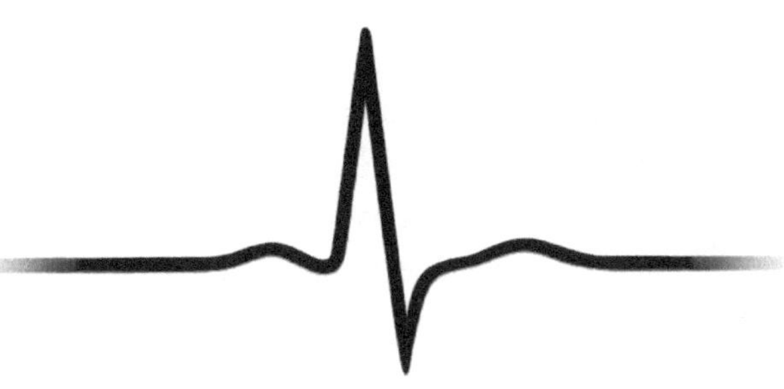

Three hundred years.

Every single one, grotesquely bloated to a painful five hundred days, each of which had the audacity to last a grueling thirty hours. Ten days a week. Five weeks a month. Ten months a year. It was absolutely insufferable and, worse, seemingly infinite.

Three hundred revolutions around the sun, a distant star whose warmth could be enjoyed by most but whose light had become deadly for me. As a Dark Elf with an innate aversion to sunlight, this wasn't much of a loss, but it hardly mattered in the end.

As long as I remained arcanely tethered to my Arch-Vampire master and his hidden fortress, there was no traveling I needed to worry about. Safely tucked away in the hollowed-out base of Mount Umbra, the highest peak of the Shadowback Mountains, the aptly named Castle Veil served as a perfectly shrouded prison for me and many others. Far too many.

No sunlight could enter, and no vassal could exit, at least not without explicit consent from Roänach, who ruled the stronghold with both iron fist and insatiable hunger. Without his cursed blessing, there was no bypassing the two containment runes on either side of the cave mouth, let alone the exterior group encircling the mountain as a failsafe. While these particular runes were unique to Arch-Vampires, the general concept was not. It was everyday practice for the common variety to be used in normal prisons and holding facilities, but unlike those occupants, vassals didn't require additional markings. The bite scars on our necks served as shackles in more ways than one.

There were many free Vampires out in the world who used to be vassals. I dreamed of becoming one of them someday.

I miss Eidolon…

The capital was one of few havens where Undead were openly welcome and able to exist as normal members of society, which I had appreciated since many of my closest friends were Vampires. I was still alive when I first moved to the city, so that welcoming attitude wasn't something I personally needed at the time. That was no longer the case.

Shame I'll never get to experience it myself.

My life wasn't perfect before I met Roänach, but it had been pretty damn close. Like many others, I'd had an active social life, a career I thoroughly enjoyed, and numerous aspirations I hoped to achieve in the future. The only thing missing was a fulfilling relationship, something I thought I had finally found with him.

Unfortunately, Eidolon was just his favorite hunting ground. The phrase *preyed upon* was the understatement of the millennium, and allowing myself to fall for him was the biggest mistake of my life. It was my only regret in moving to the city. I never would have met him if I stayed in my homeland, but I never would have found my near-perfect life either.

Near-perfect until he came along and ruined everything.

Which was my own fault. In hindsight, I knew I had been taken advantage of in multiple ways, but, even after three hundred years, I still blamed myself for being so trusting and naive. It was hard not to.

And now, I get to suffer the consequences for all eternity.

This was something Roänach found far more than just pleasing.

At least he's not here right now.

I slowly opened my eyes from where I sat on the windowsill of my room, having closed them at some point without even realizing after getting lost in thought. Normally, I would have been socializing and celebrating Roänach's absence with the other vassals until his inevitable return, but I just wasn't in the mood.

There was fresh desire in my heart to be fully numb to the circumstances, but that was a tall order while suffering emotional whiplash from Roänach's occasional trips to the capital. Every time these brief spans of peace gave us a chance to be ourselves again, they were ripped away when he came back, and he *always* came back. It was a wound that never got to heal.

I wonder if he'll show up with someone new again.

With a heavy sigh, I glanced at my dresser and eyed one of the few items scattered across the top. Specifically, a small painting in a simple yet elegant frame. A portrait of myself. It was like looking in a mirror, which was helpful in not forgetting my face since I could no longer see my reflection.

She definitely outdid herself.

I took in the details of my captured face staring back at me. Upturned eyes with red sclerae so dark they were nearly black, highlighted with softly glowing fuchsia irises split by white, feline pupils. Mid-toned gray skin tinged by the faintest hint of violet, made to look even darker by silvery white hair often likened to moonlight by my mother. Clean-shaven face defined by delicate Elven features, kept clear of silken locks by an elegant top knot while the rest cascaded over somewhat broad yet slender shoulders. Finally, pierced and sharply pointed ears tinted magenta toward the tips. I had the real ones trained on the closed bedroom door.

Even though Roänach had been gone for weeks, I couldn't help but anxiously listen to every footstep out in the hall as if expecting one to be his. It was an irrational fear at the moment but a tough habit to break, nonetheless.

He'll probably come back any day now.

Athaeïjn

Still leaning back on the open window frame, I lolled my head in the opposite direction just far enough to gaze out into the massive cavern I begrudgingly called home. I almost expected to see Roänach's opulent, black coach rolling through the cave mouth. Luckily, it wasn't.

Yet.

Despite my bedroom window being one of the highest in the anterior wall of the fortress, I had a clear but limited view of the ground just outside the cave mouth. One of the patrolling Demons briefly passed by the opening, but I was too far away to discern which one it was. At the very least, I was pretty sure I saw antlers.

One of the Fauna Demons, then.

Regardless, they were just one of many Demons forcibly enthralled with undying loyalty to Roänach. Whatever their original personalities may have been, our shared master's mind control had turned them all into huge jackasses. Fortunately, their rude behavior was limited to verbal assault. Only Roänach was allowed to touch his vassals.

Which is already too much.

I generally tried to avoid the Demons, but it wasn't personal. They were prisoners just like the rest of us. In fact, a few had been there longer than any vassal. Even when they insulted me right to my face, I couldn't hate them, not when I knew it wasn't the real them speaking. I could only imagine what they wanted to say.

Probably their names.

Unfortunately, Roänach forbade it.

As if he could be bothered to remember them all in addition to his vassals.

Other than the patrols, the easiest to avoid were the Mirage Demons due to their limited spheres of operation. Most could be found just inside the cave mouth working to hide it with their magic. Nothing blocked the view from inside, but from the outside, passersby would see nothing but an uninterrupted wall of stone. Only other Mirage Demons would be able to see through the illusion.

I wish that was my job instead.

After a minute or so of watching the two Mirage Demons on active duty, my gaze drifted to the expansive garden of bioluminescent flora that surrounded the fortress. Despite such a miserable existence, I found the glowing sprawl genuinely beautiful and often spent hours quietly lounging among the soothing foliage. It was one of the few nice things about living there.

Luckily, the Flora Demons leave me alone.

As I glanced at one of my favorite spots in the garden, my eyes caught movement heading away from the fortress. The lone figure silently passed through the flora and continued on until they reached the innermost point of the cave mouth, where they were forced to stop by the primary containment runes. I recognized their silhouette immediately.

She must be missing the sun again.

Wanting to check on her, I slipped off the windowsill and began making my way through the corridors. It was nice to see the other vassals wandering the castle instead of hiding in their rooms, and it was equally heartening to receive a smile from each passerby. Even the faintest whispers of joy were incredibly rare when Roänach was around, so I made sure to treasure every second he was gone.

Serenity lingered as I left the castle and made my way through the gardens, lightly ghosting my fingers over the foliage as I went, but my brief sense of ease quickly faded when I approached the lone figure still standing at the barrier. It was Roänach's newest vassal, another stolen from Eidolon. She was barely eighteen and had only been at Castle Veil for a few months.

The inability to walk in sunlight was mere inconvenience for me, but it was downright cruel for the Light Elf I stopped next to. The sight of her tearstained profile and trembling hand pressed against the invisible barrier was unbearable. If my hair was moonlight, her shimmering locks and glowing irises were sunlight, brilliant and golden against ivory skin with the iridescence of a freshly polished pearl. It hurt my heart to see her luminous features darkened with such misery.

A Light Elf no longer able to feel the sun on her skin. I can't even imagine...

"Are you alright, Fiella?" I asked softly.

She gasped and turned to face me. "Oh, Athaeÿn!" Her hands were still shaking as she frantically wiped her eyes. "I-I'm sorry, I didn't even notice you standing there. I'll be fine. I promise. Just— I just need a bit more time to come to terms with everything."

I gave her a moment to collect herself. "My offer still stands. Are you sure it wouldn't help you feel a bit more secure? It would only be until Roänach comes back."

"I appreciate the thought, truly, b-but I don't know you well enough to share a room. It-It's not that I don't trust you, I just— Maybe next time he goes away. I-I mean—" Her voice crumbled as she looked down and held herself. "Please don't take it personally."

"Don't worry, I never have."

She just sniffled and nodded a little.

I watched her for a few seconds. "You know, even after all this time, the castle is still unnerving for veteran vassals like me. I would understand if you never changed your mind, but my offer will always remain." I offered a supporting smile. "Having just one friend in a place like this can make all the difference in the world."

She forced a weak smile in return. "I know, and I do consider you a friend. My only one here so far, actually." Her gaze found mine again. "M-Maybe the actual reason I'm afraid to accept your offer is Roänach. Wouldn't he get mad?"

"You probably haven't noticed since you've mostly been holed up in your room, but he doesn't mind us spending time together. However, his mood can be unpredictable, which is why my offer is primarily for when he's away."

There's another reason, but she doesn't need to know that.

"We're allowed to socialize as long as we come when summoned," I added, glaring over my shoulder at the castle.

Fiella immediately teared up again and choked out a small sob. "I don't want to be his slave. I just want to go home!"

An overly familiar burning sensation came to my eyes when she started to cry. I knew exactly what she was going through.

"I miss my house. I miss my cats. I miss my boyfriend, my parents, my friends… everything…" She wrung her hands against her chest and hung her head in anguish. "Why did he have to choose me out of everyone in the whole city? Why did it have to be *me?!*" she wailed as her legs gave out, leaving her sobbing uncontrollably on her knees.

Her sudden breakdown caught me off guard and left me standing there a bit dumbly, but the sight of her bawling on the ground was too much.

This probably isn't going to go well.

After hesitating a moment, I knelt in front of her and warily eyed her hands as they trembled against her chest. Her whole body was jerking from sharp hiccups and gasping sobs. I desperately wanted to console her, but when I attempted to reach for her hands, I couldn't move.

I knew it…

Courtesy of my vile master, I had developed a severe aversion to touch over the past few centuries. Oddly enough, despite Roänach having been the one to induce this anxiety, I could actually handle him with relative ease. Maybe I was just numb to him by this point. Or maybe I dissociated with him and unintentionally kept my issues for everyone else. Either way, it was beyond infuriating. Physicality had been an integral part of my life in Eidolon, and its loss was devastating.

Not lost. Taken.

For me, the inability to enjoy physical contact was infinitely worse than the inability to walk in sunlight. I had never cared for the sun, but touch had been everything. This theft hadn't been sudden either, which was actually worse. Losing one of the most precious things in my life had been a slow, painful degradation, and I was unable to stop it. I had been forced to watch myself become a hollow shell of what I once was. An abrupt severance still would have been agonizing, but at least it would have been quick.

Fuck you, Roänach.

My touch anxiety was endless misery, but my current frustration was the simple inability to hold my friend's hands when she was upset. I wasn't about to let my desire to comfort her be stifled.

Come on.

Much to my aggravation, I still couldn't move.

You're fine.

She's obviously not going to hurt you.

Just do it.

With a shaky exhale, I steeled myself and managed to take weak hold of her hands. I knew I was playing with fire, especially since I didn't want to compound her breakdown with one of my own, but I forced myself through the anxiety anyway. Fortunately, nothing happened.

This time...

When her eyes finally cracked open, they shot wide the moment she realized what she was holding. "Oh no— I-I'm so sorry, Athaeÿn! Pl-Please, you don't have to—"

"Fiella."

Her mouth was still slightly open as she stared at me through her tears.

I offered a warm smile despite my hands trembling around hers. "It's alright."

"B-But, what about—"

"Remember how you promised you would be fine? I promise I'll be fine."

Her brows furrowed. "Are you sure?"

I nodded with an unwavering smile.

Her visible concern lingered for a few moments before a weak smile returned to her lips. "Th-Thank you, but you really don't have to do this. I remember what you told me," she muttered, glancing at our clasped hands. Hers had stopped shaking, but she made no move to pull away.

"I know, but I'm more than happy to suck it up now and then if it means easing your distress even a little bit. I only wish I could do more."

All of a sudden, our momentary peace was shattered by a familiar sound outside the cave.

I hung my head and sighed heavily.

Oh, great…

Fiella shuddered violently and leaned closer to me as if trying to hide. Her hands were shaking again. "N-No—"

Did it have to be now of all times?

Huffing angrily, I turned to see Roänach's aforementioned opulent black coach rolling into the cave. As usual, it was led by two pristinely groomed draft horses, whose shimmering coats matched the dark hue of the vehicle they pulled. Driving the horses from his exterior front seat was the Demon who served as designated coachman. He showed general disdain for us vassals like all the others but loved the horses as if they were his own children. Considering the fact he was a Fauna Demon, this wasn't surprising.

There had been a pit in my stomach all day, as if it knew Roänach would finally be coming back. I had wondered as much myself, but now that he was here, I felt downright nauseous.

Only numb to him in certain ways

Knowing the source of my touch-aversion was in that coach, I actually felt the issue fade a bit despite still making contact with Fiella. Unfortunately, this reprieve wouldn't last. Roänach was insatiable.

Better me than Fiella.

As the coach stopped uncomfortably close to us, the coachman slid off his seat and opened the side door to reveal the detestable Arch-Vampire himself casually lounging inside. I hadn't missed the oversized flap of

auburn hair, annoying soul patch, obnoxious chin-adjacent beard, and stupid forehead marked with black fangs denoting his superior status, symbols all Arch-Vampires acquired upon turning. His entire pasty face was repugnant, but the smug grin was easily the worst part.

Sprawled across his lap was an unfamiliar young woman, whose skin was equally fair yet visibly warm compared to his. The more striking contrast was icy blue eyes framed by long black hair draped over her front in thick, wavy locks, the ashen undertones of which reflected the dim light inside the coach. She was also a Human, which was unusual.

Although Roänach himself was Human, he tended to go after non-Human races for whatever reason, at least regarding new vassals. It was the opposite with his personal blood captives. I had my cynical suspicions as to why, but I didn't really care. In the end, his selfishness damned everyone he brought back, something this woman would find out soon enough.

I really wish she would stop smiling.

The ignorant bliss on her face as Roänach slowly caressed her arm was like looking in a mirror. It was infuriating. Having been in her position once, I knew any attempt to convince her to leave would be wasted effort. I had tried many times in the past, but no one ever listened.

Until it was too late…

When I looked at Roänach again, his gaze locked on mine. His creepy, pitch-black irises outlined by fiery rings and dotted with glowing red pupils were another sight I hadn't missed.

I hate his eyes so much.

With no known explanation, Vampirism made all Human eyes look like this. Unfortunately, this meant Roänach had the same eyes as my best friend back in Eidolon.

Callyn wears them so much better.

Roänach's smile never wavered as he stared at me. "Still attempting to console the new girl?"

The woman on his lap spoke first. "They're just jealous you picked me."

Yeah, that's definitely it.

I gave Fiella's hands a reassuring squeeze, ignoring the minor flare of anxiety accompanying it. "She's lamenting the sun, *actually.*"

Roänach rolled his eyes. "Why a Dark Elf would care evades me, but this pointless conversation is wasting precious time I could be spending elsewhere."

You're the one who started the conversation, asshole—

"There are far more important things to attend to," his leer finally drifted to the new woman, "and to *do.*"

She yawned widely. "Can we take a nap first, Rowy? I'm tired."

Her nickname for him made my nose scrunch up.

"Of course, my succulent sweetheart, and then we can pick up where we left off. You won't mind if I get impatient and—" he groped her breasts and flashed me a smirk "—start before you wake up, will you?"

Roänach
Lánelli

I glared at him as she confirmed and giggled in his grip. There were a few choice words I wanted to share, but I didn't want to make a scene in front of Fiella.

The already unnerving glow of Roänach's eyes turned threatening. "Don't worry, Athaeÿn," he lowered his voice, "I won't forget about you."

Even after so many years, those words still made me shudder.

He broke eye contact and knocked on the inside wall of the coach. "Alright, let's go," he looked down at the woman again, "and let's get you to bed, Lánelli."

As the coachman closed the door, Roänach glanced up just in time to show off his fangs in one final sleazy grin before he was obscured once more.

Just hurry up and leave already.

The coachman stuck his tongue out at us before hopping back onto his seat and driving the coach toward the castle. I was convinced all of Roänach's immaturity was channeled into the Demons through their enthrallment, and while that was annoying, I was just glad they couldn't touch us.

"Is he mad that you were comforting me?" Fiella asked once the coach was long out of earshot.

"No, just mocking."

I hoped she would be relieved she hadn't gotten her only friend here in trouble, so my heart sank when she said nothing and just stared at the ground.

She needs a distraction.

I smiled and gave her hands another light squeeze. "Well, since Lánelli will be keeping Roänach's mind off the rest of us for a while, would you like me to stay with you for a bit?"

Fiella managed a weak smile in return. "If you really don't mind." She then glanced at our joined hands and finally pulled hers free. "Thank you for keeping me grounded. I would love to hold your hands a little longer, but I won't ask for any more touching." Her smile brightened when she looked into my eyes again. "Sitting next to you will be plenty."

There was a frustrating but familiar mixture of disappointment and relief when she pulled away. I could have held her hands a bit longer, but severing contact was probably in my best interest, so I was grateful for her thoughtfulness. If sitting next to her would be enough, I was happy to do so.

With about six inches between us, we sat side by side and gazed out of the cave together. Even though I wasn't a fan of the sun, I had to admit the landscape was stunning when bathed in its brilliant light. It was a good distraction to keep my thoughts away from more harrowing things. Unfortunately, Roänach's return meant that would soon be impossible.

Chapter 2

Athaeÿn

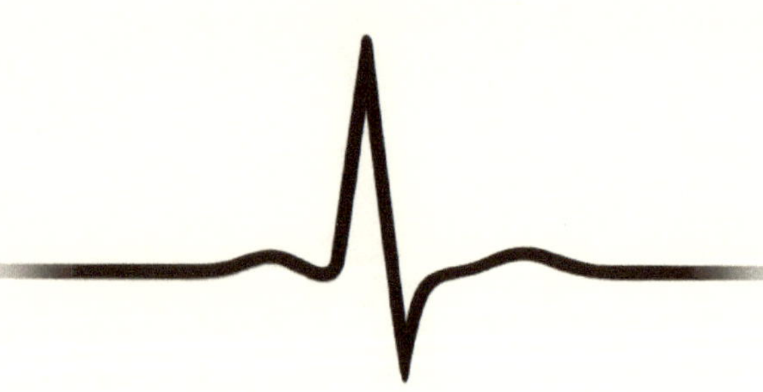

Fiella and I only remained near the cave mouth for about five minutes before relocating to the glowing gardens, where we made sure to sit in a secluded spot away from the Flora Demons. The light blue cloud moss was far more comfortable than stone.

My company and some limited conversation among the soothing bioluminescence seemed to ease her sorrow, but she slowly shut down over time. Having thought she would go completely silent, I was surprised when she spoke up again.

"Is there really nothing we can do about Roänach?" she asked quietly while slowly plucking the luminous petals from a white flower.

I shook my head as I watched her mournful activity. "Between the enthralled Demons' forced loyalty and the inability for vassals to harm their masters, I'm afraid he's basically untouchable. He would have to be killed beyond the runes or by a freshly summoned Demon he failed to enthrall. Or himself. Unfortunately, if anything was going to happen to him, it probably would have by now."

My genuine but regrettable answer was clearly a mistake as tears welled in her eyes. A few seconds later, her fingers started trembling against the remaining petals on the flower she still held.

Shit—

"But that doesn't mean his demise is impossible," I added quickly.

She closed her eyes and hung her head with a slight grimace. "It may as well be..."

Nice going, dumbass.

Guilt clawed my heart as I watched her trembling spread to her shoulders. My tendency for bluntness had gotten me in trouble countless times throughout my life, and I still struggled to regulate it. Even with good intentions, I often failed to remind myself that not everyone preferred brutal honesty like I did. I knew from experience sugarcoating things only led to more pain down the line, so I usually saw my direct approach as doing people a favor, even if they didn't see it that way in the moment.

You're clearly not doing her a favor right now.

My mind raced to turn this around somehow. "I'm sorry, Fiella, I'm letting my pessimism get the best of me. I don't think we'll be stuck here forever," I said with the most convincing tone I could manage. It may have been for both of us.

It took about a minute, but she finally lifted her head and looked at me through lingering tears.

I thought for a few more seconds. "Do you have any Vampire friends in Eidolon?"

She sniffled and nodded.

"So do I. You know what that means?"

She started to shake her head but paused. "We can be free like them someday?"

I offered a gentle smile. "That's right. Admittedly, it's rare for Arch-Vampires to free their vassals, but it does happen. My friend Callyn actually ended up in that situation when their master Vernyth let them all go. Vernyth wasn't the one who turned them, but that's beside the point." I caught myself before I could say Roänach would never free anyone.

She probably already thinks that.

And I didn't want to confirm it. "Regardless of whether or not Roänach does the same, we *will* be free someday, one way or another. Every Vampire ends up free eventually, and we're no exception." Making such a strong claim formed a pit in my stomach. Hopefully, my wishful thinking would be proven right with time.

Fiella still looked a bit skeptical but finally cracked a tiny smile. "Really?"

"Really."

It certainly didn't feel that way after three hundred years, but I kept that to myself.

Her smile brightened a little as she looked down at the flower in her hands. It had very few petals left, but instead of finishing the job, she plucked another flower and started doing something with both of them. "Can you tell me about your homeland? I've always wanted to see the Obsidian Spine."

I was more than happy to change the subject. "It's the most jagged mountain range on the continent, but that's the only noteworthy thing above ground. The interesting part is underneath, where my people live." I paused to look around the garden. "The tunnel system we live in extends for the entire mountain range, and there's actually quite a bit of glowing flora just like this," I added, lightly touching a flower next to me. "There's also endless luminous crystals of every color, size, and shape imaginable lining the walls and ceilings. Between those and the plants, we don't need to worry about firelight."

Fiella plucked another flower and continued whatever she was doing. "I would love to see the crystals."

"They're definitely beautiful. I'll take you to see them someday." I paused again to watch her expression and was heartened to see her eyes crinkle at the corners from her big smile. "As much as I loved my homeland, my family, and my people, it did become a bit monotonous over time. Everyone and everything look the same after a while in a place that secluded."

"Is that why you moved to Eidolon?"

"The main reason. I love socializing, and what better place to do that than the capital? The diversity alone was more than enough to draw me there, and I hope my people have worked on that in my absence. It would be nice to visit home and see more than just Dark Elf faces for once." I couldn't help but laugh softly. "What about you? What brought you to Eidolon?"

Fiella held up her finger for a second as she inspected her progress. She then resumed making what looked like a long string of flowers woven together. "I was going to attend The Sovereign Institute, but I never got the chance to start classes…" Her joy faltered for a few seconds, but she shook her head and smiled brightly again. "I'll just have to start when I get back."

I was relieved to see her recover on her own this time.

Maybe my encouragement is starting to stick.

Forcing optimism didn't make me feel any better about our circumstances, but if it inspired sincere hope for her, I could push through the discomfort. Just because it was too late for my spirit didn't mean it was for hers.

"Once you take me to see the crystals, I'll thank you by introducing you to my cats."

I chuckled again. "How many do you have?"

"Five, and I'm sure my boyfriend Joryn is taking good care of them."

"What are their names?"

"Beans, Cloud, Fluffy, Loaf, and Her Majesty the Queen."

I fully snorted a laugh this time. "Is Fluffy… *fluffy?*"

"He's a puffball with whiskers. A cuddly poof."

"I look forward to meeting them."

"And I know they'll love you." By the time Fiella finished her craft, she was smiling from pointed ear to pointed ear. She moved to put the ring of flowers on my head but hesitated at the last second. "Oh, you should probably put it on yourself so I don't touch you."

"I appreciate you remembering, but you can do it."

"Are you sure?"

"Positive."

Her brows furrowed with intense concentration as she reached over and carefully set the glowing flower crown on my head. She had put in noticeable effort to make sure her hands didn't touch my hair or skin.

I nearly shuddered the moment it made contact but kept it together for her sake. Thankfully, there was a big difference between flowers and fingers.

Once she was satisfied, she pulled back and clasped her hands together with a beaming smile.

I raised my brows a few times. "How do I look?"

"Absolutely beautiful. Consider it thanks for cheering me up."

"Any time."

She looked like she was about to pick some more flowers but paused and clutched her abdomen when there was an audible stomach growl. Her smile had vanished. "Oh no…"

My smile faded as well. "You were vegetarian before being turned, right?"

She nodded sullenly and looked across the garden. "I've tried eating some of the glowfruit, but they never stay down and always taste terrible. They're not supposed to taste terrible." Her gaze fell to the moss between us. "I hate that blood is all I can have now… and that it tastes good…"

"It's not your fault, Fiella. It tastes good to all of us, whether we want it to or not." I tried to think of how to spin it in a more positive light. "Listen, as long as Roänach has Fauna Demons, he'll use them to easily hunt fodder for his personal blood captives. He likes to make sure they're healthy and well-fed so his own meals are nice and rich. At least when the rest of us get the leftover animal blood, it's not going to waste."

She didn't look up. "I… I guess I'd rather drink animal blood than people blood."

I nodded before remembering something else. "You know, I've seen the Fauna Demons with the game they bring back. They may be jerks to us, but they're completely different with the animals. They put them down painlessly and are really good at it."

Fiella nodded a little as well. "The vet I take my cats to is a Fauna Demon. I watched her put down Missy, Joryn's old cat. She touched Missy's forehead and used her magic to make her sleep, then she drew Missy's soul into her claw and let it go… wherever cat souls go…" She finally looked at me again. "Do Roänach's Demons do it like that too?"

"From what I've seen, so they never suffer."

She wiped her eyes and let out a shaky breath. "I suppose that's the most I could ask for."

"It could definitely be worse."

As we slowly stood, Fiella sniffled a little and smoothed out her outfit. "I'm sorry for crying so much."

"Hey, getting it all out is much better than keeping it bottled up. I've seen people explode into a million pieces from doing that."

She smiled and looked up at me. "You really do look nice with the flower crown."

"An incredibly talented friend of mine made it for me." I grinned when her smile turned bashful. "Come on, let's get our meal over with. I'll tell you more stories afterward."

As we headed back to the fortress, I kept an eye on Fiella's expression and was saddened to see it slowly fall again, but she didn't seem overly miserable. If anything, she just looked tired, then nauseous the closer we got to the animal blood taproom.

We'll make it quick.

It was a shame Roänach's combination of paranoia and superiority kept him away from the taproom. It would have been so easy to poison the kegs with Demon blood, which was particularly lethal to Vampires, but there was no point. Roänach only drew from his personal captives. Biting was his preference anyway, but even when he used a wine glass, he would fill it directly from one of his captives and never let it out of his sight.

Even though he kept his study and bedroom locked and guarded by Demons when not in use, he didn't risk storing blood in either. We couldn't even tamper with the captives themselves due to the repellant runes around their living quarters in the dungeon. It wasn't like we wanted to since they were enthralled prisoners like the Demons, but desperate times called for desperate measures. Unfortunately, Roänach seemed to have thought of everything.

Everything is a dead end...

"Does it ever get easier?" Fiella asked as we arrived at the taproom.

"What, drinking blood?"

Please don't be asking about overall life at Castle Veil.

She rubbed her arm a little. "Yeah, but mainly not feeling bad about it."

Phew...

I retrieved two small glasses and started filling them at one of the large kegs along the wall. "I may not be the best person to ask since I wasn't vegetarian like you, but it wasn't my favorite adjustment to make either. It became much easier once I reassured myself I had no choice, er, rather that it wasn't my fault." I handed one of the half-filled glasses to her. "The fact we don't have to kill the animals ourselves makes a big difference."

Fiella barely nodded as she clutched her glass with both hands and stared at it miserably.

"Just pretend it's red wine."

"I never liked wine..."

"Alright, cranberry juice."

The corner of her mouth twitched, but she froze when a familiar, chilling voice echoed down the hallway.

Ugh, what now?

After signaling for Fiella to stay put, I crept to the side of the open doorway to listen. There were actually two voices approaching, the other of which I recognized as Roänach's lone Gravity Demon.

"I'm sorry, master. We tried everything, but his health continued to decline while you were gone."

Roänach sighed heavily. "It's fine. I've been meaning to add a fresh, young captive to my collection anyway."

"Like that woman you just brought back?"

"Ohhh no, no, no. Lánelli is prime vassal material. In fact, she can't wait to be turned."

"That eager, huh? Do you like her enough to share your captives?"

"Don't be ridiculous. You know I don't share them with anyone, not even my favorites."

"True, though I'm still surprised you never offered to Athaeÿn."

"There are more than enough kegs to go around. Besides, he prefers a different tap."

It took all of my self-control not to groan with disgust.

There was a pause before Roänach spoke again. "Are you sure he's on death's door?"

"I am, not that he even notices."

"Well then, since he's on the edge of oblivion, I think I'll give him a little *push.*"

I kept perfectly still in my hidden spot, listening to their callous laughter as they passed by.

Damn, I was hoping it would be at least a year before Fiella had to witness a summoning.

When Roänach and the Gravity Demon went their separate ways, I knew it was so the latter could spread the word. Of the Demons who cared for the blood captives, this one had exclusive permission to speak to us, but only for this purpose.

This day just gets better and bett—

"What were they talking about?"

Fiella's unexpected voice startled me a little. *"Jeez—"* I had nearly dropped my glass. "It sounds like one of Roänach's blood captives is sick, but this is the first I'm hearing about it."

"What happens if they can't save him?"

"Well…" I didn't want her to get upset, but trying to avoid this was pointless. "Roänach will put him out of his misery."

There were a few seconds of deafening silence. "He won't do it like the Fauna Demons, will he?"

I shook my head without looking at her. "It's far worse than that."

"What does he do?"

Another pit formed in my stomach as I anxiously tapped the glass in my hand. "He likes to kill two birds with one stone. When blood captives are discarded, he gets new Demons…"

Fiella gasped and covered her mouth with one hand. "I-I don't want to watch that."

"Attendance is mandatory for vassals. This doesn't happen often, so Roänach likes to make a show of what he considers a special event." My throat tightened when she clenched her eyes shut and shook her head vigorously. "I'm sorry, Fiella. We have no choice."

"C-Can't I just hide in my room?"

"He would notice your absence." I set my glass on the counter nearby, having never taken a sip. "Leave the blood. It'll still be good when you get back."

We didn't have to worry about the usual coagulation thanks to special enchantments on the kegs and glasses, but the manipulation magic used by Inverse Demons to negate blood clotting could also reverse the effects of enthrallment. Needless to say, there were no Inverse Demons at Castle Veil.

With few exceptions, Arch-Vampires could enthrall anything that possessed a soul. Arbiters, Arch-Demons, and dragons had true immunity due to the sheer power of their souls, but Inverse Demons had honorary immunity thanks to their magic's innate mastery of alteration and reversal.

Everything in here was probably stolen.

There was a soft clink when Fiella set her glass next to mine. "A-Alright, I'm ready."

I tried to make eye contact, but her gaze was fixed on the ground. "I won't lie, this isn't going to be pleasant," I forced a reassuring smile, "but I'll be right there with you."

When she finally looked at me again, it became evident my smile was either unconvincing or unhelpful. Or both. Sadly, I doubted anything better would have made a difference.

Let's get this over with…

With heavy reluctance, I led the way to the dungeon as slowly as possible. The lone access point to the blood captives' living quarters was a long staircase, the bottom of which had no doors and opened into a small courtyard of sorts. Despite the containment area having a gaping exit, the only barrier was the invisible one keeping vassals out. The captives' enthrallment was more than enough to prevent them from leaving.

Looks like everyone else is already here.

The stairs were lined with the rest of the vassals, all of whom appeared tense as they silently observed the display before them. The healthy captives' vacant eyes and hollow smiles were incredibly unnerving as they mindlessly wandered around their open enclosure, and I prayed their enthrallment clouded their awareness enough to induce blissful ignorance. The depressing sight alone was ample reason to stay away.

I have enough nightmares as it is.

Fiella was using me as a shield to block out the distressing scene, but she huddled between me and the wall when a final set of footsteps approached from behind. Her reaction alone told me who it was.

"You don't want a front row seat?"

I turned to Roänach from where Fiella and I stood at the very top of the staircase. "The acoustics are better back here."

His malevolent gaze briefly landed on the back of Fiella's head before shifting to the flower crown still atop mine, but he kept any comments about either to himself. Instead, he looked at the enclosure. "I'll have to take your word for it."

"I'm surprised you didn't bring Lánelli."

"It was a long and rather… *rough* coach ride. She's still in the midst of her recovery nap."

"You subjected the poor coachman to all that noise?"

"A bit hypocritical, darling. Besides, he was far too busy admiring his horses' polished asses."

I rolled my eyes and folded my arms. "Have you at least let her sleep unmolested?"

"For now, but I plan on doing some subtle exploring after the summoning." He showed off his fangs in a slimy grin before continuing down the stairs.

At least he left her alone.

Once Roänach was out of earshot, Fiella piped up next to me. "How do you get away with talking to him like that?"

"It's been our dynamic for a long time. He seems to enjoy the banter, and I get to openly express disapproval of his behavior. Within reason, of course."

There was more to it, but she didn't need to know that.

I added a shrug. "A perk of being his favorite, I guess."

"Why are you his favorite?"

"I'm not entirely sure."

That was a lie.

Fiella said nothing for a moment. "Does he ever use his blood captives for… *other* things?"

"No, that's what w— er, his vassals are for."

Immaculate and pointless save.

I cleared my throat awkwardly. "To quote our *beloved* master directly, he prefers his food 'fresh and unfucked.' The captives aren't even allowed to touch each other."

They barely know what's going on anyway.

Before Fiella could say anything else, Roänach snapped his fingers from within the open enclosure. After dispersing to the edges of the room, the blood captives were still smiling and swaying back and forth as they watched a beautiful Light Elf in nurse attire bring out a sickly, old Human in a wheelchair. The caretaker's appearance was convincing, but I knew it was a facade.

It was then the Gravity Demon arrived and stopped next to us. "There you are. I've been looking everywhere for you two."

A side glance in their direction was my only acknowledgement.

They just hissed with disapproval and started down the stairs, shaking their head and muttering under their breath as they went. "It's easier to find you cretins when you hide in your rooms…"

I remained silent.

When the Gravity Demon entered the enclosure, they stopped next to Roänach and pointed at a rectangular outline cut into the center of the stone floor. With an upward gesture of their claw, the outline revealed itself to be the edges of a bloodstained slab that slowly rose and stopped about two and a half feet over its nearly vacant recess. It was the perfect height for Roänach to lean over without having to bend down.

As the nurse effortlessly transferred the old man to the hovering slab as if simply moving a pillow from one bed to another, Fiella inhaled shakily and clung to my right arm.

Sh-Shit—

I shuddered even though I realized she was, fortunately, just gripping my loose-fitting sleeve and not my arm itself. The combination of dread and anxiety was making me nauseous, but I held my tongue. Fiella needed to hold something more than I needed her to let go.

It's not forever.

With the old man now lying inert on the slab, the nurse retrieved a flat wooden box that had been exposed in the floor's recess and set it next to the man's shoulder. She then moved to the side of the room and dropped her disguise. With a slight shimmering effect reminiscent of light waves over hot stone on a summer day, her illusion faded to reveal one of the Mirage Demons.

At first, I wasn't sure why she had bothered hiding her appearance, but then I wondered if they thought a sexy nurse might perk him up.

Shame that's not how healthcare works.

Meanwhile, Roänach approached and opened the box. "Let's see… Which type do I want to summon this time?"

The old man weakly lolled his head toward the familiar voice. He was smiling but could barely keep his eyes open. "Oh, hello there, master. How are you today?"

Roänach was too busy fluttering his fingers over the box's contents to return eye contact. "Just fine, and you?"

"The pretty nurse said I'm not doing too well, but I don't feel like I'm not doing too well."

"I'm afraid your blood doesn't taste very good anymore, darling."

"Oh no. I'm sorry, master. Is there anything I can do?"

"There is, as a matter of fact." He finally made a choice and pulled one of multiple sharpened Demon bones from the box. "Mind closing your eyes for me?"

"Of course, master. I promise I'll taste good again."

Roänach sighed and secured his hold on the bone. "If only…"

"Fiella, you might want to close your eyes," I whispered hurriedly. She nodded in my peripheral vision, but I didn't look to see if she actually took my advice.

With a sharp inhale, Roänach reeled back and plunged the bone into the old man's chest.

Unfortunately, it didn't kill him.

"Hmm, bit rusty." Instead of simply trying again, he adjusted his grip and started violently wrenching the bone back and forth, breaking his victim's fragile ribs and drawing horrible guttural noises from him.

I was unable to tear my gaze from the gruesome sight to check on Fiella, so I hoped her eyes were sealed shut. Unfortunately, the sickening sounds of gore loudly echoing up the stairwell were just as bad, and she whimpered and flinched with every audible jerk of Roänach's arm.

"Ugh, finally." When Roänach pulled back from his kill, the bloody Demon bone in his grip was glowing bright white with the soul it now contained. Treating the air in front of him like a canvas, he used the bone to draw a luminous circle, which filled in with a translucent pane and hovered perpendicularly to the ground. The moment he stabbed the glass-like surface with the bone, a second glowing circle appeared on the ground about five feet in front of him.

Not three seconds later, a nude Fauna Demon appeared over the second circle. The moment she was fully corporeal, both circles vanished, leaving her standing there completely bewildered.

"Where—" She gasped and froze. "Oh no. *No.* No, no, no, no, no—" She began shaking her head frantically. *"No!* I can't be summoned! I *can't!* Please! I have a newborn!" She was already hyperventilating as she desperately looked around the room. "Xixi! Please, my baby! My little Xixi! She needs me!"

Roänach calmly approached while her back was to him.

"Daemir! Daemir, please save me! Take me home! Bring me back to my baby! *Please—!"* Her scream was cut off the moment Roänach gripped her shoulder. After a few seconds, she calmly turned around and smiled at him. Her cheeks were still drenched with tears.

He grinned right back. "Welcome to Castle Veil."

Chapter 3

Athaeÿn

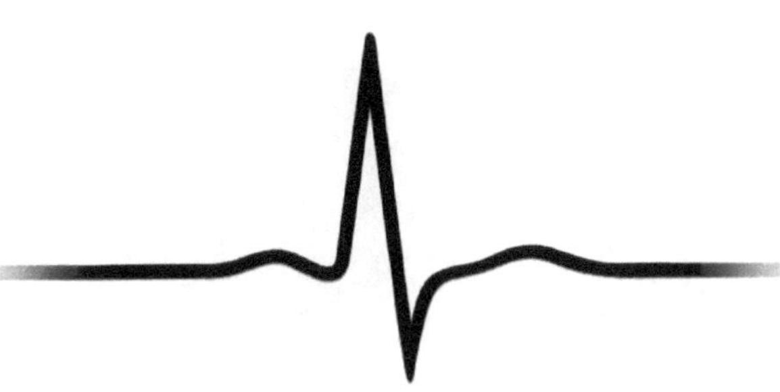

We never went back to the taproom.

No one had an appetite after that.

Fiella broke down again after the summoning, which I had a feeling would happen. Sadly, she was far from the first and wouldn't be the last.

We were both in her room after fleeing the dungeon together. I was still coming down from my own near-episode after letting her cling to me the whole way, so I sat on the far edge of her bed to give myself some space. She was crammed in the corner and curled up in the fetal position with her face buried in her pillow anyway.

It killed me to just sit there and watch her shoulders tremble, but there wasn't much else I could do. I was already pushing my own limit for the day.

At least I can keep an eye on her—

"Is everything alright in here?"

Although the voice behind me clearly didn't belong to Roänach, I couldn't help but flinch when I turned and saw similar eyes. In actuality, it was a young-looking woman with rich olive skin, two parallel scars on her nose and forehead, and sleek black hair pulled into a large bun at the nape of her neck. Haana, one of only two Human vassals at Castle Veil, though it would soon be three once Lánelli was turned.

"Better than earlier," I answered halfheartedly, returning my tired gaze to Fiella. I hated feeling so useless.

"Would you like some help?"

"Yes, please…"

Haana didn't hesitate to come in and sit on the edge of the bed next to Fiella. She had left me plenty of personal space. "Fiella, right? Do you want to talk about what happened?"

Fiella shook her head a little but otherwise didn't move.

"Do you need a hug?"

She sniffled but still didn't move.

Haana reached over and gently nudged her shoulder until she finally relented. Once Fiella let go of the pillow, Haana wrapped her arms around her and pulled her over. "Come here, sweetheart," she cooed softly as she set Fiella on her lap and swaddled her in a gentle embrace.

I smiled sadly as Fiella buried her face in Haana's neck. The inability to offer the same comfort hurt my heart, but I was just grateful Haana had showed up and was happy to do what my anxiety wouldn't allow.

No one said anything for a good ten minutes.

Eventually, Fiella broke the silence with a sniffle. "Will her baby be alright?"

Haana tilted her head down ever so slightly. "I'm sure she'll be just fine."

"How do you know?"

This time, Haana looked to me for help.

Fortunately, something readily came to mind. "Remember when you said your boyfriend was taking care of your cats? I'm sure Xixi has someone watching over her as well."

"What if she doesn't?"

"Then someone will find her. Fauna Demons have a natural talent for sensing distress, especially in the young of their own kind."

"What if no one finds her?"

"Fiella—"

"N-No, you're right. She'll be okay... I'm sorry..."

Haana and I shared a sad glance, but Fiella continued before we could say anything.

"Her mother should get to go home... I-It's not fair..."

I agreed it was unfair, but it was also too late. Daemir, the lone Demon god Xixi's mother had called out to, could neither hear her cries nor bring her home. The rest of the gods could listen, at the very least, but they couldn't send her home either. One particularly cruel member of the pantheon had made sure of that.

And had the audacity to find it funny...

Meanwhile, Fiella choked out a faint hiccup. "Will they ever see each other again?" Her faltering voice was accompanied by fresh tears. "Actually, don't answer that. I don't want to know…"

I couldn't stand seeing her so upset. Against my better judgment, I scooted closer to them and waved my hand dismissively when Haana's brows furrowed with concern. In her defense, the worry was merited. She had personally witnessed a few of my touch-induced breakdowns.

Please let me comfort her again.

Silently begging my mind and body to cooperate, I stopped about six inches from the two women and slowly reached for Fiella's arm that was wrapped around Haana's midsection. Unfortunately, taking multiple deep breaths didn't prevent my fingers from trembling before even making contact.

Come on—

Not to be deterred, I managed to place my entire palm on her arm but froze when my fingers settled.

Oh no—

Haana's eyes widened. "Athaeÿn—"

I shook my head and secured my grip even though my entire body was shaking. I wanted to console my friend. I wasn't going to let go until she felt better. "I-It's alright, Fiella."

Please—

My chest started heaving. "I promise e-everything will be fine."

Shit—

"I-I promise—"

I need to let go—

Frustration blurred my vision as I tried and failed.

I-I can't—

"Help— Help me—" I could barely get my voice above a whisper. "P-Please—"

Before my agitation could escalate further, Haana intervened and grabbed my wrist just long enough to pull my hand off Fiella's arm. I was grateful for her persistence despite my sharp gasp of terror.

Th-Thank you…

I could vaguely hear Fiella's voice somewhere in front of me, but it sounded far away and muffled as if underwater. My senses were completely shot. The only recognizable feeling was my hands trembling in my lap.

I knew this would be one touch too many.

If I were still alive, there was no question in my mind I would've had a heart attack. Even though no heartbeat meant no need for air, I still felt short of breath. Oftentimes, I only breathed when I needed to speak, but I could never control the panicked hyperventilating that accompanied these breakdowns.

I wish I would just faint instead—

All of a sudden, Fiella's voice became loud and clear. "Athaeÿn?"

I tore my gaze from my hands and felt a pang of guilt over the worried look on her face.

"Are you alright?"

The single tear coming down my cheek answered for me. Without meaning to, I glanced at my hands one more time and had to force myself to look at her again. "I'm so sorry, Fiella. I just wanted to help." My throat was so tight it hurt. "I really tried."

I felt like the biggest failure to ever walk the realm of Terraen. And the biggest liar. If this was what Castle Veil, what *Roänach* had done to me, how could I promise that everything, that *anything* would be fine? How could I say that right to her face after this pitiful display? I was "living" proof that claim was bullshit. *Undead* proof it was over when our lives ended.

What am I going to do?

Feeling utterly defeated, I closed my eyes and hung my head in shame.

There's nothing—

"I have an idea."

I looked up when Fiella spoke again.

She wiped the tears from her eyes and pointed at my head. "Hold out the flower crown."

Despite some confusion as to where this was going, I didn't hesitate to carefully remove the floral accessory and offer it draped on my upturned palm.

She managed a tiny smile and made a rotating gesture with her finger. "Turn it vertical like a coil of rope." Once I held it accordingly, she took gentle hold of the other side so the glowing ring acted like a chain link between our hands. "There, now we can still kind of touch."

After a brief moment of surprise, I returned a weary smile. "Thank you, Fiella."

Right as she was about to look genuinely happy, that awful voice ripped the chance away from her. *Again.*

"Athaeÿn."

Misery turned to rage as I watched the fragile relief vanish from her eyes.

What the fuck does he want now?

It took everything in me not to snarl as I glared over my shoulder at the newly reoccupied doorway. *"Yes?* Can I help you?"

Roänach was unmoved by my blatant aggravation. "If you're quite finished playing grief counsellor, your presence is required in my study."

"Why?"

"You'll just have to come find out."

"And what if I don't want to?" I swore I felt Fiella tense through our flower crown connection.

Roänach just tilted his head and leered at me with a half-lidded smirk. "It wasn't a suggestion." His gaze drifted to my hand. "And leave those asinine flowers, will you? I'm getting secondhand embarrassment."

My glare only intensified as he left without another word.

I swear—

"He's going to hurt you, isn't he?"

Fiella's meek voice pulled me from my anger.

"Th-This is all my fault."

I turned back to find her face twisted up with guilt. "Fiella—"

"If I wasn't such a crybaby—"

"Fiella."

There were already fresh tears in her eyes when she looked at me.

I shook my head and softened my voice. "He's not summoning me because of you. I've known him for over three hundred years, so please believe me when I say he doesn't punish us for comforting each other."

She still looked skeptical. "Th-Then, why…?"

My gaze fell to my lap.

As his favorite…

Fiella tracked my gaze and sniffled loudly. "N-No—"

"He's used to it, Fiella," Haana interjected.

Wait—

I was suddenly listening intently.

"You know why he's Roänach's favorite?"

No, don't tell her—

When Haana opened her mouth to continue, I gestured frantically to get her attention and shook my head the moment we made eye contact.

Fiella innocently turned back to me, having missed my panic while focused on Haana. "I thought you said you didn't know?"

"I said I wasn't entirely sure." I paused to glance at Haana, who averted her gaze awkwardly when Fiella looked as well. I just sighed and waved my hand dismissively. "Never mind. What matters is, now that I think about it, I doubt Roänach is summoning me for that."

Fiella turned back to me once more. She probably had whiplash by now.

"He does like to speak in euphemisms, but he happily brings up… *particular activities* whenever possible because he knows it makes us uncomfortable," I added, making another hand gesture. "I'm certain he would've alluded to such things if they were relevant."

Fiella sniffled again. "Oh… Then why didn't he just tell you why you were going?"

I forced a slight smile. "Because he's an obnoxious jackass." When she didn't respond, I leaned a bit closer and gently shook the flower crown as if shaking her hand. "I promise I'll be alright. Do you promise not to cry on Haana anymore while I'm gone?"

She finally cracked one of the smallest grins I had ever seen. "I'll try."

Her tiny smile drew a faint laugh through my nose as I let go of the flower crown. "Well, since I'm not allowed to bring this with me, why don't you give it to Haana? I'm sure it'll brighten her day, and you can make me a new one while I'm meeting with Roänach. Deal?"

Fiella pouted at first since she had made it for me, but she quickly recovered and smiled cheerfully when she put it on Haana instead. "It looks beautiful on you too."

Haana smiled and mimed fluffing her hair beneath it. "You really think so?"

"I do."

While Fiella was distracted, I gave Haana a knowing, wide-eyed look and pointed to myself before holding my finger to my lips. Once she gave a subtle nod, I nodded back and stood from the bed. "You two behave while I'm gone, alright?"

Fiella was still smiling brightly when she turned back to me. "Only if you let me show you how to make the flower crowns afterward."

"I would love that." When I reached the doorway, I paused and looked at them one more time. "I'll be back before you know it," I added before finally leaving, though my steps were slowed by guilt.

Sorry, Haana.

I hadn't meant to snap at her, albeit nonverbally, but I couldn't let her finish what she was saying. I didn't want Fiella to know yet. Not when she was still so new. Not after the abnormally miserable day she'd had. Not after promising that everything would be alright, that Roänach *could* free us someday.

He never will…

A fresh wave of dread washed over me as I slowly trudged down the dimly lit hallways. I hadn't exactly lied to Fiella, but I knew Roänach would put his hands on me regardless of why I was being summoned. I couldn't think of a time he *didn't* touch me when we were alone.

Which is partially my own fault.

Roänach was the only one at Castle Veil who had ever abused me, so I didn't understand why numbness to him then translated into visceral reactions to everyone else. Unconscious misplacement, perhaps. Either way, while I despised the fact I could barely touch anyone besides him, part of me was secretly grateful.

Out of all his vassals, I was the one who spent the most time with him. The more time he spent with me, the less time he had to terrorize the others. I couldn't save them, but I could minimize their suffering, and I knew how to keep him occupied for hours on end.

I knew exactly why I was his favorite.
I went out of my way to be his favorite.

37

Chapter 4

Athaeÿn

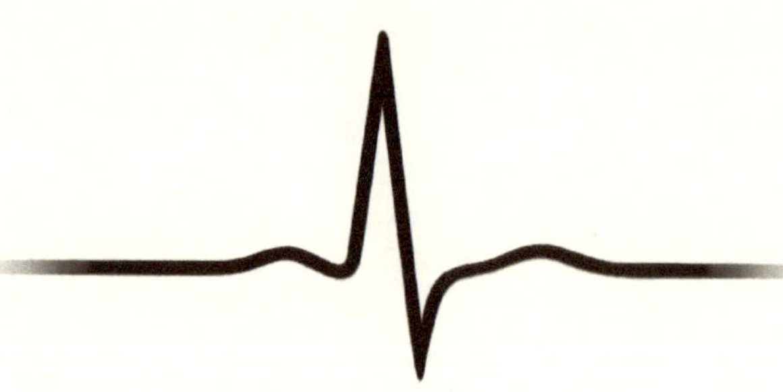

I was a statue outside Roänach's study. The tips of my boots were practically touching the door as I listened to the two voices concealed within. Two highly amused voices.

Did they have to do things in here?

It often felt like Roänach used his carnal escapades to mark his territory, as if it wasn't painfully obvious who owned the entire castle.

Might as well carve his name into the mountain while he's at it.

He regularly used his study instead of his far more comfortable bedroom, so, while irritating, this was less than surprising. At least he had the decency to keep it behind literal closed doors this time.

How thoughtful…

A few minutes passed.

Just get it over with.

I took a deep breath and finally knocked.

"Enter."

That was the last thing I wanted to do. Knowing I had no choice, I slowly opened the door.

Please be clothed—

They were not. Well, Lánelli wasn't. Roänach was, but it hardly mattered. I had seen and felt enough of his indecency to last numerous lifetimes.

"Close the door."

I obeyed a second time but stayed put to keep as much distance between us as possible. When I looked at Lánelli again, I suddenly found myself incredibly envious. Not for the cursed lap she was draped across, but rather her ease of sprawling across a lap as if it was nothing. There was a time I could do the same.

That ship has long sailed…

I acknowledged my slight bitterness toward her but did my best to push that feeling aside. She was definitely flaunting her position, just not in the way she thought.

At this rate, she'll know the same struggle one day.

"Do you expect me to shout our entire conversation across the room?"

Roänach's obnoxious question dragged me back to the present, and his tone left me bristling. There was a time his voice had been velvet against my ears. Now, it was little more than broken glass.

I hate that I used to love it.

Without a word, I slowly approached and stopped about five feet in front of the gaudy chair they occupied. I couldn't help but eye the small table next to them, where a wine glass of blood sat half-empty.

In his line of sight as usual…

"Do you expect me to do all the talking as well?"

I shook my head a little but remained silent. I wasn't in the mood for any kind of banter.

"Hmm, off to a rather quiet start. Unusual for you, Athaeÿn." Roänach stared at me for a few seconds before dropping his gaze to Lánelli. "Would you mind giving us some privacy, my dear?"

"Aww, but I'm comfy. I promise I'll be quiet."

"I appreciate your consideration, but you deserve a hearty meal after such a workout." He put on that half-lidded grin I detested. "Have the Demons in the kitchen prepare a final banquet. You'll be dining differently once I mark you as mine."

"It's about time. I thought I was going to have to beg." She met his grin with a smirk before grabbing his face and pulling herself up into a kiss.

Now I'm the one getting secondhand embarrassment.

Even though she was becoming increasingly vexing in Roänach's presence, I felt nothing but grief for the day she was slapped across the face by both him and reality. Of the two of us, the only one I was genuinely irritated with was myself.

Before I knew what trusting Roänach led to, I thought the world of him. Lánelli was annoying, but she wasn't the problem. I saw too much of my younger self in her for my liking. My stupid and naive younger self. All Roänach ever promised was love. All we ever got was betrayal.

I didn't hate Lánelli.

I hated myself.

As I stood there brooding, Lánelli finally broke the kiss and inhaled dramatically, likely to show off how breathless she had been left by their wildly romantic exchange of saliva.

Ugh, I can taste it from here.

She was still grinning when she slipped off his lap and put on a silky, black robe that had been wadded up on his desk. "See you later, Rowy." While sauntering past, she paused right behind my shoulder and leaned in close to my ear. "I'm going to be Vampire royalty."

For all of five seconds.

I then watched with great displeasure as she left the door wide open on her way out.

Seriously?

When Roänach loudly cleared his throat, I went back over and closed the door again.

Forgive me, Your Royal Impatience.

The louse in question was busy humming with delight. "What a treat she is. I do adore the eager ones."

I could feel the chill of his lecherous grin against the back of my head.

She won't be eager once you ruin her life.

Knowing he wouldn't see it, I allowed my face to be contorted by absolute loathing. This day was already terrible, and I wasn't sure how much more I could take. To say I was exhausted after three hundred years of seeking his favor to shield the others was a gross understatement.

"Any day now."

With one final grimace of hatred, I forced my expression back to neutral and approached him again. This time, however, I stopped ten feet away. It wasn't far enough to merit shouting, but I should've known better when he beckoned me closer with a few gestures of his finger anyway.

Dammit…

I kept my eyes down and took a single step.

"Why are you being so difficult? You're never this avoidant." When I didn't acknowledge his question, the haunting silence was pierced by an unnerving creak from his chair. "I suggest you get your feet to cooperate. My good mood doesn't share my boundless patience."

My neutral expression fractured. Not wanting to push my luck, I swallowed my indignation and forced myself to continue forward, this time stopping just three feet in front of him. I still refused to look up.

"Closer."

After briefly clenching my eyes shut, I moved until our feet were almost touching. What immediately followed was more than expected, but I still gasped when he grabbed the ruffled fabric around my midsection and forced me to straddle his lap.

"Ah, much better." He sounded far too pleased with himself as he leaned back and folded his hands neatly on his abdomen. His smug grin had yet to waver. "Now, I'll only have to raise my voice in accordance with your behavior."

It was a relief not to be groped for once, but I remained completely withdrawn.

"Well? Aren't you curious as to what I wanted to discuss?"

I just nodded and held myself.

He said nothing for a few moments. "Do I need to raise my voice already?"

His restrained yet chilling tone made me shudder. With great reluctance, I finally made eye contact with him but kept my own tone subdued. "What did you want to discuss?"

His smile turned eerily casual when he received both verbal reply and visual attention. "How would you like to go on a little trip?"

My eyes narrowed suspiciously. "What do you mean *trip?*"

"An extended journey to and from another location. What else could I possibly mean?"

I huffed but kept any comments to myself so he could continue.

"You serve me well here at Castle Veil, but I believe you can be equally useful elsewhere."

"How? I can't suck you off from across the continent."

"True. Not even *your* mouth is that talented." He shook his head. "No, this involves a different matter," he added, resting his hands on my thighs and caressing them with his thumbs. "Do you recall when I voiced my desire to rule the aforementioned continent?"

I had to force myself not to look down. Even though I was mostly numb to his touch, it was difficult to ignore. "On numerous occasions."

"Well, it turns out you'll be able to aid my endeavor."

"I'm not helping you lay siege to Eidolon."

"Who said anything about attacking the capital?" He feigned offense just long enough to unsettle me before grinning again. "That is the apex of *my* plan and not something you need to worry about. I'm asking very little of you, so I hope to hear minimal complaining, if any."

I said nothing for a few moments. "What exactly is my role in all of this?"

"Collateral."

"For what?"

"I've had some intriguing discussions with a surprisingly kindred spirit. For quite a while, in fact." His grin twinged with wickedness. "Are you familiar with Xythe?"

My stomach dropped. "The Demon King?"

"The same. It's been over a millennium since his failed coup, but his grudge over being exiled is alive and well. In short, we've decided to team up for mutual benefits but distinct rewards."

"Where are you going with this?"

"I was just getting to that. Xythe has agreed to a partnership, but at a cost. You're the price."

The pit in my gut deepened. "I don't understand."

He started waving his hand nonchalantly. "You know how Arch-Demons are. They love their deals and demands. Apparently, getting his revenge on the queens isn't enough, or perhaps he simply doesn't trust me. Fair enough. Consider yourself a good faith payment." He held up a finger and grinned with misguided confidence. "But don't fret, my dear. The honorable Demon King has graciously promised to return you to me once all is said and done."

My mouth fell open, but nothing came out.

Wait—

It took at least five seconds to snap out of my dumbfounded shock. *"What?!"*

"There's no need to scream in my face—"

"You really expect me to go through with this?!"

"The deal has already been made, so you will."

He can't be serious—

I shook my head. "I'm not going."

"I'm afraid it's not up to you, darling."

"It *is* up to me, *dearest.* Refer to my previous statement if you need clarification."

His brows went up a little. "Why are you getting so upset? The temporary nature of this deal wasn't a lie."

"I don't care. I'm not just some trinket you can throw away to get whatever you want," I hissed, baring my fangs to get my point across.

Unbelievable.

I knew my combative banter had become openly hostile, but I was losing control of my anger. The particularly draining incidents from earlier were not helping.

His smile became unnervingly calm. "Are you sure you want to argue about this?"

"I'm not arguing. I'm flat out refusing." Even though I folded my arms with stern defiance, I didn't actually know what to do. All I knew was I couldn't shield the other vassals from him if I wasn't at Castle Veil.

They need me.

Roänach and I stared at each other for what felt like an eternity. To an outsider, it likely would have appeared as though we were at an impasse, but he always had the upper hand in one way or another. He was definitely aware of something I wasn't, and the knowing smile on his face was making me nauseous.

Why isn't he angry with me?

"You must be wondering why I'm still composed despite your blatant disrespect."

His words made me shudder. I hated coincidences that made him look like a mind reader.

"And I bet you're also curious as to why I would send my favorite vassal on such a harrowing journey when I have ample interchangeable menials at my disposal."

The trench in my stomach was becoming a chasm.

He leaned closer and lowered his voice. "I know the *real* reason you're upset."

My chest tightened. "What are you talking about?" I asked weakly, knowing my feigned ignorance wasn't convincing in the slightest.

His eyelids fell a bit. "Oh, I think you know."

I was so shaken I couldn't move.

He leaned even closer and lowered his voice further. "I never fell for it."

Wait—

"You've been my favorite regardless of your antics, but I've known about them from the beginning." He tilted his head a little. "I'm afraid I'm not the vacuous halfwit you took me for."

When his smirk spread from ear to ear, I knew I had failed to keep the horrified disbelief off my face. There was no point trying to deny it now.

He... He's known the whole time?

"I've thoroughly enjoyed the extra attention, and my own little secret of knowing your true motive only made it better." He paused to soak in the look on my face. "Ah, but don't worry. I made sure to compensate for all that lost time with the others, not that they're even aware."

No—

He ran his tongue over his fangs. "I must say, *stealth* is much easier when I'm the only conscious person in the room."

No…

I was absolutely sick.

It was all for nothing.

He stared at me for a few seconds. "I'm not sure why this revelation has left you so incredulous. Did you really think I wouldn't notice after *three hundred years?*" he taunted, digging his thumbs into my thighs three times for emphasis.

My mind was so incoherent I barely noticed the groping.

He's right.

I suddenly felt like the most catastrophically stupid imbecile to ever exist. How could I have possibly thought he would never find out?

I couldn't even manage this one thing…

My eyes started to hurt from the burning devastation. It was a vast understatement to say I was crushed into oblivion when he betrayed me all those years ago, but this was beyond the fucking pale. My anger had simmered beneath the surface for three centuries. It finally boiled over into rage.

That's it—

I wasn't a violent person, but, in that moment, the only thing keeping me from strangling him was the arcane bond that kept his vassals docile. I had never despised it more.

I'm done.

Ignoring the tears blurring my vision, I bared my fangs again and snarled in his face. "You are *so* fucking lucky I can't kill you."

The charade was over.

His grin refused to go away. "Are we finally being transparent with one another? Good. I've been wondering when and if we would ever speak candidly again."

There is no "again."

Without hesitation, he pulled an ornate, silver dagger from a sheath on the side of the chair and began toying with it. "You won't mind if I use my negotiator, will you?"

My shoulders tensed as I eyed the decorated weapon, noting the familiar blood-red rubies laid into the gilded handle that glinted between his nimble fingers. It had been quite a while since I last saw it. The silver of its blade was the only metal that could do permanent damage to a Vampire, and while I could sense its deadly purity without even touching it, I already knew what it felt like. So did Haana. So did all of his vassals. Fiella was the only one yet to be cut.

"Now then," he vaguely pointed the dagger in my direction, "with everything out in the open, do you intend to continue arguing?"

"You wanted a discussion, *yes?* By definition, that requires some amount of back-and-forth," I spat, knowing full well he just found my rage amusing. I still wanted him to hear how absolutely disgusted and appalled I was.

"Ah, poor word choice on my part, then. I suppose this was more of an announcement." His grin never wavered as he traced circles in the air with the tip of the dagger. "You know from personal experience I'm not afraid to use this. Still wish to refuse cooperation?"

"Yes."

"You really think that's a good idea?"

"You really think I give a shit?"

His smirk turned lustful. "Mmm... You know, I've always enjoyed your audacious banter, but I think I like this raw defiance even more. I almost wish I'd let my secret slip sooner." He sighed and shook his head. "Unfortunately, this is not up for debate, so any further insubordination will result in punishment."

When I opened my mouth to continue refusing anyway, he pressed the tip of the dagger against my abdomen, indenting both fabric and flesh but piercing neither.

"Think carefully before you speak your next words," he said lowly. It was the most threatening his tone had been so far.

I dropped my glare to the blade for a moment before darting my eyes back to his. "I *think* I'll say whatever I fucking want. Torture me. Kill me. I don't care anymore. I'm done playing this game, and I'm not going to be your pawn in this ridiculous scheme. That's the end of it. *Period.*"

"Is that so?" His smile widened as he lifted the dagger and rested its tip on my forehead. Specifically, at the tapered end of a massive dark scar that extended through my left eyebrow, over my eyelid, and all the way to my jawline.

It was the same side as the two small puncture marks on my neck.

He lightly dragged the blade down my scar without piercing my skin. This time. "In that case," he repositioned the tip to the unmarred side of my forehead, "should I make your face symmetrical?"

I made direct eye contact with him. "Do it. See if I care."

His smile finally faded. "It's no fun when you give me permission."

"Cry about it."

Despite what he had just said about my abrasive demeanor, he actually seemed a bit taken aback by how persistent it was. His shock was brief, however, as his grin quickly resurfaced. "What about that special friend of yours?"

Don't you dare bring Fiella into this.

He pulled the dagger back and waved it in my face. "Would you like me to mark the Light Elf instead?"

"She has a name."

"I suppose she does. Should I carve it into her forehead?"

My shoulders heaved with renewed outrage, but I said nothing.

Regardless of how I handled the current situation, it was only a matter of time before he used her face as his newest canvas. Because of this, his threat wasn't enough to persuade me, as heartless as it sounded. On the flip side, any promise he made *not* to harm her couldn't be trusted either. His word was meaningless.

Roänach tilted his head as he waited for a response that never came. "I assume your silence indicates uncertainty. Allow me to up the stakes." He started gesturing with the dagger as he spoke. "You will act as collateral in my deal with Xythe, or I will execute Fiella and make you watch."

No—

"Or, I could send *her* as collateral instead. She would be at Xythe's mercy, and there would be nothing you could do about it." He made one final two-handed gesture and put on the most self-satisfied, shit-eating grin I had ever seen. "Your choice."

For what felt like the hundredth time, I was left gawking at him like a stupefied infant.

I can't fucking believe this.

Without question, this was now the worst day of my entire life. It even surpassed the night Roänach murdered me, as well as the following morning when I woke up Undead with neither soul nor future. I had tried to find purpose in my enslavement by shielding the other vassals at my own expense, but it had been utterly pointless. What was worse, my efforts may have actually done more harm than good.

Why did I even bother trying…

And now, I was given an impossible decision. Even though nothing I did mattered at all, I couldn't even try if I was miles away. It would have been one thing if I alone had to face consequences, but dragging Fiella into it changed everything. Her only crime was being my friend.

She doesn't deserve this.

Her safety wasn't guaranteed no matter what I chose, but I couldn't let Roänach send her to Xythe.

I guess it's actually not an impossible decision.

There was only one option.

I have to… for her sake…

All of my anger evaporated as I closed my eyes and hung my head in defeat.

Roänach's impatience resurfaced. "Well?"

Torn down and beaten, I decided to retreat into the familiar arms of banter. In dealing with Roänach, it had become second nature. In this moment of ruin, it would be comforting. Distasteful, yes, but comforting. I just needed something to cling to.

Just long enough to get this over with…

With a heavy exhale, I opened my eyes and slowly lifted my head. "Fine, I'll go."

"Excellent. I knew you'd make the right choice."

By now, all I could manage was an exhausted, half-lidded stare of indignation. "Did you have to collaborate with a fucking Solar Demon of all things?"

He glanced down over the side of the chair, only paying me half-attention. "I can't help that his magic just happens to be deadly to our kind."

I scowled as he slipped the dagger back into its sheath. The fact it was *right there* but useless to me was infuriating. "Maybe not, but you didn't *have* to team up with him. Or *anyone,* for that matter."

"True enough. However, it'll be nice to have backup when the time comes."

"You wouldn't have to worry about that if you left Eidolon alone."

"Ah, but thanks to your generous cooperation, I *won't* have to worry about it."

I frowned tiredly. "You're seriously choosing to trust him?"

"Don't mistake our alliance for amity. Neither of us would ever offer full trust in the other. Like your upcoming trip, my arrangement with Xythe is temporary. Strictly business. In fact, we've already agreed to part ways once all is said and done."

"And you already trust him too much by handing me over. What if I get on his nerves and he kills me with a single look?"

"All the more reason to behave while you're there."

Despite everything, I sighed loudly and rolled my eyes.

I'm truly blessed to be in the presence of such infinite wisdom.

"Assuming I survive, what if he decides not to give me back?"

Roänach leaned back with an easygoing smile. "Even favorites are replaceable. I do hope he returns you, but should he choose not to, Lánelli is quite eager to take your place." He slipped his fingertips into the creases where my thighs met my hips. "Don't worry about breaking my heart, darling. I promise not to shed any tears if you never come back."

My gaze fell to his hands. He still hadn't groped me as he normally would.

It's like he's already let go…

I didn't just hate him. I despised him. I had *loathed* him with every fiber of my being for so long, and yet, the ease of his decision to send me away was more painful than when he took his dagger to my face. I didn't know why his dismissal was so cutting. It hurt. I hated that it hurt.

I don't want to be here anymore.

As if reading my mind once again, he shifted one hand to my neck. "Now then, I grant sovereign authorization for you to travel beyond the runes, where the only ground you may step foot is that which lies within the solar shield around Xythe's castle."

Fuck, I forgot about that stupid shield—

My thought was interrupted by a brief, indescribable sensation in my bite scars.

Well, it did something.

"And with that," he retracted his hand, "I believe it's about time you were on your way. Do try not to take all night packing your things. The coachman isn't known for patience."

Gods, get me out of here—

I was overwhelmingly numb but could tell I was barely holding it together, so I kept my mouth shut and fled his lap in an attempt to escape.

"Forgetting something?"

After just three frantic steps, I stopped dead in my tracks and tilted my face toward the ceiling, but I couldn't see it since my eyes were closed.

Roänach and his fucking goodbye kisses.

Turning back around as slowly as possible, my animosity spiked when I opened my eyes to find his lingering, smug grin peeking over the rim of the wine glass he now held. There was a fresh trickle of blood at the corner of his mouth.

How does he remember every single time?

Delaying the inevitable was pointless, so I trudged over to acquiesce but paused halfway to his lips when a pale finger stopped me and pointed down.

You bastard—

I hissed through my teeth as I dropped to one knee and kissed the crotch of his pants, noting with intense disgust that he wasn't flaccid.

Please just let me go already.

As quickly as I had sunk down to plant the repulsive kiss, I stood back up and aggressively wiped my mouth with the back of my hand, making direct eye contact as I did so. When his vile grin predictably widened with satisfaction, I stormed out as fast as my legs would carry me. I was beyond relieved to get away from him.

I hate him so fucking much.

As I stalked the halls, I forced myself to only think about my imminent journey. Everything else had to wait if I wanted to avoid a public meltdown.

I still can't believe this.

I was less than thrilled to be going from one despot to another, but I doubted Xythe could be worse than Roänach. Even if he was just as bad, at least I would have a new face to glare at and a change in scenery.

It's the little things…

Chapter 5

Athaeÿn

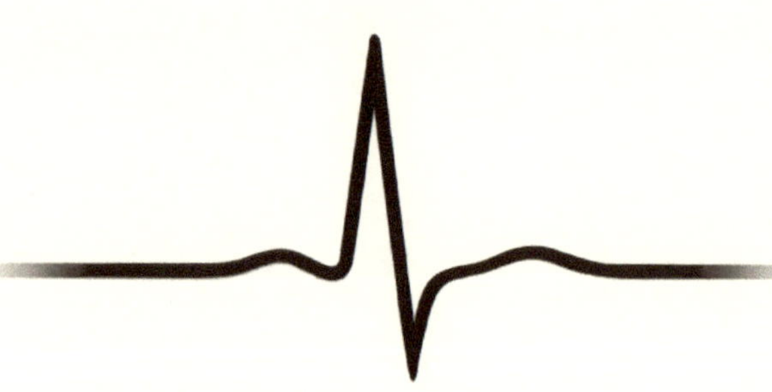

I was absolutely seething. Such contempt was effortless by now, but especially after this particular day. I thought I had reached the limit of my resentment long ago. As usual, Roänach proved me wrong.

And fucking stupid.

It was so naive to assume things couldn't get any worse, and my broken heart crumbled further at the mere thought of Fiella becoming a miserable husk of herself like I had. Her gentle spirit had already received a devastating blow. Hopefully, it would still be intact when I returned.

If I ever return…

It wasn't my intention to perish at the claws of the Demon King, but I didn't know what to expect. When not enthralled, Demons were just as diverse in personality as everyone else, but Xythe's reputation was a bad start.

Not to mention his particular flavor of magic.

I hoped his general proximity wouldn't flay my skin off, but that wasn't the primary reason I wanted nothing to do with him. I had no interest in fraternizing with someone who had attempted to overthrow Eidolon's beloved queens, and the fact Roänach wanted to do the same was just one more blemish on his already lengthy record.

The two Arbiters had watched over the capital for thousands of years, and because they made a point of introducing themselves to every inhabitant, I actually knew them personally, albeit not intimately. Although Elvylli and Sathira were sweet and caring, they could be vicious if necessary. Like protective mothers, they were willing to destroy any threat to their city and people, but only as a last resort. Above all, they were known for their instinctual grace and mercy.

From what I understood, Xythe had bypassed innocent civilians in favor of solely targeting the queens, so they had offered banishment instead of execution. Apparently, they should have just killed him to prevent further issues.

Unfortunately, there are consequences to being overly forgiving.

That was only part of what landed me at Castle Veil, but it didn't matter. Everything that led to this moment was my own fault.

I was no longer seething by the time I reached my room. I was just devastated.

I can't take this anymore...

Time stopped when I opened the door and stared blankly into my desolate cell. The only thing missing was prison bars on the threshold. I had called this dismal, gray box *home* for three hundred years, but it suddenly felt like I had never seen it before.

Have I really been here that long?

Considering the harsh truth of my wasted efforts, I may as well have never been there at all.

Don't think about it.

That was becoming increasingly difficult. Still, I attempted to keep my mind blank as I traipsed in and pulled my bulky, leather trunk out from under the bed, noting its unpleasant rasp of metal studs and wheels scraping the stone floor. The simple noise should have been innocuous but, today, carried haunting malevolence.

Everyone will be at Roänach's mercy once I'm gone.

My throat tightened as I slowly opened the empty trunk.

Stop thinking about it.

I was already failing miserably. And trembling.

S-Stop—

When I couldn't, I clenched my eyes shut and sucked in a sharp breath through my teeth.

Fuck!

Bellowing with frustration, I slammed the trunk shut and shoved it across the room as violently as possible. I barely registered its tremendous thud against the opposite wall.

Why?!

My chest was heaving when I eventually cracked my eyes open.

Wh-Why—

It took everything in me to shamble after it.

Why...

Blinded by tears and choking on my own throat, I sank to my knees and hunched over until my forehead was resting on the lid of the trunk. Digging my fingers into my hair only seemed to worsen the trembling in my shoulders.

Pull yourself together.

The combination of mind-numbing rage and suffocating misery was overwhelming.

Get up.

All I could manage was a pathetic sob.

Get. Up.

After a few more seconds, I finally let go of my head and slowly knelt upright, sniffling loudly and wiping my eyes as I did so.

Now, get a grip.

Once I had sufficiently collected myself, I closed my eyes and hung my head back with a prolonged exhale. My cheeks itched from the salt my tears had left behind.

What's the fucking point anymore?

I opened my eyes to stare at the ceiling, but all I saw was Fiella's smile when she gave me the flower crown.

She's the point.

Countless memories flooded my mind. The few months I had with Fiella. The many years with Haana and the other vassals. Even the handful of irritating moments with Lánelli.

They're all the point.

But Fiella was the one in immediate danger. Her life was the one relying on my departure. She deserved the chance to make a future for herself. She was worth it.

That's good enough for me.

After a few more minutes, I lowered my head and dragged my hands down my face.

But she can't know.

Her day wasn't the best either, and I wasn't about to compound it with more guilt. She already felt bad about me comforting her. She didn't need to know she had been used as blackmail.

Please forgive one more secret, Fiella.

I dropped my hands into my lap.

Up.

With one last sniffle and a slight groan of effort, I forced myself to stand despite feeling a bit lightheaded. My cheeks still itched.

...

I didn't have many possessions at Castle Veil, so I decided to just bring everything. There was no telling how long I'd be with Xythe.

If he doesn't kill me right away.

Once the essentials were packed, I glanced at the small portrait of myself.

Miri was such a talented artist.

Painting loved ones had been her favorite hobby, but I was pretty sure she had enjoyed giving the portraits as gifts even more. The kind woman with deep brown eyes, curly ebony hair, and skin of rich umber had been one of my closest friends, and my throat still tightened with grief when I thought about her. Sadly, as a Human, she would have passed away over two centuries ago.

I wonder if she missed me too.

My hands were a bit unsteady as I retrieved the portrait and cast a solemn gaze over it. Although in my seventies when Miri painted me, I had stopped visibly aging around thirty thanks to my Elven lineage. As a mortal

Dark Elf, I could have easily lived a thousand years. As an immortal Undead, I had all eternity to mourn the normal life stolen from me.

She really did capture my likeness perfectly.

At least my face in the portrait was from a happier time. When I was free.

And unmarked…

As I studied my younger image that looked nearly identical to my current self, my fingers unconsciously traced along the differences I now had. The massive scar down my face. The subtle yet equally humiliating legacy of Roänach's fangs on my neck. I had never seen either and was glad I couldn't. They were probably hideous.

Maybe it's for the best I can't see myself anymore.

Shaking my head a little, I nestled the portrait between some clothing in my trunk to keep it cushioned for the journey. Once it was safely tucked away, I glanced at the dusty corner adjacent to the window. It was where my zephyr harp used to sit when not in use.

I wish I still had it.

The lap-sized instrument would have been perfect entertainment for such a long trip, and I was willing to bet even the ill-mannered coachman would prefer real music to the usual symphony of slapping. Unfortunately, Roänach had taken it from me long ago.

But let me keep the portrait as a painful reminder…

Hanging my head with both frustration and defeat, I closed the trunk and just stood there with my hands braced on it.

Pretend it's a vacation.

I scoffed to myself.

Not even Fiella would believe that.

A few minutes later, I was still just standing there.

She's going to be so upset when I leave.

I was stuck in an endless loop of imagining the moment she saw the trunk. Just picturing the look on her face left me paralyzed with dread.

Maybe she's found enough peace by now to handle it.

When I looked out my bedroom window, I was relieved to see her immersed in the glowing gardens with Haana at her side. Both were wearing flower crowns and seemingly making more. Despite everything, a small smile tugged my lips.

At least she has Haana now.

The longer I watched Fiella, the more I thought about her misery over losing the sun forever and how her cold, Undead skin would never again feel that warmth.

There's nothing I can do about that, but—

I turned back to the dresser and looked at the lone item still sitting on it. A spherical, white crystal about four inches in diameter that floated over a small, metal disc. The gemstone was carved to resemble the moon and hovered a few inches above the base, where it slowly rotated and illuminated the space around it with a soft glow.

Maybe my lunelight would comfort her.

It had helped me sleep as a newborn and was my mother's first ever gift to me. It was also my only tangible reminder of her.

But if it can help Fiella even a little bit, I want her to have it.

I picked it up and hugged it to my chest.

After all, that's what it was meant for.

With the lunelight in one hand and my trunk handle in the other, I paused on the threshold and looked around my room one more time. Hopefully not the last time. Castle Veil was my prison, but it was also my home.

It's all I know anymore.

With one final sigh, I closed the door and made my way to the gardens once again. I was glad to see Fiella and Haana still smiling when I finally approached, but their joy vanished when they glanced up and saw the trunk rolling behind me. Fiella took her reaction one step further by looking over her shoulder in a panic, only to find the coach already waiting for me. When she turned back around, the horror on her face was gut-wrenching.

It's even worse than I thought it would be.

Both women's eyes were locked on mine as they slowly stood.

When Fiella managed to speak, she could barely get any sound out. "Y-You're leaving?"

All I could manage was a weak nod as I stopped in front of them and set my trunk down.

"I don't understand. Where are you going?"

"Somewhere I'd rather not, but I had very little say in the matter."

She shook her head. "But *why* is he sending you away?"

I waved a dismissive hand. "Oh, just some diplomatic nonsense. According to him, I can be useful in more ways than one."

When I glanced at Haana, I knew from her tense expression she had seen right through my vague half-answers. I had expected as much, so I was grateful she kept any comments to herself.

Meanwhile, Fiella squinted at the ground and held herself a little. "B-But… What if he pays more attention to me once you're gone?"

Wait—

I widened my eyes at Haana, but she shook her head in self-defense. It seemed genuine.

Fiella was already onto me, I suppose…

After giving Haana a nod of acceptance, I looked at Fiella again. "Try not to worry too much, okay? He's rather fond of Lánelli, and she seems pretty intent on keeping his attention all to herself anyway. As long as that doesn't change, he'll probably forget about you for the most part."

Fiella grimaced slightly while staring at the ground between our feet. "I-I didn't mean to imply that I hoped he would hurt you instead."

The shame in her tone broke my heart, but I still couldn't tell how much she knew, if anything. "I know that's not what you meant, Fiella. For what it's worth, I would gladly take his cruelty in your place."

Gods know I already tried.

She teared up and wrung her hands against her chest. "P-Please don't say that."

Hmm, maybe she doesn't actually know anything.

That would be a relief if true. Regardless, there was one more thing I wanted to share. "Did I ever tell you what my job was back in Eidolon?"

She sniffled and shook her head.

"Well, let's just say I'm familiar with people like Roänach. And, fortunately, many unlike him. I adored the vast majority of my clients, but there were definitely a few I could've lived without." I offered a reassuring smile when she looked at me. "I know how to keep people occupied. Knowing you don't have my background and years of experience to draw from, anything that could spare you from him would make me feel much better."

It took a few seconds, but she managed a small nod.

Not wanting her to get stuck on this, I gladly changed the subject. "But enough about that." My smile brightened as I held out the lunelight. "I have a parting gift for you."

She gawked at the moonlike crystal before looking at me again with disbelief.

"I know how much you miss sunlight, so I thought this might bring you some comfort." As I carefully passed it to her, I appreciated her effort to avoid touching my hand. "It's obviously not the same, but you could pretend it's your own personal sun."

"A-Are you sure?"

"Absolutely."

The faint tears in her eyes were thankful this time as she hugged the lunelight to her chest.

"Think of it as me watching over you while I'm gone, and you'll have Haana too," I added with another glance at the woman in question.

Thankfully, Haana confirmed with a smile.

Fiella was still staring at the lunelight when she suddenly perked up. "Oh, I have something for you too." She shifted the tiny moon to her left hand and extended her right arm, where another flower crown hung from her wrist like an oversized bracelet.

My grin tinged with pride as I carefully removed it without touching her and put it on my head. "It's your best one yet."

Her own smile faltered. "I taught Haana how to make them while you were busy, but I hoped it would be your turn when you were done."

"You'll just have to teach me when I get back."

She nodded sadly. "I wish I could hug you goodbye."

"Believe me, I wish I could do the same. Maybe someday."

Our surprisingly composed farewell was rudely interrupted by the coachman, who was already sitting on the driver's seat of the coach. "Today would be nice!" he thundered, cupping his clawed hands around his mouth to amplify his voice.

I see Roänach channels his impatience as well.

My reluctant gaze drifted to the coachman and his unceasing arm gestures. "Well, I guess that's my incredibly subtle cue…"

Fiella's voice weakened again. "Please be safe."

"That's the plan."

The three of us exited the gardens and made our way to the coach, the main compartment of which I hoisted my trunk into with a grunt of effort.

This still doesn't seem real.

After staring into the coach for a few seconds, I forced a smile over my shoulder. "Bye, Fiella. Bye, Haana."

Fiella shook her head. "No, just *see you later.*"

My smile turned reassuring again. "See you later," I corrected before getting into the coach and closing the door behind me. As I settled in, I looked out the window to find Haana's arm around Fiella's shoulders. The latter was still hugging the lunelight. Neither was smiling.

They'll be alright.

Haana was used to life at Castle Veil.

Fiella wasn't, but I had every confidence she would persevere. Neither youth nor fear implied weakness.

As for Roänach, despite not trusting him whatsoever, I did trust that my decision to leave had saved Fiella from execution. His threat had been genuine, but he otherwise only killed vassals when pushed to the absolute limit of patience, which hadn't happened in at least thirty years. As long as Fiella behaved, she would be alright. Marked by his dagger at some point, but not killed.

It was over before it even began.

I sighed and looked out the window again. This time, at the nearest containment rune.

Wait—

All of a sudden, I realized this was my one and only chance to get help. Unfortunately, my options would be rather limited.

Maybe I can convince Xythe to kill Roänach instead.

I had no idea how to do that or if it was even possible, but if anyone could kill Roänach with ease, it was the immensely powerful Solar Demon.

Why can't something be easy for once—

Anxiety interrupted my thoughts as the coach began passing the rune. There was no invisible wall this time.

It's working—

Before I knew it, the coach had fully exited the mountain.

I'm outside the cave!

It was the first time in three hundred years.

I can't believe it—

The sun had already set, so I took the opportunity to open the door and clamber onto the roof of the coach. Once situated, I just sat there smiling at the sky.

We could see a tiny, horizontal sliver of the sky from the cave mouth, but the view was even more limited than a barred prison window. Being out in the open and under the full expanse was something else entirely. I had forgotten how breathtaking it was. After being trapped for so long, such a simple joy was nothing short of intoxicating, and even that was an understatement.

I feel free.

The truth was pushed aside as my gaze lost itself among the fiery clouds painted across their lavender canvas. When the fading light eventually gave way to evening's first stars, I could barely contain myself. Their celestial dance was my serenity.

Despite being raised underground, I had chosen to live in Eidolon's Hillside District, the exterior portion of the city's Mountainside Region. Having been denied the sky's captivating beauty for so long, it was love at first sight. Even with the sun. Because of that lingering aversion, my preferred time of day had always been night, and my favorite part was the tapestry of stars woven across the heavens. I could stare at them for hours, which is what I planned to do as much as possible on my way from one prison to another.

At least the journey will be peaceful.

And so far, it was.

The day's prior events were still haunting me, but I managed to turn my back to them for a little while. Nothing was allowed to ruin this moment of pure tranquility, and the vastness overhead was the perfect distraction.

This is just what I needed.

I hardly ever looked away from the sky as twilight turned to dusk and dusk turned to night, when I was finally graced with the infinite sea of stars I had been waiting for. In that moment, I envied the powerful wings of Arbiters. I wanted nothing more than to glide effortlessly among the stars, high above the sweeping landscape…

...and away from Roänach forever...
My smile faltered a bit. Even miles away, I couldn't escape him.
But he's not really here.
This realization comforted me, and I refused to think about him further. Until morning, it would just be me and the stars. No one else.
This night belongs to me.

Chapter 6

Daryn

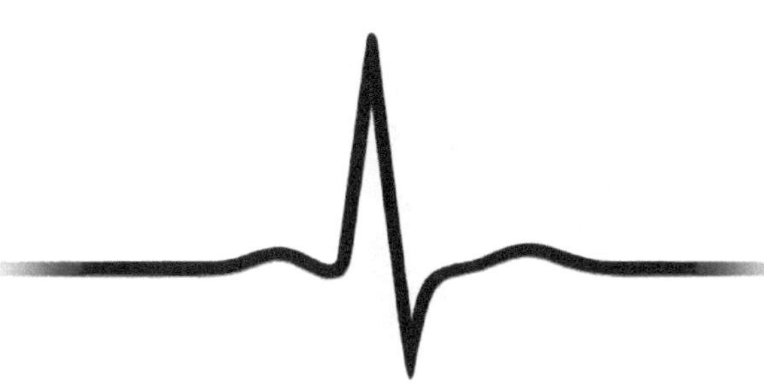

There was a petulant scowl on my face as I trudged the exalted halls of Eidolon's illustrious citadel. Much to my chagrin and immediate regret, this situation was entirely self-inflicted, and the lively city street that greeted me once I stepped outside did nothing to improve my mood.

Ugh, why did I agree to this?

In an otherwise chaotic workplace, my quiet, fragrant office in the citadel was a peaceful pocket of plants I hardly ever left. I may as well have lived there. Even though I was on my way to another of my few happy places, I was still peeved after being interrupted by a coworker.

Watering my office plants is important, Corra.

Of all my fellow Representatives, the Flora Demons were the only ones who would truly appreciate such a task.

I can't help that my leaf babies are so thirsty.

Maybe if they were carnivorous plants, she would actually value their nourishment.

Yes, how dare they not drink blood like us.

And yet, despite such blatant disregard for the wellbeing of my darlings, here I was doing a favor for none other than that same coworker.

I am far too nice for my own good.

Corra wanted to tell her best friend, a young History Fiend, about her great-grandfather's hometown, but, according to her, she didn't even have enough information to fill ten minutes of conversation.

Something about lost history and few surviving records.

The Sovereign Vault would have at least one tome on the subject, but Corra couldn't check for herself. Access to Eidolon's legendary archive of priceless knowledge and rare artifacts was a privilege granted to only the most trusted scholars and highest-ranking government officials.

And the queens, of course.

Corra had only been a Representative for five years, so she still had quite a bit of reputation building and proving of trustworthiness to do. I, on the other hand, had been one of those privileged few for a long time, hence why *I* was the one about to take detailed notes on some backwater village I'd never heard of.

She owes me big time for this homework assignment.

A wicked grin crossed my face.

I know. I'll demand another plant.

My greenhouse of an office annoyed her for some reason, so making her contribute to the foliage she detested would be delightful.

Maybe next time she'll think twice about asking me a favor.

I was still grinning to myself when I reached The Sovereign Vault's entrance. The guards on duty knew me well, but, of the two of them, it was the Mirage Demon who gave the nod of approval to go in. No identity illusions could get past him.

Upon entering, I made a beeline for the lone gravity lift and slotted the lever into the notch labeled *Index Counter.* Once the crystal handle illuminated, the hovering platform began its slow descent into the depths of the mountain where the Vault's contents were actually found. Down there, the delicate items were overly safe from the sun's harsh light.

As was I.

Can never be too careful.

And any excuse to use a gravity lift was a good excuse. I hadn't even looked at the stairs.

Pure evil.

Manual vertical travel was the bane of my existence. Considering Eidolon was a massive city with many stepped and layered districts, these elevators were a blessing for anyone with limited mobility. And me.

A much-appreciated thank-you gift from Gravity Demons.

Once the lift eased to a stop, I stepped off and went over to the directory on the nearby wall to see where I needed to go. I had a number of section locations memorized, but Boring Hamlets and Their Even More Boring Origins wasn't one of them.

Maybe I'll learn the intricate art of collecting dust.

Shaking my head a little, I turned and headed off on my jotting adventure.

Errand.

As I passed the countless, pristine shelves stuffed with tomes and collections, I enjoyed the aroma of ancient books and the cozy atmosphere provided by the many crystals glowing softly in their sconces. They were used instead of candles, as the entire vault was sealed with a fire suppressant ward to protect the artifacts. It would have been nice to add some bio-luminescent flora to the mix, but that would risk glowing mush dripping on the books.

That's alright, I have some luminous plants in my office. Mush and all.

I stopped in my tracks when a huge map in a glass case on the wall caught my eye. A map of the entire continent. It had to be at least fifty feet long and was so decrepit the crumbling paper looked like a ten-thousand-year-old tanned hide.

A single touch would probably disintegrate it.

Right in the middle was Soaring Sanctum, the lone mountain Eidolon could be found in, on, and around. It was also the highest peak in the world and had been raised singlehandedly in under a day by Galaeÿthe, one of the first Arbiters.

Just a little more interesting than what I'm here to take notes on.

Compared to the forgettable dirt pile Corra's great-grandfather had apparently grown up in, Eidolon's proud history was the most thoroughly documented of any on record. From tiny fishing village to bustling trade town known as Prosperity, to millennia as a sprawling metropolis and capital of the entire continent, this one region alone could fill numerous libraries with near-infinite lifetimes' worth of knowledge.

And the river that started it all is still here and busier than ever.

Said river being Fae's Blessing, having been affectionately named after the goddess of nature.

Shame that blessing would kill me.

To be fair to Fae, I couldn't go swimming in *any* river. Regardless, Galaeÿthe had picked a good spot for the capital and done well in founding Eidolon.

I'm sure every Demon at the time agreed.

It was a much-needed, pivotal moment for them. When Demons first appeared in Terraen, they were shunned as "unnatural abominations" and even hunted on rare occasion. When this abysmal treatment escalated over time instead of fizzling out, it led to one of only a few known instances of divine intervention.

The bare minimum, considering divine bullshit was to blame in the first place.

My gaze drifted to the top of the map, where a long row of symbols lined the upper border. One was lower than the rest. A circle around four dots arranged like the vertices of a symmetrical trapezoid, the top two of which were a bit smaller than the bottom two. The symbol for Daemir, lone god and creator of Dominion, the Demon realm.

The three D's.

There was a reason Daemir's symbol appeared as though forcibly pulled out of the sequence. Throughout the ages, delusions of grandeur had gotten people from all walks of life in trouble. Gods were no exception.

Especially with family involved.

Apparently, Daemir wasn't impressed by Terraen, but, considering our realm was his mother's work, he probably should have kept his mouth shut. Taëni, matriarchal goddess of all life, didn't appreciate her son's threat to violently take over the pantheon and "show her what a real god could do," so she banished him.

I probably would've killed him to make an example, but whatever.

Daemir had lucked out with his merciful mother. It was a different story with his siblings.

Well, one in particular.

My gaze shifted to a different symbol that was still in line with the others. A half-circle oriented like a bowl of soup and trisected by two horizontal lines. It looked suspiciously similar to a laughing mouth. Raethe, god of mischief.

God of cruelty or theft would be more accurate.

It was Raethe who had plucked the first Demons from Dominion, dropped them into Terraen, and solely cursed their kind with the ability to summon more. He was also the one who introduced enthrallment to Terraen, but he hadn't even come up with it himself. He had stolen the concept from Arch-Demons.

And then gave the worst possible version to Arch-Vampires.

I hissed under my breath.

Fucking bastard.

It was common speculation that Raethe was also the source of Vampirism, but he had only taken credit for Demon summoning.

Too busy rubbing the latter in Daemir's face.

My gaze shifted a third time to one more symbol in the sequence. A vertical line with a dot on either side, one of which was higher than the other. The much more welcome symbol for Maëlla, goddess of order.

At least she cared enough to step in.

Even if she just felt responsible for cleaning up her mischievous brother's mess, something was better than nothing.

As for Daemir, he sounded like a jackass, but I did sympathize with his isolation and the resulting inability to help. All he could do was watch as his Demons were stolen right in front of him and ripped from their home forever.

At least summoning is incredibly rare in the grand scheme of things…

Eventually, my gaze drifted back to Eidolon at the center of the map.

Aptly named as a beacon of hope in one of our darkest eras.

Maëlla couldn't undo Raethe's cruel trick or convince Taëni to intervene, so she took inspiration from Daemir and created new life in the form of Arbiters to act in her stead.

Ageless, blessed with divine blood, wielding powerful magic, and inspired by dragons, who were revered for their wisdom and peaceful nature despite possessing brute strength, Arbiters had always been seen as demigods among mortals. Although primarily sent to watch over Demons, they cared for everyone in Terraen.

What better way to turn the page than with the guiding hand of a goddess?

Arbiters didn't have literal symbols like the ones lining the top of the map, but Eidolon itself seemed to serve a similar purpose for their race as a whole.

I guess Soaring Sanctum is basically Galaeÿthe's symbol.

Although considered the city's first "king," he had never referred to or thought of himself that way, and the current queens felt the same.

Arbiters saw themselves as guardians, not rulers. They happily let elected governments run the show, but, when and if they stepped in to make decisions or changes, their word was treated as final.

I wonder what Galaeÿthe is up to these days.

If I had to guess, he was up north among the snowy peaks that stretched as far as the eye could see. Haephir, his best friend and fellow Arbiter, was probably up there too. Both had watched over Eidolon for at least a thousand years each, but the longest reigning were their married daughters, Elvylli and Sathira.

Oh, that reminds me—

With one last glance at the map, I continued on my way.

I should flip through that tome on Terraenean Flora Demon botany while I'm here.

It broke my heart that summoned Flora Demons would never again see the fields and forests of Dominion, but I couldn't decide if that was better or worse than only knowing one's original horticulture through stories and artwork, as was the case for those born here. On the bright side, they had been able to magically cultivate new, unique plants in Terraen to call their own, some of which only they could grow.

They and Fauna Demons probably have more affinity with Fae than Daemir anyway.

Unfortunately, not all were able to find such harmony. Because summoning was a one-way-trip and completely random, at least within the summoner's chosen sub-race, there had been a few, exceedingly rare, instances of Demons going on killing sprees in desperate attempts to summon their families that had been left behind. As far as I knew, those odds had never been beaten, so it was pointless misery for everyone.

To add insult to injury, both realms shared the exact same space but were invisible and intangible to one another. A Demon in Terraen could be standing right next to their loved ones still in Dominion and not even know it. My family had been out of reach when I was a vassal, but at least we were all in the same realm with a realistic chance of seeing each other again someday.

I hope a day comes when Raethe laughs himself to death.

Meanwhile, I found an old tome that had what Corra needed. I could smell how boring its contents were.

Maybe I can get her more interested in plants.

Tome in hand, I sighed heavily and made my way to the nature section.

I bet the Flora Demons would help.

As for the tome about their botany in Terraen, it wasn't there.

Um, excuse me?

I saw every title but the one I wanted, which didn't make sense. Nothing was allowed to leave the vault, and I hadn't seen or heard anyone else who may have borrowed it to read nearby.

So, where is it?

I glared at its empty spot.

Maybe it's invisible.

After a few minutes, I tilted my head back and dragged my free hand down my face.

Look at something else and try again with fresh eyes.

Huffing with annoyance, I opened Corra's tome to a random page and read the first line.

"*...it was for this reason the stone masons switched to using—*"

I snapped the book shut.

Yes, very fascinating—

When I glanced at the shelves again, I spotted the botany tome immediately.

Oh my gods.

It was exactly one shelf above its designated spot. *Directly* above. In fact, I had looked right at it several times.

I am, without a doubt, the best scholar in all of Eidolon.

Amid muttered profanities, my stomach entered the conversation with a growl.

Excellent, I can blame hunger.

With both stupid tomes tucked under one arm, I made my way to the Index Counter and set them right in front of the snippy Book Fiend who always ran the desk. He was three feet tall at most and regularly glared at me over half-moon spectacles that had to wrap behind his head and rest on his ears, as there was no protruding nose for them to balance on. The vertical slits for nostrils he had instead usually flared at me whenever I interrupted his reading sessions, which I was about to do.

My other favorite pastime.

It was a shame he was always in such a sour mood. Otherwise, we would have gotten along famously with our shared hobby.

I can already hear his breathing getting cranky.

"Hey, buddy. Setting aside a couple of tomes for later," I greeted before casually resting my elbow on the desk and waiting for his reaction with bated breath.

He didn't disappoint as he snapped his book shut and repeatedly swatted my forearm like an angry cat, having to stand on his chair and reach over to do so. "Body parts off the counter! Vault items only!" he hissed through little pointed teeth. Once he shooed my arm away, he whipped out a poofy feather duster and aggressively brushed the spot I had touched.

Never fails.

"If you stopped giving such a priceless reaction, Meech, I wouldn't be so tempted to do it every time."

"And if you just stopped touching the counter, *Daryn,* I wouldn't have to reprimand you like the ungrateful toddler you are."

"I'll have you know I'm *exceedingly* grateful for the privilege to enter the vault."

"How I do wish you would act like it…" Once he put the feather duster away, he glanced at the tomes and narrowed his solid black eyes at one in particular. "Why does a Wood Elf need to read up on botany? Haven't you memorized every fact about every plant that's ever existed?" He tapped the tome a few times for emphasis. "Even Flora Demon plants?"

"And even plants that *don't* exist." I smirked for a moment before looking at the tome as well. "Although my office could use a little Flora Demon love, I mainly wanted inspiration for some different flowers to plant in Tyrran's Shrine this year."

"Since when do you care about that?"

"Hey, I've always found its origin morbidly fascinating, but this isn't about that. It's about the *plants.*"

Meech's forehead wrinkled as his hairless brows went up, but his eyes didn't reflect any surprise. "Fair enough. Everything in the vault is far more interesting than that depressing memorial." He glanced at the tomes again. "Why are you even here if you're not reading them now?"

"The plan *was* to read them now, but my hunger has since taken priority." My honest answer was accompanied by a well-timed, second stomach growl.

"Eat any of my books and I'll tear your throat out."

"Unless there are bloody pages in them, you have nothing to worry about." I flashed a fanged grin and headed for the gravity lift, snickering to myself as I went. Meech never missed an opportunity to loudly defend his precious books with empty threats.

Understandable. I would die a second time for my plants.

"If I don't see you in three hours, I'm putting the tomes back!" he shouted after me.

"Make sure everything's in the right spot next time!"

"What?!"

My only response was an amused snort and wave over my shoulder as I stepped onto the lift and selected *Ground Level.*

The absolute horror of a tome on the wrong shelf.

To be fair, it had made me look like an imbecile.

That's the real crime.

Once the lift docked, I left the vault and began making my way back to the citadel.

Sorry, Corra, your notes will have to wait a bit.

When my stomach growled a third time, the thought of Corra brought a frown to my face.

Ugh, she'll probably insist I go out for dinner to be more social. Again.

I had perfectly good blood vials arranged in neat little rows on a narrow shelf in my office. Just because I didn't have to worry about them coagulating didn't mean they would taste fresh forever.

I don't want them to go to waste, Corra.

When I reached my office, I didn't even get a chance to look at said blood vials before hearing a familiar sound approaching down the hall.

Oh no, it's her heels—

Favorite bone straw in hand, I fled and hurried toward the citadel's exit. "Before you say anything, I'm going out!" I announced right as Corra appeared in my peripheral vision.

She scoffed loudly. *"You're* going out?"

"That's right, so I don't want to hear any comments about how I'm antisocial."

"I've never—"

"Oh yes you have. Suggestions on where to go instead, please."

She pursed her lips in thought. "Hmm, I hear The Sanguine Tap is running a special today."

"Too vague. You're not selling me on it."

"Regal Indulgence—"

"Say no more!" I was gone before I could hear any laughter. I certainly wasn't laughing.

Always teasing me.

It wasn't my fault plants were preferable to people. Admittedly, my social skills weren't the best, but I cared deeply about my work and got the job done with minimal complaints from my constituents.

They keep reelecting me, so I can't be that bad.

There would likely be a gaggle of said constituents at The Sanguine Tap, but the special they were running was worth any mingling that might be thrust upon me. *Regal Indulgence* wasn't just a pompous name for a drink. It was deliciously literal.

Gods, I love donation days.

A single drop of Arbiter blood could augment the effects of any elixir or potion, and, more importantly, it had the best flavor of any in the world. The queens freely offered some of theirs every now and then, especially to shops that needed a little boost, so the cauldrons and taps were always on the lookout for these random days of royal generosity.

Definitely the place to run a blood-based business.

It was also ideal for anyone who valued efficiency and minimizing waste, many examples of which I passed as I walked the streets. Undying forges, courtesy of Elvylli's fire magic; permafrost coolers for perishable storage, enchanted by Sathira's ice magic; clothing, jewelry, and armor enchanted by Inverse Demons to repel enthrallment; the gravity lifts—

And of course—

I tapped my chin with my straw.

Reusable drinking apparatuses.

When I reached The Sanguine Tap, there was already, as expected, a long line of Vampires waiting for a cup of Regal Indulgence, and I was mortified by the possibility of them running out before I got any. Luckily, they still had plenty when I finally reached the counter after what felt like forty years. They probably had gallons of it.

Praise Maëlla for the almighty Arbiter healing factor.

I was about to put my straw in my cup but paused when a familiar voice called out to me.

"Well, well, well. If it isn't Distant Daryn."

Oh, great…

I huffed and shook my head. "You know what would be absolutely delightful? If we could all take a moment to recognize just how unworthy of mention my reclusive nature is."

Corra's daily comments are beyond sufficient.

With another huff, I turned to face the source of the voice, a ghostly pale Human Vampire with platinum blonde hair.

And those awful eyes they all have.

I pointed between said eyes with my straw. "You're lucky your pixie cut is cute, Callyn, or I'd never indulge your smug face again."

They just smirked. "Ooooo, I'm shaking in my sandals."

"You are wearing open-toed slippers at best."

"That's rich coming from the guy in fuzzy clogs."

"Comfort before conformity, freckles. Now then, if you're quite done pestering me, I would *love* to drink my royal blood in peace," I gave a horrendously fake smile and noisily rapped the metal cup with my straw, "thank you very much."

"I just wanted to say hi, geez."

"Falsely fabricated fiction. An absolute *fib.*"

It was then I noticed the woman standing next to them. A *living* Human. We were both much darker than Callyn, but her russet-brown skin was warmer in tone and a bit lighter than mine. Additionally, while I was average height with fiery ginger hair, pointed ears, and glowing emerald eyes, she was petite with curly ebony hair, rounded ears, and non-glowing, dark brown eyes.

Much better than the creepy ones Callyn has.

This time, I pointed my straw at her. "Aha, I see you've found the latest Miri descendant to drag around."

"Her name is Kira, and I'm not dragging her around. She—"

"Alright, *encouraging* her to help you."

"Still not quite accurate—"

"Too bad. As for your endless endeavor, have you actually found anything?"

Their previously mischievous expression was falling by the second. "No. Not even with countless searches beyond the city."

"Mm-hmm. No offense, but your friend has been gone for, what, three hundred years now? Why are you still looking for him after all this time?"

Callyn frowned with offense anyway. "Because best friends care about each other, *Daryn.* Miri and I passed down all our favorite stories, hence why Kira is here, and I obviously want to see him again, but I'm not surprised *you* of all people don't understand." They were glowering by now. "I'm starting to wonder why I bothered coming to you with this in the first place."

"Don't get crabby with me. You act like I don't care at all."

"Can you blame me?"

Callyn
Kira

I was getting increasingly frustrated. And hungry. "Listen, I really am sorry about Athaeÿn, but he left of his own free will. Grown-ass adults are allowed to come and go whenever they please. What do you want from me?"

"You're supposed to look out for our kind. I know he's not one of us, so any help finding him could be considered a favor for me instead."

"That's not how my job works."

"What about the fact he left with a Vampire?"

"That changes nothing. Speaking of other Vampires," I waved my straw back and forth, "I bet you never heard from Vernyth either."

Callyn now looked more depressed than angry. "No—"

"And it was rather stupid of you to ask him for help anyway," I interrupted before finally plunking my straw into the cup with a loud clink and taking a long, dramatic sip.

Damn, it's even better than I remember—

"I told you, he's not like other Arch-Vampires—"

"*Frankly,* freckles, I don't care what he did or didn't do on purpose or by accident. His ilk are the reason you and I are Undead. I will never trust one. Ever. *Period.*"

You just don't get it, Callyn.

All Arch-Vampires had to die for the cycle to end, even supposedly "neutral" ones like Vernyth.

Neutral my ass.

Meanwhile, Kira stared at me for a few moments before turning to Callyn. "I see what you meant by him not being a social butterfly," she muttered awkwardly.

Callyn dragged their hands down their face. "Social maggot, more like…"

I pointed at them with the middle finger of my cup-holding hand. "Hey, maggots are incredibly useful for cleaning wounds and removing necrotic flesh, so I take that as a compliment." I paused to take another, much louder sip. "Besides, it's the queens' job to be the social butterflies. They even have the wings for it."

"Their wings aren't—"

"*Gods,* Callyn, would you please sink those handy dandy fangs of yours into a joke every now and then? You did so marvelously during the footwear portion of our conversation."

They ignored me and nudged Kira's arm instead. "Come on, let's leave Disrespectful Daryn to his meal."

I narrowed my eyes. "Do you just have a list of these nicknames ready to go, or—"

"Bye, Daryn."

As Callyn and Kira disappeared into the crowd, I just stood there with my arms out to the sides in disbelief. I was the one being disrespected.

The audacity.

I sighed dramatically and took another long sip of my drink. My condolences had been sincere, but I simply couldn't justify the resources necessary to look for someone who had left voluntarily and, by all accounts, merrily.

Not to mention three hundred years ago.

If this Athaeÿn *was* alive, he could be anywhere. Even more places if dead.

Like underground or at the bottom of the ocean.

I shook my head, now thoroughly bummed out.

This is why I prefer the company of plants.

To my additional dismay, I suddenly finished the last of my drink.

Noooo—

I sucked my straw so loudly a few people turned their heads in my direction, but I couldn't care less. I was going to inhale every last drop of my Regal Indulgence.

This is the real tragedy.

Only when the bottom was bone dry did I finally give up. I then stood there pouting as I waved the empty cup back and forth just enough for the straw to roll around the interior. This also made quite a racket.

I feel like I'm forgetting something.

It was then a young couple giddily walked past with armfuls of books, excitedly discussing which they were going to read first.

Oh, yeah. The tomes.

After returning the cup, I began the trek back to The Sovereign Vault, twirling my freshly blood-stained straw around my fingers as I went.

I still had plenty of time before Meech put the tomes back, but I decided to be polite and not keep him waiting longer than necessary. My decision had absolutely nothing to do with the correlation between the efficiency of my return and the length of his nagging lecture.

And I've already had more than enough socializing today…

Chapter 7

Athaeÿn

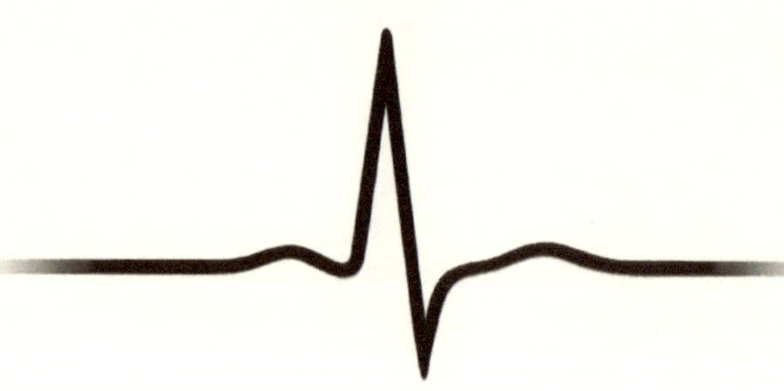

I stayed on the roof of the coach until dawn. The thick curtains inside were effective at keeping sunlight out, but sleeping the day away was more difficult than I thought it would be. The rumbling vehicle was a far cry from my motionless bed.

Not needing sleep would be a nice Undead perk.

Or at least having the choice not to. The fact we still needed rest had always seemed odd to me, but, like breathing, it was something living things did, so I didn't actually mind too much. In general, I gladly clung to anything that made me feel like I was still alive.

I'll just have to catch up on sleep when I get there.

As the long ride dragged on, I settled into a routine of reading or attempting to sleep during the day and sitting on the roof to stargaze at night. Between lengthy breaks for the horses and the vast distance of over a hundred miles to Xythe's kingdom, the journey took roughly five days. Luckily, I still had blood vials and unread books to spare.

Well, books I haven't read in a long time, anyway.

Even my flower crown remained in decent shape, and I had the Flora Demons to thank for its longevity. As beautiful as the glowing blossoms were, I wished they were bundles of lavender instead to soothe my anxiety. It was definitely starting to sink in just how real this was.

Xythe…

When it came to enthrallment, Arch-Vampires had a leg up on Arch-Demons since the latter could only enthrall other Demons, but their formidable magic easily made up for this minor deficit. In addition to their primary ability, they could also wield a secondary power from another sub-race, albeit far less potently.

I'm not sure what Xythe's bonus ability is.

Regardless, what a nightmare for whoever summoned him. There were supposedly very few Arch-Demons in Dominion, so I could only imagine the look on their face when, instead of the random, lesser Solar Demon they were hoping for, they got Xythe.

Talk about unlucky.

Raethe had infamously given Arch-Vampires a more powerful version of enthrallment than that of Arch-Demons, but he had also given a weaker, unreliable version to everyone else. If I summoned a Demon the same way Roänach did, I would only have a five-second window to enthrall them, and, to sweeten the deal, there was an arbitrary fifty-fifty chance of it not working anyway.

Because Xythe was an Arch-Demon, his summoner would have been unable to enthrall him even if they tried, but he probably took their head off before they could even register what was happening. Considering the fact he was already a king in Dominion, I could only imagine how incensed he was to lose everything in an instant compared to the average Demon.

No wonder he was drawn to Eidolon.

His attempt to take over was ill-advised at best, but, according to summoned lesser Demons who were familiar with his ilk, that was "a very Arch-Demon thing to do." He was beyond lucky the queens only exiled him, though he apparently didn't see it that way.

Should've just started a new kingdom from the beginning.

All of a sudden, I noticed an ominous light seeping between the curtains.

Oh no.

The coach had yet to arrive when I looked out the window and spotted the dreaded solar shield protecting Xythe's castle. It looked like a dome of shimmering light on the horizon. An absolutely *massive* dome. It was hard to tell how big it was from so far away, but it had to be at least five hundred feet tall.

Probably more.

The closer we got, the larger it appeared.

Definitely more.

By the time we stopped at the gleaming barrier, my final estimate was a thousand feet at its peak. Even if I was way off, it was easily the most impressive display of magic I had seen in a long time. Rather than being fully transparent like a window or opaque like a wall, it was translucent and golden, as if sunlight itself had been captured and repurposed.

Ugh, I can feel it even in here.

Despite the coach providing decent insulation from the solar magic, I could tell any direct contact with the shield would be excruciating, if not deadly. To be fair, it could've been equally harmful to non-Vampires, but I had no way of knowing and no intention of getting a closer look. All I knew was that it felt dreadful, and I wasn't even inside the dome yet.

Shame Roänach isn't here to be miserable too.

Wincing a little from the light, I peeked between the curtains and spotted a lone figure standing on the other side of the barrier. I was able to make out a pale form with a long bony tail and a serpentine face sporting four black eyes, each of which was dotted by a small but brilliant white pupil. Having seen my fair share in Eidolon, it was unmistakably a lesser Solar Demon.

Without even touching the shield, they slowly waved their clawed hand in a sweeping, vertical arc, cutting a hole in the light that was the exact same shape as their gesture but of much greater size. Once the coach passed through, the Demon fully resealed the gap with a simple, horizontal motion as if swiping something off a table.

That was that.

Well, I'm officially trapped in here now.

Even though I was still inside the coach, it felt like I was standing right next to the barrier. If this oppressive feeling of artificial sunlight was also going to exist inside the castle, the crumbling pieces of my remaining sanity would surely disintegrate.

The castle itself was even more blinding to look at. It had to be the whitest, most reflective marble I had ever seen, and the solar shield's light hitting it from almost every angle wasn't helping.

Easily the worst building in existence.

Despite being nighttime, it looked like midday within the shield. When I tilted my head to look up through the window, I was only able to see a few of the brightest stars through the distant ceiling of the dome. Somehow, my heart sank further.

I can't even see the night sky in here?

It was fortunate I had stargazed as much as possible on the journey.

This is already terrible.

When the coach finally stopped, I instinctively recoiled from the door. I didn't want this horrid light on my skin, but the coachman had other ideas as he opened the door and made a coaxing gesture. I stayed put.

His bored look turned into a glare. "Out."

I glared right back. "You have no authority over me." When I shoved my trunk out, it landed directly on his feet with a tremendous thud. I had done this on purpose but still felt a pang of guilt when he screeched in pain.

No, the coachman's attitude wasn't his fault, and, yes, I was taking out some anger on him, but I didn't care at the moment. I was so sick of everything. If he was going to be a jackass, he was going to get his feet crushed, and if he didn't want his feet crushed, he shouldn't have been standing so close.

Sorry not sorry.

Meanwhile, he yanked his injured feet out from under the trunk and rubbed them one at a time, hissing profanities under his breath as he did so. "Roänach is a sick bastard for not letting us gut you swine like the useless filth you are."

I was only paying half-attention as I reluctantly scooted toward the open door. "Aw, you poor things."

It was a nightmare the moment I stepped outside.

Shit—

I made a pitiful attempt to shield myself from the light, but it was coming from every direction other than the ground and already starting to burn me. In a bit of a panic, I grabbed my trunk and fled into the castle through the towering front doors, which, thankfully, were being held open by two more Solar Demons. Unfortunately, this meant light was spilling inside as well, so I had to keep my back to the entrance.

Still better than outside.

My tentative relief was shattered when I noticed the gilded sconces lining the entire vaulted hallway, all of which held orbs of what looked and felt like pure solar magic.

Oh, good. Suns everywhere.

Ignoring those to the best of my ability, I checked the rest of my surroundings and found quite a few Solar, Lunar, and Starlight Demons gathered nearby. Most were adults. A few were children. All were keeping their distance and watching me in silence.

At least they seem polite.

Despite the stark contrast between them and the coachman, I couldn't help but wonder if they were enthralled as well. I had yet to meet Xythe, but it was hard to imagine him as anything other than a ruthless monarch with zero patience for even the slightest bit of attitude. He didn't exactly seem the tolerant type.

I bet he ripped more Demons from Dominion to be his new subjects—

A sharp cackle from outside pulled me from my thoughts.

Ugh, why did Roänach make them like this?

Sighing and shaking my head, I pushed my trunk over with a loud, echoing thud and sat down on it with a huff, making sure to keep my back to the doors as I did so. When I carefully glanced over my shoulder, I could see the coachman laughing and pointing at me from where he remained next to the horses, enviably unaffected by the solar shield's harsh light.

Maybe there's still time to drop my trunk on his feet again.

Before I could snap at him, I was distracted by the other Demons all turning and looking down the corridor. I heard what they were looking at before I saw it.

Uh oh—

I shuddered at the distinct sound of something heavy and sharp dragging on the ground. When I finally looked, my eyes widened at the unnerving sight of a taller, more intricate Demon stalking down the hall, and it quickly became apparent what the dragging sound was. It wasn't a weapon like I expected. At least, not a handheld one. His long, segmented tail was similar to that of a scorpion, but, instead of a venomous barb, it ended in a huge, curved blade that was being deliberately scraped along the floor in a show of intimidation.

It's working—

My breath caught in my throat when he looked right at me. He had four eyes like the lesser Demons, but his were somewhat recessed in what appeared to be a horned, skeletal mask. In addition, where the others had simple, white dots for pupils, he essentially had blazing suns. I could have sworn they were audibly sizzling.

They almost hurt to look at.

The only thing more distracting than his piercing gaze, deadly tail, protruding back lined with massive spines, and lengthy claws, was the brilliant, glowing orb hovering between the two spires of his extended skull. It easily passed as a miniature star, making the upper half of his head look like a celestial crown.

Despite us making eye contact, the crowned Demon said nothing as he headed for the entryway with his tail scraping the floor louder than ever. The lack of sparks was surprising.

This noisy approach caught the attention of the coachman, who abruptly stopped laughing and tried to peer inside to see what the sound was. His curiosity then dissolved into fear when the much larger Demon appeared in the open doorway.

"What is so amusing, *pest?*"

He wasn't even talking to me, but I shivered from his chilling tone, nonetheless. Every word reverberated as though spoken by multiple voices at once.

The coachman, on the other hand, who *was* being spoken to, quickly took a few nervous steps back to put some distance between them.

"Are you laughing at my prize?"

The coachman shook his head and held his hands up in surrender.

Xythe

This response, or lack thereof, was deemed inadequate when the crowned Demon's segmented tail crackled and more than tripled in length as it whipped forward and hooked its scythe around the coachman's neck. The razor-sharp blade's searing light mirrored its wielder's fiery pupils.

"Apologize."

It took a few seconds, but the terrified coachman finally managed to speak. "I-I'm sorry—"

Without a word, the crowned Demon flung him onto the driver's seat of the coach and retracted his tail, having not taken a single step during the whole exchange. I had a feeling the coachman's presence was the only thing keeping the horses from panicking.

Meanwhile, the Fauna Demon in question snapped the reins and frantically drove the coach back to the barrier, where they were let out by the same lesser Solar Demon from before. Despite the coachman's earlier behavior, I was relieved he hadn't been killed. Shocked, but relieved.

Well, that was almost a disaster.

With a huff of superiority and slight flick of his tail, the crowned Demon came back inside and waved one of his monstrous hands to dismiss the large crowd of onlookers, all of whom obeyed without question and dispersed. His abnormally long claws would have looked almost comical had they not been glowing with the same deadly magic as his tail.

I can feel them from here.

Fortunately, the doors had finally closed and shut out the barrier's horrible light.

Unfortunately, this meant I no longer had a good excuse to avoid looking at him.

Maybe the shield's not so bad—

Taking a deep, silent breath, I turned around as slowly as possible and stared at him from where I remained anchored to my trunk.

Please don't come near me.

My chest tightened when he approached anyway and stopped just a few feet away.

Oh gods—

After a few unnerving seconds of nothing happening, he put one hand on his chest and gave a polite half-bow. "Welcome to my kingdom."

Huh?

I was a bit dumbstruck but managed a small nod. "Thank you. I presume you're Xythe?"

"The one and only." He stood upright and reinstated painful eye contact. "Roänach promised a dazzling gift," he added, tilting his head a little. "He did not disappoint."

I couldn't tell if this was meant to be a compliment or if he was just thinking out loud. Either way, it made me deeply uncomfortable.

I think I'd prefer insults…

"Th-Thank you," I repeated quietly, unsure of what else to say. When he just continued staring at me, I averted my gaze and slipped off my trunk to retrieve a blood vial, clearing my throat a bit awkwardly as I did so. Thankfully, one sip was all it took to heal the mild sunburn I had gotten from the solar shield.

"Are the lights harming you?"

I looked up and was surprised to find him already extinguishing the sconces with another wave of his hand. Even this simple kindness left me uneasy. "My burn was actually from the shield outside, but those lights were a bit uncomfortable as well, so thank you again."

"Anything to protect something so delicate."

I had to force myself not to make a noise of distaste. His off-putting comments were dripping with an overly polite aura that reminded me of Roänach a bit too much for my liking. Specifically, the Roänach I knew before he showed his true colors. This was off to a bad start.

As long as he doesn't touch me, I'll be fine.

Xythe tilted his head again and pointed at my own. "What is that?"

I unconsciously patted the blossoms a few times. "O-Oh, it's just a flower c— uhhhh… *hat.*"

His pupils sparked a little, almost like his own version of blinking. "Did Roänach believe I would find that amusing?"

My chest tightened again. "N-No, my friend made it for me. Does it annoy you?"

"It does not."

Phew…

"It is simply unfamiliar to me."

I wish your crown was flowers instead.

After returning the blood vial to my trunk, I finally stood and faced him directly, though I had to keep some distance between my skin and his various glowing body parts. He wasn't as big as I expected, but the top of his head was still at least a foot over mine, and his extended skull made him appear even taller. Regardless, I didn't enjoy being looked down on in more ways than one.

At least I'm taller than Roänach…

"Come," Xythe said plainly, starting down the hall in the direction he came from. Fortunately, he wasn't dragging his tail this time, so the only sounds were his hoof-like footsteps echoing off the polished walls.

I followed silently with my trunk, hoping to draw as little attention to myself as possible.

Please don't talk to—

"What has Roänach told you?"

For fuck's sake.

I suppressed a huff. "That you still hold a grudge against the queens and agreed to work with him to take Eidolon. Oh, and that I'm collateral for the deal."

"The bare minimum, I see."

That didn't sound good. "What else is there?"

"Details and things left unsaid."

His vague answer was annoying, but I kept that to myself. "Like what?"

"Are you certain you would prefer honesty over blissful ignorance?"

That definitely didn't sound good. "Yes… I think…"

Xythe hummed in thought as we entered a near-endless, vertical shaft and stepped onto a solid gold platform. I could tell it was a gravity lift, but instead of a lever, there was a lone solar orb on the wall. When he pointed at it and flicked his wrist upward, the small sphere morphed into a skyward arrowhead shape, causing the platform to begin slowly rising.

Ah, so that's his secondary ability.

I hadn't seen any Gravity Demons among his subjects, but, even if there were, I had a feeling the orb's dual combination of magic meant only Xythe could operate this unique elevator.

Great, trapped inside the shield and on the top floor.

Neither of us said anything for a few moments.

Fortunately, he was still staring at the wall when he spoke again. "I grant your request for honesty. What would you like to know?"

How to escape.

I glanced at the side of his head. "Everything, I guess."

He nodded to himself. "I appreciate a curious mind. It is true that I agreed to overthrow the capital with Roänach, but not to rule alongside him in any capacity. Eidolon will be his to control, and I will return here."

I already knew they planned on going their separate ways, but the implication hadn't clicked for some reason. His clarification did. "Wait, wasn't your desire to rule the capital the reason you went after the queens in the first place?"

"It was, but that is no longer the case and has not been for many centuries. With the clarity wisdom has granted me, I have come to realize leading a city of that scale and complexity would be exhausting and irritating. My time and effort are invaluable, and tedious sovereignty over Eidolon is worth neither." He stood eerily still as he spoke. "I am quite content with my small kingdom. Here, I am exempt from all jurisdictions and free to do as I please. Roänach will come to a similar conclusion one day, and his regret will be amusing to witness."

That wasn't what I had expected to hear. "Fair enough. I wouldn't want to rule the capital either," I noted truthfully. "So, you really agreed to this for the sole purpose of killing the queens?"

"Correct."

"Even though you were exiled over a thousand years ago?"

"Correct."

"That's quite a grudge."

"You will find I am capable of holding one for all eternity."

Clearly.

When the platform docked at the top of the shaft, Xythe stepped off into what looked like a small lobby with a single, ornate door in the middle of the back wall.

I followed quietly with my trunk. "Any other details or things left unsaid?" I asked after a few seconds, unsure if I actually wanted an answer.

"The final matter involves you." He stopped next to the door and turned to face me, his unchanging mask as expressionless as ever. "Would you still like to know?"

"Yes, even if it's information you think I won't like."

With a simple nod, he opened the door and gestured for me to go in first.

I reluctantly entered the room and set my trunk down off to one side. I was about to say something but froze when my eyes registered the numerous decorations meticulously arranged on the floor, furniture, walls, and ceiling. They weren't the kind I wanted to see.

That's a lot of bones.

I was completely surrounded by skeletons but couldn't tell if the majority were on stands, in display cases, or hanging from the ceiling. Scattered among them were countless preserved heads, limbs, and organs in jars; fur and skin rugs; taxidermy mounts; and pristine skulls. Most of the trophies were animals, but quite a few were not.

Oh gods—

My anxious breathing shallowed as I took in the alarming number of Humanoid artifacts. Chancing a fearful look down, my lungs gave out entirely upon realizing I had set my trunk on a leather rug made from a Human, whose eyeless face was still perceivable despite being stretched and warped.

Wh-Why—

Verging on a nervous breakdown, I swallowed my overwhelming dread and focused on some of the less nightmarish decorations. The rodent skeletons in glass cases were kind of… neat…

Just pretend they're ships in bottles.

My chest tightened when I heard Xythe enter behind me. "I, uh… This is…" I cleared my throat awkwardly. "*Quite* the collection you've got here." Before I could stop myself, I turned and gestured to his skeletal mask. "Is… Is that a trophy as well?"

Why would you ask him that?!

His pupils sparked again. "This is my face."

I nodded a bit excessively, feeling like I was about to faint at any second.

At least he doesn't seem insulted.

Eventually, he broke eye contact and headed deeper into the room. "Now then, the remaining details of your circumstances."

I'm not sure I want to know anymore.

"While I do plan to uphold my end of the bargain regarding the capital, there was another promise made to Roänach, one I never intended to keep."

My stomach dropped. "Returning me to him?"

"Correct."

So much for that "honorable Demon King" bullshit.

I'd had a feeling this would happen, but it was still a punch to the gut. "Why?"

"The value of my revenge far outweighs his misguided desire to control Eidolon. However, an entire city is a substantial, material reward, and I deserve something tangible as well. Something I can look upon each and every day with immense gratification."

As Xythe said this, he glanced over his massive bed at the back wall, which was covered from ceiling to floor by severed wings. There had to be hundreds of pairs. Half were feathered. Half were skeletal. Most of the latter were bat wings, the largest of which had a five or six-foot span and served as the centerpiece.

I wish I could fly out of here.

After staring at the wings a bit too long, I returned my wary gaze to Xythe. "If you want something tangible, couldn't you just add the queens' bodies to your collection instead? Surely, that would be a better prize than a nobody like me."

"The mere presence of those unworthy swine would defile my precious trophies. They deserve to rot at the base of the citadel with their shame on full display, a truly exquisite sight for the entire population to ridicule."

Agree to disagree.

The image of Elvylli's and Sathira's abandoned corpses putrefying out in the open was sickening. They most certainly did not deserve that.

But I know someone else who probably does—

"So, what do you say?"

His question caught me off guard. "I have a choice?"

"In either refusing or accepting my proposition."

"To, what, live here forever?"

"To be my pet."

"Forever."

"Correct."

I didn't bother hiding my look of distaste.

Wait—

All of a sudden, I remembered my idea of convincing Xythe to kill Roänach instead.

Maybe…

Once I either refused or accepted, there was likely no going back.

It's now or never.

I took a deep breath. "Can I make a proposition of my own?"

He tilted his head. "You may."

"Due to circumstances beyond my control, I can't be your pet."

"Why not?"

"I still belong to Roänach."

"Incorrect. He gifted you to me."

"He did, but he's still my master. As long as he lives, I'm arcanely bound to him."

"I do not care. His continued existence has no bearing on the fact you now belong to me."

There was a brief lull in the conversation as I tried to think. All I could come up with was an unconvincing bluff. "He's going to be furious when he realizes you lied. You really think he won't try to take me back?"

"He would be a fool to do so."

My fists clenched and trembled at my sides.

He really is just like Roänach.

I was getting nowhere fast and beyond pissed about it. If I accepted this deal, I would go from Roänach's slave to Xythe's pet. Eternal captivity either way.

But if I refuse—

When I glanced at the trophies again, a horrifying thought crossed my mind.

If Xythe doesn't kill me properly…

The mere concept of being reduced to a Vampiric skeleton that was somehow still conscious despite having no flesh to see, speak, or even move was nightmare-inducing.

Shit—

I started to panic. "I-If you agree to kill him, I'll agree to be your pet. Forever."

"If that is your proposition, I refuse."

"Why?!"

"I already have you. There is no need for me to kill him."

"What is it, *exactly,* that's so fucking important about keeping me as a trophy?!"

"It is not a matter of importance. I simply do not give up that which belongs to me."

"I don't belong to you!"

The room went dead silent.

At this point, I didn't care if I was flayed alive, mounted on the wall, gutted and stuffed, trapped as a conscious skeleton, or gruesomely killed. Escaping Roänach's subjugation just to be the Demon King's dog wasn't worth it. I was done being owned by others.

I don't belong to Roänach.

I don't belong to Xythe.

I don't belong to anyone.

Period.

My shoulders were heaving as I bared my fangs at him.

Fucking say something, already.

When he finally did, his tone was unexpectedly calm. "Are you refusing my proposition?"

"Yes."

"So be it."

. . .

I was absolutely livid, but my eyes burned with tears of frustration. None of my options were even remotely passable. Arguably, living as Xythe's pet could have been considered the "good" choice as long as I wasn't regularly assaulted, but it didn't matter. Death was preferable to being someone's property. Surviving wasn't living.

Just get it over with.

Instead of getting anything over with, Xythe continued staring at me with his head tilted like some kind of curious beast.

I threw my arms out to the sides. "So, what happens now?"

He remained silent at first before turning toward the door. "If you will not be my prize, you will be a gift for my son."

"What?! No! I'm not going to be anyone's gift! Either set me free or kill me!"

"It is not up to you."

He grabbed my arm without even looking. The instant his massive claws made contact, their honed edges sliced right through my sleeve and embedded deep into my delicate flesh, searing everything in their path with blistering solar magic.

I shrieked in agony as debilitating pain racked the entire right side of my body. It was easily the worst thing I had ever felt, *eclipsing* when Roänach took his silver dagger to my face. All things considered, that had been a relatively quick injury. Xythe wasn't letting go.

Without a word, he dragged me out of the room and back onto the gold platform, which began to descend the moment he pointed at the control orb and flicked his wrist downward.

"Let *go!*"

Tears of anguish were streaming down my face as I desperately tried to push his claws off, but all this did was harm my free hand. It was like trying to remove red-hot metal from an active forge.

Meanwhile, Xythe stood perfectly composed next to me, entirely unaffected by the pitiful barrage on his iron grip. This was infuriating but not surprising. Lesser Demons were physically stronger than other races despite only being five feet tall on average. But a seven-foot Arch-Demon?

I may as well have been an insect.

Chapter 8

Athaeÿn

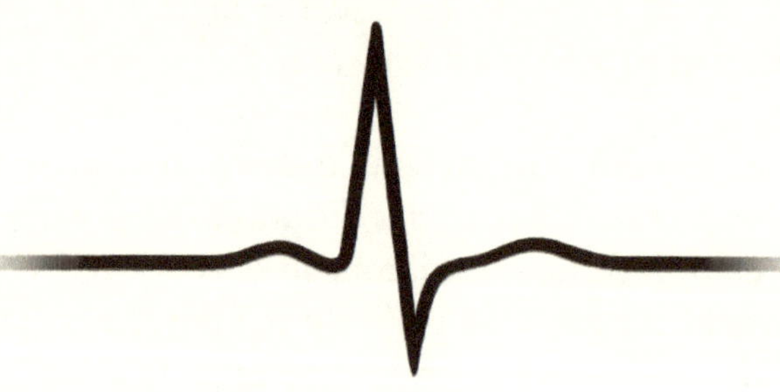

The descent felt like an eternity.

When the platform finally docked at the bottom, Xythe stepped off and continued effortlessly pulling me along, leaving me yelping and stumbling in the wake of his long gait and quick pace. I had to practically jog to keep up.

Eventually, we passed a large entertainment hall brimming with lesser Solar, Lunar, and Starlight Demons, but they were either too busy to notice or too enthralled to care about my plight. Screaming for their help accomplished nothing.

Someone, anyone—

Xythe finally spoke up when we began descending a wide, curved staircase. "I am certain my darling boy will appreciate this early birthday gift from his loving father."

"N-No—"

Without warning, he yanked me forward so hard I finally tripped and fell, but every attempt to get back up was useless. It must have looked like he was dragging a flailing corpse.

"Stop! *Please—!*"

My desperate cries were completely ignored as the world around me devolved into a disorienting blur of tears and unrelenting stairs. The pain became so agonizing it transcended any anxiety I may have felt from being touched.

Help—

I was certain one more jolt would rip my arm off.

P-Please—

...

Compared to the elevator ride, this trek into the depths of the unknown felt just as endless but twice as foreboding. My tortured arm was convinced hours had passed, but it was probably minutes at most.

It felt like days.

When we finally reached the bottom of the stairs, there was a gaping entrance to some kind of cave system. The fifty-foot-tall opening was sealed by what felt like a weaker version of the solar shield around the castle, but its light was still uncomfortable on my skin.

Not another cave with a barrier—

Regardless of the unfortunate similarity to Castle Veil, something about this was incredibly odd. I was struggling to think clearly with my arm demanding most of my attention, but my mind started racing anyway.

Xythe's son lives in a walled off cave?

Why?

Is he some kind of beast that needs to be caged?

Wait, what kind of gift am I exactly?

My eyes widened with horror.

Oh no—

Before I could protest, Xythe flung me through the barrier as if I weighed nothing.

My severely injured arm was already pushing the limit of what I could handle, but I outright screamed when it was wrenched so violently. Already drowning in agony, I almost missed the moment I went through the wall of light. Almost. It felt more like a wall of fire, but everything was starting to blend together.

The wind was knocked out of me as I landed hard on the stone ground and rolled a few times before coming to a stop. My mangled arm had ended up between my body and the coarse rock, leaving me trembling and hissing through clenched teeth.

"If memory serves, I have only ever fed him animal carcasses. You should be quite the treat indeed," Xythe announced casually from where he remained on the stairs.

N-No—

Although certain I was about to pass out at any second, I managed to lift my head just enough to look at the ground in front of me. My flower crown somehow made it through the barrier, but it hadn't survived the journey. It had been reduced to nothing more than a ring of sizzling mush, a pile of smoking, blackened blossoms shedding ash and embers instead of petals.

I'm sorry, Fiella.

With crumbling resolve, I slowly forced myself to get up. It was an arduous process.

Once standing, my shredded right arm dangled limp and useless at my side. Not only were my bones visible through the gashes cleaved into my flesh, but they were on the verge of splintering or even snapping. At least the wounds were cauterized.

Almost nothing had been spared from the wall of concentrated solar magic. My skin was charred. My hair was scorched. Even my clothing was singed. Any motion that shifted my ruined arm was bad enough, but with my entire body severely burned, every little movement inflicted further suffering.

Good thing I closed my eyes on the way through…

Shuddering and whimpering in ceaseless anguish, I painstakingly trudged back to the barrier and weakly shoved it with my functional arm. Unfortunately, it seemed impenetrable from this side.

Xythe tilted his head as he watched me. "I am uncertain if being devoured is sufficient to kill a Vampire. If not, enjoy the digestive process." His tone of indifference hung in the air like a miasma of disdain as he turned and started back up the stairs, but he paused after just a few steps. "This is your final opportunity to change your mind."

I just glared at him and bared my fangs. "F-Fuck off."

He disappeared up the stairs without acknowledging my reply whatsoever.

Despite the barrier's searing touch, I slammed my fist on it with a sharp growl of anger that dragged out into a groan of pain.

Fuck Xythe.

Fuck Roänach.

Fuck everyone and everything.

Cradling my destroyed arm to minimize any shifting, I turned away from the wall of light to take in my new surroundings.

The distant ceiling had to be at least a few hundred feet high and was split down the middle by a long, jagged crevice. The fact it was sealed by another barrier led me to believe it opened above ground, but I couldn't reach it, regardless of injuries. In contrast to this daunting vertical, the horizontal space I had landed in was just thirty feet wide and fifty feet to the back wall, where a large tunnel sat ominously vacant.

Why hasn't his son appeared yet?

Even though his absence was more unnerving than relieving, I wondered if it meant an opportunity to find another way out.

Make up your mind. Are you giving up or not?

That was apparently still up for debate. For now, I decided to keep fighting until I met some kind of end, though whether it would be from starving to death, succumbing to my wounds, or being eaten alive was yet to be seen.

I've come this far...

My extensive injuries turned stealth into a perpetual chore, but I suspected it was wasted effort anyway. Considering my bloodcurdling scream when I was thrown through the barrier, there was absolutely no way my presence had gone undetected.

He's probably just waiting to strike...

The pain was a good distraction from this likely truth.

When I reached the tunnel and peered in, I was both aggravated and hopeful to see multiple side paths branching off the main one. More paths meant more places I had to search, but it also meant more places to hide, not that I could outrun the son of an Arch-Demon anyway.

Especially not in this condition.

Catching myself just as I was about to hiss in pain, I stifled my breathing and began creeping down the tunnel. For some reason, I thought he would most likely be lurking down one of the offshoots, especially if asleep, so I decided to stick to the main path for now.

Just have to… stay quiet…

. . .

What started as feeble sneaking had long devolved into shambling. Frankly, I couldn't believe my ruined arm hadn't fallen off yet.

Has it always been this heavy?

Clear thinking was proving impossible. I had attempted to traverse the cave in a manner that would allow backtracking, but I wasn't sure if I had consistently chosen only the rightmost tunnels as intended.

I could really use a miracle right about now.

At this point, still having all four limbs attached was a miracle in and of itself.

But not enough…

My search was desperate, but there was no light at the end of the tunnel. Literally. It was an endless maze of rapidly fading ambient light. The darkness would have been comforting under any other circumstances, but what should have been soothing was becoming increasingly sinister. I had never lamented the beautiful glowing crystals of my homeland more.

I took them for granted… I took everything for granted…

Even without luminous crystals, my subterranean lineage meant I could still see somewhat decently in low light. This ability had its limits, but I had something else to pick up the slack. An actual perk of being a Vampire.

And I'm going to need it soon.

By now, the intensifying darkness and my disintegrating arm were competing for the distinguished title of *current worst thing*, but my sidelined fear of the inevitable had retaken interest. The deeper I delved into the cave, the more violently this anxiety clawed its way through my addled mind. It was a good thing I didn't need to breathe. The paranoia was suffocating.

Where is he?

As much as I didn't want to be devoured, this endless suspense was far worse than if we had run into each other right away. His solitary confinement and indicated diet had me convinced he was some vicious creature even bigger and deadlier than Xythe, and considering how poorly that confrontation went...

Gods, everything hurts.

As if my noxious arm and twitching fingers weren't bad enough, the flaking and ripping of my charred skin were getting progressively worse. Even the tiniest movement had the sensation of infinite needles digging into my flesh and pulling in every direction at once. It was unlike anything I had ever felt.

Someone, anyone, please make it stop—

The stark contrast between wanting to survive and the desire to be put out of my misery was one of the most infuriating things I had ever experienced, and it wasn't even a new phenomenon.

I feel like I'm losing my mind.

And yet, despite everything, I still didn't want to die.

H-Help...

...

After shuffling down what felt like a million tunnels, the darkness finally became too much.

Time for the perk.

With a distinct and slightly uncomfortable shift in the back of my eyes, I switched to my Vampiric thermal vision. The familiar spectrum of warm hues was marginally comforting.

At least I can kind of see again.

When I turned the next corner, my brief reassurance was vaporized by horror.

Oh no—

The tunnel was primarily deep violet, indicating a relatively cool temperature, but the far end of the passage was dominated by a massive, blindingly white figure. It was *not* the light at the end of the tunnel I was hoping for.

That's a lot of body heat—

The figure appeared to be looking right at me, but I couldn't tell from this distance. The limited detail offered by the thermal vision wasn't helping.

Why isn't he moving?

He wasn't the only one. My paralyzing fear was all that had kept me from gasping and immediately giving away my presence, if I was even still undetected.

Maybe it's just a coincidence he's looking this way.

A cautious side-step accompanied by a subtle head turn tracking my movement proved otherwise.

Fuck...

It was over.

Absolutely over.

I had no idea how often Xythe fed his son, but it didn't matter. As far as I was concerned, I was his current prey and next meal.

Before logic could stop me, I spun around with a strained yelp and made a pitiful attempt to flee. Even if I could somehow outrun this beast, there was no escape and nowhere to hide, so I didn't bother trying to stifle my whimpers of pain. It was impossible when every step worsened my injuries.

Everything is so loud down here—

With one arm cradling the other, I had little to no balance and almost fell with each corner I turned and every rock I tripped over. At this point, I was tempted to just let myself fall. Delaying the inevitable wasn't worth any of this.

My body will probably decide for me any second now.

I paused when I came upon a three-way junction, but the choice of direction wasn't why I stopped.

Wait—

An anxious glance over my shoulder revealed nothing but empty tunnel.

Is he even following me?

My cautious optimism was promptly shattered when the darkness shifted and materialized a familiar, bright silhouette just fifteen feet away.

He can move through shadows?!

Logic continued to evade me as I fled down the middle passage as fast as my wavering legs could carry me. It was anything but fast.

When I noticed a slightly warmer hue in the distance, I chanced switching back to my normal vision and nearly gasped when I saw faint, blueish green light. My remaining strength was hanging on by a thread, but I made a break for it anyway.

Wait, what's that sound?

It didn't take long to figure it out.

Oh no—

As I rounded the final curve, I was met with the horrific sight of an underground river.

No...

I just stood there staring at the deadly running water. It sounded more like cruel laughter.

So much for literally anything.

With an exhausted grimace, I readjusted the shaky grip on my destroyed arm and shuffled forward in defeat. Amazingly, I made it to the riverbank without collapsing.

Guess that was my last miracle...

When standing became too much, I sank to my knees and finally accepted my fate, something I should have done the moment I refused Xythe's proposition. Everything afterward had been such wasted effort. The resilience I had clung to was apparently just stubbornness, and all it had done was drag things out for nothing.

At least I found a beautiful place to die.

The glowing water and bioluminescent flora were calming, but they just reminded me of the gardens outside Castle Veil. And my ruined flower crown.

I'm so sorry, Fiella.

Bracing myself with my intact arm, I slowly and methodically shifted into a sitting position to wait for the violent end promised to me.

I waited for seconds.

Minutes.

It soon felt like an eternity.

Why is nothing happening?

Risking another glance over my shoulder, I was less than surprised to find the beast staring at me from where he stood motionless in the mouth of the tunnel. Now that I could see him in full detail, the sight wasn't what I expected.

Is this really Xythe's son?

Even with notable Demonic features, he primarily resembled an Arbiter. *Especially* in height. He had to be at least eight feet tall, but that was just one of many imposing details.

Defined by enormous muscles that could undoubtedly snap me in half like a twig, his hulking frame was swathed in deep red skin that darkened toward his extremities until nearly black, though some areas were split and discolored. Each hand was over a foot long, courtesy of lengthy fingers that tapered into deadly claws, and his mostly taurine legs stood atop unique, cloven feet that appeared more insectile than bovine. The protruding pelvic bone between his thighs marked the beginning of a long, segmented tail, which sported two blades much smaller than his father's scythe but of equal sharpness. Arguably most significant, however, were the large, bony spines on his elbows, knuckles, tail, and backs of his legs.

Unlike Xythe's skeletal visage, his son's face was Humanoid like mine but was still altered like much of his body. With a prominent beard, an upward horn of fiery orange above the brow, and a long mane of raven hair, the right side of his head was remarkably free of Demonic influence. Also intact were distinct markings trisecting his face that started at the hairline and angled inward toward the chin, a feature shared by all Arbiters. I could even see faint shimmering from subtle scales lining his cheekbones and forehead. As for his eyes, sclerae of solid black were illuminated by elongated, pupilless, amber irises, whose angles perfectly matched the surrounding markings. Their unmistakable, divine intensity served as indisputable proof of his Arbiter lineage.

In contrast, the left side of his head was largely encased in what looked like a fractured, skeletal helmet, which partially obscured his brow and surrounded his eye. This kept his other Arbiter horn from growing but compensated with an even larger, downward curving one that pointed toward fissured skin on his cheek and jagged protrusions along his jawline. All of this appeared to stifle the rest of his beard and hair. Even his ear looked partially eaten away.

I've never seen anything like him.

There were two more things that caught my eye. The first was four additional, much larger spines dominating his back where two, huge wings should have been.

I guess his Demon half won that battle.

Despite everything, this one little detail hurt my heart. An Arbiter without wings was like a songbird without a syrinx.

Speaking of throats—

The final thing of note was a glowing symbol on his neck. I could tell it was a magical rune, but this one was unfamiliar. What *was* familiar, however, was its golden light.

Xythe definitely put that there.

Before I could ponder it further, observation time ended when he finally approached.

Well, the respite was nice while it lasted…

His noticeably cautious movement was odd, but something else grabbed my attention.

Did I suddenly go deaf?

But I could still hear the river, so I nearly did a double take as I watched his cloven feet shift the stones on the riverbank with each heavy step. I knew exactly what that should have sounded like, but there was no sound whatsoever.

Maybe—

Looking up proved to be a mistake when my gaze accidentally overshot the rune and landed directly on his fierce, amber eyes. Even though I had accepted my fate, I was once again paralyzed with dread. The idea of being put out of my misery was one thing. Staring down my hunter was another entirely.

I changed my mind—

The reality of the situation sank in as he closed the distance between us and stopped just three feet in front of me.

I don't want to die—

As we stared intently at each other, I was certain a whisper could have shattered me.

Why isn't he tearing me to shreds?

My chest tightened painfully when his gaze drifted to my ruined arm, but my fear elevated to panic when his hand twitched.

No—

The terror of being devoured was suddenly amplified by my touch anxiety.

Don't—

To my overwhelming dismay, I was still frozen when he slowly reached for my arm.

S-Stop—

In the prison my body had become, it felt like my useless heart and writhing lungs were on the verge of collapsing in a desperate attempt to do something. *Anything.*

Don't touch me—

His hand kept reaching.

Please don't touch me—

He was going to at any second.

Stop—

My eyes were wide open, but I couldn't see through the tears that had welled up.

Stop.

Stop.

Stop.

Please—!

When there was less than an inch between his claw and one of the gashes in my arm, he paused and looked into my eyes again.

Tears began streaming down my cheeks. They were the only hint of movement besides the trembling in my shoulders. I couldn't even take in air to speak. To beg.

P-Please—

Despite my blurry vision, I could have sworn I saw something akin to confusion flash across his eyes, but I couldn't tell for certain.

Eventually, he looked at my arm once more and retracted his hand, having never made contact. After one final glance into my pleading eyes, he turned and disappeared down the tunnel, leaving me alone and shaken but untouched.

Why—

I nearly slumped over when everything hit me all at once.
I don't understand—
My body gave out before my mind had a chance to unravel further. Barely any of my thoughts were coherent as I lay there hazily staring up at the glowing plants draped across the cave ceiling. Instead of the river, I was drowning in a sea of anguish and bewilderment.
At least he didn't touch me...
The sound of running water began to fade as my vision darkened.
Maybe I can actually go out peacefully...
And with that, the world around me vanished.

Chapter 9

Athaeÿn

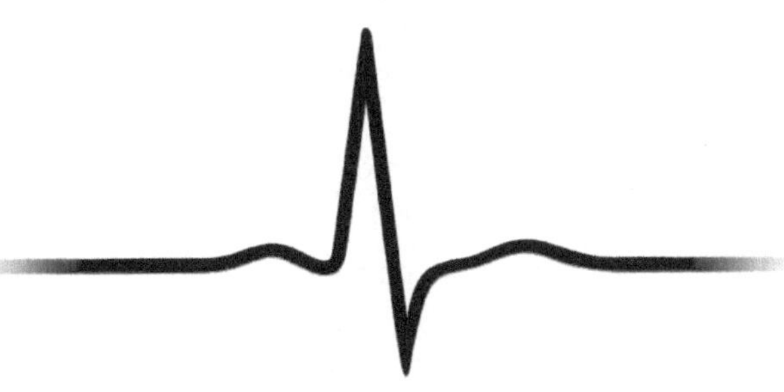

Over the next few days, I slipped in and out of consciousness. Mostly out.

On the fourth day, a familiar scent pulled me from my stupor.

Blood…

With immense effort, I cracked my eyes open and lolled my head toward the smell. The source was a severed deer leg. A rather fresh one.

Did he leave this here for me?

I frowned at myself.

No, it was the meat fairy.

Starving delirium clearly had a side effect of stupidity. Unless a deer had fumbled its way into the cave and spontaneously combusted right next to me, leaving only its leg behind, it must have been a gift from my fellow captive.

If he's willing to share, why wait days to do it?

A twinge of pain in my shredded arm reminded me of why I was languishing on the riverbank in the first place.

Maybe Xythe only feeds his son every few days.

Assuming that was true, he had actually shared as soon as he could.

And, by sparing me, waited almost a week to eat...

I had no idea what to believe, so I shoved those thoughts aside to deal with more pressing matters. Just as I was about to reach for the bloody offering, I realized one more thing. It had been left on the same side as my functional arm.

Probably just a coincidence.

Sighing heavily, I pushed this out of my mind as well. It was far too dangerous to trust even the simplest act of kindness.

Something I should've learned long ago...

With a grunt of discomfort, I reached over and pulled the deer leg onto my chest. Nothing seemed off about it, but my ravenous hunger quickly transcended any mistrust.

As I sank my fangs into the meaty end and guzzled down as much blood as possible, a wave of relief washed over me when the pain from my severe burns faded. Vampirism was a curse first and foremost, but even I couldn't deny the convenience and usefulness of my lone food source providing both sustenance and rapid healing.

It wasn't long before the severed limb was drained. When I sat upright, I was dismayed to find the horrid condition of my mangled arm unchanged, but at least the rest of my body had been repaired. Even my hair was no longer singed. Animal blood was less effective than Humanoid blood, but it was better than nothing.

Fixing my arm will have to wait, I guess.

Considering how extensive the damage was, that may have been impossible. For now, I reveled in the simple joy of unburned skin.

I need to thank him.

Keeping my butchered arm in mind, I remained seated and carefully turned until somewhat facing the tunnel, where two amber eyes glowed in the darkness. I had expected as much. Despite how creepy it was, I couldn't blame his curiosity.

Still better than touching.

We stared at each other for a full minute.

Against my better judgment, I finally broke the silence. "You can come over."

Nothing happened at first.

Eventually, he left the tunnel and sat about five feet away with his arms partially hugging his knees. He still made no sound whatsoever.

His unthreatening pose didn't stop me from shuddering, but I maintained eye contact anyway. "Do you understand me?" I asked politely, unsure if he had reacted to my beckoning tone or the words themselves.

He nodded.

I returned a nod. "Thank you for not eating me."

His gaze fell to the deer leg still draped across my lap.

"Oh, thank you for this as well, but you can have the rest of it," I added, tossing it onto the riverbank between us.

The timid man flinched as the hunk of meat landed in front of him, but his expression remained blank. After looking between me and the leg a few times, he picked it up and held it out with one hand while pointing at my mouth with the other.

"I know, but I'm a Vampire. I can only consume blood."

He blinked a few times before nodding again and chomping into the leg, which he easily tore through with powerful jaws and specialized teeth.

I was glad I couldn't hear it.

And I thought my fangs were intimidating.

The ravenous prince had sharp canines as well, but, unlike mine, his were much larger than everything else. Smoother, too. The rest of his teeth were more average in size but pointed and serrated as if from a shark. All of a sudden, I felt like a house cat next to a dragon.

Now, I'm doubly glad he spared me.

When he finished inhaling his snack, bones and all, he looked at me again but was distracted by my arm.

"Your father is to blame," I said bluntly.

His eyes widened with shock before abruptly tensing under heavy brows, which had furrowed with what looked like a mixture of doubt and confusion.

My chest tightened even though his reaction appeared more offended than angry. This was the first time I had seen undeniable emotion on his face, and the fact it was negative made me feel like an ass.

Still need to work on thinking before speaking.

I kept my mouth shut and glanced at the rune on his throat. Regardless of Xythe's involvement with that, he had clearly imprisoned his own son, so I didn't understand why the latter had gotten defensive.

Shouldn't he hate his father?

Evidently, there were layers to the situation I was unaware of.

Well, I did just get here.

Consistent with the theme of being uninformed, it was news to me that Arbiters and Demons could have young together. The prince certainly looked like a combination of both. Xythe himself was the odd part.

He doesn't exactly seem the paternal type.

Assuming he had given parenthood a genuine shot and later decided it wasn't for him, he could have just gotten rid of the problem.

Maybe his callousness falls short of infanticide.

As my mind went in circles, I realized I was still staring at the rune.

Might as well ask about it.

I looked into his eyes again. "I haven't heard a single sound from you. Can you make any noise at all?"

He shook his head.

"Is it because of the rune?"

A nod.

I can't even imagine how frustrating that is.

This just reinforced my confusion about his defensive reaction. Maybe he was in denial.

Maybe stop making assumptions.

His gaze drifted to my arm again. Even though I had upset him earlier, he seemed genuinely concerned. Or, at least, unable to ignore it.

I can attest to that.

"Drinking blood also heals my injuries," I let slip a disheartened sigh, "but I'm not sure this can be fixed."

I had barely finished speaking when he perked up and scooted closer with one arm already extended. He either didn't notice or didn't care that it hindered his balance and made his movement rather awkward.

There's no way he forgave me already—

I instinctively recoiled from his sudden approach but recovered just as fast. "I appreciate the offer, but Demon blood would kill me. I'm sorry."

He stared at me for a few seconds before slowly retracting his arm and looking at the ground.

I felt bad for refusing his offer, but I couldn't risk even half-Demon blood.

At least he can take "no" for an answer.

While this was less than the bare minimum for common decency, I couldn't deny the impact when it came from this intimidating man who could easily overpower me.

Should probably raise my standards again at some point.

Meanwhile, as the prince stood to leave, my guilt deepened when I saw how dejected he looked.

Do something.

It was at that moment I realized we hadn't introduced ourselves. "Can I at least get your name?"

He looked at me but otherwise didn't react.

Don't tell me—

My heart sank. "Do you even have a name?"

He shook his head.

I stared at him for a few seconds before groaning under my breath and pinching the bridge of my nose.

Guess naming your kid is pointless when you just throw them in a fucking hole.

Pushing this additional reason to hate Xythe out of my mind, I tried to think of a fitting name that was unique but short and sweet.

Maybe something related to his shadow ability?

After pondering for a bit, I looked up at him again. "How about Shade?"

Without hesitation, he nodded enthusiastically with a big smile.

Whoa—

His sudden cheerfulness had caught me off guard, but his grin was contagious. "Shade it is, then."

He was practically vibrating with excitement as he pointed at me and tilted his head.

My smile widened. "Athaeÿn."

To my surprise, he silently mouthed what looked like both of our names, but it was difficult to tell. Easily discernible, however, was his sheer happiness as he clasped his hands together and smiled down at them.

Okay, that's pretty cute.

His amusing delight got me wondering how often he smiled, if ever. Unfortunately, I suspected it was a rare occurrence, so it was a relief I could offer even a speck of joy.

I'm pretty sure he feels at least two specks.

As though to prove my theory, Shade was still beaming when he disappeared into the tunnel.

I just sat there absorbing the warmth of his appreciation.

He has a nice smile.

. . .

A few more days passed, during which I was frequently watched but otherwise left alone. While the opportunity to decompress was nice, tenuous relaxation soon became mind-numbing boredom, and that mental anguish was exacerbated by lingering physical agony. The only thing more annoying than my pulverized arm was the riverbank. Smooth, rounded rocks were still rocks, and my entire body demanded a more comfortable solution.

Wow, my shitty arm and I actually agree on something.

Fortunately, I was surrounded by rather plump and cushy plants that were perfect for building a nest, but I held off until one of Shade's absences so he wouldn't notice and try to help. It wasn't personal. I just wanted to do something on my own to spite my stupid arm, and I didn't want to turn him down again.

Better than wasting away as a useless slug.

The plant nest proved remarkably comfortable upon completion, but my spurned arm came back with a vengeance by starting to rapidly decompose. Sleeping had already been a grueling task. Now, it would surely be impossible.

Maybe some more blood would at least slow the decay—

I nearly jumped out of my skin when an entire, fresh deer carcass suddenly landed right next to me with a tremendous thud.

What the—

After staring at it for a few seconds, I looked up to find Shade gesturing between his delivery and my necrotic arm. Something stirred in my chest. I was still wary of his kindness, but there was distinct authenticity to his offers I couldn't ignore.

Who cares? Just drink the blood.

Hope for my arm was shaky at best as I shifted closer and sank my fangs into the deer's neck. There was a negligible decrease in pain as I sucked down as much blood as possible, but when I pulled back and inspected my arm, it looked completely unchanged.

Dammit…

"*Ugh,* why is animal blood so much weaker?" Huffing under my breath, I glared at my arm and used every ounce of concentration to try and move it even a little bit. All I got was slight twitching in a couple of fingers. My patience finally ran out.

That's it—

Just as I was about to tear the whole limb off, Shade pushed the deer aside and sat right in front of me with his own arm offered once more.

I shuddered at his close proximity. "Shade, I really can't."

There was pleading in his eyes as he lightly shook his hand, silently begging me to reconsider.

After staring at him for a few moments, my gaze fell to his wrist.

Maybe I can test a single drop without dying.

My frustration dwindled. It wasn't like I *wanted* to rip my arm off.

What have I got to lose?

I hesitated a bit longer before finally looking into his eyes again. "Alright," I held up my good hand when he started reaching closer, "but I can't bite you."

His enthusiasm faltered, but he recovered by smiling and tapping his forearm.

"I know you won't mind the pain. The problem is, I struggle with touch."

He just blinked a few times and looked at his hand as if he had never seen it before.

The familiar shame became a lump in my throat.

He must think I'm such a nuisance by now.

Instead of becoming irritated like I expected, he lit up with an idea. Looking even more excited than before, he clawed a tiny incision at the base of his thumb, dripped some blood onto a small rock, and held it out to me with another smile.

My hand only got halfway to the offering before slowly retracting and huddling against my chest. I felt like an ungrateful jerk but didn't want to risk another breakdown. The one Fiella and Haana had to witness was embarrassing enough.

Shade's smile never wavered as he set the rock down between us, slightly closer to me.

The thankful smile I returned was heavy with guilt but still genuine. When I picked up the rock and sniffed the blood, I was shocked to detect no Demonic traces.

Maybe the Arbiter half overpowers the Demon half.

Holding my breath in two ways, I cautiously touched the blood with the tip of my tongue. My eyes shot wide before the flavor had even finished processing.

That's the most delicious blood I've ever tasted.

Despite the spot being little more than a stain, I also felt minor pain relief in my arm.

Now I see what Callyn was raving about.

I could barely contain my excitement when I looked at Shade again. "I think your blood is safe."

Beaming with triumph, he pressed his hands together and began scanning our surroundings, likely for an alternative to licking a rock over and over again. It wasn't long before he homed in on my nest and plucked one of the flowers that happened to be somewhat cup-shaped.

The small cut on his thumb was already gone thanks to his healing factor, but he didn't hesitate to slice a new one and fill the flower with blood. The hesitation came when it was ready to be transferred. He tried arranging some rocks in a way that would hold the flower upright, but it refused to cooperate and almost spilled multiple times, leaving him frowning by the time he gave up. In the end, he carefully balanced it on three of his claws and held it out to me with an awkward grin.

At least he tried.

I was grateful but remained frozen as I stared at the bloody petals. It had been surprisingly easy to hand Fiella the lunelight and pull the flower crown off her wrist, so I wasn't sure why this exchange was so stressful.

Clearly, Shade's hand is too big and scary.

In the middle of internally scolding myself, I gripped the upper petals and was relieved when I managed to avoid touching his claws. The moment I took a sip, there was an instant rush from the much stronger dose.

Oh gods—

Shade's blood was nothing less than intoxicating, and I eagerly threw back the rest of the flower like a shot. After less than a second, my destroyed arm began rapidly healing before our eyes. In under a minute, it had been fully restored.

Wow, it didn't even leave scarring.

A huge smile came to my face as I repeatedly bent my healed arm and flexed my fingers. Everything worked perfectly. The singed fabric of my torn sleeve was all that remained of the violence.

I don't even know what to say.

My eyes burned when I looked into his. "Thank you."

He returned a huge smile bursting with a sense of accomplishment, but his expression slowly fell once he switched to looking back and forth between my face and neck.

I wasn't surprised my scars had caught his attention. "Don't worry, they're not painful."

His smile was long gone by the time he gestured to my restored arm.

"Yes, they were injuries too, but I think scars are technically healed already. Either way, these are unique wounds that can't be fixed." I sighed and shook my head. "They're the handiwork of Roänach, my master and the Arch-Vampire who turned me. The marks on my neck are from his fangs, and the scar on my face is from his silver dagger."

Shade's undivided attention turned into a glare directed solely at my blemishes. When he reinstated eye contact, he silently mouthed what looked like *I'm sorry.*

I was a bit surprised by the anger expressed on my behalf, but my heart skipped a beat when he asserted explicit sympathy.

When was the last time I felt that?

In addition to sustenance and healing, the consumption of blood offered my kind brief respites from undeath. These fleeting moments of life weren't literal, but they did rekindle a few irreplaceable abilities lost to Vampirism. The temporary heartbeat was expected. The skip wasn't.

My chest—

For once, it really did warm as I looked into Shade's eyes, which were still fixed on mine.

Why does he care so much?

Rather than skipping again, my heartbeat quickened. I hardly ever noticed these imitations of life anymore, but, in that moment, I felt alive.

Am I really that starved for compassion?

Feeling slightly embarrassed, I let out a slow breath and offered a more relaxed smile. "I appreciate the sentiment, but it's not your fault this happened."

Without smiling back, he retrieved the drained flower and held it up a little.

"Yes, I'm sure. Even with your powerful blood."

He nodded but looked disappointed as he limply tossed it out of the nest.

"Thank you for caring, though."

When he looked at me again, he finally returned a weak smile.

It means more than you know.

As nice as it would have been to continue sitting there with him, my restlessness suddenly caught up to me. Apparently, building the plant nest hadn't satisfied it.

Need to move.

Nodding to myself, I stood and stretched *both* arms above my head. Something else I had taken for granted. "Anyway, now that I'm no longer in excruciating pain, I could really go for a walk."

When Shade stood as well, it was impossible not to gawk up at him. I already knew he was at least two feet taller than me, but his towering stature truly registered when my standing eye level remained below his pecs. This also resulted in his bare hips coming halfway up my torso.

Don't look—

I looked immediately.

Oops.

Up close, I noticed a small detail I hadn't before. Full Demons had smooth pelvises, but Shade had a subtle slit along the top. I assumed any equipment he had was tucked inside.

Phew. That would have been awkward.

Shoving that out of my mind, I looked up at him again and felt a bit silly upon realizing just how terrified I had been when we first met. By now, gazing into his eyes was more than easy.

It's actually… pleasant.

After staring at each other for a little too long, Shade flopped the hefty deer carcass over his shoulder as if it weighed nothing and gestured between it and me a few times.

I smiled and shook my head. "Thank you, but if I drink any more blood I'll explode. It's all yours."

He returned the smile and began wading through the river, which only came up to his abdomen at the deepest point. Although rather slow-moving, it was still running water and would kill me before I even got halfway across its fifty-foot width.

Guess I won't be going over there any time soon.

There was no reason to anyway, so I settled for waving at Shade once he made it across and glanced at me over his free shoulder. He waved back before heading about thirty feet down the opposite riverbank and disappearing into another tunnel.

See you later…

My smile lingered as I looked down at my restored arm and bent it a few more times.

Shade had given me far more than just blood.

Chapter 10

Athaeÿn

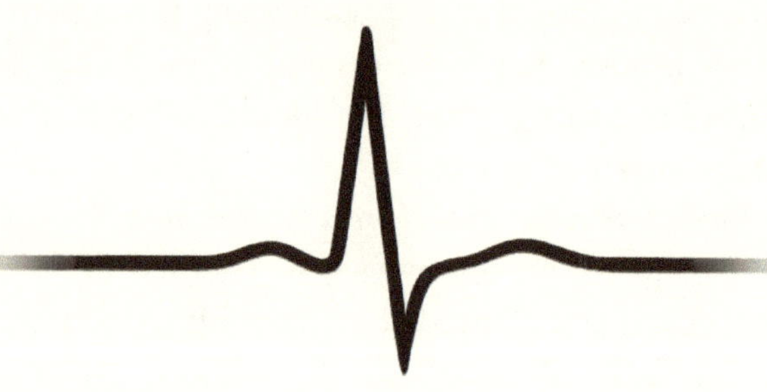

I strolled up and down the riverbank for a while before deciding to explore the cave instead. To avoid getting lost, I brought an armful of flowers and left a sparse trail in my wake, making sure to retrieve them whenever I backtracked so I wouldn't run out. The glowing blossoms were perfect for my dimly lit adventure.

It soon became really boring adventure.

How has Shade not lost his mind down here?

After what felt like hours of useless exploring, I noticed familiar golden light down one of the passages and, despite what had happened, was drawn to it like a moth. Frankly, I just wanted to see something other than dark cave walls.

As long as I don't touch the barrier, I'll be fine.

When I peeked around the final curve and saw the uncomfortable wall of light, I stayed put instead of wandering out into the open. If my assumption about the food deliveries was correct, Xythe probably wouldn't come down again for a few days, but just the idea of him spotting me sent a shiver down my spine.

I don't think he would appreciate my survival—

All of a sudden, Shade appeared right next to me.

"Gods—!"

We both flinched away from each other with wide-eyed fright.

Once I regained my balance, I clapped my hand on my chest and hung my head back with a long-drawn-out exhale. My temporary heartbeat had fizzled out a while ago, but the surrounding muscles had simulated a rather believable heart attack.

Ugh, never thought I'd miss the sound of footsteps.

Eventually, I managed a slightly tense, airy laugh. "Phew… Sorry, you scared me."

Instead of sharing my amusement, Shade frowned and gestured to my hand where it remained plastered to my chest.

"I'm fine, really. I just couldn't tell you were approaching."

Still looking a bit worried, he started checking the ground as if searching for something. It wasn't long before he picked up a rock and tossed it down the tunnel, the clattering noise of which he gestured toward with a big grin. When it eventually fell silent, he raised his brows a few times for emphasis.

I chuckled lightly. "That would probably startle me just as much."

His smile turned into a frown as he let his hand drop and smack his thigh. Unfortunately, the intended drama was lost in the soundless impact.

"Hey, it was a good idea. Really. I promise I'll get accustomed to your silence." After watching him fold his arms and pout for a few seconds, I decided to change the subject. "Anyway, does Xythe ever come down between deliveries?"

He shook his head.

"Meaning, we shouldn't see him for a few days?"

A halfhearted nod.

I still don't get it.

Feeling slightly less anxious, I left the tunnel but stopped halfway to the barrier so I could peer up at the sealed crevice. My gaze drifted to Shade when he appeared in my peripheral vision. "Have you ever been outside the cave?"

There was a subtle nod as he stared at the ceiling.

"*Outside,* outside?"

He shook his head before pointing at the main barrier and nodding again.

"Just the castle?"

A final nod.

"When was the last time?"

He looked at his hands for a few seconds before thumb-pointing over his shoulder and mouthing two or three words.

I wasn't a professional lip reader, but my guess was *Last year.* "Was it your birthday by any chance?"

This time, he nodded cheerfully.

It was nice to see him smile again, but something was bothering me. Quite a few somethings, actually. "Same gift every year?"

His grin widened as he pointed to the rune on his throat and made a gesture as if wiping it away.

"And Xythe lets you speak?"

Shade looked oddly excited as he pressed his hands together then moved them in opposite directions, almost as if something invisible was expanding between them. Additionally, he mouthed something that appeared to include the word *month.*

I wanted to share his enthusiasm, but I just felt more and more uneasy with each new piece of information. Temporary freedoms weren't gifts.

This doesn't make any sense.

"Why does he keep you down here?"

Shade's smile never wavered as he patted his chest and silently mouthed something else, but it was too long for me to decipher.

"Sorry, I missed that."

His smile faltered before turning into a full frown when he looked at his hands again. Instead of making another gesture, however, he went to the closest wall and clawed his answer into the stone.

Now feeling downright apprehensive, I hesitantly followed to read what he wrote.

"I have to earn my birthday month in the castle."

Outrage boiled in my chest as I read the words over and over again.
Is that what he thinks?
I shook my head.
No, that's what Xythe told him.
Swallowing my disgust proved impossible as I looked up at him. "How long has he been doing this?"
Still appearing unbothered, Shade moved toward the barrier but stopped to the right of it and gestured to a distinct, textured area on the wall.
I followed again to get a closer look. The unique, scratchy texture was actually numerous gouges that resembled tally marks arranged in rows and columns. I hadn't noticed them before.
There are so many—
I counted the number of marks in the top row.
One hundred…
My chest tightened as I counted the rows, each of which appeared to have the same number of marks as the first.
Ten…
I slowly turned back to him. "Please tell me those aren't years."
He was still staring at the wall when his neck muscles visibly tensed. His smile was gone.
My voice fractured. "You've been down here for a thousand years?"
He half-glanced at me before scanning over the marks again. After a minute or so, he turned back to me with no expression whatsoever.
I couldn't tell if the blank look on his face was from shock, apathy, or indifference.
This can't be his first realization.
As much as I wanted to conduct a full-blown interrogation, my desire came to a screeching halt when I remembered Fiella's emotional reactions to my blunt statements. The absolute last thing I wanted was for Shade to cry.

Ask him something less miserable.

I had to think for a bit.

Speaking of questions, I'm surprised he hasn't asked why I'm here...

I sighed and waved my hand dismissively. "Never mind all that. What about me? Is it odd having someone down here with you?"

His smile resurfaced as he shook his head.

That wasn't the answer I expected, but before I could inquire further, he headed for the tunnel and gestured for me to follow.

Is he not actually alone?

When we reached the river, Shade got about ten feet in before pausing and glancing over his shoulder to find me still on the bank.

"I can't touch running water." An awkward grin crossed my face. "More Vampire nonsense. Sorry."

He blinked a few times before perking up with an idea, but once he looked at his hands, he jammed his fists into his hips and glared at the water. Eventually, he made a *wait-here* gesture, finished his trek across the river, and practically ran into the opposite tunnel.

While I sat in the plant nest to wait, I couldn't decide if I was disappointed or relieved that he couldn't carry me across. Either way, his scowling at the river was amusing.

A few minutes later, he reappeared with something on his shoulder. Once he crossed back over, he sat next to me and cheerfully gestured to the small, glowing creature he had brought.

There are spirits down here?

It almost reminded me of the solar orbs throughout the castle, but this little sphere was only two inches in diameter and, much to my relief, emitted harmless light.

As I gazed at the spirit, it looked back at me with pupilless, sky-blue eyes and waved a hovering, mitten-like hand in greeting.

That's the cutest thing I've ever seen.

Shade was still grinning as he turned his head and gently nosed the spirit, who squinted happily and nuzzled his face before pulling back and cooing softly.

Wait, what kind of spirit is that?

My assumption was some kind of light spirit, but I couldn't remember what they were supposed to look like.

I guess it doesn't really matter.
"Does your friend have a name?"
Shade briefly glanced at me before looking back at the spirit. His smile had faded.
Hmm...
All of a sudden, I recalled something else it reminded me of.
The lunelight I gave Fiella.
"How about Lune?"
As Shade mouthed my suggestion, the spirit cooed brightly and did a little twirl of approval before flying over and swirling around my head.

I chuckled when all I saw was a blur of light repeatedly zoom past my eyes. "You're welcome, and it's nice to meet you," I added when Lune finally settled down and hovered over my palm to look up at me. Despite the cool blue of its eyes, its light was warm and comforting on my cold, Undead skin. "Shade is lucky to have a cute companion like you."

Lune gleefully rolled around on my hand before returning to Shade, but, this time, it hovered over his head instead of his shoulder. It looked like it was waiting for something. When Shade began swaying side to side, Lune held on to his Arbiter horn and ended up waving back and forth like a tiny, glowing flag.

I'm so glad he already has a friend.

Despite Xythe and Roänach still lurking in the back of my mind, I found it surprisingly easy to smile as I watched Shade and Lune. For just a moment, everything actually felt… alright.

Chapter 11

Athaeÿn

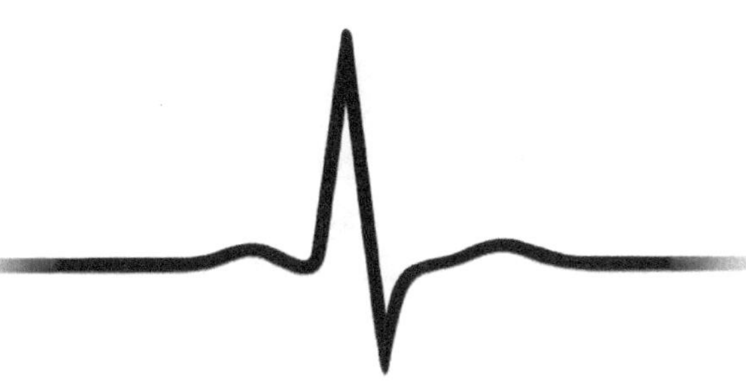

With both arms now fully functional, I set about improving my plant nest to make it even more comfortable. As I suspected he would, Shade offered to help the moment he saw what I was doing, but I politely turned him down. Luckily, he didn't seem offended.

The completion of such a menial task was anything but impressive, but it was still an achievement. After so many failures in life, my stupid little nest made me feel good, and no one could take that from me. It probably shouldn't have meant so much, but it did.

It really is the little things.

Meanwhile, Shade and Lune played a highly amusing game of tag on the riverbank. It was still odd to hear nothing from his rapid, heavy footsteps, but Lune's enthusiastic coos made up for it.

I finished improving my nest just in time to sit and watch them move to the river. The sight was bittersweet. Even celebrating Roänach's absences, we never reached the authentic cheerfulness of Shade and Lune's interactions. My heart ached more than ever for the other vassals.

They'll take care of each other.

It was difficult to reassure myself of this, but my sorrow eased when I remembered Haana and Fiella making flower crowns together in the gardens. Just the image of their smiles brought a weak one to my face.

Fiella wouldn't want me to worry.

The longer I dwelled on her, the more I wanted her to meet Lune.

She would probably squeal from cuteness overload.

I couldn't help but pretend she was sitting there watching as well. Her imaginary joy was contagious, and I was smiling brightly by the time I refocused on the scene in front of me.

Shade and Lune were playing hide and seek among the bio-luminescent flora, which was perfect for the glowing spirit. There were numerous occasions when Shade thought he found his friend, only to furrow his brows when he parted the plants and found nothing. The befuddlement on his face was priceless. If he took too long, Lune would fly out of its hiding place with a loud coo and impact his nose at high speed, which was hilarious every time.

Their final activity involved Shade swimming face-down with Lune perched on one of his back spines. To me, it looked like the little spirit had tamed a giant sea monster.

They're adorable together.

Eventually, they rejoined me on the riverbank. Some of Shade's hair had gotten tangled around his horns during their antics, but Lune was already sorting that out as he sat next to me.

I smiled knowingly. "Did you have fun?"

He nodded and flashed a huge grin.

"I had fun watching."

His smile somehow got even bigger, giving me a clear view of all his razor-sharp teeth.

Which reminds me—

"Does it bother you that Xythe only delivers food every few days?"

His smile relaxed but remained steadfast as he shook his head.

"Hmm… I guess a whole deer is enough to last multiple days, now that I think about it."

He shook his head again. This time, there was distinct mischief in his grin.

I narrowed my eyes. "What do you mean *it's not enough?*"

As my confusion mounted, it became increasingly obvious he was trying not to laugh.

"You did *not* eat that whole deer already."

By now, he looked like he was about to implode into a giggling fit.

Lune and I just stared at him.

How—

I cleared my throat. "That's an impressive appetite, but doesn't it leave you starving by the next delivery?"

He was still grinning when he shook his head once more.

Well, alright then.

I was relieved he wasn't on the brink of starvation all the time, but I was more confused than ever regarding his relationship with his father, especially with the additional context of only getting one month a year in the castle.

For a thousand fucking years.

All of this was really starting to get to me, but I tried to stay light-hearted for his sake. "Well, he definitely keeps you nourished. I mean, look at those muscles." I forced a smile and made an animated gesture toward him. *"Clearly,* he cares about your protein intake."

He blinked before staring down at himself as though noticing his physique for the first time.

"Anyway, you seem to love your father dearly. Do you spend a lot of time with him during your birthday months?"

Once he returned his attention to me, he nodded with a cheerful smile and mimed some different activities. Reading. Writing. Cooking. Playing the harp. Even dancing.

Ignoring the unsettling mental image of Xythe even tapping his foot to music, I was perplexed by Shade's happiness as he went through this list. Apparently, he genuinely enjoyed spending time with his father. My instincts were still screaming that no loving parent would isolate their child for the majority of the year, but I was starting to second-guess myself.

Am I being too judgmental?

Just because I thought Xythe was incapable of love and compassion didn't mean that was true. This was definitely not typical child-rearing behavior for a Demon, but Xythe wasn't a typical Demon either. Maybe he really did love his son and this was just his misguided, unintentionally cruel method of parenting. I even started to wonder if he was so afraid of losing his patience that he kept Shade isolated for his own safety.

Maybe, but…

While that seemed *kind of* plausible, I had a feeling I was giving Xythe too much credit and benefit of the doubt.

He couldn't at least name his son?

That in particular still infuriated me and made no sense, but Shade didn't react at all when it first came up, so it must not have been a big deal.

And yet, he was super excited when I gave him a name.

Regardless of my confusion, Shade seemed more than fine with the way things were, and I wasn't about to give him a hard time for no reason. The whole *earning his birthday month in the castle* thing still rubbed me the wrong way, but maybe that was just Xythe covering his impatient ass.

What about the silence rune?

That was the one thing that felt needlessly cruel, and not a single excuse came to mind.

Ugh, I don't know what to think anymore.

Everything about this bothered me, but I forced myself to try and let it go. If things weren't as rosy as they seemed and Shade wanted my help, that would be his decision to make.

Just have to roll with it for now…

I dragged myself back to the present. "He really does all that with you? Well, as nice as that is, pretend for a moment he's not in the picture. What's *your* favorite thing to do?"

He hesitated before indicating reading and playing the harp again.

Damn, another reason I wish I still had mine.

"What do you like to read about?"

This time, he smiled wide and made a big, arcing gesture with both arms.

"Everything?"

He nodded.

Despite my lingering unease, I couldn't help but smile as well. His enthusiasm really was infectious. "You know, I'm from the outside world. Is there anything in particular you want to know more about that isn't in your books?"

Still odd he doesn't seem curious as to why I'm down here in the first place...

His big smile never wavered as he made another grand gesture.

I couldn't help but chuckle. "I'm afraid I don't know *everything...* Hmm, are you familiar with Eidolon? I lived there for about ten years, so I have plenty of stories to tell. Would you like to hear some of that?"

He nodded even more eagerly this time, and Lune cooed with interest as well from where it hovered just above his head.

"Alright, let's see..." My gaze wandered as I tried to think. The first thing that came to mind was my career as an escort, as that was the primary focus of my life and how I spent most of my time, but I doubted he wanted to hear about that.

What's something he could relate to?

When my gaze drifted back to him, his appearance gave me an idea. "Actually, quick question, first. Do you know who your other parent is?"

He shook his head.

Odd. Not sure what to make of that.

"Do you at least know what an Arbiter is?"

He nodded this time but didn't look very confident, as though he had only heard of them.

"Did you know you're half-Arbiter?"

His eyes got huge.

"That's right. I can tell just by looking at you." I repeatedly pointed at him and grinned when he leaned forward a little. "You know what that means? You have divine blood that was a gift from the gods themselves."

A gift for my arm, that's for sure.

I could barely contain my amusement when he stared at his hands with awestruck wonder. They were far more Demonic than Arbiter, but he didn't need to know that. It was just nice to see him feel special.

"In case you don't know, Eidolon has *two* Arbiter queens, and it's possible you're distantly related to one of them." I leaned forward as well and lowered my voice to just above a whisper. "Meaning, you could be *double* royalty."

He was still staring at his hands when his eyes widened again.

"I only met the queens once or twice, so there's not much I can share about them personally, but I do know they make a lovely couple and are great protectors of the city."

Their relationship is enviable…

"As for me, other than my job, my friends were the most important part of my life. Two of my best were Miri and Callyn. Miri was probably the nicest person I'd ever met and was an amazing artist. She even made me a portrait of myself. I'd show you, but it's, uhhh… somewhere else…" I cleared my throat a bit awkwardly. "As for Callyn, they're a Vampire like me, but I was still alive back then."

They would be devastated if they found out.

Maybe it was for the best that I would probably never see them again. I didn't want to break their heart.

Focus.

I cleared my throat again. "Anyway, Callyn and I hung out almost every day, and one of our favorite things to do was play music. You mentioned doing the same with your father, right? If I ever get my hands on another zephyr harp, I'll gladly play it for you."

Shade's irises seemed to glow even brighter when I mentioned playing music, but right as he began making an excited gesture, he tensed and looked over his shoulder at the main tunnel.

My smile evaporated. "What's wrong?"

He ignored my question and remained perfectly still. After about ten seconds, he shooed Lune off his head and signaled for us both to stay put before vanishing into the dark passage.

I cupped my hands around Lune when it cooed worriedly and moved to follow. "It's alright, Lune. He probably just heard something," I reassured, turning my palm upward so the spirit could see. As Lune held my fingers, we both settled for anxiously watching the tunnel.

I hope he doesn't tell Xythe about me.

Considering how unsettled Shade seemed just now, I doubted he would.

I knew there was more to this.

With a reserved sigh, I glanced down and began gently petting Lune to distract myself. The spirit's warmth was soothing, and a relaxed smile came to my face as I listened to the softest cooing I had heard yet. It almost sounded like Lune's version of purring.

Well, whatever Xythe is up to, at least Shade can easily hide.

His ability to literally disappear into the shadows was incredible.

And maybe a little attractive…

Unfortunately, it didn't help pinpoint his other parent since every Arbiter had unique magic. He could have been related to any of them, but I could only recall the ones tied to Eidolon.

Galaeÿthe has earth magic.

When he wanted to move on, he entrusted the capital's safety to his best friend Haephir.

Haephir has air magic.

He eventually stepped aside for his daughter Elvylli.

Elvylli has fire magic.

At some point, Galaeÿthe's daughter Sathira married Elvylli and joined her rule.

Sathira has ice magic.

And now there was Shade, whom I counted even though he was only half-Arbiter.

I can't tell if his magic is shadows or just darkness in general.

Regardless, I was no closer to figuring out who his other parent was, and I still couldn't think of any other Arbiters. It felt like the more I tried to remember, the less I could recall.

Wait, doesn't Sathira have a sibling?

My memory suddenly clicked. Sathira had a sister named Aëlla.

I'm pretty sure she has… water magic… I think…

I vaguely recalled her having a child as well, but that was where my brain gave up.

Maybe she's Shade's mother.

It was hard to imagine Xythe in a romantic relationship, especially with an Arbiter, but if he and Aëlla had any kind of history, his attempted coup against her sister probably would have led to a falling out. He failed to beat two Arbiters, but if he had gotten into it with just Aëlla…

I think she's been missing for centuries.

All of this was just speculation, but everything seemed to fit. I was half-tempted to share my thoughts with Shade.

Speaking of which—

I started to worry when I realized he hadn't come back yet.

How long has he been gone?

As if sensing my growing concern, he finally reappeared and joined me on the riverbank.

I silently exhaled with relief. "Was it Xythe?"

Shade still looked a bit tense but nodded while running his claws through his hair.

"Did he want something from you?"

He shook his head.

I swallowed nervously. "Was he looking for something… or… or *someone?*"

He shook his head again.

My second wave of relief was tinged with confusion. "Why else would he be down here?"

After a brief pause, Shade gestured for me to follow and reentered the tunnel, this time without dissolving into the shadows.

Maybe I'll bring up the Aëlla stuff later…

Following as directed, I grinned with amusement when Lune zipped over and perched on his shoulder again. The glowing spirit was basically a tiny lantern in the darker parts of the cave, which I appreciated even though all the tunnels looked the same to me.

Adorable and handy.

Since I was behind Shade, I freely let my eyes wander over his body. His height and muscles were hard to ignore, but I kept getting distracted by the numerous bony spines, especially the four biggest ones. They easily prevented him from lying on his back in any capacity.

I wonder if they could be shaved down or removed.

As long as that wouldn't be painful, I didn't see why not. They didn't seem to be hurting him, something his healing factor would likely suppress anyway, but there was no way they were comfortable, especially with his bulky muscles trying to shift around them.

He would probably enjoy a massage.

I would have gladly offered him one if I wasn't drowning in touch anxiety, as I actually had quite a bit of experience to pull from. Of the many services I offered as an escort, that had always been one of my favorites. Now, sadly, just thinking about it made me nauseous.

Maybe I could ask—

I shook my head and averted my gaze.

My problems aren't his responsibility.

Before I could argue with myself, I spotted familiar golden light once again.

Another barrier?

We were nowhere near the castle stairway, so if this was another way out, Xythe had probably been making sure it was still sealed. Clearly, that was the only other thing worth coming down for.

Prick.

Around the final curve, we came into an open area similar to the one by the stairs. There was indeed another barrier, but instead of blocking some kind of exit, it was shielding a deep alcove in the back wall, inside of which sat what looked like a miniature sun on a pedestal.

Shit—

I darted behind Shade's massive frame to avoid the brilliant light. Fortunately, it hadn't gotten a chance to burn me, but I still huffed with annoyance.

Yes, by all means, send me to the one fucking place that has eternal sunlight outside and inside.

It was a good thing solar magic was artificial, otherwise I probably would have been incinerated the second I stepped out of the coach.

The fake light still sucks.

After a moment, Shade turned and looked at me confusedly.

"I'm fine. It's just the light." I gestured vaguely in the orb's general direction. "Sunlight and solar magic are deadly for Vampires, but I'll be alright back here. Your *shade* is protecting me."

His immediate half-lidded frown was priceless.

I knew that name was a good choice.

With a faint snort of amusement, I carefully peered around him to try and get a second glance at the alcove. Even though the barrier was a good fifty feet from us with the pedestal another thirty behind it, the orb's light was still oppressive. It looked to be about three feet in diameter, and its sizzling, undulating surface was occasionally and erratically rupturing arcs of pure energy.

That has to be the power source of the barriers and solar shield.

I wasn't sure what else it could have been.

But why keep it all the way down here?

When I glanced up at Shade, he was already staring at the orb. "Do you know what it is?"

My question wasn't acknowledged whatsoever.

I tried waving in his peripheral vision. "Shade?"

No reaction.

"Shade!"

Still nothing.

"Shade!"

It wasn't until I practically thundered for his attention that he finally looked at me, but he still seemed far away. When his eyes eventually widened with realization, he shot a brief glance at the orb before focusing on me with guilt scrawled across his face.

"Don't worry, I'm not mad. Are you alright?"

He nodded and turned back to the orb. All expression had gone from his face.

"Do you know what it is?" I asked again.

He continued staring at it but at least shook his head in response this time.

I quietly watched him while pondering the trancelike state he had gone into. The orb was mesmerizing, but it didn't seem spellbinding in a literal sense.

Unless it only works on Shade.

Whatever the case, he was clearly drawn to it for some reason.

"Is this where you were coming from when we first crossed paths?"

He was only paying half-attention but did nod in response. After another minute or so, he transferred Lune to my shoulder, thankfully without touching me, and gestured back down the tunnel before going over to the barrier and sitting right in front of it.

I recoiled into the shadows as my giant shield walked away. Knowing better than to try and convince him to leave, I sighed in defeat and glanced at Lune instead. "I assume you know the way to the river."

Lune cooed in affirmation before hovering into the light to check on Shade one more time. After watching him for a few seconds, the spirit turned and started down the tunnel with far less enthusiasm than usual.

As much as I wanted to check as well, I didn't want my face to disintegrate, so I trusted Lune's judgment and followed without a fuss.

That orb also sucks.

Power source or not, I was highly suspicious of its magnetic effect on Shade.

Hopefully, he won't sit there for hours.

It was a bit embarrassing how much I already liked being around him, but maybe I was just glad to have another friend who respected my boundaries and was interested in what I had to say. His extra effort to communicate was particularly charming. He didn't have to do anything, but he wanted to do everything.

He already means a lot to me.

My throat got a little tight.

Gods, I'm pathetic.

All things considered, being trapped under the castle wasn't so bad. Obviously, I still wanted to escape, but Shade made things more than bearable. In fact, he was the best thing to happen to me in a long time.

Chapter 12

Athaeÿn

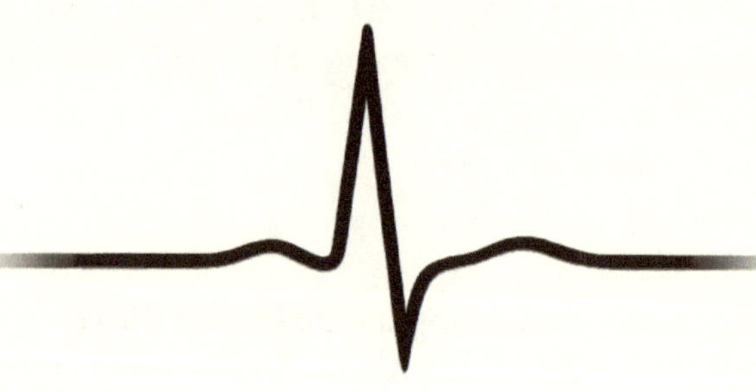

When Lune and I made it back to the river, I was hit by a wave of exhaustion.

Nap time.

Making a beeline for my plant nest, I plopped down and rolled my neck back and forth to crack it, stretching my legs out in front of me as I did so. Meanwhile, Lune perched on my knee and tilted slightly to one side as it gazed up at me.

Painfully adorable.

I mirrored the spirit's body tilt with my head. "Do *you* know what that orb is?"

Lune rotated back and forth.

"Do you think it's dangerous?"

This time, Lune cooed softly with what sounded like uncertainty.

"Well, if he's sat near it for a thousand years without consequences, I guess it can't be *that* bad," I reassured, probably trying to convince myself as well. The orb was still concerning, but the only one it seemed to hurt was me. Maybe Shade just enjoyed its warmth and found its hypnotic surface relaxing to watch.

And yet…

I glanced at the tunnel.

There's nothing I can do about it either way.

Shaking my head a bit, I returned my attention to Lune to distract myself. It was nice to have company even when Shade wasn't around. Incredibly cute company.

Could Lune possibly be any cuter?

My gaze drifted to the plants surrounding me. Already grinning, I plucked one of the smallest cup blossoms I could find and set it upside down on the spirit like a little hat.

The answer is yes.

At first, I was highly amused by Lune twirling around and playing with its new accessory, but my smile faded when it reminded me of the flower crown Fiella gave me.

Stop bumming yourself out.

I forced a new smile and refocused on the spirit. "Do you sleep at all?"

Lune stopped dancing and rotated back and forth again.

"That's what I figured. You don't have to stay if you'll be bored."

This time, Lune hovered up and nudged my nose.

"You sure?"

A happy coo.

Once I got comfortable in the nest and closed my eyes, I felt Lune perch on my shoulder.

Thank you, Lune. I feel safer already.

Unfortunately, this peace vanished the moment I was asleep. Most nights, I was blessed with relatively normal dreams. This wasn't one of them.

Don't touch me—

I couldn't move or even struggle.

My heart was pounding, but my lungs had stopped working.

Nightmare Roänach gripped me from behind with both hands, but rather than groping me like I expected, he held me even tighter to his chest and inhaled sharply behind my ear. Without warning, he latched onto my neck with such precision his fangs reopened the scars from his original bite. I was still frozen when the sound of a hard shell cracking open reverberated against my back, which turned out to be additional arms erupting from his body. They were unusually long and segmented like spider legs, but instead of wrapping me in silken web, they began undressing me.

Stop touching me—

My clothes had only been partially removed when they fizzled away like a fine mist, leaving me fully nude and welded to Roänach's bare front. His arousal was pressed up against me.

Please stop—

I was already trembling when nightmare Xythe appeared. His skeletal face was upside down and had dozens of eyes instead of just four, all of which were pitch-black with no blazing pupils to be found. As he slowly raised his hands, his exaggerated claws began winding toward me through the air like snakes, twitching and multiplying with the echoing sounds of crunching bone. Upon reaching me, they effortlessly impaled my chest as though it was nothing more than butter under a hot knife. They seared all flesh and fractured every rib in their path, even slipping between my organs like vines overtaking ruins. My lungs had been speared. I couldn't make a single sound.

Help me—

Behind Xythe, a third figure appeared.

Oh gods—

It was a nightmare version of Shade. The warm, friendly smile I remembered had been replaced with a hideous grin dripping with so much saliva it cascaded down his chest like a viscous waterfall. Instead of teeth, hundreds of needles filled his gaping maw and cavernous throat, all of which were clearly visible thanks to his stretched mouth literally splitting his face from ear to ear. He had doubled in height, and his bulk was no longer muscle. To my horror, all of his flesh had been replaced with an undulating sea of writhing hands and broken fingers.

Wh-What—

He began stalking forward.

No—

When he reached Xythe's back, he phased right through him and continued approaching.

Don't—

By the time he stopped in front of me, I could smell his putrid breath even though he towered ten feet over my head. He reeked of a mass grave.

Please don't—

His lifeless eyes were solid white, but when he finally blinked, his eyelids painted Roänach's haunting irises all over his sclerae.

P-Please—

After staring at me for what felt like an eternity, he started reaching for my face.

Stop—!

When the tips of his thumb claws were less than an inch from my eyes, I snapped awake with a painful jolt.

...

I wanted to scream but couldn't.

I was shaking violently but couldn't move.

My eyes were wide open, but I couldn't see anything.

I was hyperventilating even though I didn't need to breathe.

My fingers were gripping my head so tightly my nails were digging into my scalp.

Tears were streaming down my face with such fervor I could hear them hitting the plants as they dripped off my cheek and landed next to my ear.

Everything was spinning.

Time had stopped.

It felt like I was about to fall through the ground into oblivion.

...

Half an hour later, I finally convinced myself I was awake.

There was some kind of frantic sound above my head.

What... What is that...?

I was so disoriented I had no idea where I was, and the sound fled before I could get a closer listen. When I managed to let go of my head and lower my arms, I looked in the direction the noise had gone but could only vaguely discern a small white glow darting back and forth in front of a large, red figure. My vision was still too blurry to tell what either thing was.

Sniffling rather grossly, I wiped the tears from my eyes to try and see clearly. The moment I could, a sharp gasp of terror clawed my throat.

I-It's him—

I immediately hid under my arms again.

W-Wait—

Mustering my courage, I peeked over my elbow and looked a second time. The figure was familiar, but it wasn't the same one from my nightmare. It looked like Shade. The *real* Shade. I didn't see any writhing hands, and he wasn't stalking toward me or reaching for my eyes.

Shade…

All of a sudden, reality came rushing back.

It took a few extra moments, but I finally registered everything in front of me. Shade was sitting about ten feet away, leaning sideways on the cave wall with his eyes closed and arms folded, and the white glow was a rather panicked and frantically cooing Lune. Shade wasn't stirring, so he must have been deep asleep.

Oh…

The wave of relief nearly made me go limp.

Thank the gods…

I trembled my way into a sitting position but glanced down when something else caught my eye. My heart broke when I realized it was Lune's flower hat lying abandoned next to me.

I'm sorry for making you so worried.

Meanwhile, Shade finally stirred but was still half-asleep as he watched Lune repeatedly gesture in my direction. When he groggily looked over to see what all the fuss was about, he snapped wide awake the moment we made eye contact.

I guess I still look like shit.

He almost tripped himself as he scrambled to his feet and rushed over. Once sitting in front of me, he tilted his head and gestured to my mess of a face.

"I'm alright," I muttered, wiping my eyes again. "Just nightmares."

The skeptical tension in his brows was less than subtle.

I forced a smile this time. "I promise I'm okay."

My reassurance seemed to ease his concern, but he remained visibly worried as he pointed at my head and rotated his wrist a few times.

"How often? Rarer than I'd expect but always horrific. This time was no exception."

He frowned heavily before perking up a bit and gesturing between us a few times.

"I appreciate the offer, but I'm afraid you can't help this time. It's just something I have to deal with."

There was a pause before he nodded sullenly and looked at the ground.

"Do you ever have nightmares?"

After a few seconds, his gaze drifted to the ceiling.

I said nothing for a moment. "Are you afraid a day will come when you're no longer allowed in the castle?"

He just continued staring overhead.

I reconsidered pushing him about Xythe but decided to quietly observe instead. His frantic eye darting betrayed a racing mind, but the eventual jaw quiver was proof of inner turmoil, at least to me. It was the first time I had seen distinct heartache regarding his isolation.

And it's still barely anything.

When he looked at me again, he pointed at my head instead of acknowledging his sorrow.

I guess he's still not ready.

"What are my nightmares about?"

A nod.

I opened my mouth to answer but closed it before saying anything.

Would he even understand the full explanation?

My gaze fell to the subtle slit along his pelvic shelf. If he truly spent one tenth of each year in the castle, then he had actually lived a hundred years up there.

It probably doesn't feel like it.

Either way, a hundred years was a long time. The extent of his knowledge was a mystery to me, but between reading books, watching the Demons, and having a thousand years to explore himself, *surely* he was at least familiar with the concept of sex.

Assault is another story…

Regardless of what he knew, I didn't want to traumatize him with my own trauma. He didn't need those mental images. Maybe he was the one person who could remain blissfully ignorant about such things.

"Well," my chest tightened a bit, "let's just say my arm and scars are far from the only instances of violence I've suffered. Over the years, I've developed anxiety regarding physical touch, but the severity is situational and often unpredictable. Usually, it's mild paralysis. Sometimes, it's a full breakdown." I sighed and shook my head. "Touch used to mean everything to me. Now, it's nothing but a nightmare. I can't escape it no matter what I do…"

Shade never once broke eye contact and looked increasingly sad as he listened. When I finished speaking, he blocked my healed arm from view and tilted his head the other way.

"The other violence? Trust me, you don't want the details."

His gaze slowly fell until it landed on my hands. After staring at them for a bit, he looked into my eyes again and earnestly gestured between us while mouthing some kind of phrase.

It was a bit difficult to catch, but I was pretty sure the final word was *help*.

Wait—

My eyes widened. "What? No, Shade—" I cut myself off and took a deep breath. "Forgive me. I appreciate the offer, really, but it's not your job to help me."

He just smiled and put his hand over his heart, then extended that same hand to me.

All I could do was stare at him dumbly.

I don't understand.

Completely bewildered, I looked at his hand instead.

I haven't earned this.

My throat tightened with uncertainty. Despite my nightmare, I wasn't afraid of him and hadn't been for a while, but my mind was still split. Half of me desperately wanted to touch him. The other half was screaming I would just end up hurt again.

I'm so sick of this.

Amid my frustration was slight guilt for using him, but I tried to replace it with gratitude. I hadn't asked him for help. He had explicitly offered. From the very beginning, he had been nothing but considerate.

There's no one I would rather have sitting in front of me offering their hand.

Shade was everything I could have asked for.

Please let me make even the smallest amount of progress.

With a shaky exhale, I began reaching for his hand but paused and glanced up when his other one waved to get my attention.

Once I was looking, he pointed at the rune on his throat.

"I know it'll affect me, but I don't mind."

Thank you for asking.

Taking a deep breath this time, I resumed slowly reaching forward. My fingers trembled before even making contact, but I pressed on and managed to take hold of his hand without hesitating or freezing. It was the first time we had ever touched.

Progress—

Unfortunately, my hand began shaking almost immediately.

Or not—

My shoulders started heaving as I glared at my hand with increasing aggravation. It was odd not hearing my usual strained breathing, but I was preoccupied with impatiently begging my mind and body to cooperate.

It's not working—

Even though I felt a breakdown approaching, I bared my fangs and refused to pull away.

Dammit—

My eyes were burning when I let go at the last possible second and slammed my fist on the ground with a bellow of frustration.

Fuck!

Trembling with anger and defeat, I closed my eyes and choked out a sob before hanging my head back and inhaling sharply through my nose. Tears were already streaming down my face.

I can't take this anymore.

With a few gasping breaths, I rolled my head forward until my chin hit my chest. I barely noticed the tears dripping onto my hands.

What's the point in even trying...

After a few minutes of wallowing in misery, I remembered I wasn't alone.

Shit—

I frantically wiped my eyes and looked at Shade. My vision was blurry, but I could still see the pity on his face.

He must think I'm pathetic.

"I'm sorry, Shade," I muttered, closing my eyes and hanging my head. "I think it's too late…"

It's been too late for a long time.

Before I could withdraw further into myself, a series of vibrations prompted me to crack my eyes open. It was Shade's hand silently thumping the ground to get my attention. When I looked up at him again, he switched to pointing at my hands and shaking his head.

I felt like a corpse as I stared at him with the emptiness of crushing failure.

When I didn't indicate any willingness to try again, he furrowed his brows with something akin to denial and picked up the smoothest rock within reach. After carving something into it with his claw, he held it out so I could see.

"Don't give up."

I read it a few times before tiredly gazing into his eyes again.

He now looked more determined and shook the rock for emphasis.

Unfortunately, my defeat was insurmountable. "It doesn't matter how much I want this or how many times I try. The result is always the same."

Nothing ever changes.

I shook my head and buried half of my face in one hand. "I don't know why I thought it would be different this time." My shaky voice crumbled to barely above a whisper. "It was stupid to get my hopes up."

I never learn…

Shade waited for a change of mind that never came. Eventually, he lowered the rock and halfheartedly toyed with it in his lap.

Meanwhile, I rested my cheek on my palm and stared down at the ground, though I wasn't really looking at it.

It was evident neither of us knew what to do.

There's nothing to do...

Shade was still gazing at the rock a few minutes later. When he finally looked at me again, he stared for a moment before turning the rock over and carving something new into the back. This time when he held it up, there was nothing forceful or commanding in his movement.

"It does matter."

My resistance started to crack, but I still couldn't fully latch onto his encouragement.

Unlike before, his demeanor remained soft despite my persistent stubbornness. He first gestured to my scars and shook his head. Then, he indicated my hands and pointed right at my chest.

There was a sharp pain in my throat when I looked at my trembling fingers.

I want it to matter.

Even if I hadn't deliberately spent extra time with Roänach, my wounds never would've healed at Castle Veil. Not the ones that mattered.

But I'm not at Castle Veil.

I finally had a real chance. I had to at least try.

Especially when I have Shade.

I closed my eyes and exhaled deeply.

Don't give up.

When I opened my eyes, I looked directly into his. "Alright."

The warm smile Shade offered was the antithesis of what I saw in my nightmare. It radiated what I could only describe as tender admiration.

Is he... proud of me?

All of a sudden, I felt like I could do anything.

Maybe I really can this time.

Choking up a bit, I managed to return a fragile but genuine smile.

He was visibly delighted when I finally smiled, but his enthusiasm faltered when his own hand caught his eye. After turning it over a few times, he looked at me again and made a turn-around gesture over his head.

"What for?"

He briefly covered his face and pointed at my hands again.

I wasn't sure if his suggestion would help, but I doubted it could make things worse. It seemed like a decent idea.

Frankly, I'm willing to try anything at this point.

I nodded mostly to myself. "Sure, we can try that."

He smiled again and turned around. Once his back was to me, he sat perfectly still.

I can do this.

As I shifted onto my knees and scanned over the wall of muscle in front of me, I was hit by a wave of attraction. There was definitely a lot of him to work with.

Focus.

Huffing under my breath, I shoved those unhelpful thoughts aside and concentrated on his bony spines instead. At least, I assumed they were bone. The bleached white of Xythe's lengthy mountain range of spines was obviously skeletal, but Shade's were something between sand and slate in color. Upon closer inspection, they actually looked like stone.

Maybe those won't trigger my issues as much.

Unsurprisingly, my fingers still trembled when I slowly reached for the closest spine, but, to my immense relief, there was only a faint tremor of fear when I lightly touched the jagged tip.

That's... better than usual.

My anxiety tended to manifest in the form of phantom sensations. The most common was numerous invisible hands touching and stroking along my skin, even under clothing. During the severest episodes, it often escalated to feeling like I was being strangled. Just now, however, I only felt one hand glide across the back of mine.

W-Wow—

I couldn't believe it, but, obviously, when I tried to vocalize my excitement, no sound came out.

Idiot.

Shaking my head at myself, I pulled back just enough to sever contact. "I touched one of your spines. Did you feel it?"

He shook his head but otherwise remained still.

When I brushed my fingertips against it a second time, I realized it felt as stony as it looked. It was almost like the cave itself was growing on him.

Yeah, there's no way those are comfortable.

As I slid my fingers along the length of the spine, I smiled when my anxiety remained a whisper. The illusion of touching nothing more than a rock definitely helped.

Progress… progress…

With another deep breath, I wrapped my fingers around until I was actually holding it.

Oh gods—

I shuddered a little but kept it together. When I took hold of the adjacent spine as well, I gripped both tightly and closed my eyes with a shaky exhale, the silence of which helped me stay focused on what my hands were doing. I felt bad that Shade's curse was a temporary blessing, but at least it wasn't the concern he feared it might be.

Maybe he'd even be glad to hear it's actually useful for something.

When I opened my eyes again, I was thrilled to find I was still holding both spines.

It's working—

I wasn't sure if this qualified since the spines were just rocky bone or actual stone he couldn't even feel, but they were still part of his body. That had to count for something.

I'm touching him!

As much as I wanted to feel his muscular back, I decided to avoid his skin for a little longer. Instead, I let my right hand drift toward his thick, raven mane. With only brief hesitation, I ghosted over a few flyaways before lacing my fingers into the actual bulk of his hair. It was surprisingly soft and clean as well as untangled and tame despite how long and freely it flowed.

He probably grooms himself in the river.

A surprisingly relaxed smile came to my face as I gently combed through his hair and watched the dark locks repeatedly swallow my fingers. The less surprising fear lurking in the back of my mind was irritating, but I was taken aback by how well this second attempt was going.

This is… nice…

After a minute or so, I noticed his head was slightly tilted to the same side as my hand.

And that's adorable.

When my gaze shifted to his back, however, my smile fractured.

Maybe…

Before attempting any skin-to-skin contact, I pulled back to speak again. "Are you doing alright? We can take a break if you want."

There was no reaction.

He must have zoned out.

I snickered when he suddenly perked up as if realizing he had been spoken to.

A few seconds later, he offered a big grin over his shoulder.

"You sure?"

He nodded and turned forward once more.

I was thankful for his patience, but my smile faltered again when I refocused on his back.

I'll be fine.

I closed my eyes and took a deep breath.

It's still Shade.

It's just skin.

I'll be fine.

I'll be fine.

I'll be fine…

Exhaling shakily, I opened my eyes and rested my fingertips on one of his sculpted back muscles. To my annoyance, I froze immediately.

Come on, don't be a baby.

I frowned when my hand began trembling.

No, be nice to yourself.

Swallowing hard, I focused on my hand instead of the surface it was touching.

You can do it.

I nodded to myself.

I can do it.

Still watching my hand, I slowly rotated it down until my palm made contact. My entire handprint was now pressed against his back. As expected, there was a nauseating wave of terror, but it actually began fading rather quickly.

Wait—

It continued easing until it was just a faint simmer.

I… I'm doing it.

My eyes widened.

I'm touching his skin.

Not wanting to lose momentum, I put my other hand on his back as well. There was another surge of anxiety, but this one was much smaller and faded even more rapidly.

He's so warm.

There had been too much panic when holding his hand to notice.

No wonder he was so blinding in my thermal vision.

I had enjoyed the body heat of many throughout my life, but Shade had the most by far. It was the exact opposite of Roänach's icy touch.

Shade's warmth is so comforting.

My throat tightened.

I can touch him.

My vision blurred.

I can touch him!

This was overwhelming in the best possible way, and I choked out a few silent laughs despite being moments away from sobbing.

I-I can touch him—

Trembling with elation, I slowly dragged my hands across his back in every direction I could, watching my fingers dip in and out of the deep contours between his defined muscles.

I can't believe it—

Afraid I might finally overdo it, I pulled back and tended to my face instead. A few light sobs slipped past my joy anyway.

Shade whipped around the moment there was audible crying, but his worry turned into confusion when he saw the smile on my face.

"D-Don't worry, I'm alright. Way better than alright, actually," I reassured with a shaky laugh. When his expression remained uncertain, I put my hands on his broad shoulders to prove my claim. There was another spike of fear now that we were facing each other, but this one faded as well.

His eyes widened as he glanced back and forth between my hands, and that shock lingered when he looked at me again.

I let go so I could speak. "I still have a lot of work to do, but this is the most I've been able to touch anyone in over a century."

Besides Roänach.

My jaw quivered a little. "Thank you."

He smiled brightly and pressed a hand to his chest. After watching me for a few moments, he tilted his head and extended that same hand to me once more.

I took a deep breath.

Let's try this again.

Chapter 13

Athaeÿn

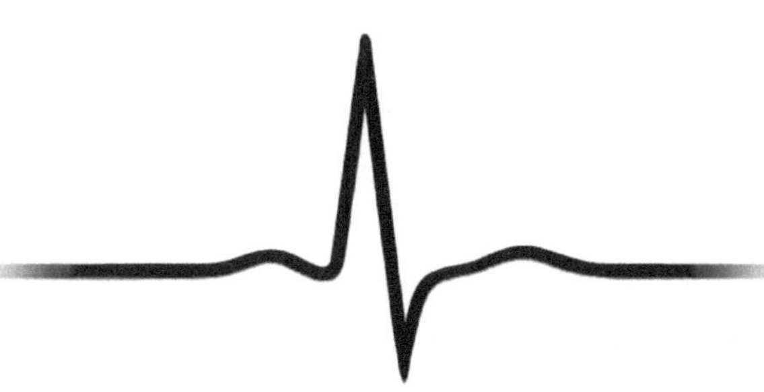

There was still triumphant wind in my sails, but the longer I stared at Shade's hand, the more my ship threatened to sink beneath the waves of progress I'd made.

I had countless good memories of touch from when I was alive, but they were buried under three centuries of Roänach. His hands had done far more than just assault me. They had taken one of my defining qualities, and I desperately wanted it back.

Shade just restored a small piece.

Despite lingering unease, my determination remained intact. And my gratitude.

I'm glad I let him help.

Part of me was still afraid to trust him, but the rest of me was sick of distrusting everyone.

It's exhausting.

All of a sudden, Roänach's hands were gripping my wrists. I saw nothing, but it felt far too real for my liking. The instinctual fear was no longer acceptable.

You will NOT hold me back.

I aggressively wiped my hands down my arms to push him off. Obviously, nothing had actually been removed, but I still felt better.

That probably looked ridiculous.

When I glanced at Shade, he was still just sitting there with a gentle smile on his face. He hadn't even blinked.

I guess he's letting me figure things out...

Clearing my throat a bit awkwardly, my gaze drifted back to his patiently outstretched hand. I wholeheartedly believed he would have held it there for at least an hour before giving up, but I had no intention of making him wait that long.

Just give me a little more time.

I started comparing hands from recent memory. Fiella's were smaller and more delicate than Roänach's, but they effectively looked the same. Xythe's were comically large and painful to both look at and touch. Shade's were somewhere in the middle. He had ten fingers like Roänach but no deadly solar magic in his claws like Xythe. Now that I was over the first hurdle, I hoped Shade's hands were unique enough to be just what I needed.

Please continue being patient with me.

Clinging to my progress, I used my middle finger to gingerly touch the tip of his middle claw. It wasn't as sharp as it looked, but it could still do serious damage if needed. Fortunately, my anxiety was minimal compared to the first time. I didn't even need the rune.

More progress.

I slowly dragged my fingertip along his claw until I reached his palm. His *huge* palm. It was difficult to see the creases since his hands were almost black, but I was able to trace along them by feel alone. His palms were somewhat callused but otherwise surprisingly soft, even with the subtle, reptilian texture of his skin.

Still so warm...

Feeling courageous, I turned his hand over to inspect the far more rugged back. My favorite details were the raised tendons as strong as steel and pronounced veins woven around thick knuckles. I had always been a sucker for such sculpted features, so I was disappointed the latter were mostly covered by stony growth.

He could probably punch Roänach's head clean off.

While true, the image wasn't amusing. I wanted to strangle him in his study, but the thought hadn't brought me joy. It still didn't. However, knowing he would never free us and would always be a threat, I reluctantly acknowledged that any new beginning would require his end. He didn't deserve to live, but I wasn't sure it meant he deserved to die.

Isn't that the same thing?

I shook my head with uncertainty. All I knew was I never wanted Roänach to touch me ever again. Now that I could hold my friend's hand and truly appreciate his gentleness, there was no going back. Shade was already the start of a new beginning.

He has no idea how much this means to me.

I planned on making it clear, but, for now, I was still lost in his touch. For the first time in centuries, I was reminded of why I loved it. I couldn't believe I had almost forgot.

It's everything I remember.

I had to fight back joyful tears as my throat tightened again.

And more…

Now feeling surprisingly relaxed, I held his hand with my left and glided my right fingers over the back toward his wrist. When I paused and lightly caressed the prominent bone, I was pretty sure I felt an extra surge of heat in his exceedingly warm skin, but I kept that to myself.

Hopefully, that means he's enjoying this as well.

I continued leisurely sliding my hand up his forearm, taking note of each and every muscle I could discern. When I reached his huge bicep, I paused again and struggled not to gawk.

Pretty sure it's bigger than my head.

As my fingers explored the contours of said bicep, I started to feel slightly drained.

Alright, maybe I'm finally pushing it.

Before I could retract my hand, I felt the faintest tremble in his arm.

Wait, is this the first time he's ever been touched like this?

That was just my knee-jerk concern, but if true, his offer to help was even more generous than I thought.

Why is he so willing to—

I shook my head again. What mattered was he wanted to help, and I hoped he would let me return the favor someday.

Please trust me, Shade.

Finally withdrawing from his bicep, I turned his hand back over and neatly layered both of mine on his palm. It was probably time to let go for both our sakes, but I couldn't bring myself to pull away just yet.

At least his tremble is gone.

I watched his claws twitch with desire before carefully folding over my delicate fingers, cradling them in what felt like a protective embrace. When I looked up, there was still a warm smile on his face. I smiled back.

I actually feel… safe.

Chapter 14

Athaeÿn

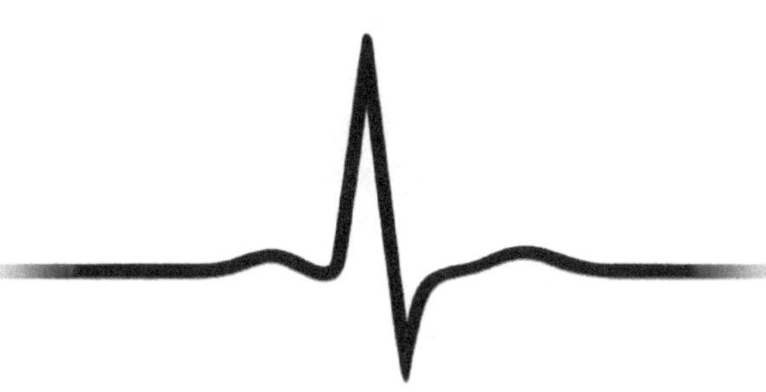

We sat there holding hands for what felt like forever, but it was a good forever. Shade made me feel alive. What hurt was the fact Roänach had given me a similar feeling once.

When I was actually alive…

My mortal life had been nearly perfect except for one thing. Romance. I found nothing but failure back home, and things were no better in Eidolon. When it came to dating, no combination of gender, race, occupation, personality, *anything* ever made a difference. Nothing lasted. And then, Roänach fooled me into thinking he was finally the one.

How wrong I was.

At Castle Veil, it wasn't long before I deemed myself unworthy of love. This primarily concerned romance, but I included familial love. After ungratefully fleeing to Eidolon seeking a more exciting life, I failed to visit my parents once during my ten years there. I didn't even write. They loved and housed me for almost seventy years, and that was how I thanked them. If they were still alive, they probably hadn't thought about me in at least a century.

I wouldn't blame them.

Having now been discarded by Roänach and Xythe in rapid succession, I was getting a taste of my own dismissive medicine. Clearly, I wasn't worth anyone's time and effort, at least not in any meaningful way.

And yet...

Shade seemed to think otherwise, even though I had done nothing to deserve the care and patience he was giving me. I gave him and Lune names, but that hardly counted.

It seemed to make him happy, though.

We were still looking at each other, but my smile was long gone. When I forced a new one, his widened cheerfully until his eyes squinted shut. The adorable sight turned mine genuine.

Why is he being so nice for no reason?

Shade's unconditional compassion stoked an ember in my heart, and it made me want to reconsider my lack of worth. After so long, the idea was almost disconcerting.

But also, kind of... pleasant.

I already cherished Shade's friendship, but that was where my feelings had to stop. Falling one too many times had destroyed my life. My memories were begging me not to do it again.

What if it's different this time?

I shook my head and glanced down at his claws, trying to sense an ulterior motive. All I felt was warmth and affection.

Does he really want nothing in return?

With great reluctance, I finally pulled my hands free of his gentle grip. "This is probably a good stopping point for now, but I can't express enough how much I appreciate your help. Thank you, Shade." I tilted my head a little. "By the way, are you alright?"

He gave a relaxed nod and grinned when Lune hovered over and nuzzled my forehead.

I smiled and lightly petted the spirit's face with my thumbs. "Are you happy for me too?"

Lune cooed in affirmation and rolled around on my palms a few times before returning to Shade, who was still amused as he watched the spirit perch on his shoulder. Eventually, his gaze drifted to my shoulder. His hand briefly shifted toward me but planted on the ground to help him get up instead. Once standing, he was no longer making eye contact.

I guess he wants to touch me in return.

Shade was far from the first, so it was his reluctance that caught my attention. At first, I assumed he was just giving me space, but then I recalled his nervous tremble. Whether he was shy, touch-starved, or a bit of both, I suspected he wasn't sure of what to do with himself.

Maybe he doesn't actually know what he wants.

I glanced down at my hands and sighed a little.

You and I both...

Eventually, I smiled to myself and touched my shoulder for him.

What I do know is I want to want.

Touch had been a curse for so long, but the desire remained. Even though that was the one thing Roänach couldn't take from me, I had convinced myself I would never again find someone to share it with. That was no longer the case. All of a sudden, I realized just how much I wanted to touch Shade.

And for him to touch me...

I cleared the yearning from my throat and forced a chuckle. "Well, I think I'm going to stay here and decompress for a while. That was a lot."

When Shade turned back to me, he gestured between himself and the ground.

"As much as I enjoy your company, clearing my head will probably be easier if I'm alone. Why don't you go for a walk after sitting for so long?"

Disappointment flashed across his eyes, but he just smiled and waved before turning again and heading down the tunnel with Lune. This was his slowest departure yet.

Sorry...

By now, it was obvious he liked being near me, but it felt different this time.

Almost like—

My anxiety suddenly flared up.

Someone's touching me—

When I glanced down, my hand was resting on my chest. I didn't remember putting it there.

Oh, for—

Groaning under my breath, I dropped it into my lap with a loud smack.

Okay, now I'm glad I sent him away.

I would have been mortified if he saw that, but once the embarrassment passed, I couldn't help smiling a little. For just a moment, I felt like my younger self.

When I was alive and full of hope.

My smile faded when I glanced at the ceiling.

Alive or Undead, neither of us are really living down here.

Unfortunately, there were far more important things to worry about than my feelings.

Like Xythe.

I sighed heavily and dragged my hands down my face.

What am I going to do?

Regardless of his and Roänach's plan or the fact he nearly ripped my arm off, I didn't want him dead. I just wanted him to let go of his ridiculous grudge and live happily ever after in his stupid solar castle. The problem was, his happily ever after demanded revenge. It was his way or no way.

Even if I wanted Xythe dead, I was useless. Direct confrontation would be a death sentence, and I didn't have the tools to rig some kind of trap to better my odds.

Right, because that's definitely a skillset I have.

I doubted anything I cobbled together would slow him down anyway. It seemed like the only one who stood any kind of chance was Shade. I wasn't sure if Xythe needed to die for us to be free, but I had a feeling he wouldn't give us much of a choice.

How could I possibly ask Shade to kill his own father?

Even if they had hated each other, it was an unthinkable solution.

What if it's the only solution?

Frustrated with my lack of ideas, I groaned loudly and flopped onto my back with a thud. I was half-tempted to just give up and make a nice life with Shade right there on the riverbank, but I knew I couldn't do that. Xythe and Roänach were far too big a threat to innocent people.

Maybe that's how I can convince Shade to help.

Just thinking about the necessary conversation made me nauseous. Nothing had been said, but I already felt gross and manipulative. I had finally seen a crack in the supposed acceptance of his circumstances, so maybe I still had a chance to prove he was a prisoner. Unfortunately, I didn't know how much time was left before Xythe and Roänach made their move.

And it's entirely possible Shade will never turn against his father no matter what.

With another groan, I rolled onto my side and crossed my arms in front of my face.

I hate not knowing what to do.

All of a sudden, I wished my parents were there to guide me, but I would have settled for just seeing their faces. I hadn't loved or appreciated them nearly enough.

I wonder if they ever went to Eidolon to look for me.

My knees came up as I curled in on myself.

Probably not…

I felt more vulnerable than ever.

Centuries old but still behaving like a pitiful child.

I closed my eyes and exhaled a bit shakily.

I'm supposed to be decompressing.

That certainly wasn't happening.

And I'm lonely.

With my mind refusing to calm down, I regretted asking Shade to leave. His presence had become soothing.

Relying on him is a bad idea.

I opened my eyes and stared at nothing.

But having someone to rely on would be nice.

After glancing at the tunnel to make sure I was alone, I untangled my arms and clasped my hands together. It wasn't the same as holding Shade's hand. Not even close.

I really am pathetic.

There had been a groan of frustration when I first sprawled out, and there was a groan of frustration again when I got back up and entered the tunnel to find Shade.

What a waste of time and mental energy.

It was a bit easier to navigate this time, but I dropped flowers again just in case. Eventually, a faint echo of distant music led me to the castle barrier, where it was reverberating down the stairs and throughout the cave. The combined acoustics produced an almost haunting sound.

Meanwhile, Shade was sitting right in front of the barrier, swaying back and forth while Lune danced in the air over his head. It was nice to see they still had some access to music.

I wonder if Xythe knows he can hear it.

Shaking my head a little, I went over and sat next to Shade despite the barrier's uncomfortable light. It was nothing compared to the orb. "Do they play music often?"

He just smiled and continued swaying to the rhythm.

To my dismay, the music suddenly faded and left us with nothing but cave ambience.

Figures…

After a few moments of awkward silence, I glanced at Shade again and found his gaze still locked on the barrier. He was no longer swaying. Or smiling.

How does he stand this?

I looked back up the silent stairwell.

Now I really wish I had my harp.

My gaze drifted back to Shade once more. "You said you danced and played music with your father, right? Is this all you can do during the rest of the year?"

I was surprised when he smiled brightly and shook his head, but before I could inquire further, he got up and gestured for me to follow. We were back on the riverbank in record time, where he had me and Lune wait while he crossed and disappeared down the opposite tunnel. When he reappeared, he was carrying a zephyr harp.

Wow, it looks just like mine.

I was overjoyed to see something so familiar, and Shade was equally cheerful when he rejoined us and proudly displayed the instrument.

Did Xythe actually—

It was then I noticed his mischievous smile, which brought a tiny smirk to my face. "Did you steal that?"

He clutched the harp to his chest and averted his gaze, but the huge grin gave him away.

His smile is so cute.

We sat across from each other in the plant nest and watched Lune pluck soft but crisp random notes on the harp. The spirit was adorable no matter what it did.

I looked at Shade again after a few minutes. "Is it safe to assume you've memorized every song ever written after all this time?"

He smiled knowingly and mimed a writing gesture.

"You wrote some too?"

There was no hesitation as he nodded and moved the harp to his right thigh.

My brows furrowed a little. "You play even when you can't hear it?"

He just smiled again and tapped his head. Turning his attention back to the harp, he began playing something that appeared calm and peaceful, but, as expected, the instrument remained completely silent. The only sound to be heard was the river beside us.

My smile was already long gone.

How has he lived like this for a thousand years?

The longer he played, the slower his already faltering movements became. Eventually, his claws began trembling against the strings and even missed them now and then.

Oh no—

His smile was hanging by a thread when I glanced up from the harp, but there was something worse. For the first time since we met, there were tears in his eyes.

Shade—

He was barely playing by now and soon slowed to a stop. His smile had finally broken.

My throat became painfully tight, but I didn't know what to say anyway.

Other than the river, the only sound was a sad coo from Lune.

Meanwhile, Shade just sat there staring at the harp. When he looked at the ceiling and touched the rune on his throat, both of his hands were trembling. It wasn't long before he hung his head and clenched his eyes shut, causing tears to stream down his face.

It took all of my willpower not to cry as well.

This is too much—

I wanted nothing more than to comfort him and hoped my progress would let me. "Shade, do I have permission to touch you?"

His head remained hanging as he gave a single, weak nod.

I briefly hesitated before putting my hands on his shoulders and slowly working my way up to his face, where I used my thumbs to wipe away his tears. My fingers were still a bit unsteady, but this was almost easy compared to last time.

Shade was staring at the ground when his eyes slowly reopened, and it wasn't until a minute or so later that he realized what was happening and looked at me with surprise.

The moment we made eye contact, I offered a reassuring smile and continued gently caressing his face. Fortunately, my thumbs were no longer trembling. Even though his cheeks were dry by now, I wasn't going to pull away until he smiled back. To my relief, he managed a fragile one.

Thank the gods…

I was still smiling when I let go. "I bet your playing is beautiful."

He raised his brows a little before shyly averting his gaze. His smile had turned bashful.

At least he's alright.

I thought for a moment. "Would you like me to play something for you?"

He perked up even more and eagerly passed the harp to me.

I set the harp on my thigh like he had. "Fair warning, I haven't played in a few centuries," an awkward chuckle slipped out, "so this might be terrible."

He had already given me his undivided attention and a big smile.

"I appreciate your faith in me," I added, though my amusement turned to nervousness when I looked at the harp.

Please don't let me disappoint him.

As I began carefully tuning the instrument, I couldn't help but smile wistfully. Every note took me back to when life was simpler and more carefree. As much as I regretted my mistakes, I didn't regret them leading me to Shade.

Once the harp was tuned, I played some random chords to awaken more memories. Preferably, muscle memories. I was delighted when they rushed back as though the last time I had played was mere weeks ago.

Now, what to play for him…

My gaze lingered on the harp as I tried to think. Drumming my fingers didn't help.

It has to be something special.

All of a sudden, I remembered one song in particular.

That's perfect!

I began playing without hesitation.

He'll love this, I know it.

My hands moved as if tenderly caressing the instrument, weaving a gentle melody that echoed all around us and down the illuminated waterway. Amid the intro, I glanced at Shade and was relieved to see him still smiling without a tear in sight.

This is just for you.

I refocused on my hands so I wouldn't miss the transition into the first verse. As I joined in with the lyrics, I made sure to play slightly louder so my voice wouldn't drown out the harp. It had been so long since I last sang.

"When memories fade, and time slips away,
One thought remains, and that's you.
When all I see is dark, and all I feel is pain,
One light remains, and that's you.

Colors pale, hearts cease to beat,
Oblivion is calling out to me.
Earth shakes, gone beneath my feet,
Stumbling, but I don't fall.

I fly, I can touch the sky,
All it takes is one look from you.
I fly, I feel so alive,
All it takes is one single hue,
From only you.
Amber eyes, amber eyes,
Your amber eyes…

When my hope is weak, and every dream is gone,
One wish remains, and that's you.
When all my strength has failed, and all my soul's laid bare,
One love remains, and that's you.

I fly, I can touch the sky,
All it takes is one look from you.
I fly, I feel so alive,
All it takes is one single hue,
From only you.
Amber eyes, amber eyes,
Your amber eyes…

Amber eyes, amber eyes,
Your amber eyes…

If there was only one thing I could remember,
It would forever be your eyes of amber…"

After the final lyric, my playing gradually softened until I finished the song with a small hand flourish. My voice had nearly fallen to a whisper by the end.

I did it.

Gripping the harp and exhaling shakily, I glanced at Shade and found him gaping at me. I couldn't help but smile. "You know, you have some rather beautiful amber eyes of your own."

The deep red of his face darkened substantially as he closed his mouth and swallowed hard.

His heavy blush was amusing at first, but I started to worry when he clutched his chest in a wide-eyed panic.

Oops—

I set the harp down and scooted closer to him. When I reached over and slipped my fingers between his hand and chest, his heartbeat could have been mistaken for hummingbird wings. Now fully concerned, I looked up at him and patted the back of his hand with my free one.

Fortunately, he nodded and offered a reassuring smile. Once he had calmed down, he just sat there gazing at me with half-lidded eyes and a relaxed head tilt.

My breath caught in my throat when he gently pressed my hand to his chest.

I envy his heartbeat.

Not having one at that moment was devastating, but I knew mine would be racing as well.

It shouldn't.

My feelings were getting away from me, but I didn't know how to stop them. All I knew was I cared deeply about Shade. He already meant the world.

I hope I mean something to him too.

Chapter 15

Athaeÿn

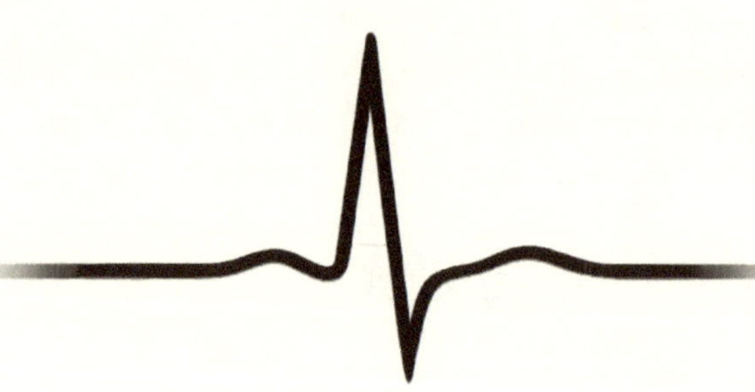

As we sat there smiling at each other, Lune floated over and hugged our joined hands.

My smile tinged with amusement as I pulled my hand free and held the cheerful spirit, gently petting it with one finger. "Did you like the song too?"

Lune cooed in affirmation and tried to pull my hand back toward Shade, uttering tiny noises of effort as it did so.

I raised my brows but didn't hesitate to press my palm to the back of his hand. My chest tightened a little when Lune immediately hugged our joined hands again and squinted happily.

Maybe my feelings are more obvious than I thought.

Shade was still gazing at me when I glanced back up.

His amber eyes really are beautiful.

Eventually, he perked up with an idea. After gesturing between my hand and his face, he indicated the reverse and shyly held up his own hand.

Here we go—

The progress I had made was astonishing, but it wasn't enough. I wanted him to be able to initiate contact as well. I wanted it more than anything.

I think I'm desperate for it, actually.

My anxiety lingered, but I was tired of it getting in the way.

Shade would never hurt me.

I took a deep breath and nodded with a slightly forced smile. Despite swallowing my fear to the best of my ability, it still clawed through me as I warily eyed his approaching hand.

I'll be fine.

I'll be fine.

I'll be fine—

Shade hesitated before carefully touching my scarred cheek with the backs of his fingers.

Shit—

I clenched my eyes shut and tensed almost painfully. The moment I started trembling, his hand retracted.

Wait—

I opened my eyes to find a worried look on his face. "I-I'm alright. You can try again."

He shook his head and pulled back even further.

I added a smile. "I promise I'll be fine."

It took about ten seconds for him to finally nod and reach forward again, but he didn't even get halfway before stopping and looking between the huge scar on my face and his massive claws. To my dismay, he retracted his hand once more and averted his gaze, now looking rather downcast.

As much as I appreciated his desire not to hurt me, there was a small pang of frustration. I didn't want to be treated like glass.

We're so close—

"Shade, listen. I understand your hesitance, but you have nothing to worry about. Even if you do accidentally cut me, a small sip of your blood would fix it right away, remember?" I reassured with another smile. "Please trust me. It would mean the world."

He still looked worried but did manage a hesitant smile. A full minute later, he once again slowly reached forward and rested the backs of his fingers on my scarred cheek.

Even though I tensed and closed my eyes again, he didn't pull away this time.

Thank you for trusting me.

The longer we stayed frozen like this, the more my brows furrowed with aggravation.

Please let me enjoy his touch.

My throat tightened.

Please…

When I slowly opened my eyes, a smile spread across Shade's face.

Wait—

I gasped soundlessly when I realized his claws were still touching my cheek.

It's working!

His smile shifted to intense focus as he carefully slipped his fingers under my ear and laced them into my hair, but his hand kept going until it was cradling my head.

I melted into his warmth. The touch was so simple, but the longer he held me, the more my nerves were overtaken by ecstasy.

When was the last time I felt like this?

My eyes were barely open by the time my throat vibrated with an embarrassing but, thankfully, silent whimper. I prayed he hadn't noticed.

I forgot what this was like…

Smiling blissfully, I caressed the side of his face until my fingers disappeared into his hair as well. I was secretly hoping he would lean into my hand.

He did.

Gods, I wish I could hear his voice.

As nice as that would be, our wordless touch was magical in more ways than one.

And I still wish I had a heartbeat.

There was a simple way to remedy this.

But…

My chest tightened as I pulled back and gently removed his hand from my head. "May I humbly make a selfish request?"

He looked a little confused but nodded.

"So, drinking blood offers more than just healing and sustenance for Vampires. I'm not sure what, if anything, you know about my kind, but we're classified as Undead. In simple terms, neither alive nor dead. I haven't had a living heartbeat for three hundred years, but drinking blood gives me a temporary one," I explained as simply as I could.

Shade pressed his hand to my chest and furrowed his brows when there was indeed nothing to be felt. When he eventually severed contact, he offered his wrist without hesitation.

I gawked for a second before shyly meeting his gaze. "I didn't even ask yet."

He just smiled and held his arm closer.

"Are you sure? You don't have to do this just to make me happy."

His smile widened as he tapped his chest then gestured to the center of mine.

After what was probably way too long, I finally returned a slightly awkward smile. "I know you don't mind the pain and can heal right away, but I feel bad enough just asking for this... And, I don't think I've made *quite* enough progress to bite you."

He waved away the issue and sliced the usual spot at the base of his thumb. When he held his hand in front of my mouth, the small wound was trickling blood for me.

It smells so good.

I wondered if my Vampiric thirst could override my issues for just a sip, but I decided against trying for now. There would surely be future opportunities.

Stemming from desire rather than injuries, I hope...

Meanwhile, Shade had seemingly noticed my hesitation. He signaled for me to wait and plucked one of the cup blossoms, which he managed to fill about halfway before his cut finished healing. This time, when he held it out to me, his claws weren't restricted to the bottom.

My fingers effortlessly brushed against his as I took the flower. After downing the blood and discarding the empty blossom, I closed my eyes and hung my head back with a deep inhale of satisfaction through my nose.

There it is.

I put my hand on my chest and smiled when I felt a calm heartbeat.

Alive again.

Not literally, but close enough.

When I opened my eyes, I looked at Shade and eagerly gestured for him to feel my chest again. My heart wasn't just beating. It was soaring. The difference between mourning touch and actively wanting it was night and day.

He returned his hand to my chest and smiled brightly when he found what hadn't been there before. The longer his hand remained, the faster my heart beat.

Oh gods—

My eyes were already half-lidded when I leaned forward and pressed his warm palm harder against my chest, but they fell closed the moment his other hand resumed cradling my head.

I love his touch so much.

Getting a bit lightheaded, I nearly went limp when his claws got lost in my hair again, and it wasn't long before my unnecessary breathing escalated to desperate panting. I couldn't control it.

How I've wanted this—

Somehow, this was more intimate than anything in my past, even my career as an escort.

Can barely... think...

I was so immersed in euphoria I barely noticed his hands shift until both were holding my head. When my eyes slowly reopened, he was taking in every detail of my face, but I was caught off guard when his gaze paused on my lips before quickly averting.

Huh?

I gaped at him as he pulled back and confined his hands to his lap.

Wait—

My heart skipped a beat.

I...

The hammering in my chest verged on frantic, and I could tell Shade was equally affected when he wrung his hands together and refused to look at me.

I guess I wasn't the only one getting overwhelmed.

As disappointing as it was to stop, I knew it was probably for the best.

For now…

After letting the air clear for a few minutes, I smiled and put my hand on my chest. "I don't know about you, but I loved every second of that."

Fortunately, Shade had collected himself enough to return a smile and mirror me with his hand on his own chest.

I wonder if his heart is racing too.

Instead of asking, I cleared my throat and glanced down at the plant nest. "Well, I think it's about time I went to bed for real. My nap earlier wasn't exactly the most restful," I said with an awkward chuckle, but when I looked at Shade again, he was no longer smiling.

Maybe…

I swallowed a bit nervously. "You know, this nest thing I made is actually pretty comfortable. Do you… want to stay here with me?"

His smile came back right away, but rather than agreeing to my proposal, he pointed to the opposite tunnel across the river.

There was an instant surge of heat in my cheeks and ears.

When was the last time I blushed?

I got up and approached the water's edge so I could glare at the deadly current. It was just a coincidence my blush had been turned away from him.

Such a stupid—

My brooding ground to a halt when Shade appeared next to me and made a carrying gesture. With all my progress, it finally seemed like a viable option.

Get over one fear just to drown in another…

I had never personally witnessed the effects of running water on my kind, but the horror stories from my friends were a sufficient warning. Everything about Vampirism felt so arbitrary, not to mention obnoxious.

It was definitely Raethe.

Once Shade lowered to one knee and bent over so I could reach him better, Lune perched on his shoulder and cooed at me.

I just stared at them and inhaled a bit shakily.

Please don't drop me.

As I reached over his shoulder and gripped one of his back spines, he secured me with one arm behind my back and the other under my knees. The moment he stood up, most of my body leaned against his broad chest.

This is a lot of touching—

Fortunately, I managed to keep my composure despite being more overwhelmed than anticipated.

It's not forever—

To my surprise, Shade lifted me even higher when he entered the water. It was more than necessary, but I appreciated the excessive caution.

At least it seems effortless for him.

The journey across was a stressful eternity. Thankfully, we reached the other side without incident, and I still half-clung to him as he set me down on precious dry land.

Wow, I hated that.

Specifically, the threat of watery death. Shade's brawny chest was another story.

I probably enjoyed that more than I should have...

When I glanced up at him, his brows looked a bit tense. "Don't worry, I'm alright." I side-eyed the river and waved dismissively. "I always preferred puddles anyway."

He took a moment to smile with relief before chuckling so hard his shoulders bounced, making Lune bob up and down in the process.

I had just enough fading heartbeat left to blush again.

That was adorable. I need to make him laugh more often.

When he turned and headed for the tunnel, I followed with a quiet sigh.

If only I could hear it...

Lune zipped ahead but had to keep pausing to wait for us. I wasn't sure what the rush was about, but its impatient darting back and forth was amusing. Eventually, we approached what looked like an impenetrable wall of dark blue vines, which were decorated by luminous, white flowers.

Shade was already smiling when he gently touched one of the small blossoms.

When he pulled back, the flower cooed softly and turned around just enough to look at us with pupilless, light green eyes, though it tilted its petaled head at me in particular. A few seconds later, the floral spirit let out a more trilling coo that roused the others, whose glows brightened as they stirred one after the other.

Eventually, the vines untangled and drew to the sides like curtains. Shade passed through right away, but I hung back to pet some of the spirits while Lune took the time to greet all of them individually. Once we followed and were sealed in by the vines, I stopped in my tracks and gawked.

A spirit den!

We had entered a rounded cave with a thirty-foot diameter and fifteen-foot ceiling, which was concealed by more vines as well as glowing crystals. These vines were also covered in floral spirits, and among them were a few gemstone spirits slowly milling about. While normally considered rare, the latter were actually quite abundant in the crystalline depths of my homeland.

The circular wall around us was lined with small alcoves stacked with rock spirits, and over these piles hovered magical flames surrounded by dancing fire spirits. The upper layers of rock spirits were noticeably delighted as they sat warm and toasty right under the intense heat.

Finally, along the base of the wall were numerous glowing pools, all of which were full of water spirits splashing around and leaping out to meet air spirits soaring overhead.

It's beautiful in here.

When I eventually caught up to Shade, my footsteps were silent thanks to the familiar cloud moss. "So, this is where you normally sleep?"

He nodded with a big grin and approached the far side of the wall, where he made a show of falling forward like a heavy plank of wood onto a particularly fluffy patch of moss. Even with his immense bulk, he still bounced a little on the cushioned growth. It almost looked more comfortable than a real bed.

Much better than the riverbank, that's for sure.

As Shade turned onto his side, Lune flew over and rolled around on the moss in front of him. Now that we were surrounded by a variety of spirits, its cheerful coos jogged one of my memories.

Oh, that's right—

I looked around to see if any matched Lune.

Nope.

There were, however, six, non-elemental spirits I hadn't noticed before. Three white with golden eyes. Three black with deep violet eyes. These life and death spirits were sometimes called soul and void spirits but were most often referred to as Wisps and Wights. Although the Wisps resembled Lune the most, they still weren't a perfect match.

Maybe Lune is one of a kind.

When the Wights noticed me, they hovered over and playfully swirled around my head. Instead of cooing, they murmured softly in a low-pitched, resonating hum.

"Hey there, little ones. You must be thrilled to finally have an Undead around, huh?" I held my hand up to see if they wanted to be petted like Lune, but the only one that took interest phased right through my palm as if it wasn't even there. Fortunately, it didn't seem upset and simply rejoined the others in their dance around me.

I guess it was just saying hello.

The Wisps hadn't acknowledged my presence whatsoever, which made sense, but it was strange they hadn't greeted Shade yet.

Maybe they don't bother after all this time.

To my surprise, it was the Wights who hovered over to him.

Wait—

I was befuddled once again. As far as I knew, any sentient being in the mortal realm couldn't survive without a soul, even the most powerful like Arbiters and Arch-Demons. Undead like me were just reanimated corpses, but Shade was very much alive. I could tell from his blood.

If anyone could bend the soul rule, it was a half-Arbiter-half-Arch-Demon, but it still seemed like a stretch. Pointless, too, if I pretended Xythe was responsible. Even if Shade had hated his father, he couldn't get through the barrier to hunt him down. Soul or no soul, he wasn't much of a threat.

He seems fine, so maybe these Wights are just abnormally friendly.

I sighed and rubbed my temple.

Good thing Undead can't have aneurysms...

Shade waved in my peripheral vision right as I sat down. When I glanced over, he stood and gestured between me and the extra fluffy patch he had been lying on.

"I appreciate the offer, but you can keep your spot. This is already way better than the riverbank," I grinned and dragged my hands back and forth on the soft moss, "maybe even the plant nest I made."

A big smile came to his face as he shook his head and pointed to the fluffy patch again.

My chest tightened a little. "Are you sure?"

He just nodded and stepped aside, unwavering smile fully intact.

I stared at him for a few seconds.

Stop feeling guilty every time he does something nice for you.

Trying to be grateful instead, I sat on the indicated spot and nearly fell over when I sank down more than expected.

Whoa—

It was embarrassing how long it took to find my balance. Once I got situated, I chuckled at the patch's exaggerated cushioning. It really was like a bed.

At least he's had a comfortable place to sleep all this time.

I was about to change my mind again but caught myself at the last second.

I didn't take his spot. He gave it to me.

Instead of arguing, I just smiled up at him. "Thank you."

He returned a smile and waved a polite goodbye before lying on his side about ten feet away.

Even though his back was to me, I remained facing his direction when I settled down as well.

You can turn around if you want...

Meanwhile, Lune perched on his shoulder and watched the Wights swirl around his back spines as though they were an obstacle course. I couldn't help but grin at the amusing sight.

At least someone enjoys those giant spikes.

I was still smiling when I closed my eyes and drifted off to sleep.

Chapter 16

Athaeÿn

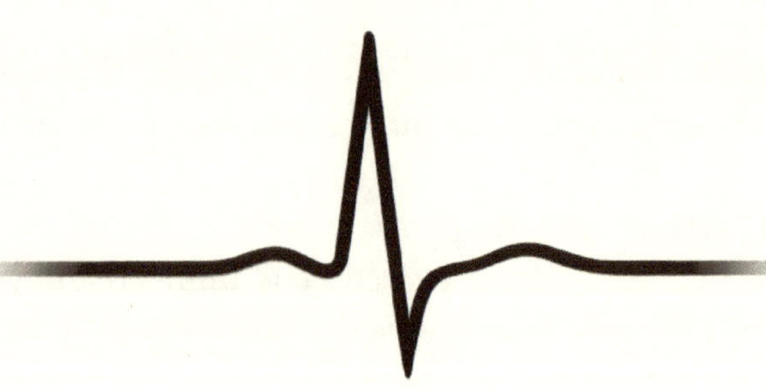

I wasn't blessed with pleasant dreams this time either, but instead of horrific nightmares, my unconscious mind dredged up every depressing revelation possible. Unfortunately, while different in effect, the impact was of similar magnitude.

The day I left my parents behind.
The fact I never wrote or visited them.
Every failed relationship.
Miri's long-gone passing.
Knowing I would never see her or Callyn again.
Or any loved ones from my old life.
Roänach's betrayal and my subsequent murder.
Three hundred years of fearing touch.

Everyone held prisoner at Castle Veil.
My failure to protect the other vassals.
The fact Roänach knew all along.
Being thrown away as collateral.
Being discarded to die.

Being nothing.

Everything went pitch-black, followed by silent darkness for what felt like an eternity. All of a sudden, Roänach's horrid eyes appeared right in front of mine. Only his eyes.

"Even favorites are replaceable."

…

My cheeks itched from salt when I woke up.
Dammit…
Huffing under my breath, I wiped my eyes and slowly sat upright.
Gods, I'm such a—
All of a sudden, I noticed Shade sitting right in front of me. *"Shit—* Did I wake you up?" I paused to sniffle and clear my throat. "I-I'm sorry. I didn't mean for this to happen again."
Can't even go one minute without disturbing him with more bullshit.
Instead of answering my question, he gestured to my tear-stained face.
"Just more upsetting dreams… Different from last time…"
His brows were already tense when he tilted his head.
"I appreciate your concern, but I've dumped enough problems on you. Way too many, actually."
He frowned for a moment before tapping his ear and pressing his palm to my chest.
Why…
I just stared at him.
Why does he want to listen to this?
Eventually, my sullen gaze fell to his hand. There was no heartbeat for him to feel this time.
It would be a waste anyway…

Almost numb from misery, I clung to the comfort in his touch and slipped my hand under his so I could feel even more warmth. My throat tightened when he gently pressed my palm against my chest.

Maybe it's okay to finally let everything out.

If I could trust anyone with my pathetic history, it was Shade. I trusted that he wanted to listen. I trusted that he cared about what I had to say. I trusted him wholeheartedly.

Thank you, Shade.

He retracted his hand when I gave a subtle nod, but I remained silent.

How do I even start?

I was still hesitant to bring up sexual violence, but trying to skirt around the topic would just make things needlessly difficult.

And this will be painful enough as it is.

Eventually, I took a deep breath and met his gaze. "Before I start, are you familiar with sex and romance?"

He nodded and pointed up.

My eyes widened. "You've been intimate with the Demons?"

I'm surprised Xythe allows that.

This time, he shook his head and pointed to his own eyes before pointing up again.

"Oh, just observed them."

Another nod.

Well, I guess that's familiar enough.

My gaze fell as I mulled things over. Even though Shade seemed a bit more open to acknowledging his father's cruelty, I wasn't going to mention that incident again. In the grand scheme of things, it was a drop in the bucket and hardly worth mentioning. Everything before Xythe was the true source of my misery.

Here goes…

I took a deep breath and forced myself to make eye contact with Shade, just for the sake of being polite. It already felt like too much. "My homeland is a mountain range known as the Obsidian Spine, but my people, the Dark Elves, live underneath in an extensive cave system." I paused and glanced up at the decorated ceiling. "Ironically, if there were glowing crystals like these throughout the tunnels down here, I would've felt right at home," I added with a weak smile.

"Life was pleasant enough for a long time but slowly dulled until it became unbearable. It felt like I hadn't seen anything new in over half a century and was missing out on the rest of the world, so I decided to move to the capital. Things looked up as soon as I got there. I could see the sky every day, made tons of new friends from all different backgrounds, and even became a professional escort like I always wanted, just to name a few examples. Life had finally gone from boring to fulfilling.

"The only problem was I couldn't find lasting romance. That probably sounds whiny and ungrateful, but I wanted love that went beyond friendship. Everyone else seemed to have it. Most of my friends were in happy relationships, as were almost all of my coworkers. In fact, the head of the Escort Union got married right after I joined."

It was a lovely wedding...

"Of everyone I knew, it often seemed like I was the only one who couldn't figure it out. A few breakups were because of my career, but most were unrelated. Either way, I was rarely the one who ended things, and my confidence suffered as the rejections piled up." My throat began to tighten. "Unfortunately, someone I never should have trusted was waiting for me to become desperate, and he knew exactly when to strike."

I wish he hadn't been so patient...

"The day I moved to Eidolon, I had the misfortune of crossing paths with Roänach. At the time, he was one of the nicest people I had ever met," I shook my head, "but it was just a flawless act, one he showed off by regularly supporting my career. He sat front and center for all my stage performances, tipped better than anyone else, and even bought numerous companionship dates I offered as one of my services."

I averted my gaze in shame. "He only visited the capital a few times a year, but we still grew close. I was too blinded by what felt like genuine affection to notice how much time and money he spent on me, especially once I stopped charging him. I should have realized what was happening...

"During one of our final dates, he revealed the Arch-Vampire symbol on his forehead. I was appalled, to say the least, and I should have clung to that initial sense of betrayal. Instead, I gave him a chance to explain himself."

Like a fucking moron.

"Quick aside for some context. Callyn's master is an Arch-Vampire named Vernyth, but he didn't turn them. They were actually fellow vassals until he replaced their shared master by feeding from his corpse. This was supposedly a panicked attempt to ensure he could never be controlled again, but he didn't think about the consequences until it was too late. Fortunately, he let everyone leave the moment he realized what he had done. Callyn and the others remain his inherited vassals to this day, but as long as he never shows up in their lives again, they're effectively free.

"All this to say, Roänach tearfully claimed he did the same thing and promised he had never turned anyone. He also professed desperation for intimacy, which I found believable since Arch-Vampires are shunned by society for obvious reasons." My eyes started to burn with anger toward my past self. "According to him, I was the one person in *all* of Eidolon he trusted enough to confide in, and I not only believed his sob story but had the gall to actually feel *special.*

"I was used to friends and clients alike telling me their darkest secrets, but an admittance like that should've been too much. That's how much I trusted him. That's how desperate I was to be someone's favorite." I shook my head again. "My heart already went out to Vernyth, and I wanted to give Roänach the same benefit of the doubt. He knew I would believe everything he said. He knew exactly what he was doing…"

Tears welled in my eyes. "On our final date, he asked me to be his partner. I gave up *everything* for him, and the moment we reached Castle Veil, he knocked me unconscious and killed me while I was defenseless. I woke up as just another one of his vassals. Undead. No soul. No future. Nothing more than a doll for the true Roänach to use however he pleased."

My shoulders started to tremble. "Many of my friends had suffered at the hands of other Arch-Vampires, yet I ran off with one and was too cowardly to tell any of them. This is what I get. Death and an eternity to think about what a lonely, pathetic cretin I was."

And still am…

"I threw my whole life away. Sure, Roänach was the one who took it, but I put myself in that position. I basically handed it right to him." I paused to sniffle and scoff bitterly. "Despite everything, I wanted to help the other vassals. I don't know why I thought I could. Apparently, I was in denial over how useless I was."

A single tear fell. "I used everything at my disposal to try and keep him occupied, including becoming his favorite, but it just turned into three hundred years of assault with a slow development of severe touch anxiety. I couldn't even hug the other vassals without breaking down, and I was afraid to spend time with them anyway since it could draw attention back to them... I was so lonely..."

Everything is my fault.

Tears were streaming down my face when I looked at Shade again, but I couldn't see his expression through the blur. "And the best part? Roänach knew what I was doing the whole time. The whole *fucking* time. I put myself through all that extra misery for *nothing*. He even made up for it by abusing the others while they slept. For all I know, he did the same to me too."

Everything...

I shook my head and glanced at the ceiling, but all I saw was an undulating sea of colors. "I'm s-so... tired..." My face slowly twisted into a grimace as I hung my head. "I threw away a great life, and my Undead existence is meaningless. I couldn't help anyone. If anything, I just made things worse." Tears were fervently dripping off my chin. "A-And now that I'm here..."

I can't even help you, Shade.

My throat was so taut it could have split down the middle. One of my shaking hands came up as if to soothe it, but all it could do was clutch the scars from Roänach's fangs.

I did this to myself—

By now, I was gasping for enough air to speak. It felt far more like choking.

This is all my fault—

"I was stupid in life, a-and... and even stupider in death..."

A-All my—

I clenched my eyes shut. "I'm completely worthless."

I deserve everything Roänach ever did to me.

This was the breaking point.

Everything around me vanished the moment I broke down sobbing uncontrollably, clutching my chest and hunching so far forward my arms pressed against my thighs. The gentlest breeze could have shattered me like glass.

I really am forsaken.

I thought by standing up to Roänach and Xythe I could regain some semblance of control, but it hadn't changed anything. Nothing ever changed.

I deserve to be forsaken.

I couldn't do anything for myself, much less others. I couldn't do anything for anyone. I should have just stayed home and rotted in my childhood bedroom. That would have been a better use of my time, of my pathetic excuse for a life.

Shade deserves a better friend than me…

When I cracked my eyes open, there was just a blue blur instead of moss.

Wait—

A gasp clawed its way out of my throat.

Pull yourself together—

There was no point. Not even Shade would be able to stand such incessant rambling and woeful sobbing.

He probably left already.

In case he was still there, I composed myself just enough to speak. "I-I'm so sorry, Shade. I didn't mean for this to become such a disaster." I paused to wipe my eyes and take another gasping breath. "I know you said you wanted to listen, but I would understand if you didn't want to put up with this shit anymore."

Maybe it would be for the best…

I was too ashamed to look up from the ground.

Just get it over with.

With a sniffle so heavy it turned into a hiccup, I fearfully lifted my gaze.

Huh?

Shade was still sitting right there.

Why hasn't he—

My thought cut off when I noticed what he was doing.

Rather than looking at me, he was clawing something into a foot-long piece of slate.

After staring dumbly at the unexpected sight for a few seconds, I glanced at the cave wall nearby and spotted a shallow recess where a chunk was missing.

He must have a lot to say.

When I turned back to him, all I could do was anxiously watch his furrowed brows twitch with every word he etched into the stone.

Oh no—

My chest tightened when he finished and offered the slate with an almost stern expression. I had never seen his eyes so intense.

He's probably going to chastise me for being so stupid.

I wasn't sure he would actually do that, but I was terrified my new friendship was about to end. A tender but impassioned friendship I already cherished dearly.

Please don't discard me like the others.

My hand trembled as I hesitantly took the slate and set it in my lap. When I forced myself to read the words, they weren't what I expected.

"I'm sorry you suffered for so long and that I couldn't be there for you.
I don't know anyone from your past, but I don't need to for this.
The actions of others are irrelevant to your inherent value.
You are worthy of love, you are not stupid, and nothing
that happened to you was your fault. Period."

As I read his message over and over again, the fresh tears in my eyes made it increasingly difficult to see the words. The sentiment was almost too much.

I want to believe him...

After reading it one more time, I looked up just enough to make eye contact. "But—"

He shook his head and tapped the last few lines with his claw.

"You are worthy of love, you are not stupid, and nothing
that happened to you was your fault. Period."

Before I could argue, he brushed the words with his fingers as if trying to wipe them away.

They remained.

When I glanced up and received an encouraging nod toward the slate, I looked back down and mimicked his brushing gesture.

The words still remained.

After about ten seconds, I stopped and stared at the declaration I couldn't erase. A full minute later, a sad smile tugged my lips.

I guess it's my turn to listen...

As I attempted to dry my eyes, Shade transferred the slate to the ground and pulled me into a firm yet gentle embrace on his lap.

I immediately froze in shock.

He's—

The moment I snapped out of my daze, I buried my face in his chest and eagerly returned the hug. It became desperate clinging when my fingers dug into his back.

When was the last time I hugged someone?

My anxiety was barely a whisper as I focused on the soothing rhythm of his powerful heartbeat.

I've needed this for so long.

Shade's touch was the most comforting of any I could remember. I had never felt so safe.

Maybe... it would be okay to fall one more time...

I shivered and let slip a silent whimper when one of his hands tenderly cradled my head. There was no way he didn't feel it this time.

I don't care...

...

We stayed like this for at least half an hour.

Shade only adjusted his arms once, and it wasn't until after my trembling faded. Otherwise, the only movement between us was his deep breathing.

I want him to hold me forever.

Before I could melt further into his embrace, he shifted us both until we were gazing into each other's eyes. Our faces had never been this close before.

Wait, is he—

I didn't know what to do when he slowly leaned in. To my surprise, he just smiled and nuzzled my cheek with his unmarred one. He hadn't even looked at my lips.

Oh gods—

My whole body tensed as our faces touched for the first time, but I quickly relaxed and leaned into him again. Despite the smallest speck of disappointment, my fragile heart was beyond appreciative of this subdued but equally intimate gesture.

Thank you, Shade…

All of a sudden, I slumped against him as my body practically gave out.

Ugh, that breakdown was more exhausting than I thought…

Without prompting, Shade carefully laid me on the extra soft patch of moss and gazed down at me with a knowing smile.

I cracked a fittingly tired one in response. "Is it that obvious?"

His grin tinged with amusement as he nodded and turned around on his knees.

Don't go—

My hand unconsciously reached for him. "Wait!"

There was a small pang of guilt when he flinched and glanced back with surprise.

"S-Sorry. Uh, I just wanted to say you can stay here if you want." I glanced down and shyly patted the moss. "N-Next to me."

He beamed and enthusiastically flopped onto his side just two feet away, which bounced me a little through the shared cushioning. His eyes were closed by the time I settled, but there was still a smile on his face.

Not close enough.

After some internal debate, I turned over and shifted until my back pressed against his front. When he stirred from the contact, I was afraid he had decided to leave, but he just draped his arm over mine and held me to his chest.

Phew…

Smiling bashfully, I hugged his thick forearm and closed my eyes as well. His warmth and steady heartbeat were more calming than ever.

I think I've already fallen…

Chapter 17

Athaeÿn

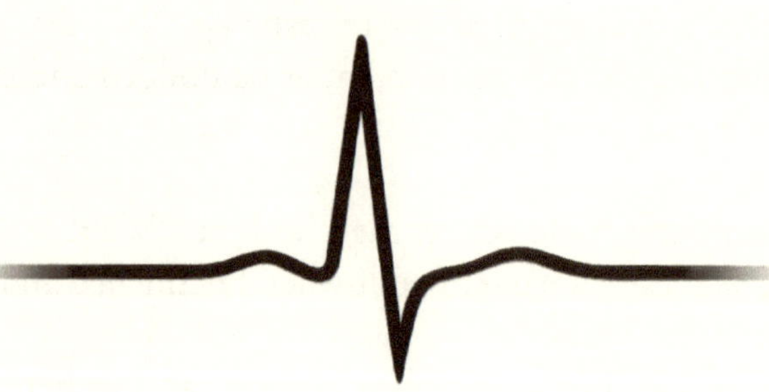

I had no idea what time of day it was when I awoke. All I knew was I finally felt rested after some much needed peaceful sleep.

Wait, what's—

There was brief panic when I registered a wall of heat against my back, but a familiar rhythm reminded me it was just Shade. With a sigh of relief, I turned over and buried my face in his warm chest, which was a bit of an endeavor under the weight of his heavy arm.

Thank the gods Roänach never made me do this with him.

When Shade eventually stirred, he gave me a light but affectionate squeeze before pulling me up until we were face-to-face. He was already smiling.

I returned the smile and nuzzled his face with mine.

Whatever this is between us, I adore it. And him.

As I reached up and threaded my fingers into his hair, my bliss was intersected by sorrow.

I still wish I could hear his voice.

My smile faded when I glanced at the jagged rune on his throat. Unfortunately, it was also a reminder of the conversation we needed to have about Xythe, but I still didn't know how to broach the topic without upsetting him.

That may not be possible.

I figured an indirect approach would be best. Knowing Shade's birthday was imminent, I forced a smile and tapped the rune since it would supposedly be removed.

He seemed to understand as he nodded and rapidly articulated something in response. It was enthusiastic but incomprehensible.

Eagerness to speak, no doubt.

I couldn't help but silently chuckle. Other than the harp incident, he didn't usually seem too bothered by his auditory shackle, but I could only imagine how frustrating it was being limited to hand gestures and scratching phrases into stone.

Regardless, it's nice to see him excited.

Meanwhile, Lune hovered down from his shoulder and shoved itself between us. As I petted the spirit's tiny face, it squinted happily and hugged my thumb.

Lune should get to see the world too.

I sighed and shook my head a little.

This is going to be a difficult conversation…

After a few more minutes of enjoying Shade's embrace and Lune's cuteness, I finally pulled free and sat up to stretch my arms over my head. I grunted a little when my shoulders cracked.

Damn, I could use a massage too.

I watched Shade sit upright and stretch his arms as well. "So, you've really never been outside the castle? Not even within the solar shield?"

He shook his head.

"I'm assuming you could at least *see* outside."

This time, he nodded and made a vague gesture overhead.

"Is that the sky?"

He smiled brightly and pointed at the crystals on the ceiling.

"And stars?"

There was pure joy in his eyes as he pressed both hands to his chest.

As usual, his smile was contagious. "I love the stars too."

He looked thrilled upon hearing this, but his elation faltered after a few moments. Instead of trying to gesture his thoughts, he retrieved the slate from earlier and carved something into the other side before handing it to me.

"I can only see the stars during my birthday month."

My heart sank as I read his note. I remembered seeing just a few of the brightest stars through the solar shield. There was no way he could see any through two layers of barrier.

So, he's never seen a true starry sky?

All of a sudden, I felt bad for my indulgent nights on the roof of the coach.

If only I could make illusions like Mirage Demons…

Sighing with disappointment, I set the slate down and tried to think of something to cheer him up. "Can you at least see the moon since it's much brighter?"

As though my question had set fire to the moss beneath him, he scrambled to his feet with such urgency he almost tripped. Twice. Once standing, he only paused to make a *wait-here* gesture before rushing out of the spirit den.

I just sat there blinking in shock.

Wow. I wish I got that excited about literally anything.

A little later, he returned and eagerly signaled for me to follow.

I fought to contain a knowing grin as I got up and went over to him. "What is it?"

He could barely contain himself and simply fled again.

It's nice to see him so happy.

Wondering if our little friend was going to join us, I turned just in time to see Lune cram itself between a few of the rock spirits in one of their wall piles, cooing with effort as it did so. Once settled in, Lune squinted with delight just like the others under the intense heat.

Lune clearly has very important business to attend to.

I was still grinning to myself when I left the spirit den and caught up with Shade, who was impatiently shuffling in place as he waited on the riverbank.

He's adorable.

Once he carried me across like last time, he led the way to the castle barrier but stopped halfway to the stairs and pointed up. Instead of the jagged gap through which the sky was somewhat visible, his claw was aimed at a crevice at the very top of the cave wall where it met the ceiling. He beckoned me over to said wall before I could say anything.

Wait, is he—

A pit formed in my stomach. "You want to climb all the way up there?"

He responded with a big, toothy grin.

I gaped at him. "Not to sell myself short, ignoring the fact you're two feet taller than me, I don't think I'm quite strong enough to climb that high."

His grin never wavered as he got down on one knee and thumb-pointed to the spines on his back.

Oh. Well, that makes things easier.

After securing myself to his back by gripping the two largest spines and wrapping my legs around his midsection, he began climbing a path of handholds that were way too evenly spaced and chiseled to be natural. Regardless of my presence requiring manual ascension, I wondered if the light from the barrier prevented him from shadow-scaling the wall.

Maybe he could but finds this more fun.

I shifted my focus to the man I clung to. His talented hands and feet made the climb seem effortless, but I was distracted by his powerful muscles flexing and shifting beneath his textured skin. The combination of skill and physique sent another surge of attraction through me.

I'm so glad I can actually enjoy this.

When we reached the top, Shade hoisted himself into the crevice and sat with his legs dangling over the edge to catch his breath and soothe his hands.

Meanwhile, I slipped off his back and sat next to him with a grin. "So, you come here often?"

There was a tiny smirk on his face as he peered sideways at me.

"You made that look easy."

He dismissively flicked his wrist but failed to hide a flattered grin.

"No, really. I'm quite impressed."

It looked like he was about to blush when his eyes suddenly widened. With renewed excitement, he gestured for me to follow again and began heading down the narrow tunnel we had ended up in, having to duck down a bit due to the low ceiling.

Fortunately, I could remain upright as I followed.

We eventually reached a small alcove that opened above ground, but, of course, it was enclosed by another barrier. Because the solar shield was fully visible through the translucent ceiling, I could only glimpse the moon before having to retreat around the corner with a hiss of pain.

Well, I got to see it for a whole second.

When Shade rushed over in a panic, I waved my hand to shoo away his concern. "I'm alright… *Phew,* I just forgot how intense the shield was," I reassured through a grunt of discomfort after being slightly burned.

He still looked worried but did manage a sad smile as he gestured toward the moon.

I smiled back to ease his guilt. "Yes, I saw it."

There was a pause before he mouthed *I'm sorry* and pressed his hand to his chest. The effort behind clearly articulating these words in particular was evident.

"It's not your fault sunlight hates me, but it was worth it to see the moon anyway. I just wish you could see a real night sky. There's nothing more breathtaking."

A small smile returned to his face.

"And I don't even need to breathe, so imagine the effect it would have on you," I added before poking his chest.

He visibly chuckled when I jabbed him, but his amusement faded when he refocused on my minor burns. As usual, he offered his arm.

And, as usual, I just stared at it dumbly.

I'm a sorry excuse for a Vampire.

My gaze found his after a few moments. "Since we don't have any backup flowers, we can try what you suggested last time."

He looked almost too thrilled as he sliced the usual spot at the base of his thumb and held it right in front of my mouth.

All of a sudden, I couldn't move.

Come on—

Just as I was about to backtrack, I got a whiff of his intoxicating blood and latched onto the incision a second later. My eyes closed as I began drinking him in, and my legs nearly gave out from the rush that almost instantly healed my burns and rapidly spread to my heart and loins. This was the first time I had ever fed directly from a living person.

Gods, yes—

An unfamiliar instinct had my fangs sinking into his hand before I could stop myself.

Alright, that's enough—

My control kept slipping.

Stop!

As quickly as this compulsion took over, I snapped out of it and pulled back with a trickle of blood at the corner of my mouth. My heart was pounding in my ears. "Shade, I-I'm so sorry. I didn't mean to—" I cut off when I looked up and saw his shoulders bouncing with silent laughter.

Huh?

There was still a huge grin on his face as he wiped the blood off my chin, but when my horrified confusion lingered, he softened his smile and patted his chest.

Phew…

I felt like an idiot for how relieved I was. Not only had he offered this from the beginning, but he actually seemed dissatisfied while gazing at the bloody spot on his hand with something akin to yearning. A few moments later, his hips shifted ever so slightly.

I saw that.

His heart was already beating frantically when I put my hand on his chest, but it intensified to panic and brought an intense blush to his face when my lips curled into a knowing smirk. Without warning, he spun around and took a few steps away to hide his embarrassment.

Or something else.

My grin lingered as I thumbed the indent under my bottom lip.

Noted…

Hoping to ease some tension, I groaned like an old man and slowly sat down against the cave wall just out of the light. "Who would've thought

I'd find a friendly first aid kit down here?" I joked with a glance at the back of Shade's head.

He just gave a thumbs-up and heaved his shoulders.

I had to stifle a chuckle.

And I thought some of my clients were shy.

In reality, I had a feeling he was just trying to be considerate.

Cute either way.

Five minutes of awkward silence later, he turned back around but avoided eye contact. It looked like he was still blushing a little.

My grin resurfaced. "You good?"

His hands were on his hips as he nodded and puffed his cheeks out. When he finally looked at me, he mouthed *sorry* again.

"It's alright. You didn't do it on purpose."

He smiled with relief and sat in the middle of the alcove to gaze at the moon, which, sadly, had been reduced to a plain, white silhouette in the brilliant light of the barriers. His entire being radiated with profound longing for what lay just out of reach.

I almost wish he couldn't see it.

A few minutes passed.

The air had long cleared, but I just sat there watching him.

Ten minutes passed.

He had pulled his knees into a partial hug but hadn't looked at me once.

Half an hour passed.

His gaze remained locked on the sky. He had barely moved.

I guess now's as good a time as any.

Despite giving myself shit in the past about brutal honesty, I had a feeling it would be necessary under these circumstances. There didn't seem to be any way around the truth.

No thanks to Xythe.

I took a few extra minutes to steel myself.

Please forgive me…

"Shade?"

His head turned about one degree, but he was still looking up.

"You should be allowed to go outside."

This time, there was no movement at all.

I waited for acknowledgement that never came. "Do you really think it's fair you have to earn your birthday months in the castle?"

He still didn't look at me, but his shoulders visibly tensed.

My throat tightened as I watched him. "I know this is what you're used to, but as someone from the outside world, I have to tell you this isn't normal."

He shook his head so subtly I almost missed it. I wasn't even sure if he did it consciously.

I can't tell if that's good or bad.

"For the sake of honesty, I don't like your father... for quite a few reasons..." My gaze fell as I fiddled with my tattered sleeve. "I believe your love for him, but I'm skeptical of his love for you. I have been from day one." When I glanced back up to see his reaction, there was none.

Probably bad...

"Even though Xythe didn't care for me, I hoped he at least cared for you. The problem is, loving parents don't isolate their children for nine hundred years out of a thousand. It doesn't matter how nice they are for the other hundred." I felt manipulative, but I needed him to understand the severity of his nightmarish existence.

Shade finally lowered his gaze and stared straight ahead at the cave wall. When he turned his head, there was faint mist in his eyes.

I hate this.

His brows slowly furrowed over the next few minutes. After one more glance outside, he refocused on me with what looked like genuine confusion.

I was starting to think he'd never ask.

"Why am I here?"

He nodded.

No point holding back now.

I shook my head a little. "Roänach made a deal with your father to take over Eidolon, and I was sent as collateral. When I refused to be Xythe's pet," my fingers brushed against my sleeve again, "he dragged me down here to be your next meal."

Shade's eyes widened with horror as he listened, especially when his gaze followed my hand to my arm. He looked increasingly devastated the longer he stared at the scorched gashes in the fabric, and it only got worse when his own hand drifted to the rune on his throat.

My heart shattered when his fingers began trembling. "You deserve to be free, Shade. You deserve to have a real life beyond this gods-forsaken cave. There's a whole world out there."

I'm trying to help you.

My voice crumbled to a whisper. "This isn't living."

Please…

There was an excruciatingly long pause.

Come on, Shade.

When he finally reacted, he just closed his eyes and hung his head.

No—

This outcome wasn't unexpected, but it was still a punch to the gut.

Dammit…

I sighed heavily and ran both hands through my hair. As much as I wanted to get over this hurdle, he clearly needed a break.

We can talk more about this later.

With another sigh, I got up and took a step away from the light. "Let's go back to the spirit den. I'm sure Lune misses you by now."

Shade stood without looking at me and trudged back down the tunnel. His tail was dragging lifelessly behind him.

This could've gone better.

I hesitated before following him to the ledge and securing myself to his back. As we descended the wall, I couldn't think of anything that might change his mind. I had already listed the worst details.

Maybe a thousand years is too many to overcome.

By the time we reached the ground and separated, my shattered heart had turned to dust.

I don't know what to do…

Shade hadn't even taken a single step when music began echoing throughout the cave. As his head slowly turned, all I could do was clutch myself and watch in shame.

Great, because he needed to feel worse.

I hung back to watch as he approached the barrier and looked up the stairwell. When he walked over to his thousand years carved into the stone, he stared at them for a few minutes before returning to the wall of light and pressing his palm against its blistering surface. He didn't even flinch.

I was glad I couldn't hear his skin burning. The rising smoke was bad enough.

His arms and shoulders were trembling by the time he clenched both fists at his sides, and it wasn't long before blood seeped between his fingers and dripped onto the ground. If he was aware of the damage his claws were doing, he ignored it.

I can't stand this—

But I didn't get the chance to speak.

All of a sudden, Shade reeled back and slammed his fists on the barrier, spattering it with blood that audibly sizzled once no longer making contact with his hand.

But the slam itself made no sound.

The fact this was expected only seemed to enrage him further, and he began repeatedly striking the translucent pane with such force that his feet stuttered backward.

Every hit was silent.

When beating the wall of light accomplished nothing, every muscle in his neck strained to unhinge his jaw in a desperate attempt to scream.

He couldn't even whisper.

As quickly as his rage erupted, it evaporated, leaving him shaking with failure and staring up at the barrier as if nothing had even happened.

It was pointless.

The music's volume never changed, but it became deafening when Shade hung his head and slowly sank to his knees, dragging his bloody fists down the light as he went. He hadn't even fully settled when he began sobbing uncontrollably into his hands.

This is unbearable.

Everything blurred as I rushed over and knelt at his side. "Shade… Shade, look at me."

He just continued breaking down.

My throat was so tight I could barely get any sound out. "Why does Xythe torture you with that sadistic rune?"

Shade finally uncovered his drenched face, but instead of looking at me, he reached down and painstakingly carved something into the ground. His hand was shaking so violently he could barely get his claw into the stone. By the time he finished, the words were barely legible.

"He got tired of hearing me cry."

In that moment, I knew what it would feel like to have a stake driven through my heart.

This can't be real.

And yet, I could easily imagine a three-year-old Shade standing all alone at the barrier and crying for his father, only to be unduly silenced when Xythe finally came down.

There's no reason for this.

When I looked at Shade again, he had already reburied his face in his hands.

This nightmare has to end.

For now, all I cared about was consoling my friend.

It's a start...

I softened my tone until it was just above a whisper. "Shade, do you remember comforting me with that hug?"

His face was still hidden as he nodded weakly.

"It did wonders for me. Can I try the same for you?"

Another nod.

Feeling an ember of hope, I moved in front of him and coaxed his hands away from his face. He was still trembling when I draped my arms over his shoulders and stood so the base of my neck gently pressed against his forehead.

It's alright, Shade...

With him secured in a tender embrace, I cradled the back of his head and felt him shiver when my fingers began lightly combing through his hair.

You're alright...

He practically shoved his face into my chest as he clung to me. I could hardly blame him.

I'm here...

Having both reached our limits, I was more grateful than ever we had found each other.

I wish I could talk while hugging him.

I settled for resting my cheek on top of his head and holding him even tighter.

Hopefully, this is more than enough...

...

Similar to my breakdown, we stayed like this for at least half an hour.

He hasn't trembled for a while.

Taking care not to startle him, I slowly lifted his face with both hands and used my thumbs to wipe the tear stains from his cheeks. When I offered a warm smile, I received a weak but thankful one in return.

Thank the gods...

To my surprise, the music had yet to stop, but its gentle melody gave me an idea.

Maybe this will cheer him up.

I finally let go to speak. "Would you like to dance with someone new?"

He perked up a little but remained kneeling.

"Do you know how to slow dance?"

This time, he stood and nodded with a bright smile.

We moved to the center of the area and fell into the appropriate stance as if we had done this a hundred times. He was too tall for me to comfortably put my hand on his shoulder, so I rested it on his arm that was around my waist instead.

Our height difference probably looks absurd right now.

I couldn't care less as we began a leisurely twirl far slower than the music itself.

No one else is here anyway.

Time seemed to stop just for us.

Everything else can wait...

As I lost myself in a haze of serenity, I realized I still had a heartbeat. Sadly, it began to fade the moment I noticed, but I was too busy melting under Shade's half-lidded gaze to care. It was a relief to see such a relaxed smile on his face.

I could watch him smile for hours.

Thanks to the rune, all we could hear was the soft melody that had enveloped us. No breathing. No footsteps. Just music. It was almost eerie, yet somehow ethereal.

I love this.

We only got to dance for a few minutes before the music finally died out, but Shade didn't seem upset when we eased to a stop. In fact, he looked quite content as he took the opportunity to lift me off my feet until we were face-to-face.

Is he—

His smile softened as he slowly leaned in.

Yes.

Shivering with anticipation, I closed my eyes and parted my lips.

Finally…

All of a sudden, he froze and shuddered violently.

What the—

My eyes snapped open when I felt a familiar third presence.

"Happy birthday, son."

My heart stopped.

Chapter 18

Athaeÿn

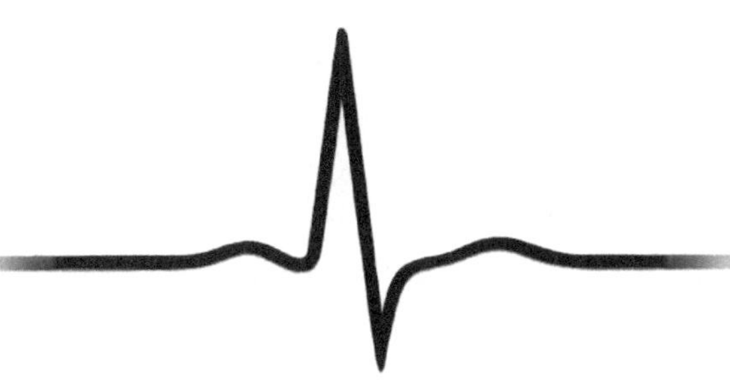

Shade was still holding me inches from his face, but I slipped a little when his hands began trembling. Our eyes were locked in paralyzing dread.

"Drop it."

He flinched and let go without warning, but it was evident he didn't mean to.

I was still in free fall when Xythe's tail hooked around my abdomen and yanked me backward. My feet didn't touch the ground until I impacted his chest, where he kept me pinned with my cheek jammed against his protruding, claw-like sternum. Luckily, it didn't ooze solar magic like his actual claws. These two rough jolts knocked the wind out of me, but my touch anxiety forced mild hyperventilating before my lungs had even recovered.

With me securely held hostage, Xythe refocused on his son. "I raised you better than to play with your food." His tone was flat, but his layered voice was chilling as it reverberated off the walls.

I shivered a little but was distracted by the look on Shade's face. He was staring at his father as if some nightmarish abomination had split him down the middle and clawed its way out of his mangled corpse. The visceral fear in his eyes was unlike anything I had ever seen.

Meanwhile, I attempted to pry Xythe's tail away from my chest as it started crushing my rib cage, but it was my strained grunt of discomfort that caught Shade's attention. He looked increasingly horrified the longer he stared into my pleading eyes.

Do something—

That something was darting his gaze to my scorched sleeve, but the turning point came when his brows furrowed with realization. *Acceptance* may have been more accurate. Either way, the immediate betrayal that contorted his normally cheerful features was heartbreaking.

I'm so sorry, Shade. I wish it wasn't true.

By the time he homed in on Xythe, his trembling had boiled over into enraged shaking. He already looked terrifying with his massive fangs bared in a vicious snarl, but his death glare became something else entirely when his luminous amber irises vanished into the pitch-black of his sclerae.

Even though I wasn't his target, I couldn't help but shudder. This was what I had expected to find when first thrown into the cave.

Thank the gods he was the opposite.

Shade moved as if to lunge forward but froze when Xythe held up his hand.

"One step," his tail shifted until the searing blade was hovering in front of my throat, "and his head will land at your feet."

Shade's shoulders heaved as his own tail began furiously whipping back and forth. I could tell it was taking every last ounce of his self-control not to move.

Please don't get me decapitated.

Xythe slowly tilted his head. "I am afraid the misuse of your gift has been known to me since the moment you spared him." His palm came to rest on my shoulder. "Nothing goes unnoticed in my castle. No pathetic song played on a stolen harp, no misguided attempt to turn my son against me," he pushed my shoulder down just enough to cause discomfort, "and no mental breakdowns."

Shade looked like he was about to explode, but he still didn't move.

"Despite such conspicuous misbehavior, my darling son, I still have every intention of celebrating your birthday. There just so happens to be some long-overdue information I would like to share, and I look forward to how little you will enjoy hearing it," he added ominously before making a turn-around gesture with his claw. "We are going on a field trip to the orb. Lead the way."

Instead of testing his father's patience, Shade made brief eye contact with me and turned around without a fuss.

Xythe followed with me still pinned to his chest. "Look back and he dies."

Slamming the ground with his tail was Shade's only response as he stalked into the tunnel.

I struggled not to trip over my own feet as Xythe pushed me along. Unless he relinquished his hold on me, I didn't see a way out of this, and I *really* didn't like the implication of why we were going to the orb.

He's probably going to shove my face into it and make Shade watch.

At least he wasn't ripping my arm off this time.

Yet...

...

Like every previous trek with Xythe, the journey to the orb felt like an eternity.

When we arrived at the cavern, he pointed to the side opposite the barrier. "Be a dutiful child and wait over there. You also have permission to look."

Once Shade begrudgingly planted himself by the wall as directed, he whipped around only to see me squirming in his father's grip. With Xythe's blade still at my throat, he was forced to just stand there and watch me be pushed toward the wall of light.

Meanwhile, Xythe strode past his son without even looking at him. When we reached the barrier, he cut a hole in it and shoved me through with his foot before I could try to get away. He turned after resealing the gap to find Shade rushing him, but instead of fighting, he simply back-stepped through the barrier as if it wasn't even there.

Now safely inside the alcove, he didn't even flinch when Shade's fists impacted the pane a split second later. Mere inches separated them as he just stood there calmly gazing at his son's snarling face.

Behind Xythe, I groaned from where I lay after landing hard on the stone. The orb's light had already been insufferable outside the barrier but was downright excruciating up close, so I tried to keep my back to it as I slowly sat upright. Regardless of how much protection this served, I knew my efforts would be wasted once Xythe returned his attention to me.

And now Shade can't help…

Xythe watched his son pummel the barrier and silently scream for at least a minute before finally turning around, but instead of grabbing me like I expected, he strolled right past and stopped in front of the orb. "The time has come for me to return to Eidolon."

I turned my head slightly toward his voice but kept my face out of the orb's harsh light. Fortunately, the barrier between me and Shade was harmless in comparison.

But still shit.

My patience was already hanging by a thread. "You really can't let go of your stupid vendetta against the queens, can you? It was over a thousand fucking years ago, *and* it's your own damn fault you were exiled," I hissed over my shoulder. "You're lucky they didn't execute you on the spot."

"If I let go, they win. That is unacceptable."

I rolled my eyes but didn't get a chance to comment.

"Besides, it would be quite a shame to trip at the finish line. Elvylli and Sathira have already suffered greatly by my hand, though they do not know it."

"How?"

"Their warranted extermination is merely the final verse in my song of retribution."

Very informative, jackass.

He continued being uninformative. "Do Elvylli and Sathira have any children?"

I nearly sputtered at the random topic shift. "You didn't answer my question."

"Answer mine, and you will find I am."

There was a pause as I huffed to myself. *"No, they don't have any children."*

"Why not?"

"That's none of my business. Maybe they just don't want any."

"Try again."

Despite groaning with annoyance, I did try to think of anything relevant I may have forgotten. Eventually, a sinister but hazy memory resurfaced. "Actually, didn't they lose a child? Maybe it was too painful to have more after that."

Xythe said nothing.

But I thought... Wait—

It suddenly clicked.

Tyrran's Shrine.

I was flooded by long lost memories of visiting the mournful site in the citadel to pay homage to the queens' murdered son. Three hundred years of Roänach had completely pushed it out of my mind.

If he's bringing that up—

"*You* killed their son?"

"I did not, but they believe someone did."

"What do you mean *they believe someone did?* I remember what happened now. Their son was slaughtered in his crib. How can his murder be something they just *believe* when they personally found his pile of gore the next morning?"

"Who killed him?"

"How the fuck should I know?"

Xythe hummed in thought. "So, they never shared any details... even after all this time..." he muttered to himself. "Perhaps this will shed some light. A note was left on the remains of their infant. It simply read, 'Your son for my daughter.'"

It clicked immediately this time.

Sathira's sister—

I remembered some of what I couldn't before. Aëlla and her daughter Sae had attempted to take over Eidolon after Xythe's failure, but Sae was killed in combat. *She* was the child of Aëlla I had vaguely recalled, not Shade.

That doesn't mean Sae was the only or last one.

Maybe Aëlla saw Xythe as a kindred spirit, tracked him down, and had Shade with him to fill the void her daughter left behind. *If* that was what happened, I didn't understand why she would then abandon Shade.

Unless—

I circled back to the note Xythe mentioned.

If Aëlla killed Tyrran to avenge Sae but was then hunted down by the queens—

My eyes widened.

That would definitely explain why she hasn't been seen in centuries.

It would also explain why she never came back for Shade. As for Xythe, his role slotted right in. He clearly had no interest in being a father, but shacking up with Aëlla to spite one or both of the queens seemed like something he would do.

Everything fits.

I was about to voice my theory, but the note he had mentioned was bothering me.

Hold on—

"Assuming that note is real, how do you know about it?"

"First, I am curious to know what you ruminated on for so long,"

The knowing tone of his voice reminded me way too much of Roänach. I hated it. "Fine. Were you and Aëlla ever a couple?"

"No."

"Is she Shade's mother?"

"No."

Well, so much for that theory.

"Alright, then. Who's his other parent?"

"A pointless question. I will instead address your previous inquiry."

Wish you would've just done that from the beginning, but go on.

"That note is very much real. I wrote it."

Wait—

"But, what about—"

"Aëlla was simply a scapegoat with a convenient dead child."

Charming.

"So, you killed Tyrran and left that note to trick the queens into thinking Aëlla did it?"

"Incorrect. I was not lying when I said I did not kill him."

I started to feel like I was losing my mind. "Okaayyy, you *sent someone* to kill Tyrran, and *they* left the note to trick the queens."

"Closer."

"The fuck do you mean *closer?* What other option is there?" I snapped, thoroughly aggravated. "Would you just tell me what happened already? I'm sick of not knowing what the fuck is going on!"

Xythe said nothing.

"Who killed Tyrran?"

"No one."

Oh my gods—!

I dragged my hands down my face and forced myself to take a deep breath. Yelling at brick walls like him never accomplished anything.

I don't get it.

His claim that no one killed Tyrran was absurd. Note or no note, the queens found his eviscerated remains in his crib. Their son was *dead.*

What if he's telling the truth?

I glanced at Shade where he remained outside the barrier. He still looked angry, but his fists were just braced on the wall of light instead of trying to bash it in.

If Tyrran is alive…

A chasm formed in my stomach. "My question about Shade's other parent. Why did you say it was pointless?"

"It cannot be answered."

"Why?"

"Your use of the word *other* implies involvement in his creation."

Please don't let me be right.

I was becoming nauseous. "You're not his father?"

"No."

The confused shock that took the place of Shade's anger was heart-wrenching.

The gore in the crib wasn't their son…

I had finally pieced it together but was in denial. I needed to hear it out loud. "What did you do?" I muttered fearfully.

Xythe let the dread fester for a few seconds before replying. "Tyrran was not killed."

I heard him turn around to face the barrier.

"He was stolen."

No…

I grimaced and clutched my chest.

Shade—

When I forced myself to look at him, it was just in time to see his amber irises reappear. They were accompanied by tears.

"My revenge may be incomplete, but I have reveled in the dual misery of the queens every single day for a thousand glorious years," Xythe announced proudly, his tone dripping with satisfaction. "Not only do they believe their precious son to have been tragically annihilated in mere infancy, but they are wholly unaware he yet lives and wallows in isolation while believing his captor to be his loving father." He paused for a moment. "Even when my prize is not in my line of sight, there are reminders of his presence all around me."

My eyes started to burn as I stared at the horror on Shade's face.

How can this possibly get any worse?

"Whether it be severed wings mounted on my bedroom wall—"

I swallowed painfully.

Those weren't bat wings…

"—or the impenetrable shield guarding my castle."

Xythe, you fucking bastard.

Cutting off infant Shade's wings was enough to make me sick, but I got caught on the second thing he said. "What does Shade have to do with the solar shield?" I demanded angrily.

"Allow me to show you." Xythe dragged me over with his tail but used his hand to grab my arm and yank me to my feet. Just like last time, he effortlessly cleaved both fabric and flesh.

I screamed in agony from the combined solar magic of his claws and blinding light that was now right in my face, but turning away from the orb did nothing to stop my skin from charring and sizzling. The more I tried to pull away, the tighter his grip became.

"You are not looking." He used the searing tip of his tail blade to puncture my scorched cheek and force me back around. "I suspect you believe this artificial sun to be what generates the shields. That is correct. However, it is also a shield in and of itself, one which protects its own power source," he added, waving his hand in front of the orb.

I could barely see anything through my tears of anguish, but I was able to discern the orb's surface splitting down the middle to reveal a second, smaller orb inside. In contrast to the solar generator, this inner sphere could have fit in the palm of my hand and appeared to be made of pure darkness.

Wait—

After a few seconds, the concentrated void undulated and began reaching for me but remained trapped when Xythe quickly resealed the opening.

It can't be—

I glanced over my shoulder at Shade, whose eyes shot wide as he clutched his chest.

No wonder he was so drawn to the orb.

Hissing in pain and anger, I whipped back around and glared at Xythe. "You've been using his soul this whole time?!"

He was unmoved by my shriek of enraged disbelief. "Were you two somehow able to escape, my sweet, silent prince would not get far without perishing."

I couldn't believe what I was hearing.

The fucking gall—

If Shade's soul was powerful enough to fuel the solar generator for a thousand years, it was no wonder Xythe didn't want him to have it.

What an absolute coward.

Something was still bothering me. "Hold on, if he's pure Arbiter, why does he have all those Demonic features? Did you do that too?"

"Unintentionally. I believe that, without his soul, his growing body was corrupted by the potent magic of my kingdom. It was rather amusing to witness. Now then," he turned us both toward the barrier, "the time has come to finish this. I still have two loathsome queens to dispose of."

I glanced up to find him staring at Shade, and his reason for doing so became clear when he made a show of crushing my arm with a deafening crackle and explosion of embers. It was indistinguishable from a rotten log snapping in a bonfire. My scream eclipsed the previous as my bones and flesh were reduced to an almost charcoal-like material, leaving my arm unrecognizable as a limb and crumbling in Xythe's grip.

Despite being on the verge of passing out, I managed to see the moment rage overtook Shade's horror. My broken heart nearly imploded when he resumed slamming his fists on the barrier and silently bellowing over the fact that he couldn't reach me.

I'm s-sorry—

"Son, or should I say *souvenir,* you are going to watch in vain as your worthless friend disintegrates before your eyes. Then, I am going to exterminate your real parents, the mothers who actually loved you. And, finally, you will remain alone in this gods-forsaken cave until the end of time, knowing you have never been anything more than a trophy," Xythe detailed coldly as the small orb between his horns started to brighten.

Tears were streaming down Shade's face as he continued his useless assault on the barrier. No matter how hard he struck it, the only damage dealt was to his hands, which repeatedly spattered the wall of light with blood. It was hard enough to watch the first time.

This has to stop—

I turned my head just enough to see the solar generator in my peripheral vision. There was no way out of this for me, but there was for Shade. He deserved to have the life that was stolen from him, and I finally had the chance to help. I could finally make a difference for someone I cared about. My life would *finally* be worth something.

Shade is worth it.

I swallowed my fear.

I'm putting an end to this nightmare.

My throat tightened as I made eye contact with Shade one last time.

Forgive me—

With a sharp inhale, I wrenched away from Xythe and stumbled toward the orb, howling in pain as the charred flesh between my shoulder and upper arm frayed and tore until the connection finally severed. I didn't look back to see the amputated remains of my discarded limb still in his grip.

Don't stop—

My balance was so uneven I accidentally dodged a swipe of his tail just by stumbling. When I reached the generator, I shoved my intact arm through the plasma and grabbed Shade's soul, roaring in agony as I forcibly pulled it through the orb's blistering surface. Despite still being attached, this arm was now in even worse condition than the one left behind, having been reduced to crumbling, blackened bones narrowly held together by brittle threads of muscle and tendons.

Move—!

Left with nothing but raw instinct, I lurched around and ducked under another swipe of Xythe's massive tail blade. Unfortunately, I had no balance this time and immediately crashed to the ground with a painful jolt. The only reason I still had a grip on Shade's soul was because the fragments of muscle on my skeletal hand had essentially petrified and locked my fist in place.

"Vermin—!"

Hearing Xythe's thunderous voice behind me, I made a pitiful attempt to shove myself forward with my legs. I didn't get very far. A sickening gurgle trickled from my mouth as his scythe impaled me all the way through from above, cleaving right through my back and gouging into the stone beneath me.

N-No—

I choked on a congealed mixture of cold blood and hot air as I was slowly lifted upright by the searing blade, a foot of which was coming through my chest when I glanced down. Knowing I was finished, my gaze drifted to Shade's soul where it quivered in my deteriorating hand.

G-Go... Please—

As though hearing my silent plea, the sphere of darkness streamed between my withering fingers and passed through the barrier that had nearly faded after losing its power source.

You can finally be free, Shade—

The instant his soul reached him, I was violently yanked backward as if nothing more than a harpooned fish. Nightmares became reality when Xythe positioned us face-to-face with his claws piercing my battered torso from what felt like every possible angle, lacerating each internal organ and breaking every bone in their path.

"A noble but wasted effort." His tone was eerily calm as the orb between his horns blazed so radiantly it completely disintegrated the rest of my hair and skin.

With both lungs completely shredded, I couldn't even scream as I was flayed alive. My jaw nearly unhinged as I tried, but the only sound that came out was the rolling boil of blood in my esophagus from the heat of his searing claws.

"I will simply remove his soul once more," he continued, watching my eyes rupture and vaporize in their sockets, "but, unfortunately, you will not be here to see it."

My ability to comprehend anything was fading fast. For a split second, I thought I heard something behind me, but before I could listen for anything else, there was a concentrated flash of solar magic—

Chapter 19

Shade

Shade clutched his chest and sucked in a sharp breath as his essence was restored. Despite his immense physical strength, the overwhelming surge of power from sudden reunification of body and soul brought him to his knees with a tremendous thud.

An audible thud.

He gasped and clutched his throat.

The silence rune was gone.

And so were Athaeÿn's screams of agony.

Before he could help his friend, he nearly lost consciousness and slumped forward. Down on all fours, he trembled violently as the strongest wave of restoration he had ever felt swept his entire frame, and he watched with disbelief as the rocky formations on his hands and around his eye fizzled away like sand in the wind. In mere seconds, his entire body was free of stone.

Without warning, his arms gave out. Landing flat on his chest, his strained breathing was interrupted by an anguished cry as his back erupted with some kind of rapid growth. When this surge of healing finally ebbed, he weakly glanced over his shoulder to find two massive draconic wings settle into place.

The moment he began shakily pushing himself upright, a familiar blade pierced the back of his shoulder and yanked him across the ground. When hoisted up like a carcass on a meat hook, he found himself face-to-face with his false father.

Xythe reached for his trophy's chest. "I will be retaking your soul now."

Shade just snarled in his face and dissolved into the shadows.

"Come out, coward." Sounding unimpressed, Xythe attempted to use the glowing parts of his body to eliminate the darkness beneath him. He was unsuccessful.

As silent as the shadows in which he had hidden, Shade reformed behind Xythe, ripped the scythe off his tail with a spray of black gore, and flung the now-useless weapon to the far end of the alcove. The severed blade was still coated in Athaeÿn's dried blood.

"Filthy Arbiter spawn—" Xythe hissed as he whipped around and raked his massive claws across Shade's abdomen, leaving three devastating slashes in his flesh. As his target's lacerated organs began falling out, Xythe shoved his hand through his innards and gripped his reinforced vertebrae.

Shade pushed through the agony just long enough to break Xythe's wrist, which weakened the latter's hold and allowed the former to shove him backward to put some distance between them. Having prevented his spine from being ripped out, Shade took the opportunity to quickly collect and shove his organs back into his abdomen, where they neatly settled into place and healed over as his gaping external wounds rapidly closed.

Xythe smacked the ground with his injured tail after regaining his footing. "I should have mounted your *head* on my wall," he growled, charging with even greater intent to kill.

Despite being shaken by the traumatizing assault on his abdomen, Shade managed to intercept Xythe's new attack by catching his intact forearm, which he shattered just like the other with a single clench of his fist. His assailant's claws were now effectively useless.

Time seemed to stop as they stared at each other.

Shade was briefly pierced by crushing despair before unmitigated rage took over. He glared at Xythe with every ounce of resentment in his soul before grabbing the back of his head and repeatedly slamming his face into the cave wall, gasping and hissing through gritted teeth as he did so. Anger and betrayal had completely overwhelmed him.

Xythe grunted and hacked as he was brutally thrashed against the stone. Despite his skeletal face having been pulverized, he started laughing when there was a pause in the assault. "You cannot kill me."

Shade's hand started trembling.

"You lack the resolve to take my life. Just like your weak-minded mothers."

Tears welled in Shade's eyes as he struggled to finish the job. He knew everything was a lie, but it still felt like he was killing his father.

"Prove me wrong."

He couldn't.

Clenching his eyes shut and baring his massive canines in a heartbroken grimace, Shade whipped around and threw Xythe across the alcove with a roar of devastation. He watched him impact the back wall with a sickening crunch then crumple to the ground in a broken heap, though his twitching and faint wheezing indicated he was still alive.

With heaving shoulders, Shade walked over to Xythe's twisted body and watched the orb between his horns flicker and dim as his strength faded. Even though he was suffocating under the weight of his resentment, he just stood there and stared down at the Arch-Demon who had done nothing but abuse and lie to him for a thousand years.

All he could do was sniffle and wipe his eyes with the back of an unsteady hand. The rune was gone, but he had nothing to say.

Meanwhile, the silence behind him became deafening.

When his teary eyes widened with realization, he whipped around but froze upon spotting Athaeÿn on the ground in the middle of the alcove.

Or what was left of him.

Shade could barely move as he slowly approached the remains of his friend.

Amid tattered heaps of singed clothing was nothing more than a partial skeleton of blackened bones reminiscent of charcoal, only a few of which were intact. Most had been reduced to crumbling fragments and piles of ash.

Nearly paralyzed with disbelief, Shade slowly sank to his knees and hovered his trembling hands over what remained of the cremation. His shallow breathing suddenly turned painful. He didn't know what to do, but there had to be something. He refused to accept this.

Blinded by denial, he sliced a huge gash down his entire arm and frantically poured blood over the remains, but this only dissolved more of the bones and turned the ashes into coagulated paste. Panic soon took over as he picked up the skull and desperately tried to get his friend to drink his blood like before. Instead, the mandible turned to dust and sifted between his fingers while the teeth eroded like loose sediment in a river, encrusting his palm with congealed, murky residue. Only the cranium and a few upper teeth remained intact.

This was the only way he knew how to heal him.

He had seen it work before.

It had *always* worked.

But it didn't this time.

His throat was far too taut to speak, but Athaeÿn hadn't needed spoken words to understand him. Shade was confident his friend would hear the silent pleading in his heart, would hear his soul begging him to be okay, begging him to come back.

He waited.

For so long.

But it was too late.

Athaeÿn was gone.

Shade lost all control and broke down sobbing violently. He ended up hunched so far forward his nose almost touched the skull, which was starting to fracture and drop what few teeth remained into his shaking hands.

His entire world had fallen apart.

Even though he could barely take in enough air to stay conscious, he threw his head back with one final gasp and unleashed a blood-curdling, soul-shattering scream of anguish that seemed to pierce the fabric of reality. His divine blood wailed with despair, but the cry went unheard.

The entire realm of Terraen shuddered.

In the midst of his deafening shriek, pure darkness exploded from his body. This unknown phenomenon swallowed all light in its path as it overtook the castle in less than a second and rapidly expanded in every direction. In outward appearance, it was an immense, black dome that quickly reached a mile in radius.

Then two miles.

Five miles.

Ten.

It wasn't stopping.

Chapter 20

The city of Eidolon was already wide awake when morning arrived. Normally, the queens would have been flying over the streets on their first security round of the day, stopping now and then to assist an elderly citizen or help the city guards deal with a scuffle, but today was different.

During the middle of the night, some unknown force had woken everyone who was asleep and startled everyone who was awake. It was as if something had shifted, but it wasn't an earthquake. No one knew what it was, not even Elvylli and Sathira who were still going door to door making sure everyone was alright. They had never gone back to sleep.

By dawn, the city guards were politely urging the queens to take a break, and the latter finally agreed when the former promised their superior numbers would finish the welfare checks in record time. Still wanting to help, Elvylli and Sathira stationed themselves right in front of the citadel so they were easy to find. In the heart of the mountain, far out of the sun's reach at any time of day, everyone could safely get to them. However, with next to no information, the most the queens could really offer anyone was reassurance.

Elvylli

Sathira

Fortunately, the unrest settled after a while. Even though things seemed back to normal by sunrise, the queens still remained outside the citadel. They would have gladly stood there all day if it meant giving even one passerby a sense of security after such an unfamiliar event.

In the midst of watching people go about their business, they heard laughter nearby and turned to find a large gathering of children about fifty feet away. Most of them were huddled around one in particular. The spectators were a jumble of Human, Elf, Fiend, and Demon younglings actively cheering on their friend, a little Mirage Demon practicing their magic by making illusions of nonsensical wildlife hybrids. Some of the onlookers had real animal companions with them. One tiny Fiend even had a Wisp on their shoulder.

Both queens found the sight highly amusing, but their smiles were bittersweet. After all, the anniversary of their son's murder had just taken place the previous day. Their hearts still ached. Even after a thousand years, the grief was always fresh around the mournful occasion.

Watching the children, they imagined a tiny Tyrran somewhere in the rowdy mob, small but still towering above the others and accidentally knocking a few over with his wings. It was painful to think about what could have been, what should have been, but they couldn't help it.

He never got the chance to be a kid.

He never got the chance to run and play.

He never even got the chance to live.

When the children ran off to play somewhere else, Elvylli and Sathira shared a glance before leaning on each other with the sides of their heads resting together.

Although both had an equal hand in Tyrran's creation, his deep red skin had been closer to Elvylli's rich maroon compared to Sathira's dark violet. All three shared abyssal black sclerae, but where Tyrran had amber irises, Elvylli had light gold and Sathira had gentle peach. For the most part, the wives' only identical features were their wings, tails, and shared seven-foot height.

Elvylli was crowned with rose-tinted horns that curved upward and angled outward, accentuating her friendly, heart-shaped face. She had short, pointed ears, which were decorated by numerous silver piercings and clearly stood out against the shaved sides of her head, the top of which sported a thick braid that started black and ended in a fuchsia loop on the back. Every bit of striking beauty was only complimented by her somewhat slender but gentle, flowing curves.

Next to her gracile wife, Sathira's voluptuous silhouette was equally gorgeous, giving her a captivating elegance all her own. Her rounded face was crowned with downward-sloping lavender horns, and while she wore similar earrings to her wife, hers were far fewer in number. Even though Elvylli's hair was long when let down, its length was eclipsed by the braid that wrapped around the left side of Sathira's head and draped over her front all the way to her knees, where it finished blending from black to soft blue.

The one other feature they shared was thick lips as dark as a starless night.

Sathira used hers to place a kiss on her wife's ear. "Are you alright, my love?"

Elvylli nodded and turned her face toward Sathira's warm cheek. "I'm fine. What about you?"

"Significantly better than yesterday, but I'm still concerned about what happened last night. I wish I knew what it was."

"Maybe one of the gods finally shed a single tear over Tyrran," Elvylli huffed, pulling back and glancing in the direction the children went. "At least everyone seems fine."

Sathira looked as well. "Which is a relief, considering it felt like the whole realm shifted."

"I'm surprised Haephir and Galaeÿthe haven't shown up yet."

"They know we're here for Eidolon. Besides, I'm sure they're busy sweeping the continent making sure others are alright." Sathira managed a small smile. "There are quite a few locations to check, after all."

Elvylli returned a smile and lightly clacked her horns against her wife's. "Too true. If we ever retire like they did, a small house on the beach is still my first choice. We can pretend to be old ladies who collect shells and make jewelry."

Sathira's smile became more playful. "We're already old ladies."

"In years, maybe, but I still have the looks of a perky princess and the energy to build my own sandcastle," Elvylli noted, batting her dark eyelashes. "I could even make it glass if I wanted," she added with a big grin, summoning flames at her fingertips and fluttering them at her wife.

"I'm not sure beach sand would suffice, love."

"Don't squash my fun."

As the queens chuckled and leaned on each other again, they heard rapidly approaching footsteps and turned to find one of their many scouts running toward them.

"Elvylli! Sathira! There's something you need to see!" the Light Elf shouted as he skidded to a stop in front of them.

Just as they were about to respond, a wave of intrigue rippled through the crowd as people began heading toward the exterior districts.

"Want to place bets on if it's related to the realm shift?" Elvylli asked with a tiny smirk.

Sathira shook her head but failed to hide a grin. "Hush, this could be serious," she chided before thanking the scout and taking off to fly over the crowd.

Elvylli snickered and flew after her, but all amusement faded when she caught up to Sathira just outside the mountain and found confused alarm on her face. Tracking her gaze to the west explained why.

The sun had finally burned off the morning fog, revealing some kind of towering black dome on the horizon. It was easily miles in height.

Elvylli pursed her lips and rubbed the back of her neck. "Okay, maybe you were right about this being serious…"

Sathira shook her head a little. "I've never seen anything like that."

"I knew we should've placed bets…" Elvylli muttered under her breath.

"We have to investigate, but if that darkness is as intense as it looks, we may need to borrow a Vampire or two."

"The sun literally *just* rose. We'd have to wait all day before flying with any of them."

Sathira thought for a few moments. "I don't know what that thing is, but I'm going to assume it's dangerous until I learn otherwise. If we need to evacuate the city, time is of the essence."

"Want me to check it out while you stay here and spread the word? I can see if we'll even need thermal vision."

"Only if you promise to be incredibly careful."

Elvylli grinned and playfully poked Sathira's nose. "Caution is my aesthetic."

"You pronounced *chaos* wrong," the latter retorted, thumbing the former's bottom lip. "Now then, get a move on before the entire continent is swallowed up."

They shared a quick kiss. "I'll be back before you know it," Elvylli reassured before turning and making haste for the distant void.

Despite the grim task ahead, she couldn't help but smile as she ascended higher and higher until soaring above the clouds in the morning sun's warm embrace. It had been a while since she got to fly so free, and she was going to make the most of it.

The darkness was still a good distance away when she passed over the Shadowback Mountains two hundred miles later, and the void had loomed high overhead since the beginning. She guessed it had to reach at least fifty miles into the atmosphere.

Her wings were relieved when she finally landed about ten feet from the endless black wall, which was slowly expanding at about one foot per minute. As she cautiously approached and hovered her fingertips mere inches from the void, something hazy stirred in the back of her mind, but she pushed that aside after remembering the importance of her mission.

The moment she stepped into the darkness, she was brought to her knees by a suffocating aura of despair that left her gasping and clutching her chest. She wasn't sure what she expected, but it wasn't that. In her thousands of years, she had only felt such anguish once before, and she was still a bit shaken when she got back on her feet.

One hand remained on her chest as she attempted to look around, but there was just pitch-blackness in every direction, even when she glanced down where her body should have been. Putting her other hand right in front of her face made no difference. It was as if her eyes were closed.

As a final test, she extended her arm and cloaked the entire limb in fire. She could feel the heat but still saw nothing. Thoroughly confused but glad she hadn't dropped dead, she dismissed the flame and backstepped into the comforting light of day, noting how the darkness was unpleasant but seemingly harmless. Either way, she knew the investigation was far from over.

She looked up at the void one last time before taking flight again. When she made it back to Eidolon hours later, she went right to the citadel and found Sathira out front just like before, this time talking to some guards.

When Elvylli landed, Sathira urgently but politely excused herself and pulled her wife into a hug. "Elvylli! Thank the gods you're alright."

She eagerly returned the hug but became a bit concerned over the anxiety in Sathira's embrace. "I'm fine. Did something happen?"

"No, no, sorry. You were gone for over eight hours, so I started to worry." She pulled back and looked Elvylli up and down to confirm her safety. "Were you able to reach the darkness?"

"I was. The edge was fifty miles past the Shadowback Mountains."

"Oh my, no wonder your journey took so long. Will we need help seeing inside?"

"Definitely. I couldn't see anything at all. Not the ground, not my body, not even fire. It's more than just a lack of light. I think it actually absorbs it."

Sathira furrowed her brows. "I see. That's... interesting... I'm relieved it's not a dome of death, but now I just have more questions." She shook her head and turned to the guards. "Can you two fetch Daryn for me, please? I believe he's in his study."

Once the guards left, Elvylli rubbed her cheek and looked at the ground. "There's a bit more to it," she muttered distractedly.

Sathira turned back to her. "Like what?"

"A couple of things. First, it wasn't just darkness. When I stepped inside, there was also an overwhelming feeling of misery and depression, and I mean an *extreme* feeling."

"Hmm... Well, I suppose that fits the visual, but it doesn't really narrow down what the darkness itself is. What was the other thing?"

Elvylli said nothing for a moment. "It felt like Arbiter magic."

Sathira's eyes widened. "Are you certain?"

"Pretty certain, but wouldn't we have heard of them by now?"

"It's possible they wished to remain unknown and were successful until last night."

"I guess. Kind of seems like odd behavior for an Arbiter, though."

Sathira hummed in thought. "Maybe the pressure made them nervous. After all, our existence demands quite a bit of responsibility."

Before Elvylli could respond, they were interrupted by a carefree voice.

"Afternoon, my lovely queens. I hear you're in need of some Vampire vision," Daryn greeted, sauntering over with a casual grin.

Sathira smiled politely. "We would appreciate your help exploring that giant void on the horizon. Do you think you could find time in your busy schedule to lend an eye or two? If not, we can always ask around."

He averted his gaze and stroked his chin. "You know, I'm supposed to attend a *very* important meeting today, but I've been dreading it all week. If I wasn't already Undead, I would surely die of boredom. Killed by tedium. *Deceased.* Wouldn't it be a shame if I were to be whisked away on some critical mission and rendered wholly unable to attend said deadly meeting?"

The queens shared a quick glance with matching tiny smirks.

Elvylli then peered at him with a knowing grin. "It would indeed be a shame, you being such a vital member of the council and all."

His eyes widened and darted back to them. "On second thought, I have been known to exaggerate the gravity of such things. They won't miss me. I'm sure of it."

"Hmm, we probably shouldn't interfere—"

"Please save me," he whispered, clasping his hands together.

Elvylli snorted with amusement. "When is your boring meeting?"

"Just after sunset."

"Perfect, that's exactly when we plan to leave. Lucky you."

Daryn exhaled with relief and dramatically hung his head back. "Thank the gods…" He then straightened up and splayed his fingers across his chest. "Fear not, I will be ready when the time comes. I await your summons with bated breath."

"You don't even need to breathe."

"Hence why I'm so good at bating it." He then turned and left with a flamboyant hand gesture.

The queens smiled as they watched him go.

Elvylli casually folded her arms. "He's extra sassy today."

"Meeting days are his sassiest."

"Can't say I blame him."

"Me neither."

As the day went, they continued spreading the word and answering questions about the possibility of evacuation. Sathira had already used Eidolon's vocal rune network to make a citywide announcement, so they were able to take their time talking to people directly. This easily kept them busy until after sunset.

When they made their way back to the citadel, Daryn was already waiting out front.

"Did you know time moves slower than a dead snail when you're waiting for a particular hour of the day? Well, now you do. Come back next week for more not-so-fun facts with Dismal Daryn," he announced with his hands on his hips.

Elvylli grinned and wrapped her arms around him from behind to secure him for flight. "Apparently, even ancient Arbiters can still learn new things. How ever did you amass such impressive wisdom?"

He gripped her arms to hold on. "You know me. I'm a bottomless well of knowledge. An endless ocean of tidbits, even."

"That, I do know. You're an asset to the citadel for a reason, my friend."

"For many reasons, Your Shrewdness. Feel free to list them off as inflight entertainment."

"I'll see what I can do."

The trio took off and began making their way toward the distant void, which didn't seem to have grown much larger since that morning. If anything, it was oddly static.

When they neared the wall of darkness, Elvylli glanced down at the top of Daryn's head. "So, does that bottomless well of yours have any knowledge that might shed some much-needed light on this situation?"

"Afraid not."

"What about your endless ocean?"

"Not a single tidbit."

"How disappointing."

"Hey, I never claimed to know *everything.*"

Elvylli laughed through her nose but turned a bit more serious when entrance to the void became imminent. "Alright, since Sathira and I are going to be flying blind, we're counting on you to prevent us from crashing into anything."

Daryn took in the landscape. "So, trees." He nodded to himself. "Considering those are nature's anti-Vampire installation art, I'm happy to avoid every single one," he added warily, shifting a hand to his chest.

Elvylli nodded in agreement then realized something else. "Sathira, this might be really awkward, but you should probably hold my tail so you don't drift away."

"Good idea." She moved behind her wife and took hold of her tail as suggested. "Shame I won't be able to admire the view."

"Gods, get a *room*—" Daryn wheezed as Elvylli playfully crushed him in her arms.

As they entered the darkness, Sathira faltered in the overwhelming aura. "Ugh, I see what you meant," she groaned, sounding nauseous.

Daryn turned his head. "What are you grousing about back there?"

Elvylli was the one to respond. "You didn't feel that?"

"Feel what?"

"The oppressive aura of despair?"

"Nope."

She said nothing for a moment before smirking to herself. "Ah, perhaps it only affects living beings with souls."

He gasped and clutched his chest. "Ooooo my *feelings*—"

The three went quiet to focus, but the silence lasted three seconds at most.

"This is weird," Daryn noted before finally switching to his thermal vision.

"More like awful," Elvylli added.

Sathira tightened her grip on her wife's tail. "I second that."

"Sucks to be you two."

Elvylli looked ahead to focus on flying straight. "What can you see?"

"Mostly an endless sea of dark colors since the sun's heat set with it… Uhhh… Oh, I see a deer."

"What's it doing?"

"Walking *very* slowly."

"Anything unusual about it?"

"I don't think so. Let's see… Walking… Still walking… Aaaaaand it fell on its face."

"See anything informative?"

"Excuse me, that detailed synopsis was very informative."

"Let me rephrase that. Anything useful?"

He gasped to feign offense. "No one appreciates my observation skills." When he looked ahead as well, there was something rather large in the distance. "Remind me… Which kingdoms are in this direction?"

"Daryn—"

"Yes, I know my memory is immaculate. Humor me."

Elvylli sighed. "The only notable *monarch* in this area is Xythe," she answered, her tone heavy with distaste.

"That's what I was afraid of. We're heading right for his castle."

"What? Are you certain?"

"I have never been more certain about anything in my entire life, unfortunately."

"Is that where the darkness is coming from?"

He tilted his head a little. "I can't tell, but it's the only major landmark for miles in any direction. Consider my suspicions aroused."

It wasn't long before they landed safely in front of the castle, where, instead of panic or confusion, they heard nothing.

"Why is it so quiet?" Sathira asked uneasily.

Daryn looked around at the many lesser Solar, Lunar, and Starlight Demons scattered throughout the area, all of whom were lying motionless on the ground. He checked a few and was relieved to find steady pulses. "I was about to comment that dead bodies aren't very talkative, but I think these Demons are just unconscious."

"Says the chatty corpse," Elvylli muttered under her breath.

"Eheh*eheh*—"

"*Anyway,*" Sathira interjected, "I think it's safe to say the darkness erupted from this location or somewhere nearby. Rather violently, it would seem."

"Rather *oddly,*" Daryn suggested, looking up at the sky. "It's as if his eyesore solar shield reversed properties and exploded." He shook his head and returned to the queens. "Only one way to find out," he added, taking hold of their hands and leading them toward the entrance that stood wide open.

Elvylli nodded the moment they stepped inside. "This is definitely Arbiter magic."

Sathira was about to agree but noticed something first. "Wait—" She stopped and turned her head. "Daryn, do you see anything unusual?"

"Nothing besides even more unconscious Demons and a long-ass hallway."

"Take us to the right. I sense..." She shook her head. "Elvylli, do you feel that?"

She looked as well. "I... Yeah, I do..."

Daryn pursed his lips. "Is this something else I need a soul to feel?"

Sathira ignored his quip and tugged his hand. "Take us that way. Please."

"Alright, alright, we're going." He began leading them down the hall as requested but got a bit ahead of himself and fell without warning, yelping in shock and losing grip on both of their hands.

Sathira listened worriedly. "Daryn? What's happening?"

"Ow— *Fuck—!* I'll be ri-*right* with you— *Gah*— currently falling down— *Stairs—!*" he shouted amid a bunch of pained grunts and tumbling sounds. After a solid ten seconds, the hall went silent other than a long-drawn-out groan that echoed up the stairwell.

"Are you alright?" Sathira asked loudly.

"I would be better had I paid more attention to my feet, one of which is now twisted at an odd angle," his distant voice answered. "Hang tight, I'll be back in a minute," he added before starting to crawl back up, grumbling to himself as he went. "This is why I hate stairs..." Eventually, he reached Elvylli and used her leg to pull himself to the top step. *"Phew...* Mind if I get a nibble for my ankle?"

"Not at all."

"Thank you." He bit her leg and drank just enough blood to heal before standing with a sigh of relief. *"Ahem.* Well, with that embarrassing episode out of the way..." He paused to brush himself off. "There's actually enough room in his huge stairwell for you two to flap your wings, but I don't feel like directing you in such close quarters. Instead, we'll descend the normal way, *very carefully,* and try not to do what I just did. Sound good?"

Elvylli nodded. "Works for me."

Daryn watched his feet intently this time as he led them down the stairs. Even without flying, their wings were still useful for dragging along the inside wall to remain oriented.

After quite a while, Elvylli lightly tugged his hand. "This is taking forever. Can you see the bottom of the stairs yet?"

"Funny you should ask right at this moment, because I do. In fact, there's some kind of gateway." He looked back down at his feet. "Don't worry, we're almost there."

Once they were safely through the gateway, Sathira let go of his hand and took a few steps into the darkness. "This feeling…" Her heartbeat rapidly picked up. "What do you see now?"

"A cave with a stupidly high ceiling and a big tunnel in the back wall."

Elvylli let go of his other hand and blindly felt around until she found her wife. "Sathira, this aura is really bothering me. Something's not right."

"Because it's more familiar than you thought?"

"… Yes…"

Sathira nodded to herself. "Daryn, will you help us follow the aura? We'll tell you which direction it's coming from."

He could feel their shift in demeanor. "Of course. That's why I'm here," he said with a more reserved tone as he took their hands again and led them into the tunnel.

After five minutes or so of traversing the cave system, Elvylli came to a screeching halt and clutched her chest with her free hand. "W-Wait… This aura… Th-This feeling, I… I know what—" She shook her head. "N-No, that's not possible… Sathira, do you—"

"Y-Yes," she interrupted, her voice trembling.

Daryn remained silent and gently tugged their hands to continue forward. When they ended up in another open space, he spotted a large figure in a deep alcove in the back wall. "There's something over there," he whispered, nearly blinded by how bright it was.

Elvylli squeezed his hand a bit too tightly. "What is it?"

He swallowed a grunt of discomfort and cautiously led them to the edge of the alcove.

The stranger's back was to them where they lay curled up in the fetal position with their arms covering their head. It looked like they were trying to hide beneath their massive, trembling wings.

"I… I think it's an Arbiter."

Elvylli covered her mouth with both hands. "It-It can't be—"

The stranger flinched.

Daryn let go of Sathira's hand. "They moved. Keep talking."

The queens found each other and took a few wary steps. Both had tears in their eyes.

Elvylli struggled to breathe. "Hello?"

There was another flinch.

"They moved again."

Before Elvylli could say anything else, a drastic shift in the aura pulled them forward so abruptly they nearly fell over. When the crushing feeling of despair vanished, they knew the magical darkness was gone. The void fifty miles in radius had retracted in under five seconds.

This part of the cave was still pitch-black, so Elvylli summoned a small flame in each hand and flung them in opposite directions to act as makeshift sconces. With the alcove lit, the queens could finally see the stranger with their own eyes. They knew the deep red of his skin.

Sathira gasped but could barely manage a whisper. "Son?"

His trembling faded as he gradually lowered his wings. A few moments later, he sniffled and stiffly pushed himself into a sitting position before turning his head to reveal heavy tear stains and dark smudges. The desolation on his face was impossible to overlook, but his brilliant amber irises were what really caught the queens' attention.

Tears began streaming down their cheeks as they spoke in unison. "Tyrran?"

Time stopped when his eyes widened.

Their son was alive.

Chapter 21

Shade

Shade couldn't move as he stared at the women in front of him. He had never seen another of his kind before, let alone two at once. His soul was practically humming. Little did he know, the surges of warmth in his chest were the memories his mind couldn't recall.

After what felt like an eternity, he slowly got up and approached with caution. Time remained frozen when he stopped in front of them. It hurt to watch the tears streaming down their unfamiliar faces, but he remained still and silent to see what they would do.

Elvylli and Sathira briefly hesitated before placing their hands on his chest, where all three felt something resonate. The two mothers had contributed small pieces of their souls when giving him life and could now feel those long-lost remnants cradled within his own. Regardless, they recognized their son's soul immediately.

It really was Tyrran.

As Elvylli completely broke down, Sathira maintained enough composure to reach up and hold his face. "My baby—"

However, this was all she could manage, so Elvylli collected herself as best she could and took her turn holding him. "You're alive. M-My sweet boy is alive—" She could barely see him through her tears, but she was smiling with the purest joy she had felt in a thousand years.

All Shade could manage was an involuntary, choked laugh as he sank to his knees and promptly fell apart. He didn't mean to, but his legs had decided for him.

Elvylli and Sathira knelt as well and locked him in a trembling hug with his head tucked under their chins. They had lost the strength to remain standing anyway.

Time finally resumed in the midst of their sobbing.

When the queens eventually pulled back to look him over, their elation fractured upon noticing the Demonic shapes of his hands and legs.

Elvylli could barely take in enough air to speak. "What... What happened to you?"

He glanced down at his claws but flinched when the silence was pierced by weak laughter from the far end of the alcove.

Both queens pulled him close and gasped when they noticed the crumpled figure in front of the back wall. All of a sudden, they remembered where they were.

Xythe lay a broken husk of his former self. The orb that once hovered between his horns was gone, and all four blazing pupils appeared to have died out with it. The black voids he now had for eyes made him look like a soulless corpse, but his fractured head bobbed with residual life as he continued laughing. Each raspy cackle sounded like it could be his last.

Elvylli's teary eyes widened. "Y-You—"

He inhaled deeply with a painful wheeze. "I never knew darkness could be so *delicious.*"

She struggled to steady herself as she slowly got up and approached. "It was *you?*"

"And yet... it was Aëlla who paid the price."

Sathira flinched where she remained kneeling with Shade.

Xythe was still chuckling weakly between strings of arduous speech. "The absolute despair I could taste in the soul of that pathetic wretch," he paused to wheeze again, "was worth every second I wasted in his foul presence."

Elvylli's horns were glowing red-hot by the time she stopped a mere five feet from him. "How could you?" she choked out, her breathless words made uneven by her trembling fists. "We let you live," she pointed a shaky finger at him, "and *this* is how you show your gratitude?"

Xythe's head continued quivering with amusement as he tilted it to listen.

Fresh tears welled in her eyes. "You had *no right* to take him from us," she hissed through bared fangs.

"The theft of my dignity was an unforgivable slight. I had every right to take something in return." His breathing devolved into gasping. "I could have slaughtered your putrid spawn in response to the insult levied against me. I *should* have. *You* are the ones who should be grateful."

Her fists caught fire the moment he finished speaking.

"Elvylli, wait."

She whipped around and glared at her wife. *"Why?!"*

Sathira knew better than to take her anger personally. "We need to consider what Tyrran wants."

Elvylli's fury remained steadfast, but she restrained herself for her son's sake and his alone.

Sathira glanced down where Shade's face was buried in her neck. "Sweetheart, if you don't want Xythe dead, just say the word, and we'll spare him."

He shuddered but kept his face hidden.

She waited a few seconds for a response that never came. "Is there anything you wish to say to him first?"

Shade turned just enough to see his false father over his shoulder but quickly shook his head and reburied his face in her neck.

Xythe chuckled through a labored exhale. *"Coward."*

With that, Sathira met her wife's impatient gaze.

Elvylli didn't hesitate to turn around and square up to a defenseless Xythe.

The fading Arch-Demon in question was only enjoying himself more with each passing second. "You will never get those thousand years back."

Inhaling sharply through clenched teeth, she used both hands to light him up with a concentrated stream of the hottest fire she had ever summoned. Intent to kill would have sufficed, but the desire to utterly annihilate him fueled her magic to a whole new level.

And yet, he barely reacted to being torched alive. "Instead of you, *I* am the one who got to raise him."

Her hands began shaking as she took a step toward him.

"Not a single day will pass where your precious child does not think of me."

Despite overwhelming rage, tears once again streamed down her face.

"And every time you gaze upon his twisted, misshapen body, you will remember how you failed to protect him."

She nearly choked on her throat. *"Enough—!"*

Behind her, Shade desperately hid from the sounds of Xythe's burning flesh, splintering bones, and relentless cackling, the last of which only seemed to get louder with further incineration. Even if he wanted to turn and look, Sathira's iron grip on the back of his head would have prevented him from doing so. He didn't bother fighting her protection.

Even once Xythe's laughter died out, Elvylli continued her vicious onslaught. She wasn't going to stop until he had been completely erased from existence.

When all that remained were ashes and bone fragments, she screamed at the top of her lungs and finished her execution with one final surge of power. This left absolutely nothing. Not even a Demonic dust particle.

Xythe was finally gone.

She just stood there with heaving shoulders and glared at the spot he had occupied. His taunting had been forever seared into her memory. Without warning, she screamed again but held this one until a gasp for air forced her to stop, which just turned into a choked sob as she sank to her knees and buried her face in her hands.

Xythe's final words had cut her to the core.

The moment Sathira loosened her grip, Shade got up and rushed over to Elvylli. When he reached her, he knelt and gently pulled her hands away from her face, but she couldn't bring herself to look at him.

"I'm so sorry, Tyrran." She could barely breathe as she clung to his forearms. "W-We don't deserve to be your m-mothers... I... I-I don't—"

She hadn't even finished speaking when he shook his head and pulled her into a crushing hug. As he nuzzled her temple, he hoped his embrace would offer even the slightest comfort or reassurance. He finally had his real parents and wasn't about to lose them. Not for any reason.

Eventually, Sathira made her way over and knelt beside them. "My love, I think it's pretty clear our boy wants you to be his mother," she said with a warm smile.

Elvylli glanced at her before looking up at Shade. "Can you ever forgive us?"

He just smiled and pulled Sathira into their embrace.

Enveloped in the warmth of her wife and son, Elvylli finally managed a small smile despite lingering tears. She turned her face toward Shade's neck one more time before pulling back and looking up at him. "Thank you."

He tenderly cradled her head as a silent *you're welcome,* but his smile fractured when he realized what he was doing. He had made similar gestures before.

She noticed right away. "Are you alright?"

His smile was gone by the time he looked at his trembling fingers.

When a verbal reply never came, she realized something else that had been pushed aside until now. "You haven't said a word since we found you." She held his face with both hands. "Are you able to speak?"

He nodded faintly.

"Then why have you been so quiet?" She paused to offer a small, reassuring smile. "You know, the last time we heard your voice was when you were a baby. We would love nothing more than to hear it again now that you're all grown up."

Barely able to see her through the mist in his eyes, all he could do was shake his head.

She was heartbroken by his refusal to speak. "Why don't you want to say anything?"

This time, he closed his eyes and hung his head. Tears promptly followed.

"Oh, sweetheart, what's wrong?"

Without a word, he slowly got up and knelt beside the disarrayed mess of tattered clothing and withering remains in the middle of the alcove. His hands were shaking as he tried to sweep them into a more cohesive pile, and he whimpered softly when some of the few intact bones crumbled to dust in the process. He didn't know what to do with the ashes.

Or himself.

The queens knelt across from him and watched sadly as he carefully picked up the fractured skull and cradled it to his chest. It was now evident where the dark smudges on his face came from.

Elvylli's throat tightened. "Was this a friend?"

Her innocent question was too much for his last, fraying thread of composure. As he broke down sobbing violently, clutching his chest did nothing to ease the pain, and his claws threatening to draw blood at any second weren't helping.

The sight was unbearable, but the queens didn't know what to do.

All Sathira could think of was reaching over and gently taking the skull from his shaking hand so he wouldn't drop it. Upon closer inspection, she noticed one of the few remaining teeth was quite distinct. "Daryn, come look at this."

As the man in question began making his way over, Elvylli watched the endless tears streaming down Shade's face. "Is this why you lost control of your power?"

He nodded weakly and hung his head again.

Meanwhile, Daryn stopped behind Sathira and leaned over her shoulder to peer down at the skull. "Definitely a Vampire." He glanced at the rest of the remains and sighed heavily. "Definitely incinerated by Xythe's solar magic…"

Shade looked over but still said nothing.

Daryn's gaze drifted right past him to the back corner where Xythe himself had been cremated. After thinking for a few moments, he finally made eye contact with Shade. "Did your friend die trying to help you?"

Shade's eyes shot wide before clenching shut with guilt. In his heart, he already knew this to be true, but hearing it out loud shattered him unlike anything else. He knew it was all his fault.

Eventually, he took the skull back from Sathira and stared into its crumbling eye sockets, longing for the vivid, glowing fuchsia they once held. The memories weren't enough.

Still in denial and out of other ideas, he held out the skull to Daryn with a look of desperation. His tears had become silent pleas for help, for anything to fix this.

The intended recipient shook his head sadly. It hurt to see one of his kind reduced to a pile of ashes and crumbling bones. "I'm sorry, Tyrran, there's nothing I can do. If your friend had died from starvation, *maybe* the combined blood of three Arbiters could have revived them, but I don't think anyone can fix this."

Shade just stared at him with crushing devastation. A few minutes passed before he finally retracted the skull and set it on the pile of remains, but his trembling hands couldn't let go. He wasn't ready to say goodbye.

Sathira reached over and put her hand on his arm. "Sweetheart, I think it's time you left this all behind… I fear keeping your friend's remains might be too much for your heart to take," she paused before continuing softly, "but if you really want to bring them, we won't stop you."

Before he could acknowledge her, faint sounds began echoing throughout the alcove, sounds he could tell were rapidly approaching. He recognized them right away as frantic coos.

Not a second later, Lune zipped around the corner and made a beeline for Shade, completely ignoring the other three and flying right past them. When the spirit reached him, it hugged his face and got to work wiping away his tears.

Sathira tilted her head. "Daryn, isn't that…?" When she glanced back at him, he was already staring at the spirit with wide-eyed recognition.

All of a sudden, Lune noticed the pile of remains and cried out with dismay. It hovered down and frantically sifted through the ashes for a few seconds before looking up at Shade and cooing sadly.

It felt like his soul was going to implode as his oldest and dearest friend looked at him with such sorrow. He attempted to cradle Lune to his chest, but the spirit abandoned his hands and went right back down to the remains with unusual determination.

Daryn snapped out of his shock. "Tyrran, do you know what that is?"

Shade was busy watching with confusion as Lune began glowing brighter.

"That little friend of yours is the solution you were looking for." When Shade finally looked over, Daryn gestured between Lune and the remains. "That's a Sacrifice Spirit."

Shade's eyes immediately filled with terror.

Meanwhile, Elvylli glanced up at Daryn. "Bet you never thought you'd see one of those again."

"At least this one's not trying to revive my old master." He sighed and shook his head. "Shame that one's sacrifice was wasted when Rialla got herself killed a second time."

Now in a full-blown panic, Shade frantically enclosed Lune in his hands so it couldn't reach the remains. His entire body was shaking.

Daryn swallowed hard. "Tyrran—"

He vigorously shook his head and grimaced until his eyes were forced shut. The more Lune struggled against his fingers, the more difficult it became to breathe. Every coo of protest was a needle to his heart.

The spirit's muffled cries were distressing to listen to, but no one had the heart to say anything.

Eventually, Daryn tried again. "Does your spirit have a name?"

Shade still refused to speak but did silently mouth *Lune.*

"Lune?"

He barely managed a nod.

Daryn gave him a moment. "Tyrran, this is what Lune wants."

Shade's vision was a solid blur when he reluctantly cracked his eyes open and looked at him.

"Sacrifice Spirits usually bond with just one person, that being you in this case, but they can bring back anyone they love. They wait their whole lives for this moment, knowing full well it means their end. It's a sacrifice they gladly make."

Shade stared at him before looking down at his trembling hands. His fingers relaxed ever so slightly but still kept Lune from getting out.

"I know you don't want to lose another friend, but allowing Lune to bring back someone you both care about is the highest honor you could bestow." He softened his voice. "If you truly love Lune, you'll let it go."

Tears fell the moment Shade closed his eyes. Despite being one gasp away from a breakdown, he gathered all his remaining strength and relented. He had never stopped shaking.

Lune was hugging Shade's thumb when he finally opened his hands, but instead of going to the remains, the spirit hovered up to his nose and tapped him a few times, cooing softly to get his attention. When Shade opened his eyes, Lune squinted happily and nuzzled his face with a more cheerful coo.

Despite everything, his lips pulled into a quivering smile as he cradled his dearest friend with trembling fingers. Not even the strongest despair could withstand Lune's affection.

After their embrace, Lune went to Shade's chest and pressed one of its little mitten hands over his heart, leaving a glowing white imprint that began slowly fading once it pulled away. When the spirit hovered back up, it chirped the moment they made eye contact.

Shade actually wanted to speak this time, but his throat was far too taut. Instead, he silently mouthed *I love you, Lune.* To his surprise, Lune made four coos that almost sounded like *I love you too.*

His broken smile clung to life as he cradled the spirit one last time. By now, the handprint on his chest was gone, but he could still feel the warmth. It had merged with his soul.

When they released each other for the final time, Lune went back to the remains and perched on the skull, where it glowed exponentially brighter until the others had to shield their eyes. It practically sang with elation as its light consumed everything within reach, and its ethereal song echoed joyfully throughout the cave even after the spirit was gone.

Once he was able to see, Shade lowered his hand and hesitantly looked down. Instead of charcoal bones and coagulated ashes, there lay a slender figure made of Lune's pure essence, the fading light of which slowly revealed what appeared to be a peacefully sleeping Athaeÿn.

Shade froze mid-gasp. Other than his clothes, which remained in tatters on the stone beneath him, his friend had been restored exactly how he remembered, scars and all.

Having never seen him undressed, he treated his exposed body like hollow glass as he carefully picked him up and laid him across his lap. He even shifted into a sitting position, hoping it would be more comfortable for his friend when he woke up.

If he woke up.

As Shade anxiously watched Athaeÿn's face, he became increasingly worried the longer nothing happened.

An eternal minute passed.

Just as he was about to panic, his breath caught at the sight of subtle movement.

Another excruciating minute later, his friend finally awoke.

Shade smiled with pure relief the moment they made eye contact. His throat was almost too tight to speak.

Almost.

A single tear came down his cheek. "Hi, Athaeÿn."

Chapter 22

Athaeÿn

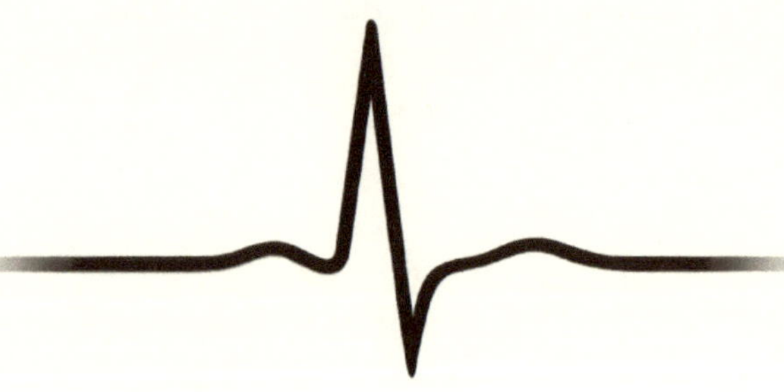

I gawked up at Shade.

Did he just—

My gaze darted to his throat.

The silence rune is gone. That must mean—

Something else caught my attention.

Wait—

My hands unconsciously touched my face.

I'm not dead.

Which was strange, but I was still preoccupied with the first thing I noticed.

Shade—

I looked into his eyes again. "You said my name."

His voice is so deep… and comforting…

My throat tightened as I reached up and held the side of his face with a trembling hand. "Y-You're really speaking."

He leaned into my touch. "Thanks to you."

Everything hit me all at once.

After choking out a breathless laugh, I flung my arms around his neck and pulled myself into a desperate hug, not caring in the slightest that I was sobbing grossly into his chest. I couldn't control my overwhelming relief. I didn't want to anyway.

Shade swiftly wrapped his arms around me in a loving embrace unlike anything I had ever felt. A faint gasp escaped my throat as he lifted me up and buried his face in my hair, but a whimper slipped out when one of his hands cradled the back of my head. We were both trembling.

Is this really happening?

I had been certain my goodbye was the end.

This can't be real.

It was then I felt his powerful heartbeat. That was all the proof I needed.

This must be real.

I smiled through my tears and dug my fingers into his back.

This is real...

...

It took at least ten minutes for us to collect ourselves.

Shade took the opportunity to adjust our embrace so he could look at me. There were still tears in his eyes as he caressed the side of my face. "You're alive."

"As alive as an Undead can be." I paused to rub the bare half of his head, chuckling as I did so. "And I see your soul did a little maintenance."

"Something else I have you to thank for." He nuzzled my temple with his cheek. "I can't believe you're really here. I thought you were gone forever."

My hand drifted to the other side of his head. "We're both here."

He just nodded and buried his face in my hair again.

I could feel a lingering tremble in his arms. Knowing it had soothed him in the past, I began slowly combing my fingers through his thick mane. Fortunately, my efforts didn't go unnoticed as his breathing steadily slowed until he seemed much more relaxed.

I finally made a difference…

As nice as it was to realize this, I shouldn't have been able to.

I'm supposed to be dead.

I was relieved not to be, but the gap of the unknown was starting to bother me.

Now feeling somewhat uneasy, I pulled back so I could see his face. "What actually happened?"

He draped some of my hair over my shoulder. "It was the worst thing I've ever seen. My father—" he let out a shaky a sigh, *"Xythe* reduced you to a pile of bones and ashes. Needless to say, pouring blood on your remains didn't help."

Oh.

After a slight pause, I offered a smile to lighten the mood. "Well, it was certainly the worst thing I've ever *felt."*

Something's still missing.

My smile faltered. "I can see why you thought I was gone forever, but if your blood didn't help, how am I here?"

His jaw started to quiver.

A pit formed in my stomach when he hung his head. "Shade?"

He said nothing for a few moments. "I found out what kind of spirit Lune was."

… Was?

When he lifted his head, there were fresh tears in his eyes. "Lune was a Sacrifice Spirit."

Wait—

My eyes widened with horror.

He can't mean—

I could barely take in enough air to speak. "Lune is gone… because of me?"

No—

It felt like Xythe's blade had impaled my chest all over again. This time, right through my heart.

I-It can't be—

Before I could unravel, Shade's firm voice abruptly refocused me. "No."

Having frozen in shock, all I could do was stare at him in disbelief.

He shook his head and lightly ran his claws through my hair. "No," he repeated, his tone much softer this time. "Because of Lune, I get to see your face again."

I opened my mouth to argue but didn't get the chance.

"Bringing back someone they love is their purpose." He briefly glanced past me before reinstating eye contact. "When Xythe wasn't around, Lune was all I needed. We were more than content with our love for one another," he cradled my head with one hand, "but then you came along and became something special to both of us." He managed a small smile. "Lune didn't even hesitate to give its life for yours."

My voice was feeble with guilt. "I'm so sorry, Shade. I-I didn't know this would happen."

He shook his head. "Don't be sorry, Athaeÿn. We both desperately wanted you back. I'll miss my friend dearly, but I could feel how happy Lune was in those final moments. You were clearly worth saving."

I could barely see him through my tears.

His smile brightened as he tucked a stray lock of hair behind my ear. "Besides, Lune wouldn't want you to blame yourself."

It was almost impossible to cling to his words of comfort. Gods knew I was trying.

I'm honored, Lune.

My eyes closed as I let the full weight of my head rest in his hand. It felt so heavy, but he held me with ease.

Why do they both think I'm worth so much grief?

Even if everything he said was true, it didn't make the news of Lune's passing any easier.

How could I possibly deserve this...

I shook my head a little and felt a tear roll down my cheek. Shade's hand had yet to move, so mine found his wrist and held on tightly. He was even warmer than I remembered.

Lune really did this for me?

Despite my broken heart, I wasn't going to let the misery consume me. Shade was right. Lune wouldn't want that, and I had no intention of lessening the impact of its sacrifice.

I promise to make the most of this.

It was still hard to see him when I finally opened my eyes. "I wish I could've at least said goodbye."

He just offered another gentle smile. "Maybe part of Lune is still with you."

I touched my chest to see if I could discern anything. As expected, there was no heartbeat, but I swore there was faint warmth where there didn't used to be.

Maybe he's right.

I fully leaned on him and managed a fragile smile.

Because of Lune, I get to be with my friend…

A few minutes later, Shade brushed his cheek against the top of my head. "By the way, there's something you'll want to see. I think it'll cheer you up."

I pulled back to look at him. "What is it?"

He just smiled and nodded in the direction he had glanced earlier.

After wiping the remaining tears from my eyes, I turned and did a full-on double take when I saw the queens. "Wh-What? But— It's your— How did—"

Shade chuckled and pressed his finger to my lips. "It's a long story."

I escaped his hand by whipping back around. "And I missed the reunion?!"

He was still grinning. "If it makes you feel any better, I doubt it'll be over for quite a while."

Fair point.

When I turned back to the queens, both were crying but had smiles on their faces. I could only imagine the moment they found their son.

And his face when he first saw them…

Shade looked at his mothers again. "I'm sorry for refusing to speak earlier. I was… Well, let's just say I was used to not talking for long periods of time. I didn't usually mind too much, but that changed when this one came along." He held me even closer. "All of a sudden, I wanted nothing more than to talk every second of every day."

A bashful smile tugged my lips as I hugged his arm.

"When he died, I didn't just lose that desire. I lost everything." He leaned his head on mine. "Nothing could ever replace him."

I shivered a little when he gently tucked my head under his chin.

Nothing could ever replace you either.

When his hold loosened, I turned on his lap to find both queens looking at me.

Sathira's eyes were still misty. "Is it true you sacrificed yourself to save him?"

I couldn't help but grin. "To be fair, there was a panicked attempt *not* to die."

She shifted closer and pulled me into a tight hug. "You have no idea how much this means to us." Her arms were trembling. "Thank you."

I shuddered from her touch but managed to return the embrace without incident.

At least my progress was resurrected as well.

Once she let go, I retreated to Shade's lap but noticed Elvylli still staring at me. Her intense gaze was almost unnerving. "What's wrong?"

"We remember everyone we've ever met. Now that I recognize you, I realize I haven't seen you in a long time." She turned to an unfamiliar Wood Elf standing behind Sathira. "Is this the missing Athaeÿn you told us about?"

"That depends." The emerald-eyed man raised a brow and looked directly at me. "Are you the Athaeÿn that Callyn never shuts up about?"

"You know Callyn?!"

He nodded to Elvylli. "Yeah, it's him." When he refocused on me, his tone sharpened without warning. "You weren't a Vampire when you left Eidolon. Who turned you?"

At first, I was taken aback by his stark shift in demeanor, but the indignation on my behalf made a bit more sense when I noticed his fangs. Between that and his accompanying the queens, I figured he was a high-ranking government official. Specifically, a Vampire Representative.

A little misguided, but at least Callyn tried to get help.

My chest tightened.

Wait, have they been looking for me this whole time?

Regardless of how unbelievable that was, I pushed it aside for now and looked at the stranger again. "Can I get *your* name first?"

"Daryn."

"Nice to meet you, Daryn. As for your question, I was turned by an Arch-Vampire named Roänach."

He briefly narrowed his eyes before hanging his head back and groaning loudly for a solid three seconds.

Elvylli looked at him again. "You were hoping he'd say Vernyth, weren't you?"

"*Yes,* but far more importantly, we have yet *another* Arch-Vampire skulking around."

I could taste the venom in his tone.

Wait—

"Oh, Roänach! He's half of why I'm here in the first place." My gaze darted to the queens. "I was unwilling collateral in a deal he made with Xythe to invade Eidolon, but Xythe just wanted revenge on you two. Roänach is the one who wants to take over this time."

Elvylli and Sathira shared an unamused glance.

The latter sighed and shook her head. "Another who will have to learn the hard way…" She eyed the scorched corner of the alcove. "At least Xythe didn't get the chance to try again."

Elvylli looked as well. "We should've killed him the first time," she growled through clenched teeth. After taking a deep breath, she noticed Sathira was still staring at the spot Xythe had been. "Are you alright?"

She tensed but said nothing.

"You're thinking about Aëlla, aren't you?"

Sathira's gaze fell to her hands where they rested in her lap. "We killed her for nothing." She swallowed hard. "We didn't even give her a chance to claim innocence."

Elvylli watched her for a moment. "Even though the note left behind was a lie, we believed it without question. Maybe we were just blinded by rage, but… Could that note have become reality?"

Sathira's voice crumbled to a whisper. "I don't know…"

It hurt my heart to see her so upset. "Why *did* she invade?"

"Envy…" She took a minute to collect her thoughts. "When we were young, Aëlla was more than just my big sister. She was my role model, my best friend… but she changed as we got older, especially when our father entrusted Eidolon to Haephir. She was furious he had gone to a friend instead of her, and I found her entitlement distasteful.

"When Haephir passed the responsibility to *his* daughter," she took hold of Elvylli's hand, "Aëlla went from angry to incensed, but when I married in, she disowned me outright." She shook her head again. "Even with her sense of betrayal, she never indicated a desire to take over by force until Xythe's failure. I have an idea of what went through her head. I just don't understand."

She closed her eyes and hung her head. "I'm the one who killed her daughter... my own niece..." Her shoulders began trembling. "It was never clear if she supported the invasion or was coerced, but all I cared about was protecting my wife and the city. At some point during the confrontation, Sae moved to strike Elvylli with lightning, a-and," she inhaled shakily, "and I put a shard of ice through her skull. She was dead before she hit the ground." A few tears came down her cheeks. "I should have just incapacitated her somehow, but I panicked." She leaned on Elvylli, who put her arm around her. "I don't care if she was complicit or not. I wish I hadn't killed her."

Sathira paused to compose herself. "That's when Aëlla fled. We had every reason to go after her, but I didn't want her dead. I just wanted her to realize invading wasn't worth it... I just wanted her to stay away... Despite everything that happened, I never stopped loving her." She choked out a small sob. "I *still* love her..."

Elvylli cradled her wife's head and slowly stroked her hair. "For what it's worth, thank you for protecting me."

Sathira's only response was a subtle nod.

No one said anything for a few minutes.

I made sure my voice was gentle when I broke the silence. "I'm so sorry, Sathira. I don't even know what to say."

She shook her head miserably. "I'm the one who should be sorry... and I am..." Another minute or so passed before she took a deep breath and looked at me. "Some circumstances are beyond words, but I appreciate your sympathy. Truly."

All I could do was offer a reserved smile.

Her gaze fell again. "It seems a thousand years wasn't enough to get over my sister either."

Elvylli placed a soft kiss on her temple. "The truth reopened the wound."

"I'm not sure it ever closed..." She toyed with her hands in her lap. "I grieved her long before her death," her gaze lifted to Shade, "but the thought of her killing our baby boy was too much." She gazed at him for a moment. "It hurts to learn her fate was unjust, and yet," she managed a weak smile and reached out to him, "I'm relieved she wasn't involved."

He smiled back and took her hand. "As am I."

It was heartening to see some joy return to Sathira's face, even if it was fragile.

At least she has one less family member to mourn now.

Hoping to lighten the mood, I smiled up at the person in question. "You see, Shade? I knew you were related to them."

He returned a grin. "You said it was possible I could be distantly related to one of them."

"I'm pretty sure you're twisting my words."

"I'm directly quoting you."

"Hmm, should I be annoyed or flattered that you remembered what I said…"

Meanwhile, Elvylli tilted her head. "Why do you keep calling him Shade?"

"Huh?" My eyes widened a bit as I turned to her. "Oh, sorry, that's just how I think of him. He didn't have a name when we met, so I gave him one. It was inspired by his shadow magic."

She closed her eyes and dragged her hands down her face with a loud groan, but instead of commenting about Xythe like I expected, she reopened her eyes and smiled warmly. "I'm glad he finally got a name from such a wonderful friend, and Shade is a rather nice one."

"Thank you, but I'll gladly call him by his real name if you want," I paused and turned to him, "or rather if *you* want, since it's your name we're talking about. It might take me a bit to break the habit, but I'll try."

He stared at me for a few moments before looking at his mothers.

Elvylli was still smiling. "It's your choice, sweetheart."

It took mere seconds for him to return a smile. "I think I'll go by Tyrran for you two and everyone else," his gaze returned to mine, "but continue going by Shade for you."

I gaped up at him. "Are you sure? You don't have to do that just for me."

"You gave me a name when I thought I had none, and it meant more than you'll ever know. I want to be Shade for you and only you." His smile widened. "Please."

For some reason, I struggled to process his simple request.

Is that really what he wants?

Both queens smiled when I glanced at them. With their approval, I turned back to Shade with a smile of my own. "I would love that."

He pulled me into a tight hug. "Thank you."

I shivered a little and buried my face in his neck. "You're welcome."

For me and only me...

As much as I wanted to melt in his embrace and never let go, a dark cloud still hung overhead. Xythe was just passing thunder. Roänach was the real storm.

And I can finally do something about it.

I turned back to the queens once Shade loosened his hug. "Listen, I need your help. This is my only chance to do something for the other captives without Roänach getting in the way. I tried turning Xythe against him, but we all know how that turned out." My hand found and gripped Shade's for support. "Now that you're here, we can stop Roänach before he does any more harm."

"Will he come here to check on Xythe?" Elvylli asked.

"I'm not sure why he would. He has no way of knowing there was an altercation."

"No, not because of that. I meant—" Her eyes widened. "Ohhh, you never saw it."

My brows furrowed a bit. "Saw what?"

Shade rubbed the back of his neck. "I, uhhh, *may* have had a bit of a meltdown when you died..."

Elvylli continued before I could look at him. "To put it simply, there was some kind of shift in the whole realm, and his unstable magic erupted into a massive dome of darkness. We could see it from Eidolon."

I slowly peered up at him. "Shaaaade—"

"I didn't mean to!" He averted his gaze and blushed heavily with embarrassment. "I was really upset, okay? I didn't even know I could do that..." he added under his breath. "Wait— Oh no," he suddenly looked at his mothers in a panic, "please tell me it didn't hurt anyone."

Sathira shook her head. "The Demons overhead are unconscious but appear unharmed."

"Also, a deer fell on its face," Daryn chimed in. "So, you know," he splayed his fingers across his chest, "pretty serious stuff."

After a brief pause, Shade sighed with relief. "Thank goodness…"

Elvylli returned her attention to me. "I know it's not much context, but it's all we have. Hopefully, my question makes a bit more sense now."

"It does, thank you. There's no way Roänach would have missed something like that, but I highly doubt he'll show up to investigate. He'll probably just send a messenger raven. At most, a Demon or two if the raven returns with no reply or doesn't return at all."

Would be nice if he accidentally handed himself right to the queens.

I sighed and folded my arms. "He has a weird dichotomy of confidence and paranoia, but I'm certain he would at least be wary of an unfamiliar, towering darkness that can be seen from hundreds of miles away. If anything, he'll avoid this area at all costs. Personally, at least."

Elvylli nodded. "Fair enough. We weren't exactly thrilled about flying through the void to get here, even with Daryn acting as our eyes," she said with a vague gesture toward him. "What would Roänach do if he thought Xythe was dead?"

"Probably ditch their plan and come up with something else. They may be two arrogant peas in an audacious pod, but I don't think Roänach has the nerve to attempt something of that scale without a partner in crime. Otherwise, he would have tried by now."

Not to mention he admitted the desire for backup right to my face.

I repeatedly looked back and forth between the queens, hoping my desperation was obvious but not pitiful. "Even if he never pursues invasion again, he's still a threat on a smaller scale, and I can't kill him myself. Please help me free everyone."

Sathira smiled and nodded. "Of course we'll help."

Daryn held up a finger. "I'm not a fighter, but I'll gladly watch."

"There's leftover anger toward Xythe I could take out on him," Elvylli added, flashing her large canines in a big grin.

I just sat there gawking at them.

They… Do they really mean it?

A dual wave of disbelief and relief hit me like a tsunami.

We could finally be free—

"The other Demons. What was their role in all of this?"

I glanced at Elvylli as she asked this, but she was looking at Shade.

He shook his head after a moment. "Nothing, as far as I can tell. They always ignored me."

Her horns began sizzling. "So, they were complicit?"

Uh-oh—

I quickly waved to get her attention. "Actually, I think there's a good chance they were enthralled. I have no proof, but Xythe had more in common with Roänach than just ambition."

"A shame Rialla missed out," Daryn mumbled, folding his arms with a huff. "I guarantee Xythe was fed up with being 'disrespected' and wanted to ensure it would never happen again, at least in his own kingdom. A monarch can be as shitty as they want if their subjects can't leave or fight back."

When I glanced at Elvylli again, her anger had already faded.

Phew….

Shade sighed a little. "I'm not familiar with this *enthralled* thing you guys are talking about, but, now knowing the truth about Xythe, it definitely seems like something he would do…"

I looked up at him but said nothing.

You only saw what he wanted you to see.

My gaze drifted back to Elvylli. "I doubt the other Demons wanted anything to do with Xythe, let alone Shade's imprisonment."

She seemed satisfied as she turned to her wife. "We should make sure they're alright."

Sathira nodded in agreement and looked at me. "Can we afford to take additional downtime? It would be a few days at most."

"My guess is Roänach will lay low for quite a while. His fortress is well-hidden, so he can hide carefree as long as he wants."

Daryn's shoulders hiked all the way up to his ears. "*Ugh,* this is bringing back so many awful memories. I look forward to this Roänach's timely demise." He paused and made oddly intense eye contact with me. "By the way, would you like to borrow my pants?"

A smirk crossed my face. "What, you don't like what you see?"

"I can't judge what I've politely refused to look at, so you'll have to forgive my respectful ignorance."

I was still grinning when I looked at my tattered clothing on the ground. "I can probably salvage enough of this to reach Xythe's room. If my trunk is gone, I'll just swaddle myself in curtains or something."

"Fitting for a reborn."

Elvylli smiled and shook her head before turning back to me and Shade. "I think it's about time we got out of this cave."

Chapter 23

Athaeÿn

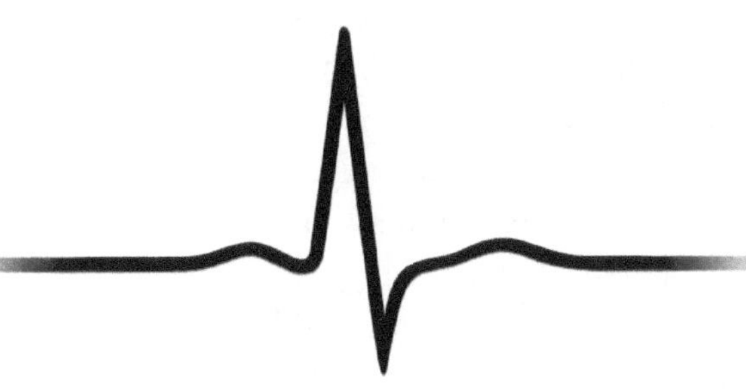

Covering up proved easier than expected. In the end, I tied what remained of my outfit's innermost layer around my hips and slipped on my surprisingly intact boots to make walking more comfortable. It wasn't the most secure arrangement, but it was serviceable.

And temporary.

When our group made it back to the castle stairway, Daryn stopped dead in his tracks and vehemently shook his head. "Ohhhh no. *Nuh-uh.* I counted nine billion steps on the way down, and that was after falling down half of them. I absolutely *refuse* to climb all the way back up."

"Gods, you are such a drama queen," Elvylli muttered under her breath.

"No, *you* are the queen of drama, and that illustrious display of screeching whilst immolating Xythe served as your coronation. What a performance. I, on the other hand," he splayed his fingers across his chest, "am reasonably refusing to exert myself when there is an obvious and preferable alternative to giving myself a leg cramp."

"You do realize I could just fly up the stairwell without you, right?"

"Empty threats. *However,* if you speak with sincerity," he turned to Sathira, "I can just ask your wife instead."

She was already smirking. "No."

He threw his arms out to the sides before jamming his fists into his hips. "You two are so mean to me." After pouting for a moment, he perked up but was beaten to the punch by Elvylli.

"Don't enable him, sweetheart," she whispered to Shade.

Daryn pointed right at her face. *"Hey."* He then pointed at Shade. "He's a grown-ass adult who can make his own decisions!"

Much to Daryn's wide-eyed horror, Shade glanced at his mothers before offering him an awkward, toothy smile.

This time, Daryn threw his hands up in exasperation. "Oh, good. We got a momma's boy."

Elvylli grinned and pinch-tugged his ear. "I was never going to make you walk up the stairs, dumbass. You're the one who brought it up and proceeded to make a scene."

He averted his gaze and scratched his cheek. "I, uhh… *ahem,* have been known to be a bit dramatic on occasion…"

"Rare occasion."

Meanwhile, Sathira smiled at me and Shade. "We'll be tending to the Demons upstairs. Take all the time you need and join us when you're ready."

Shade nodded and pulled his mothers into a group hug. "Thank you. We shouldn't be long."

Elvylli and Sathira each took a turn gently pulling his head down and kissing his forehead. After sharing one more loving smile with him, they took off with Daryn and disappeared up the stairwell.

The echoes of their wingbeats were still reverberating throughout the cave when I glanced up at Shade, whose eyes were misty as he stared after them.

Damn, I really wish I hadn't missed their initial reunion.

Shaking my head a little, I smiled and held his hand. "So, is it nice to finally have your real parents?"

He wiped his eyes with his free hand. "They're everything I could have hoped for."

"And now you have the wings to match." As I pulled back and caressed one of them, my smile faded over the lingering corruption. "Your soul fixed quite a bit. Why not everything?"

"I'm not sure." He turned his hands over and peered down at his pelvis and legs. "Maybe because there's technically nothing wrong with them? I mean, everything works just fine," he added, sticking his foot out and rotating it a few times. His tone became a bit anxious when his gaze drifted back to mine. "You sound disappointed. Does it look bad?"

I waved my hands to shoo away his concern. "No, not at all. I'm just upset because the original change happened without your consent, but if you're happy, I'm happy." I offered a smile to prove it. "Either way, your uniqueness is one of a kind. I think that's pretty cool."

He blinked a few times before grinning at his feet. "Works for me! Besides, I'd probably have to relearn how to walk if I suddenly had legs like yours."

"True, I hadn't even thought of that. Well, I'm just glad you got your wings back. They really complete the Arbiter look."

His smile slowly morphed into a frown. "Wait a minute. Wings mean I have to learn something anyway."

The scowl on his face drew an unattractive laugh through my nose. "I'm sure your mothers will happily teach you. What better way to bond and catch up on lost time?"

His big smile came back as he hugged himself with his wings.

I grinned with him. "*And,* learning to fly sounds way more fun than relearning to walk."

"Yeah, but at least walking doesn't risk falling to my death."

"It does if you walk off a cliff."

He took his turn snorting a laugh. "I should probably avoid those regardless." After chuckling for a few seconds, he glanced at the tunnel in the back wall. "Before we head up, want to say goodbye to the spirits with me?"

My joy promptly disintegrated.

Lune…

I put my hand on my chest again. The faint warmth was still there, but it only made me feel marginally better. "Yes, of course…"

Shade said nothing for a moment. "You know," he put his arm around my shoulders, "Lune touched my soul before bringing you back."

My throat tightened. "Really?"

He smiled and put his hand over mine where it remained on my chest. "I truly believe Lune is still with both of us."

As always, his smile was contagious. "I hope you're right."

With that, he led the way to the riverbank once more. It was an odd feeling, knowing it was probably the last time, and I hadn't even been there that long.

I can only imagine how he feels.

Upon arrival, he retrieved the zephyr harp and flopped me over one shoulder to cross the river. Despite his one-handed grip, not even the most powerful hurricane could have ripped me away from him.

Thank the gods he's so strong.

The moment we set foot in the spirit den, we were rushed by the Wights and Wisps.

Shade was startled when the latter made a beeline for him. "What the—" He stood gawking at the white, golden-eyed spirits dancing around his head. "These three have never shown interest in me before."

"Those are Wisps. They're drawn to living things with souls."

"Ohhh, no wonder they always ignored me." As his hand drifted to his chest, he looked at the three dark spirits twirling around me. "What are those called?"

"Wights. They prefer dead things but are primarily repulsed by souls, hence why they still liked you even though you were alive."

His brows furrowed a bit. "I remember you saying you didn't have a soul."

I nodded. "Its absence is part of what makes me Undead."

"Is yours hidden somewhere like mine was?"

I shook my head this time. "Mine's been long gone for three hundred years. When Roänach killed me, he used it to summon a new Demon. He does the same with all his vassals. Everyone he kills, actually." I held my hand up and watched one of the Wights phase through my palm like last time. "I'm nothing more than a reanimated corpse. Twice over, now…"

My explanation was followed by depressing silence.

Yeah, I wouldn't know what to say either…

Eventually, Shade turned to me and held my shoulders with both hands. "Well, at least this time it was Lune who brought you back." He smiled warmly. "That's better than Roänach, right?"

It…

After a few moments, I managed a small smile.

Yeah, it is.

As I gazed into his brilliant amber eyes, I realized just how grateful I was to do so. Without Lune, I never would have seen him again. I was still Undead, but all Roänach did was reawaken me. Lune had restored me. *Revived* me.

Lune did more for me than it could ever know.

My smile brightened. "I'd much rather be here because of a friend than a master."

He pulled me into a hug. "Am I selfish for being glad you ended up here?"

I melted into his warm embrace. "Some might think so, but I don't regret finding you."

"Even though you died again?"

"Saving you was worth it," I muttered into his chest, feeling him shiver a little.

We just stood there hugging for a few minutes. A few wonderful minutes.

Thank you, Lune…

Shade finally pulled back just enough to smile down at me. "Would you like to hear the song I silently played on the riverbank?"

"I would love that."

He sat on the soft cloud moss and patted his left thigh for me. Once I settled there and leaned back on him, he rested the harp on his other thigh and gave it a quick strum. I could feel him vibrate with joy when it actually made a sound.

And from now on, it always will.

Once he wrapped his left arm around me to get both hands on the harp, he began playing one of the most intricate songs I'd ever heard.

He really wrote this himself?

It was nothing less than a professionally written piece that had me shivering with rapture in under a minute.

His playing is beautiful.

The gentle melody was a soothing whisper to my senses, something akin to midnight fog drifting through a sleeping forest, or a meadow of wildflowers shimmering with morning dew. I had never heard such serene tranquility in a song before. Every note had its own heartbeat.

I could listen to this for hours…

My eyes fell closed as my head slowly lolled sideways on his chest. Part of me wished there were lyrics so I could hear his deep, alluring voice layered into the song, but the instrumental music was more than enough.

It's already perfect…

A few blissful minutes passed.

"Athaeÿn, look."

When I cracked my eyes open, almost all the spirits were dancing around us in a hovering circle. Even the water and rock spirits were swaying in their luminous pools and squinting happily in their stacked piles. The endearing sight brought a smile to my face and warmth to my heart.

Wait—

By the time I pressed my hand to the center of my chest, the small flicker had become a steady, comforting heat that reached my shoulders. All of a sudden, I remembered Lune's joy when I played the harp for Shade.

It really is Lune.

My throat tightened as I glanced up at Shade. "Do you feel that?"

He was smiling despite the mist in his eyes. "I do."

I kept my hand on my chest as I lounged against him and watched the spirits dance.

The perfect excuse to play long and often.

When Shade finished the song, he sniffled quietly and slipped his hand between my back and his chest. "That was for you, Lune."

I gave him a moment before speaking. "I'm not exaggerating when I say that was the most beautiful piece I've ever heard."

He smiled and wiped his eyes. "Thank you." After watching the spirits disperse, he gently removed me from his lap and got up. "I'm leaving the harp for them to play with, so I'll have to get another one someday," he added, setting the instrument in the middle of the den.

I stood as well. "There are entire shops dedicated to music in Eidolon. I'll gladly take you to all my favorites that are still in business."

This caught his attention right away. "Are there really? Can I learn how to play other instruments too?"

"Yes and yes."

He rushed back over and pulled me into a tight hug. "Thank you!"

"Y-You're welcome," I wheezed in his crushing embrace, "but you don't need my permission."

"Oh, right." He let go and dropped to one knee so we were eye level with each other. "Sorry for making it weird," he added with a slightly awkward chuckle.

I coughed out a laugh of my own. "It's alright. I appreciate that you value my opinion."

His amused smile relaxed. "I value far more than just that."

I shivered a little but said nothing.

After a minute, he cradled my head with one hand and caressed my cheek with his thumb. "I'm so glad I got you back. I don't know what I would've done if I'd lost you forever."

With him kneeling at my height, it was impossible not to stare into his eyes. "You haven't known me very long." My voice weakened a bit. "I'm sure you would've been fine…"

He shook his head. "I don't think you understand just how much you mean to me," he leaned forward and held my face with both hands, "and not just because you saved my life."

"Y-You're just saying that."

"I assure you my feelings go far deeper than just words." The closer he got, the softer his tone became. "Let me prove it to you."

"You already have," I muttered, gripping his forearms in case my legs gave out.

How is he doing this—

My fingers started trembling. "I-I thought you had no experience with intimacy."

I can't breathe—

He paused with less than an inch between our lips.

No, don't stop—

A smile crossed his face. "Maybe it just comes naturally—" His lips met mine before he even finished speaking.

O-Oh gods—

I inhaled sharply through my nose and clenched my eyes shut.

He's kissing me—

An embarrassing whimper slipped out as I eagerly reciprocated. *Desperately* was probably more accurate.

I can't believe it—

During my career, I had often taken the lead and always enjoyed doing so, but Shade's initiative swept me off my feet and left me reeling. I couldn't think clearly whatsoever. All I knew was that I had never felt so cherished in my entire life.

Don't cry on his face.

It was becoming increasingly difficult not to.

And don't overdo it.

As much as I wanted to have a full-blown make-out session, I knew we had important things to do. There would be better times and places.

This is more than enough for now.

With every intention of stopping before things escalated, I grabbed his face and deepened the kiss while I had the chance. Everything about him was powerful, and his lips were no exception.

He tastes so good—

I failed to contain a soft moan when his fingers slipped into my hair, but his deep inhale that followed almost brought me to my knees. It had become evident his ravenous hunger extended far beyond appetite. And yet, he remained gentle.

Don't let go… not yet…

I succumbed to ecstasy over and over again, only to be resuscitated every time his hot breath hit the back of my throat.

He makes me feel so alive.

My hands were trembling when I reluctantly drew our kiss to a tender close. "We should probably go before we get too carried away," I murmured, resting my forehead against his.

He smiled and nuzzled my cheek. "We can always pick up where we left off."

I hope that's a promise.

After we separated, I watched him say goodbye to all the spirits individually. The endeavor left us both teary-eyed. On the way out, he paused to give them one more bittersweet smile before finally turning and leaving the den, perhaps just indefinitely rather than forever.

Maybe we can visit them someday.

Meanwhile, my hand drifted to my chest as he disappeared into the tunnel.

I've definitely fallen for him.

I waved to the spirits and followed him out.

He's the one.

Chapter 24

Athaeÿn

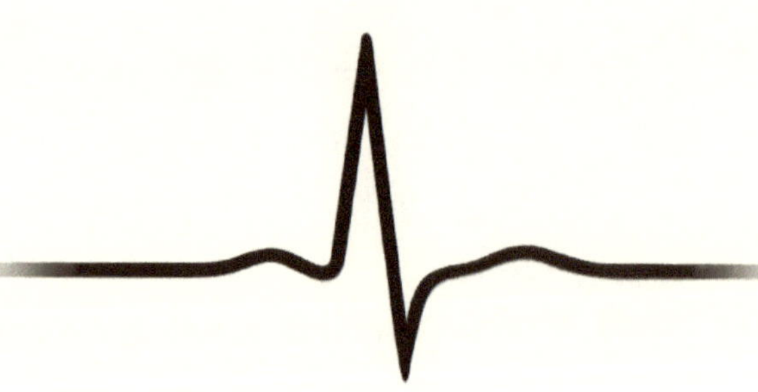

The castle stairwell almost felt ominous as we stood in front of the bottom step, staring up the daunting yet beckoning passage. We had been standing there for at least five minutes.

My gaze drifted to Shade. "Has it really been a year since you were last up there?"

He nodded and glanced back at the tunnel. "Is it weird that I might actually miss this place?"

"I don't think so. It may have been your prison, but it was also your home."

He nodded again and smiled wistfully at the towering wall we had scaled. "I *will* miss the rock climbing."

I smiled with him. "I think you'll like mountains."

"Climb up, fly down," he mused before turning back to the stairs. "Speaking of flying, I don't know how yet, so I guess we're doing this the hard way."

"And if my legs get tired, you can carry me."

"Okay, Daryn."

Now eager to get out of the cave, I started up the stairs but paused after just five when I noticed Shade wasn't following. I glanced back just in time to see him turn and look off to the side, but before I could ask what was wrong, he went over to where his thousand years of imprisonment were etched into the wall and just stood there staring at them. A full minute later, he smiled and clawed something new underneath. I couldn't see it from my angle.

"What did you write?" I asked when he came back over.

His grin never wavered as he passed me on the stairs without looking back. "Nothing you don't already know."

I was overcome with curiosity but decided against looking and followed him instead.

A scribble for closure, maybe.

We climbed the stairs for a few minutes. It had stopped being fun after the first.

I broke the silence with a huff. "As painful as it was to be literally dragged down the stairs by Xythe, at least I didn't have to do any work."

Without hesitation, Shade scooped me up against his chest the same way as our first time crossing the river. "Allow me to do the opposite."

I grinned to myself. "If you insist."

The ascent went much faster with him carrying me.

"Speaking of Xythe, I'll be fucking pissed if he ditched my trunk."

Shade chuckled. "Change your mind about the curtains?"

"Wearing curtains *would* be a pain, but no. There's something irreplaceable in it."

"Oh. Well, if it makes you feel any better, I doubt he got rid of it."

"What makes you say that?"

"He valued efficiency, so, if anything, he probably just made use of it somehow."

By emptying it first.

A pit formed in my stomach.

Or maybe he didn't bother and just set more trophies on it like a table.

My shoulders relaxed a little but remained somewhat tense.

Shade seemed to notice and smiled down at me. "But if it's not in his room, we'll search the castle until we find it, okay?"

Despite lingering uncertainty, I smiled back and rested my head on his chest. "Thank you."

When we finally made it to the top of the stairs, he set me down and started brushing himself off, muttering a tiny *ew* under his breath as he did so.

"Oh, I'm sorry, did my loincloth shed on you?" I teased, making sure the item in question was still securely tied around my waist.

"It *is* a little ashy." His grin fractured after a moment. "Also, I just noticed how much dried blood is on my stomach," he added, trying to rub some of it off without much success.

I hadn't noticed until now either. It blended right in with his deep red skin. "Xythe injured you, didn't he?"

"Just a little bit."

I knew he was downplaying what happened. "Well, I'm glad you have that healing factor."

"Me too…"

As we headed down the vaulted hallway, the unmistakable ruckus of a large crowd got louder and louder. Eventually, we stumbled upon a chaotic sea of activity, at the center of which stood Elvylli and Sathira. It looked like every Demon in the castle was packed into the hall.

A lone figure stood apart from the rest, which turned out to be Daryn leaning on the wall a good twenty feet from the edge of the crowd.

I grinned and went over to him. "Not feeling particularly social?"

"Huge crowds are the queens' field of expertise, not mine," he replied without looking at me. "Besides, keeping an eye on the situation from afar is a highly specialized task few are qualified to undertake. I just happen to be one of those select few."

"Uh-huh."

Meanwhile, the queens looked over and smiled when they saw Shade, prompting the crowd to look as well and swarm us. Daryn retreated before they could get close. The sheer number of voices all speaking at once was nearly incomprehensible, but I was able to discern some apologies and grateful exclamations. Luckily, they kept their hands to themselves despite the frenzy of excitement.

Shade recoiled from the sudden wave of attention but recovered just as quickly. After watching the commotion for a bit, he waved his hands until they quieted down. "H-Hi there. Um, I'm sorry for knocking you all unconscious. I didn't mean to. Is everyone alright?"

They briefly confirmed and went quiet again.

A Starlight Demon in the front lifted her hand to speak. Her four celestial eyes showed peaceful nebulas but were wide with horror. "The queens told us everything. Is it all true?"

"It is." He shook his head a bit. "Despite how things ended, Xythe was actually kind during my birthday months. Well, to me, at least. Please tell me that didn't change when I wasn't around."

"Our enthrallment kept us obedient, meaning there was nothing for him to punish, and, fortunately, he wasn't cruel for no reason." Her voice saddened. "To us, at least."

Shade sighed with relief. "Thank you, that makes me feel better."

She stared at him for a few seconds before shaking her head. "I'm so sorry, Tyrran." Tears welled in her starry eyes. "I wish we could have helped you."

"There's no need to apologize for what wasn't your fault. As far as I'm concerned, we were all prisoners." He smiled and offered his hand, which she took without breaking eye contact. "I'm just glad we're free."

A single tear came down her cheek as she smiled back.

After gently pulling his hand free, he glanced down and spotted a much younger Starlight Demon standing in front of her legs.

The little one was gawking up at him with the biggest eyes of childlike wonder I had ever seen, and the fact they literally twinkled made it even better.

"Hey, look who it is!" Shade crouched down so he was closer to the youngling's level. "I've seen you around the castle. You turned five this year, right?"

The little Starlight Demon shook his head. "Nope. Just four."

"Four?! No, that can't be right. You're almost as big as me!"

There was a tiny giggle.

Shade smiled and gestured to the adult he had been talking to. "Is that your mother behind you?" When the youngling nodded, Shade sat him on his shoulder and stood all the way up. "Those are mine," he added, pointing over the crowd at Elvylli and Sathira.

"You get to have two?!"

"I know, aren't I lucky?"

The youngling beamed at everyone from his towering shoulder perch and started kicking the air when he glanced down and waved at his mother. "Momma, look how tall I am!"

She waved back. "I bet you could touch the clouds from up there."

Shade chuckled when his chest got kicked as well in the little one's excitement. "Alright, I have to take care of something with my friend Athaeÿn, but we'll be back soon. Here, catch!" Instead of actually tossing the youngling, he handed him back to his mother but made a show of it to amuse them.

As the crowd refocused on the queens, Shade and I began making our way to the elevator shaft that led to Xythe's room.

"That wasn't as scary as I thought it would be," he said once out of earshot.

I smirked up at him. "Multifaceted natural talent, it would seem."

He averted his gaze but failed to hide a tiny grin.

"In all seriousness, this may be the first time you've interacted with them, but I'm sure their general familiarity soothed your nerves."

His smile faded. "I wish I already knew them." He shook his head a little. "I never understood why they always ignored me, but now that I know about enthrallment…"

I said nothing for a moment. "Xythe forced you to rely on him and him alone."

By now, Shade looked miserable. "If his goal was to make the big reveal as painful as possible, he succeeded."

Yeah, it couldn't have been much worse.

The look on Shade's face when Xythe showed his true colors would haunt me forever.

Better me than his mothers…

When we reached the elevator and stepped onto the gold platform, my stomach dropped when I spotted the lone control orb on the wall. I had completely forgotten this lift was unique.

Shit—

As I petulantly mimicked Xythe's wrist-flicking gesture, Shade looked up the elevator shaft and sighed heavily. "Even if I knew how to fly, it's too narrow in here," he mumbled, turning and scratching the wall with his claw. "I can probably climb up…"

His dejected tone broke my heart. "Shade, we don't have to—"

"Yes, we do. Your trunk with the irreplaceable thing in it could be up there, and you shouldn't have to walk around in shredded rags." He shook his head without looking at me. "Besides, climbing will take my mind off things…"

I stared at him for a few seconds. "Are you sure?"

He just nodded and sank to one knee so I could reach him better.

I had to use his front this time since his wings took up most of his back. After securing my legs around his waist and my arms around his neck, I leaned my head against his and softened my voice. "Everything will be alright."

There was a quiet sniffle as he buried his face in my hair and hugged me tightly.

I promise.

Once he let go, he began the arduous task of climbing the elevator shaft. He used every appendage at his disposal, including his wings since they had impressive reach and claws of their own. Even without handholds, he still made the ascent look easy. The only evidence of a struggle was the numerous gouges left in the walls.

Meanwhile, my mind spun like coach wheels stuck in fresh mud. I wanted nothing more than to make him feel better, but I didn't know how.

Probably by getting him professional help.

A weak smile crossed my face. I was confident the queens would get their son the best counseling Eidolon had to offer.

Maybe they'll put in a good word for me too…

Regardless, I reassured myself the same way I did for Shade.

Everything will be alright.

When we finally reached the top, Shade gave his wings one big flap to boost us onto solid ground. The moment we separated, he rolled onto his back and clapped his hand on his heaving chest to soothe his panting.

It took him at least a minute to catch his breath. "That sucked."

I leaned over his face and chanced a mischievous smile. "Not sure what you're complaining about. I'm not tired at all."

"Shhhhh—" He pressed his finger to my lips before dropping his hand back onto his chest with a thud. "At least one of us is having fun…"

"Fun is a strong word." I got up and readjusted my hip covering. "Now then, you stay here while I check for my stuff."

"What? Why?"

"Because I don't want you getting even more upset."

"Why would I?"

My brows went up. "Have you never seen Xythe's room?"

"No." He sat up and glanced over his shoulder at the door. "What's in there?"

I think he forgot about the wings…

"Believe me, you don't want to know." I was about to take a step but didn't get the chance.

"Hold on," he took hold of my ankle, "you can't just say something that cryptic and expect me not to look," he complained, pouting and giving my leg a few light tugs.

I sighed and leaned down to look him dead in the eye. "Shade, I'm not trying to be annoying. Going in there will *not* make you feel better right now."

His eyes widened a little, but he remained quiet.

I put my hand on his shoulder and softened my tone. "You need to trust me on this."

He stared at me for a few seconds before looking at Xythe's door again. Eventually, he turned back around and lowered his gaze with a reluctant nod.

Thank you…

I leaned closer and kissed his cheek. "Try to think about something else for a minute, alright? I'll be right back."

Especially if my trunk isn't in there.

Once Shade's back was to the door, I quickly slipped through and closed it behind me.

I hate this room so much.

It felt like every trophy was staring at me, but most were actually facing Xythe's bed. I hadn't noticed the first time.

Yeeaaahhh, I didn't need that insight.

Heading in the direction I left my trunk, I kept my gaze down to avoid seeing the morbid decorations as much as possible. Unfortunately, this more or less resulted in direct eye contact with the Human leather rug.

Fuck, I forgot about that—

After a sharp inhale and violent shudder, I noticed my trunk still sitting on said rug.

Phew…

Despite what Shade said in the stairwell, I was still amazed Xythe hadn't ditched it.

To be fair, he does like holding on to things for a long time.

Shaking my head a little, I opened the trunk and was relieved to find the contents seemingly untouched. Even though the spare outfits were just identical copies of my destroyed Castle Veil uniform, clothes were clothes.

I can't wait until I can wear my own again.

With a heavy sigh, I got dressed, fixed my hair, and replaced my various ear piercings to the point of looking exactly the same as when I first showed up. It was nice to be clothed again, but the real joy came when I fished out the small portrait of myself.

Thank the gods it's still here.

I was about to flee the horrid room but paused when my gaze landed on the wall of severed wings. Specifically, the large pair right in the middle.

Unbelievable—

Huffing in disgust, I stormed over and climbed onto the headboard so I could reach the skeletal remains of infant Shade's wings, which I carefully pulled off the wall and laid on the bed. After staring at them for a few moments, I concealed them under the sheets. This was probably weird, but I couldn't stand the sight of them as such a demented trophy.

Rest in peace.

Portrait in hand, I eagerly left the room and sealed it behind me. When I looked at Shade, he was sitting on the edge of the elevator shaft with his legs dangling over the edge and his back still to the door. He hadn't reacted at all when it opened and closed.

I'm definitely glad I made him wait out here.

With a deep but silent breath, I went over and sat next to him. "Are you alright?"

His voice was feeble when he finally spoke. "Is it possible Xythe secretly loved me but refused to admit it? Even just a little bit?"

My throat tightened. "I think we both know the answer to that."

He nodded sullenly and watched his hands as he toyed with them in his lap.

"Do you wish he had?"

There was no reply at first. "I don't know…" After a long pause, he shook his head. "I don't think so…"

"You can say yes."

He shook his head again. "I don't want to."

"And you don't have to."

Neither of us said anything for a few minutes.

Shade was the one to break the silence. "I know he only wanted me for the worst reasons, but he always enjoyed himself when we spent time together. I mean, now I know he was faking it, but…" He let out a shaky exhale. "I just… I guess I just thought after a thousand years he might've taken a liking to me…"

I almost wish he did.

It broke my heart to see him like this. "If it's any consolation, I don't think he liked anyone. Even his own subjects."

Shade said nothing as he continued staring at his long, Demonic claws.

I'm sorry. I know that doesn't mean much…

A few more minutes passed.

He broke the silence with a sniffle this time. "I can't believe I fell for his lies my entire life. I can't believe I thought he loved me." He shook his head again. "I loved him from the very beginning. I loved him *so much.*" Tears welled in his eyes as he watched his hands start to tremble. "Why couldn't he just love me back? *Why?*"

My chest tightened so much it hurt.

He clenched his eyes shut and choked out a quiet sob. "Why was I so stupid?"

I felt completely useless as tears began streaming down his face.

Is this how I sounded to him?

It took a moment to find my voice. "Shade, look at me."

He just hung his head more.

I turned his face toward mine. "Please."

There was a pause before he slowly opened his eyes.

I held his face with both hands and used my thumbs to wipe away his tears. "Do you remember what you wrote for me in the spirit den?"

He nodded weakly.

"Out loud."

There was another pause, this time accompanied by a sniffle. "That you weren't stupid, and nothing that happened to you was your fault."

I raised my brows and tilted my head toward him.

He just looked more upset. "This is different."

"How?"

It took at least ten seconds for him to come up with an answer. "Roänach didn't reveal his true nature until he had you at his mercy. Xythe isolated and silenced me for most of my life, but I still loved him."

I pulled his face a little closer. "How could you have known any better?"

He almost sounded desperate. "I never saw the other kids isolated or silenced."

"Shade—"

"I-I should've realized something was wrong—"

"*Shade.*"

He froze and stared at me with wide eyes.

I shook my head and softened my voice. "You're never going to convince me, your mothers, *anyone,* that you were stupid or that this was somehow your fault, so stop trying to convince yourself. Don't you think you've been lied to long enough?"

Another tear came down his cheek, but he said nothing for quite a while. Eventually, he sniffled again and nodded into my hands. "It just seems so obvious in hindsight."

"I know, but it doesn't change who's at fault. The blame lies solely at Xythe's feet, no one else's, and especially not yours."

Despite lingering tears, he managed the ghost of a smile. "I'll try not to blame myself for what Xythe did if you promise not to blame yourself for what Roänach did."

The corners of my mouth turned up a little. "If I could promise that, I would have by now. We'll both just have to try our best."

His smile remained intact as he rested his forehead on mine. "Thank you for arguing with me about this."

"Any time."

He silently leaned on me for a few minutes. "Is it okay if we talk about something else?"

"Of course."

With one last sniffle, he pulled back and glanced down at my lap. "Is that the portrait you told me about?"

I nodded and held it upright so we could both see it. "I wish you could have met Miri. She would have loved painting you."

"You keep using the past tense. Is she gone?"

"She was a mortal Human, so she would have passed away a couple of centuries ago. This is all I have left of her."

"I can see why it's so important to you."

"Yeah, but for a slightly selfish reason too."

"What do you mean?"

I traced my painted jawline with my finger. "Vampires don't have reflections, so this is the only way I can see my face. Without the portrait, I probably would've forgotten it by now."

Shade was speechless for a moment. "Oh… Well, it's really good. It looks exactly like you."

"Almost."

"Why just *almost?*"

I turned my head toward him. "Notice something different?"

His brows slowly furrowed as he glanced back and forth between my face and the portrait.

"Do you really not—"

"Wait, wait, wait, don't tell me."

I watched him struggle for a few seconds. "Shade—"

"N-No, I can do it!"

I waited for an answer that never came.

Eventually, he stopped on me and twiddled his thumbs awkwardly. "Okay, tell me."

Without a word, I pointed to the scars on my face and neck.

His eyes shot wide. "I-I knew that."

I frowned at him. "You don't have to pretend you don't see them."

He frowned right back. "I wasn't. Why would I do that?"

I blinked a few times. "I… I guess I just figured most people would lie to avoid hurting my feelings."

"You never made a big deal out of them, so I thought they didn't bother you."

Oh.

"Fair enough, I suppose that's on me." I paused and let slip a quiet sigh. "If I'd seen them, I probably would've fixated on them more."

"Why?"

My throat tightened as I ran my fingertips down the massive scar on my face and over the marks on my neck. "I can tell they're hideous."

It probably looks like someone threw an axe at me…

Shade tilted his head. "I don't think they're hideous."

"Please don't lie just to—"

"I'm *not.*" He pointed right at my face. "Listen, if you're allowed to say nothing was my fault, I'm allowed to say nothing makes you hideous. Especially your scars."

"But—"

"*Ahp,* this isn't up for debate." He flashed a smile. "Sorry."

I didn't smile back.

His grin faltered after a few seconds. "Why do you think they're hideous?"

My gaze fell. "Maybe this makes me vain, but I like to think I was relatively attractive back in the day. How could I look even halfway decent with this huge gash in my face?"

Like damaged goods…

He said nothing for a moment. "If other people had similar scars, would you consider them unattractive?"

I shook my head weakly.

"Alright, so why are you the exception?"

It took a full minute for me to finally look at him again. My throat was still tight.

This time, his smile was soft instead of playful. "Maybe I just get lost in your eyes, but I barely ever notice your scars. Even when I do, they change nothing." He caressed my cheek as if the huge blemish wasn't even there. "When I look at you, I see a beautiful man who makes my heart race with just a smile. You're stunning, you've always been stunning, and you'll always be stunning."

My whole body shivered as I stared into his eyes.

No arguing, remember?

A fragile but genuine smile tugged my lips as I hugged him tightly. "Thank you, Shade."

He nodded and returned the embrace. "I meant every word."

We just sat there hugging for a few minutes.

All of a sudden, he chuckled and squeezed me in his arms. "And if anyone insults you, I'll glare at them until they apologize."

I grinned into his neck. "I'm almost positive a death glare from you would be literal."

"Oh, come on, I'm not *that* scary."

"You're pretty scary."

"And yet, you're hugging me."

"Maybe I like scary."

"You just like my giant muscles."

I shifted enough to smile at him. "It *is* rather satisfying when you carry me around as if I weigh nothing, but I like you for *at least* one other reason."

He grinned back and effortlessly hoisted me up for a kiss. "Nope, it's just one reason, and it's how tall I am. Don't bother denying it."

"Damn, you got me."

"I knew it."

We both laughed and shared another kiss. My heart wasn't beating, but the butterflies in my stomach made up for it.

His presence just gets more and more comforting.

I was the one to break the kiss. "Alright, we should probably head back before the others get suspicious."

"Is the portrait all you're bringing?"

"Would you like to carry my heavy trunk?"

"I mean… We *did* just acknowledge my giant muscles…"

But we left it behind anyway. I didn't want the spare uniforms, and I could replace everything else. The portrait was all I cared about.

Once I was secured to his front like before, Shade carefully dropped over the edge of the elevator shaft and slowly descended by dragging his wingtip claws down the walls.

The sound was unpleasant.

Most of the Demons had dispersed by the time we arrived at the entrance hall, but a few small groups lingered here and there. The most recognizable figure was Daryn, who was looking outside from where he stood near the wide-open main doors. Fortunately, it was still dark out, so it was safe for him to do so.

He turned and looked me up and down as we approached. "Nice outfit."

Shade and I stopped next to him. "It's the uniform Roänach makes me wear."

He flicked his wrist without missing a beat. *"Terrible* outfit."

I couldn't help but grin a little.

"Is it at least better than being almost naked?"

"Marginally."

He briefly eyed my scars before turning back to the open doorway, thumbing the bite marks on his own neck as he did so. "Well, for what it's worth, you look good regardless."

My smile widened.

I guess Shade was right.

"Where are the queens?"

He nodded outside. "Talking to some Starlight Demons. Shame it's cloudy, but, stars or no stars, they can finally enjoy real nighttime with that gods-awful solar shield gone."

Which reminds me—

I went over to the doors but stopped on the threshold, uncertain if my travel restrictions had been restored with me. The solar shield had been gone for a while, but I hadn't disintegrated yet.

It's technically the same ground, I guess…

A grunt of annoyance slipped out as I shook my head.

This is stupid.

I hesitated a few more seconds before gingerly touching the ground with the toe of my boot.

Nothing happened.

Thank the gods…

There was a huge grin on my face as I confidently strode outside and took a deep breath once out in the open. I didn't care that I didn't need to. The fresh air was delightful.

That cave was more suffocating than I thought.

It wasn't long before the queens and group of Starlight Demons looked over. Elvylli and Sathira smiled at first, but their joy faded when they peered around me at the open doorway. When I turned to look as well, Shade stood frozen on the threshold, his gaze locked on the ground where I had tapped my boot. He looked genuinely terrified.

"Shade? What's wrong?"

His wide eyes were darting back and forth. "I've never stepped foot outside the castle."

Shit, I forgot about that—

"Xythe forbade it, and I didn't want him to get mad at me…"

The queens joined me before I could say anything.

Sathira waved to get his attention. "It's alright, sweetheart. We're safe and sound out here." When he looked over, she gestured to the three of us. "See?"

He just shuddered and looked down again.

I smiled despite knowing he wouldn't see it. "I promise nothing bad will happen."

Come on, Shade. You can do it.

After what felt like forever, he cautiously tapped the ground with one foot the same way I had done.

Keep going, you're right there—

Eventually, he took one step and clenched his eyes shut.

His mothers froze next to me.

It took at least a minute for Shade to crack an eye open. When he finally opened both and took in his surroundings, his visible dread eased a little. "I'm outside."

My throat tightened when Elvylli covered her mouth with both hands.

Shade looked up at the clouds and smiled brightly. "I'm outside!" He started toward us but stopped halfway and began spinning around with the purest elation I had ever seen. *"I'm outside!"*

As I took my turn covering my mouth, Elvylli and Sathira rushed their son and pulled him into a shared hug. Both were crying tears of joy.

Shade nearly collapsed into them and broke down sobbing. "I-I'm outside—"

Sathira pulled his head down and nuzzled his face. "You're finally free, sweetheart."

I could barely see through my own tears as I watched the three of them.

This moment alone was worth everything.

Chapter 25

Athaeÿn

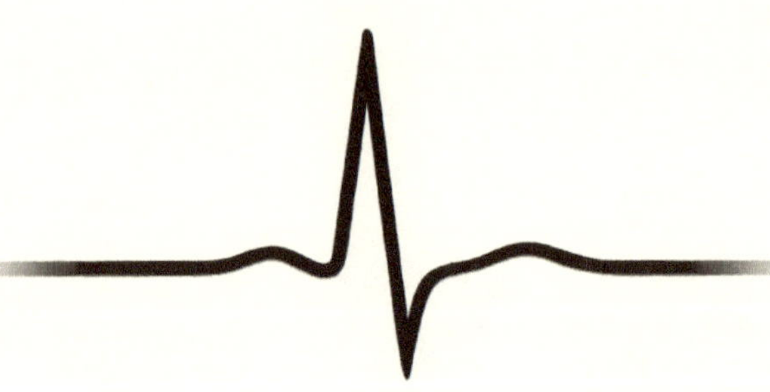

As soon as Shade let go of his mothers, he rushed over and snatched me up into a crushing hug. With my arms pinned to my sides and my feet dangling helplessly, the embrace was rather one-sided. It was a good thing I didn't need to breathe.

There was, however, just enough air already in my lungs to wheeze into his chest. "Y-You're going to snap me in half—"

"Oops, sorry." His smile tinged with guilt as he set me down and smoothed out my clothing. "So, what happens now?"

Sathira answered as she and Elvylli came over. "We're going to teach you how to fly and control your magic before we confront Roänach."

Shade's smile faded. "Will that be difficult? I don't want to slow everyone down."

"Flying cuts week-long trips down to hours, and knowing how to wield your magic properly is crucial for everyone's safety, including your own."

He nodded hesitantly. "Okay. What are we starting with?"

She looked to the side and hummed in thought for a moment. "Flying is vital for taking swift action, especially if plans change. Learning about your magic is still important, but it can wait if necessary." Her gaze drifted back to him. "In the event of a delay, we would ask you not to use it until we can resume study and confirm your understanding and control."

He nodded again but now looked a bit confused. "But, wouldn't my darkness be useful to blind Roänach?"

I shook my head. "It would be, if he was literally anything other than a Vampire."

"What do you mean?"

"Remember when Elvylli mentioned Daryn acting as their eyes?"

"Oh, yeah. I meant to ask about that."

"She implied he was using his thermal vision, something all Vampires have that allows us to see heat instead of light. I was using mine when we first crossed paths in that pitch-black tunnel. It's the only reason I could see you."

He frowned at his hand. "Figures. I finally have all my magic but can't even use it…"

"We haven't explored it yet, sweetheart," Sathira chimed back in. "Arbiter magic works on a spectrum, and we only know one small piece of yours. I'm sure we'll find something for these circumstances." She offered a reassuring smile. "We just have to look."

Shade beamed with renewed confidence. "When do we start flying lessons?"

"Tomorrow. I think it's safe to assume everyone needs some good, restful sleep."

He nodded and yawned widely. "Fine with meeee…" Without warning, he once again hugged me to his chest so my feet couldn't touch the ground, and there I remained as he turned and headed for the castle.

"Excuse me, I have two functioning legs."

"Sorry," he gave me a light squeeze, "I'm just really happy."

All I could do was grin to myself.

This is what I get for admitting I enjoy being carried.

...

Surprising no one, Daryn made a fuss about sleeping on the floor. Luckily for him, two Demons offered to share one of their beds so he could have the other, and he accepted without hesitation. The Arbiters and I didn't mind sleeping on the floor in the main hall, but we did accept offerings of spare pillows and blankets. The three of them were too big for normal beds anyway.

Shade tried to convince me to borrow a bed as well, but I was happy to sleep next to him the same way as in the spirit den. Sleeping against his chest was better than any bed. I hardly even noticed the lack of soft cloud moss.

The Solar Demons had extinguished the orbs lining the hall so we could sleep better, but they didn't bother making new ones when morning arrived. Even with full cloud cover, there was ample daylight to see clearly, especially with the towering entry doors standing wide open for fresh air. Daryn and I certainly didn't mind the lack of miniature indoor suns.

Meanwhile, mothers and son were outside discussing various wing mechanics. Thanks to the clouds, I was able to sit and watch in relative safety, though I remained just inside the doorway to be sure.

My breath caught when Shade spread his wings for the first time. His full span had to be at least thirty feet. Arbiters were known for their dragon inspiration, but he truly had the presence of one. It was difficult not to stare at him. Embarrassingly so.

Wow, he really is—

"Should I give you some privacy?"

Daryn's voice startled me so bad I gasped and clutched my chest.

For fuck's sake—

Once I collected myself, I glared at him over my shoulder. "Shut up."

He snorted a laugh from where he sat leaning on the wall nearby. "Relax. I won't tell him you were ogling."

"I wasn't og—"

"Oh yes you were," he tilted his head smugly, "but don't worry, I'm not judging."

I frowned at him. *"Ogling* sounds crass."

"Forgive my word choice. Would you prefer *admiring?*"

"Yes, but now I feel weird about it either way."

"Indeed, so imagine my rapture having to witness your repressed titillation."

"You know," I spun around to face him better, "this castle *is* rather large."

"I would prefer to keep you in my line of sight."

"Seems a bit contradictory."

"Big Red is busy," he gestured outside, "so I'm keeping an eye on you."

My brows furrowed a little. "Did he ask you to?"

"No. Watching over other Vampires is quite literally my job." He started casually inspecting his fingernails. "Besides, there's nothing better to do."

A grin crossed my face. "You just want to show me off to Callyn."

"Lies and slander."

I laughed through my nose. "Have they really looked for me all this time?"

"They have."

"And repeatedly pestered you about it?"

"Much to my annoyance."

"That definitely sounds like Callyn."

"Unfortunately for me." He shook his head. "Their determination was admirable, but I was displeased when they reached out to Vernyth for assistance." His gaze drifted to me. "I assume you know who that is."

"I do."

He nodded and resumed scrutinizing his nails. "I look forward to shoving you in Callyn's face with no Vernyth in sight."

"So, you *do* just want to show me off."

"Nonsense. I'm genuinely chuffed to see you in one piece, Callyn or no Callyn." He said nothing for a moment. "But my concern for your well-being goes beyond that, and I'm not happy about it."

My smile faded, but I could tell he had more to say, so I waited for him to continue.

He finally did a minute later. "I may be a respected government official, but I'm far from a paragon. My shame is that, at least in general, I care only for fellow Undead despite valid plights of the living. The fact I'm a Vampire Representative is no excuse." He shook his head and glanced at me again. "You were supposed to be someone I could overlook."

Ah, I see...

I offered a bittersweet smile. "I wish I was still alive too."

We both averted our gazes and fiddled with our hands for a while.

Eventually, I looked at him again. "Down in the cave, when I was talking about Roänach, you brought up someone named Rialla. Was that your master?"

He nodded, still focused on his hands. "The first and only Arch-Vampire I've ever been cursed to know. Personally, at least."

"Same with Roänach in my case. How long have you been free?"

"Longer than you've been Undead. To be exact, four hundred fifty-seven years."

"What happened to Rialla?"

"Got herself killed twice. She had a Sacrifice Spirit as well, which is why I knew what Lune was the moment I saw it," he glanced at me, "and why I was pretty sure it could bring you back."

"Just *pretty sure?*"

"Rialla wasn't cremated like you. Her throat was a bit torn open, and by *a bit* I mean her head was nearly taken off."

"A near-severed head does sound easier to fix than a pile of bones."

He nodded and glanced down the hall at a small group of Lunar Demons. "The result of a summoning gone wrong. Well, the summoning itself went smoothly, just not the aftermath, and I'm proud to say I had a hand in that. The Fauna Demon she had summoned was freaking out more than most, which I heard and came running to investigate.

"Fortunately, by the time I showed up, he had managed to avoid her touch. I distracted Rialla with a shout, which gave him an opening to claw her neck. While she was incapacitated, I told him to impale her heart with one of her own stakes," he relayed proudly.

I was enraptured by his story. Maybe even a little envious. "That's amazing."

A heavy frown replaced his smile. "It *was* amazing... for a whole minute. I felt our connection sever, so I knew for certain she was dead. I *finally* tasted freedom." He huffed and shook his head. "But then her stupid Sacrifice Spirit ruined everything."

"I'm surprised one would bond with an Arch-Vampire."

"Normally, I'd agree, but I don't think spirits care about morality. Either way, Rialla was back on her feet with fully restored control in no time at all." He sighed heavily. "At least the Demon was able to escape…"

"Did you get the chance to thank him?"

"I did."

"And were you able to get his name?"

He nodded. "Xiir. Couldn't forget if I tried."

Hmm, doesn't ring a bell.

"Do you know what happened to him afterward?"

Daryn flashed a cheeky grin. "Only one incident. Before he fled, I gave him a quick rundown of how to kill Vampires in case he ever needed to defend himself."

I think I know where this is going.

"A year later, Rialla went out to find another blood captive. Guess who she ran into."

I smiled back. "A certain Fauna Demon she failed to enthrall?"

"Yes!" He clapped his hands so loudly it sent a thunderous echo down the vaulted hallway. "Of *all* the villages she could have targeted, she just happened to pick the one Xiir had ended up in."

"And he had a bone to pick."

"More like a whole skeleton. He recognized her immediately and attacked on sight."

"Did he keep stakes on him?"

"No idea. All I know is he knocked her unconscious and threw her in the local river." He barked a laugh that echoed like his clap. "She would have disintegrated in seconds," his smile suddenly vanished, "meaning *no one* got the chance to pull the shit Vernyth did."

Whoa—

I smiled to try and lighten the mood. "So, Xiir saved you twice."

"All of us." He sighed and shook his head. "Unfortunately, I wasn't able to thank him a second time. He left that village long before we found out what happened, so I haven't seen him since he was first summoned." His gaze fell. "Wherever he is, I hope he's alive and well."

"It sounds like he can take care of himself. I'm sure he's fine."

He nodded faintly. "You're probably right. I just wish I knew either way…"

There was a moment of silence.

I offered another smile. "Well, it's nice to hear you've been free for so long. I look forward to being free again as well."

He slowly looked at me. "It's about time another Arch-Vampire dies."

My smile faded as quickly as it had surfaced.

He's right. What's your problem?

I knew Roänach needed to die, but there was a dread in my heart I couldn't shake. It was infuriating. I hated feeling so conflicted even after he threw me away. After *everything* he had done.

At least I'll never have to worry about killing him myself…

Before I could withdraw into familiar misery, I was startled by a tremendous thud outside that shook the ground beneath me.

Daryn glanced at the open doors. "I believe the actual flying lessons have begun."

The three Arbiters strolled inside a few moments later.

"Lunch time!" Shade announced cheerfully.

I stood up to ask something I already knew the answer to. "What was that noise?"

"Oh, that was me. I fell."

"Are you alright? It felt like an earthquake."

"Don't worry, I'm just really heavy."

I nodded reluctantly. "Fair enough. Were you jumping out of trees or something?"

"Off the castle."

"What?!"

His smile never wavered. "It wasn't the top or anything."

"Shade—"

"It was fun!"

I nearly sputtered with disbelief and looked to his mothers for an explanation.

"We were right there," Elvylli reassured with a grin. "Besides, he practically begged us. How could we say no?"

Shade chimed back in. "No actual flying yet, just catching air and landing safely." He scratched his cheek a bit. "In my defense, I was actually doing pretty well. I just messed up the last jump…"

I sighed and put my hands on my hips. "Well, practice makes perfect, I suppose."

"That's what my mothers said!" He was practically vibrating with excitement. "Do you want to see my progress later?"

The enthusiastic grin on his face was contagious. "Of course."

"Yes!"

As a beaming Shade ran off, Daryn waved his hand from where he remained seated against the wall. "Sathira, my selfless and succulent savior, Dehydrated Daryn needs a drink." He batted his eyelashes. "Mind if I get a suck?"

She sighed heavily but went over to him without protest. "Must you phrase it in such a vulgar manner?"

He just snickered and sank his fangs into her thigh.

"I'm far too tolerant of your nonsense." She glanced at Elvylli. "We both are."

There was a hummed laugh as he pulled back and wiped his mouth. "Divine as always."

"Your charm is your saving grace."

He put his hand on his chest. "And your flattery makes my heart flutter."

I couldn't help but grin at their exchange.

Maybe I'll ask Shade for a bite when he gets back. Politely.

…

Shade made substantial progress with his flying over the next few days, becoming more and more like a majestic dragon with every wingbeat.

It took quite a bit of convincing on his end, but I was eventually persuaded to let him make the ultimate leap of faith from the top of the castle. I made sure to fast beforehand so I wouldn't have a heart attack. Despite his mothers being right there to help if needed, I was drowning in anxiety as I watched him climb the castle until he was nothing more than a tiny dot on the tip of the tallest spire.

Please be careful.

I held myself and took a deep breath.

He can do it.

And yet, paralyzing terror gripped my chest when he leapt off.

Please—

My fears were swiftly abated when he spread his wings and curved upward in a giant arc as though commanding the wind itself to obey. It didn't look like he had struggled at all.

Wow—

Even with the deafening cheers of the Demons around us, I could hear Shade's howls of triumph as he soared confident and free. His mothers only watched for about a minute before joining him high overhead, where the three of them effortlessly whirled around each other as if they had been born among the clouds. Shade was nothing less than a natural.

Meanwhile, my cheeks hurt from how hard I was smiling.

What an incredible family.

In that moment, I was more determined than ever to find my own.

And thanks to this one, I'll finally have that chance.

. . .

I had thought for certain Shade would sleep soundly after such a momentous occasion.

I was wrong.

That same night, I woke from a dead sleep to find myself being slowly crushed. Normally, I loved being held tightly against his chest, but this embrace was abnormally strong.

And painful—

It wasn't long before he started shaking and whimpering, but right as I was about to try and wake him, the most intense darkness I had ever seen spilled from his body and swallowed up everything around us.

This is what they could see from Eidolon?

Ignoring how terrifying that sounded, I switched to my thermal vision and cranked my head around to see his face. Not only was his visage somehow even brighter than usual, but his grimace was also clearly visible despite the limited detail I had to work with.

All of a sudden, Elvylli's startled voice pierced the darkness. "What the—"

I glanced over to see both queens now wide awake and looking around blindly.

"Not again— Tyrran!"

"Don't worry, I'll wake him up," I reassured, turning my head back around. "Shade!"

The only response I got was hyperventilating and even more violent shaking.

"Shade!"

This time, his eyes snapped wide open and began darting around frantically. "Athaeÿn?!" He sat bolt upright but looked over my head as if I wasn't even there. "A-Athaeÿn, please—"

"Shade, I'm right here."

"H-Huh?" When he looked down, he appeared genuinely shocked to find me in his arms.

"Your darkness is spreading."

He blinked at me a few times before looking around again. "Oh no— Wait, how do I—" He shook his head with increasing panic. "I don't know how I stopped it last time—"

"Sweetheart," Sathira interrupted gently, "the more you panic, the less control you have. Calm your mind, and your magic will follow."

Even though he closed his eyes to try, I could tell he still struggled to breathe.

It was only a matter of time before he had a nightmare about that...

I shook my head a little and held his face with both hands. "Shade, look at me." When he reopened his eyes, I had a smile waiting for him. "I'm safe."

He just stared at me with wide-eyed horror.

As much as I wanted to watch him, I switched back to my normal vision so I could tell when and if his darkness retracted, making sure to keep my face toward his as I waited in the strange void. The world around me didn't reappear until a few minutes later, but the tears streaming down his face were all I could see.

Oh no...

His eyes were now almost squinted shut. "I'm so sorry."

I could barely hear his feeble whisper. "It's alright—"

"No, it's not alright." He pulled my hands off his face and averted his gaze. "I'm completely useless," he added, his voice steadily rising.

"Shade—"

"I can't control my magic. I can't contain my emotions. I can't protect the people I care about. I can't even help strangers." He shook his head. "I can't do *anything*."

"Shade, listen—"

His shoulders started to heave. "It's all my fault. I let Xythe take everything. My soul, my wings, my freedom… my entire life…" He looked devastated when he turned back to me. "Even you."

I tried to hold his hand. "That's not what hap—"

"It doesn't matter. I was right there and couldn't protect you. My incompetence got you killed." He repeatedly jabbed himself in the chest. "If I had just stood up for myself, for *you*, none of this would've happened. If I had just kept you safe, you wouldn't have had to sacrifice yourself, and if you hadn't died, Lune would still be here."

There was a sudden, heartbroken quiver in Lune's warmth, and I knew Shade felt it too when he froze and clutched his chest. I forced myself to stay quiet this time.

When he snapped out of his shock, he grimaced and hung his head miserably. "I lost two friends but only got one of them back." His voice had crumbled again. "All I had to do was hold on. If I hadn't dropped you when he ordered me to… If-If I hadn't…" His hand was trembling on his chest when he lifted his head and looked at me again. "Please forgive me."

The despair in his eyes was unbearable, but Lune's sorrow over him blaming himself was even worse. My chest hurt from every angle.

Don't worry, Lune. I'll speak for both of us.

I took hold of Shade's face again. "Apparently, my previous words didn't sink in, so listen carefully." My stern tone mirrored my firm grip and intent eye contact. "The only one to blame for what happened is Xythe. End of story. Period. You didn't *let* him do anything. That's now how this works."

Please listen.

I pulled his face closer and softened my tone. "This is *not your fault*. Xythe is the one who put us in that situation, not you. He may have taken advantage of your fear, but, in doing so, he also handed me an opportunity to save you. I took that chance, and Lune did the same for me. We *chose* to give our lives and would do it again in a heartbeat." My vision blurred as I pulled him even closer. "You were worth everything."

Time froze as we stared into each other's eyes.

Without warning, Shade broke down sobbing and pulled me into a trembling hug. The familiar, desperate clinging broke my heart. I wasn't sure if my sentiment had finally sunk in, but I didn't care at the moment. I just wanted to comfort him.

He could use your warmth, Lune.

I shifted in his embrace until I was kneeling on his thighs with his head cradled against the base of my neck. As I hoped, his shaking began to ease the moment my fingers laced into his hair.

You're alright…

Even after he calmed down, he kept his face buried in my chest and his arms locked around me, refusing to let go. I could hardly blame him.

He did lose me once, after all.

Still combing my fingers through his hair, I glanced over my shoulder to find his mothers smiling, sadly, but with genuine relief. My gaze drifted between them before landing on Sathira, who put her hand on her chest and silently mouthed *Thank you.* I just smiled back.

You're welcome.

Lune's warmth was at peace once again.

Chapter 26

Athaeÿn

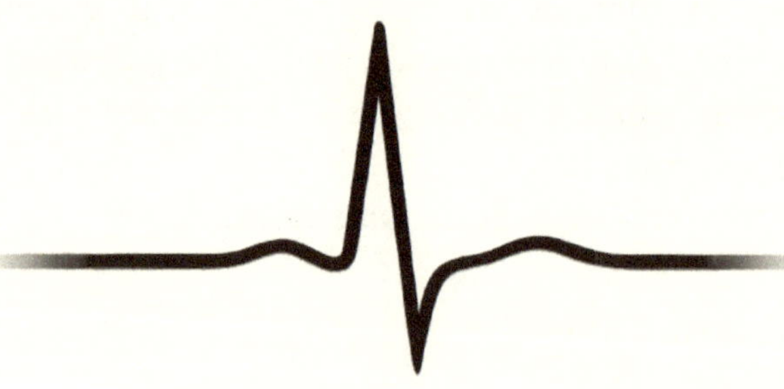

None of us went back to sleep after Shade's nightmare.

By now, I was sitting on just one of his thighs with my back against his chest. We hadn't separated once since waking. I had his right hand cradled in my lap and his left in my hair, which did feel nice, but the intent was to keep him relaxed.

Seems to be working so far.

Unfortunately, it was at this moment he stopped playing with my hair to glower at his hand instead. "I don't like my magic…"

Sathira looked at him sadly. "You just don't understand it yet, sweetheart."

His misery turned into a scowl. "I *understand* that it can knock people unconscious if I'm upset." He suddenly looked at her with wide-eyed terror. "Wait, that massive darkness you could see from Eidolon… could I have killed everyone inside it?"

"Maybe, but I doubt under those circumstances."

"What do you mean?"

"Arbiters are meant to be guardians, benevolent protectors who wield compassion and powerful magic for the people of Terraen. Violence is supposed to be a last resort. Sadly, there are exceptions…" She sighed and shook her head. "Our magic is deeply emotional in nature, but the deciding factor is intent."

"So, no one died because I didn't want to hurt anyone?"

She nodded. "I'm sure you were angry, but, above all, you were devastated, especially over Athaeÿn's death. We could feel it." She put her hand over her heart. "Unchecked rage may have led to a different outcome, but there's no guarantee. Not all anger is destructive."

He just stared at his hand again.

Sathira said nothing for a moment. "You know, I'm not actually sure if your magic has a harmful side. The Demons were knocked out, yes, but not injured, the raw emotion we felt was dreadful but otherwise benign, and the darkness is just, well, darkness. At least from what we've observed." She tilted her head a little. "If there is capacity for harm, how it would manifest is unclear."

Shade was unmoved. "Well, either way, I've seen nothing positive or worth exploring…"

A few minutes of gloomy silence passed.

Eventually, Sathira spoke again. "Would you like to see how our magic can help people?"

There was a delayed, halfhearted nod.

"Hold out your arm." With one flowing gesture, she summoned snowy fog at her fingertips and wove it around Shade's outstretched wrist, where it solidified into a thick cast of crystal-clear ice. She smiled when he gawked at it. "How does it feel?"

He turned his hand over a few times. "It's not even cold."

She chuckled lightly. "Securing a broken limb would be pointless if it died from frostbite."

As Shade tried and failed to bend his wrist, Elvylli summoned a gentle flame and used it to slowly melt the ice. "Admittedly, our ice and fire are often helpful in a state that could harm people if we're not careful, but if we want it to be harmless," with the ice gone, she collected her flame over his upturned palm and lowered it onto his skin, "intent goes a long way."

He flinched at first but smiled after a moment. "It's not burning me."

"I enjoy teaching kids not to play with fire," she chuckled as well, "but sometimes they touch before they think."

Shade's weak smile died out with the fire. "It's comforting to know I could have that much control someday, but at least fire and ice have real uses, good and bad. What use is disappearing into shadows and generating darkness? Who does that help?" He shook his head glumly. "If the only real use could be something harmful, I don't want to wield it. I don't want it to come out ever again."

The queens' brief joy faded with the sad glance they shared.

We're just going in circles.

After another minute of uncomfortable silence, I squeezed his hand and glanced up at him. "I agree with your mothers about exploring your magic."

He narrowed his eyes at me. "Why?"

"You need to know the full extent of its capability. Let them help you."

"But I don't want to use it."

"And you can make that choice *after* you know what you're dealing with. At the very least, you should know how to control it. Wouldn't it be nice to not have more incidents like tonight?"

He averted his gaze without saying anything, but his hand fidgeting in my lap betrayed how conflicted he was.

Sathira spoke when he wouldn't. "Athaeÿn's right, sweetheart." She waited until he looked at her. "We would never force you to use your magic, especially not to hurt anyone, but fundamental knowledge and unwavering command of your abilities are absolutely crucial. In everyday life, interpreting our emotions helps us avoid lashing out at others. The same applies to your magic."

Shade pressed me to his chest as he listened, but I wasn't sure he even noticed. Regardless, I hugged his arm supportively.

"We can't always choose our emotions, but we can decide what to do with them. Simply put, you're in charge of your actions." She offered a patient smile. "If your magic is capable of harm, you must be able to recognize the feeling that comes with it."

I felt him swallow hard as he stared at her.

Come on, Shade.

When he looked at his hand again, his glance was accompanied by a shaky sigh and reluctant nod. "Okay."

Phew…

I lightly jostled his other hand and smiled up at him. "For what it's worth, I think your ability to disappear into shadows is really cool."

As his gaze drifted to mine, the corners of his mouth turned up ever so slightly. "It *was* useful to defend myself against Xythe."

"I'm sure it was. As for your darkness, I promise there'll be a perfect time and place for it without hurting anyone. You just have to find it."

"You really think so?"

"I know so."

He smiled and nuzzled my forehead. "Thanks, Athaeÿn."

"Any time, Shade."

After hugging me tightly, he returned his attention to his mothers. "Can we fly a few miles away first? I don't want to endanger anyone here."

Sathira smiled. "I was going to suggest the same thing."

I looked at them as well. "I doubt Daryn and I would have much to worry about, but we'll hang back in case the sun finally burns through the clouds." I thought for a moment and glanced up at Shade again. "Hey, maybe that could be a use for your darkness."

He looked a bit skeptical. "Shielding you from the sun?"

"From what I've seen and heard, it absorbs *all* light. I don't see why it wouldn't work."

"I… guess that makes sense."

"Don't worry," I paused to kiss his cheek, "we wouldn't try until you were confident."

He smiled bashfully and held the spot I kissed. "You make me feel like I can do anything."

"Because you can," I kissed his lips this time, "so hold on to that feeling and run with it. Or fly, your choice."

He crushed me against his chest in another tight hug. "I will."

I was glad to feel his heart pounding with excitement. Hopefully, his enthusiasm would make things easier for him.

You got this, Shade.

Once he had gotten his fill of squishing me, he set me down and beamed at his mothers. "Can we leave now?"

Sathira smiled proudly. "Of course."

...

The three Arbiters didn't stop by the castle once all day, not even for lunch or an afternoon snack. I started to worry when evening arrived without them, so I tried to convince myself they had just lost track of time. Exploring Shade's magic was probably an intensive task.

I'm sure they're fine.

Daryn and I were still in the large entry hall after spending most of the day there, but one of us had been far busier than the other. He was sitting on a stack of pillows in front of a huge gathering of what had to be every youngling in the castle, all of whom were enraptured by his stories.

Meanwhile, I was lounging against the wall nearby with a grin on my face. Apparently, he was happy to put aside his dislike of crowds if it meant showing off his extensive knowledge. To be fair, it was impressive.

I might be as amazed as the kids.

Currently, the little ones were awestruck by tales of his homeland, the sprawling and revered forest known as Fae's Embrace.

One of the more inquisitive Solar Demon kids spoke up. "Are the trees there really alive?"

Daryn held up a finger. "All flora are living things, Xian, but yes, the Soulwoods have a bit more life to them than the average tree, which is why we live among them so effortlessly. Not only are they the largest trees in the world, but their thick branches form natural bridges and open areas to walk. They even weave houses for us in the canopy," he made a big, enthusiastic gesture with both hands, "but we also live inside the trunks, which open and close all on their own.

"It's believed they contain the souls of departed Wood Elves, hence their name, and that even the oldest are still held deep within their roots. Normally, the Soulwoods only respond to our kind, but they have been known to open for outsiders in immediate danger. Their protection rivals the walls of any castle, as their bark can harden like steel and is completely fireproof. Even their leaves can shrug off stray embers in the wind."

Xian was beaming. "So, I wouldn't have to worry about my magic burning the trees?"

"That's right. In fact, trees love sunlight. I bet the Soulwoods would welcome you and your solar magic with open branches."

"I wanna go!"

"You'll get the chance someday. I'll be sure to put in a good word for you."

As the kids broke out in excited conversations, my thoughts drifted to my own homeland. Specifically, the endless glowing crystals lining the tunnels. I had no memories of discourse regarding souls of departed Dark Elves or the crystals' possible involvement, but I found it hard to believe the concept had never crossed anyone's mind.

Maybe the notion came and went long before my time.

If it had, it was probably shrugged off as wishful thinking.

A nice idea, though.

I ruminated for a few more seconds before glancing at the back of Daryn's head. "Do you believe the Soulwood theory?"

He turned a bit to see me better. "There's no definitive proof, but it seems like a reasonable explanation for their lifelike behavior, at least in my eyes. There's still much about souls we don't know or understand, so who's to say the Soulwood phenomenon isn't possible?"

"Do you think your soul found its way there? Or did Rialla use it to summon a Demon? That's what Roänach did with mine."

"She did, so I've always assumed it's gone forever." His brows furrowed heavily. "If true, the Soulwoods will never know I existed…"

The forlorn haze dulling his eyes had my chest tight with regret. "Well, like you said, we don't know everything about souls. Maybe they're not actually lost when used to summon Demons. Maybe they're more of a catalyst and are free to go once they've set things in motion."

He sighed and shook his head. "From what I understand, and to put it rather crudely, souls are essentially used as currency to purchase Demons from Dominion. I don't see how they could survive such a violent transaction."

"I think Raethe is more interested in the before and after. He finds cruelty entertaining, right? Our murders and summoned Demons' misery are what he's interested in. Souls are just a means to an end."

There was no response.

I tilted my head a little when his gaze fell. "You know, Xythe used Shade's soul to fuel the solar shield for a thousand years. We may not have had powerful Arbiter souls, but if his could survive an ordeal like that, I don't see why ours couldn't handle a few simple summonings."

His head lifted ever so slightly.

"Even without proof, the Soulwood theory seems believable to me. I see no reason why my theory has to be any different." His eyes were still downcast, but I offered a reassuring smile anyway. "I bet once Rialla borrowed your soul, it was free to go home."

He finally looked at me again. "You really think so?"

"I do."

His gaze fell once more but, this time, was accompanied by a small smile.

It was clear this had bothered him for a long time, so I was relieved to see his tension ease.

I hope my theories are right.

He looked at me a few minutes later. "What about your soul?"

"There's no consensus among Dark Elves, but I like the concept of the Soulwoods. It got me thinking about the crystals in the Obsidian Spine. Maybe their light is actually from departed souls of my people."

"Sounds plausible to me."

Another smile tugged my lips as I fiddled with my hands in my lap, but it faded when thoughts of my people led to memories of my parents. Ten years without contact was bad enough. Now that three hundred years had passed, it was difficult not to drown in guilt, regardless of who was at fault.

Maybe my soul went home and has been watching over them.

My throat tightened.

Please don't let them hate me…

I was dragged out of my thoughts by the sound of approaching wingbeats, and it wasn't long before the three Arbiters landed and came inside.

Daryn looked over and made a sweeping hand gesture. "Ah, the dragons return."

"Athaeÿn!"

Shade's cheerful voice brought a smile back to my face. "How'd it go?"

"It went great! Want to see what I've been practicing?"

"Of course."

He could barely contain himself as he sat in front of me and put his hand between us. A moment later, a black dot appeared on his palm and slowly expanded into a sphere about a foot in diameter, making it look like he was holding a ball of darkness.

I waved my hand through it and smiled when nothing happened. "I'm really proud of you."

A slight blush darkened his face as he dispelled the sphere. "Thank you. I'm still not sure how to help anyone with this, but at least I can control it a bit better."

"Like I said, you'll think of something." With the sphere gone, I took gentle hold of his hand. "Did you get a chance to push into harmful territory? If your magic even has it, that is."

He nodded. "It was a lot harder than I thought it would be."

"I imagine you were afraid to hurt your mothers."

"Probably, but I'm not upset about it." His gaze fell to his massive claws. "I don't want harm to come easily."

I watched his eyes for a moment. "You still feel bad about hurting Xythe, don't you?"

His nod was sullen this time.

"In your defense, he didn't give you much of a choice."

"It became a choice toward the end."

"But you didn't kill him."

He said nothing for a few moments. "I just wanted everything to stop…"

I shifted onto his lap and hugged him tightly. "At least he can never hurt anyone again."

There was a shaky exhale as he returned the embrace and leaned his head on mine. "He had a thousand years to let go of his grudge. All that effort he put into lying to me, why couldn't he have used it to become a better person instead?"

"Unfortunately, people like Xythe justify every action they take, regardless of circumstances. He was never going to fix what he considered unbroken."

Shade nodded reluctantly and buried his face in my hair. "I'm so tired."

I know…

"Well, it is bedtime. You must be exhausted after working on your magic all day." I heard a faint exhale of amusement, but Shade didn't get the chance to reply.

"I'll tell you who's tired," Daryn butted in loudly. *"Me."*

Elvylli snorted a laugh. "Looks like you've been sitting on your ass all day."

"Excuse me, I've been running Daryn's Demon Daycare all day, thank you very much," he snapped, gesturing wildly to the giggling kids in front of him.

I spun around on Shade's lap so Daryn could see my smirk. "The only thing that's been running is your mouth."

"Which was *exhausting."*

"I didn't hear any complaining."

"I'm not one to disappoint my fan club." He gestured to the large gathering again. "Right kids?"

"Right, Uncle Daryn," they replied in unison.

He clutched his chest and choked out a melodramatic sob. "I'm legendary."

Elvylli pursed her lips. "Your ego certainly is."

Sathira put her hands on her hips. "How are you so antisocial yet so desperate for attention?"

He splayed his fingers across his chest. "I'm a man of many talents." There was still a grin on his face when he turned back to the kids. "Alright, you ready? Three, two, one," he threw his arms forward, *"disperse!"*

The crowd of children laughed and squealed as they scrambled to their feet and scattered in both directions down the hall, tripping over themselves and each other as they went.

Elvylli raised a brow. "I didn't peg you as someone who would be good with children."

"You have never pegged me in any way, shape, or form, and I would respectfully ask you keep it that way."

"Ew, Daryn—"

"No, *ew* would have applied if I requested the opposite. Nothing personal, of course."

"Too late, I'm already insulted."

"Lies. If you were actually insulted, you would have—" his mouth was still open when he glanced at Shade. After a brief pause, he shook his head and cleared his throat. "Never mind. Anyway, I agree about bedtime. Farewell, friends," he added as he got up and wandered off, stretching his arms above his head as he went.

I was glad Daryn hadn't finished his immolation joke.

Hopefully, Shade is oblivious.

When I glanced up at him, he was just blinking in confusion as Daryn walked away.

Good...

He looked down at me once Daryn was out of earshot. "What was he going to say?"

"Something else gross about pegging, I'm sure."

"What's pegging?"

"I'll tell you when you're older."

"But I'm—"

I grinned and pressed a finger to his lips. "Shush."

He pulled my hand down. "Is it—"

"Still bedtime? Yes."

The giant frown on Shade's face was highly amusing. *"Fiiiiine..."*

Once everyone settled down to sleep, I smirked up at him from where I lay against his chest. "Try not to have another nightmare," I teased, keeping my tone light and playful.

He chuckled and squeezed me in his arms. "You're one to talk."

"Ouch."

"Arms or words?"

"Yes."

We had a tiny giggling fit before finally going quiet, but there was still a smile on my face when I hugged his arm a few minutes later. The soothing rhythm of his heartbeat was already lulling me to sleep.

I can't wait until I'm free to be with him forever.

Chapter 27

Athaeÿn

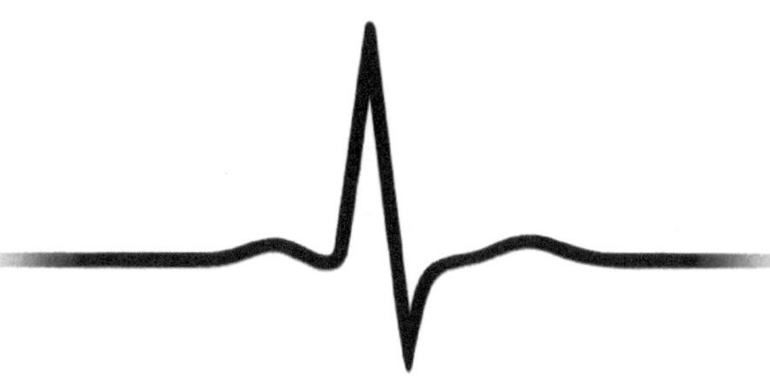

The next morning was anything but peaceful. In a good way, this time.

Daryn, Elvylli, Sathira, and I sat watching a bunch of kids running around the hall. At first glance, it looked like they were being chased by some invisible entity, but they were actually fleeing an amorphous shadow on the ground. Every now and then, a clawed hand would shoot out of the darkness and grab one of their tails just long enough for them to squeal with laughter before letting go and vanishing again.

Definitely the most unique game of tag I've ever seen.

While exploring his magic the previous day, Shade had discovered the ability to turn into an artificial shadow in any amount of light. This hadn't been possible without his soul, and he wasted no time making up for it.

The kids are certainly enjoying his new ability.

I glanced at the queens every now and then as they watched, and I couldn't help but smile at the faint tears of joy in their eyes. I knew exactly what they were thinking and feeling.

Better late than never.

Eventually, Shade reformed his full body and scooped up ten or so kids in a big embrace. It was an easy feat with his strength and huge arm span. "I win!"

"No fair!" Xian complained from within the bundle.

"You're just jealous of how cool my shadow magic is."

"Am not! My solar magic's *way* cooler!"

Daryn scoffed and shielded his eyes. "My thermal vision dictates otherwise."

"Why are you taking his side?!"

"I'm just stating facts."

"Traitor."

Shade snorted a laugh and set all the kids down. "Alright, that's enough for now."

Xian folded his arms and looked directly up at him. "You didn't say the magic word."

"Please?"

"No."

Shade thought for a moment before grinning and mimicking Daryn's two-armed gesture from the previous night. "Disperse!"

With that, the kids scattered and ran off laughing just like last time.

Daryn pretended to choke up again. "Still legendary."

"Still egotistical," Elvylli mumbled.

"Still *mean.*"

Now free of children, Shade came over and sat with us. "What's the plan for today? Are we practicing my magic again?"

Sathira nodded. "We are, and then we're heading to Castle Veil once the sun has set. It's still cloudy, but we're playing it safe."

He looked alarmed before she even finished speaking. "Wha-really? Already?"

"Yes, two days of practice will suffice for now. I know that sounds irresponsible, but I'm starting to regret leaving Eidolon without at least one Arbiter. The city is in good hands regardless of our presence... and yet..." She shook her head. "I can't shake the feeling we've been gone too long."

"Oh..." His gaze fell. "I'm sorry for being such a slow learner..."

"No, sweetheart, don't apologize. You're actually quite an efficient learner. Even if you weren't, Elvylli and I are the only ones to blame if something bad happens in our absence." She offered a reassuring smile. "Pay no mind to my anxiety. I've always been a bit of a worrier, often without merit, but I admit Roänach has been haunting my thoughts from the moment I learned of him." She sighed and shook her head. "I'm sure I'll feel better once he's dealt with."

Shade still looked concerned. "Alright... You're sure you don't want to go now?"

She nodded this time. "I believe it will be best to approach under cover of night, though we may wait until sunrise to confront him. At the very least, that would prevent him from fleeing if we had trouble killing him."

"What if it's still cloudy?"

When Sathira looked to me for input, I glanced at Shade to reply for her. "I'm honestly not sure if he would risk escape during the day, even if it was dark and stormy. Maybe if he was desperate enough. Regardless, I agree we should wait until morning."

He stared at me for a few moments before sighing at his hand. "Magic or no magic, I thought I would be more excited to get rid of him, but I've never killed anyone before." He dropped his hand into his lap. "I don't look forward to confronting him."

"I don't think anyone does. Not even me." I hung my head a little. "Despite how much I hate him, I dread his fate even more. I can't articulate every reason why, but I accept his end if it means saving countless others."

Daryn glanced between us. "I'm sure our capable queens will gladly snuff him out for you." He side-eyed Elvylli. *Hopefully,* with a little less screaming this time. However, if my assumption is proven wrong, I'll gladly kill him myself."

Elvylli smirked at him. "Since when are *you* capable of violence?"

"Since I took personal umbrage with every single Arch-Vampire in existence. This is simply the first opportunity handed right to me."

"I know you choose playful violence in conversation, but I was under the impression you were otherwise harmless."

"*Peaceful,* not harmless. True, I'm generally not a fighter, but, given the chance, I would drive a stake through Roänach's heart before he could even open his cursed mouth. The only reason I didn't kill Rialla was the fact I literally couldn't as one of her bound vassals." He sighed heavily. "I owe Xiir everything…"

After a brief lull of silence, Shade glanced at me again. "Everything will be better once Roänach is gone, right?"

Gods, I hope so.

I offered a smile that was a bit forced. "Yes. I promise."

He fiddled with his claws for a second before nodding and turning to his mothers. "Alright, let's go practice some more."

Sathira returned a nod then smiled at me. "We'll be back a little before sunset."

Once the Arbiters were gone, I turned to Daryn with a smirk. "So, are you running Daryn's Demon Daycare again?"

Before he could answer, a small group of kids all shouting various questions ran up to him. "I don't think it's up to me," he whisper-hissed in my general direction, looking pained as he did so.

His pretend agony didn't fool me. I had witnessed firsthand how much he enjoyed telling stories to them.

Either way, he's in for another long day of talking.

...

Just as promised, the three Arbiters returned when the sky began to darken, and the queens requested everyone gather in the entry hall for an announcement. They would be sending quite a few of Eidolon's most experienced counselors to speak with them. In particular, those specializing in post-enthrallment recovery. The Demons promptly expressed sincere gratitude.

Afterward, all the kids crowded around Shade and Daryn.

Xian looked angry, but he was betrayed by the tears in his eyes. "Do you really have to go?"

Daryn nodded. "I'm afraid so, sunshine."

"I don't want you to."

"I know, but there are more enthralled Demons and other captives who need our help. Surely, you can appreciate the importance of freeing them."

Xian folded his arms and halfheartedly kicked the floor. "I guess…"

Daryn almost looked sad as he watched him. "Hey, don't be such a pouty puss." He put his hands on his hips. "You really think this is the last time we'll see each other?"

Xian slowly looked up at him.

"I said I would put in a good word for you to visit Fae's Embrace, but… What if I took you there myself someday?"

"Really?!"

"Perhaps." Daryn waggled a finger. "*If* you promise to behave until then." He had barely finished speaking when Xian hugged him tightly, drawing a sharp gasp from him. "This was a mistake—"

A wave of secondhand touch anxiety washed over me just from watching him freeze. "Are you alright?" I whispered just loud enough for him to hear.

He nodded and glanced down at Xian. After hesitating a moment, he awkwardly returned the hug and patted the little Solar Demon's head. "You're welcome."

Hopefully, he doesn't have the same issues I have.

As Daryn partook in what looked like the first affectionate hug in his entire life, Shade and I were distracted by the tiny Starlight Demon youngling he had interacted with the first day.

The little one barely reached Shade's knee as he hugged his leg. "You'll come visit, right?"

Shade smiled down at him. "Of course, Xyn. You know I would never abandon you."

Xyn let go and reached up with both arms. "Can I be tall one more time?"

Shade beamed and sat Xyn on his shoulder like before. "Look out, everyone!" He spun around and ran outside. "Tallest Demon in the world coming through!"

Daryn sighed with relief when Xian let go and followed Shade with all the other kids. "Phew. Thank you, Tyrran…"

I smirked at him. "You really are a drama queen."

"Naturally."

When the rest of us also made our way outside, Sathira signaled for Shade to rein it in. His reluctance was obvious when he stopped running and set Xyn down, but he didn't hesitate to kneel and use his wings to sweep the children into a big group hug.

Xyn clung to him. "You really promise to come back?"

"I do." After gently prying Xyn off, he slowly got up and smiled at the kids. "Like you did for Daryn, you all promise to be good while I'm gone, right?"

"We do!"

Shade's eyes were misty by the time he turned to the adults. "Please be well."

Xyn's mother spoke for everyone. "You as well, Tyrran. Thank you for helping set us free."

"Thank Athaeÿn." He pulled me into a side-hug. "Without him, neither I nor my mothers would have gotten the chance."

My chest tightened a little but was quickly soothed by a small surge of warmth.

And I have you to thank for my second chance, Lune.

I could have sworn there was the faintest whisper of a familiar coo from deep in my chest, but I was probably just imagining things.

Meanwhile, Sathira waved from nearby. "Are we all ready to head out?"

Instead of answering, Shade just stood there gazing at the castle.

I looked up at him and hugged his arm. "You alright?"

He stayed silent for a moment. "This place is all I've ever known. I've already come and gone a few times, but…" He let out a long, shaky exhale. "Yes, I'm alright. I'm ready to leave."

"Are you sure?"

He smiled down at me. "I promised I would visit, so this isn't really goodbye. Besides, it already feels different," he gestured to the Demons, "and they're worth coming back for."

I smiled back. "I'm glad you think so."

As Shade and Elvylli secured me and Daryn for flight, all the kids waved to us. "Bye, Tyrran! Bye, Uncle Daryn!"

Daryn waved back. "Farewell, children!"

Shade did the same. "Take care, everyone!"

This is it—

Fortunately, the small portrait of myself fit snugly into my thigh-high boot, so both hands were free to grip Shade's arms when he launched into the air. The moment his feet left the ground, I gasped and dug my fingernails into his skin. Luckily, he didn't seem to mind.

If he even noticed.

Once the initial shock faded, a huge smile came to my face as we cleared the canopy and ascended high above the forest. There had been a sense of liberation atop the coach, but this was something else entirely. I had never felt so free.

But I'm not yet.

A pit formed in my stomach.

And I won't be until Roänach is dead.

For the first time in three hundred years, an end to my ordeal was in sight. Unfortunately, it didn't come with the elation I wanted. It was old news that everyone's freedom would cost Roänach his life, but as reality began to set in, my persistent dread was heavier than ever.

I just want this over and done with…

...

Our two-hour journey to Mount Umbra felt longer than my five-day trip to Xythe's castle, and every second was riddled with twice the anxiety. The nausea was becoming unbearable.

Please let this end quickly.

I swallowed my discomfort and waved to get the others' attention. "I'm not sure how far the patrolling Demons go, but I think we can get away with hiding around the side of the mountain until morning. If the sun finally comes out, I trust Shade to protect me and Daryn."

Elvylli nodded. "Works for me."

Because her hands were free, Sathira was able to gesture to us. "Would you and Tyrran like to remain outside when the time comes? It wouldn't hurt to have external backup, but I mainly ask in case it would be too much to witness Roänach's death."

I swallowed hard and shook my head. "No, I… I want immediate proof." A shaky exhale forced its way out of my tight throat. "I need to see him die with my own eyes."

"Wish I could've seen Rialla die both times," Daryn chimed in flatly.

I glanced over at him but said nothing.

For once, I envy your coldblooded attitude.

It wasn't long before we landed in a sheltered location away from the cave's hidden entrance. Fortunately, there were no patrolling Demons in sight.

Hopefully, that means this spot is secluded enough.

As we settled in, I glanced at some large rocks a ways out from where we were. They had no markings, but I could sense the familiar magic oozing from them. "Well, I'm stuck inside our containment runes again, so I hope this goes smoothly."

Daryn hummed in thought for a moment. "If I ever have the displeasure of meeting Vernyth face-to-face, *maybe* I could be persuaded to let him live, *if* he offers to locate and shut down more of these runes."

"Are you even capable of giving him a chance?"

"I promise nothing."

"Did I use the word *promise?*" I smiled before I could stop myself. "Either way, one Arch-Vampire at a time."

He just folded his arms and blew a raspberry at me.

"And we should probably be quiet while we wait."

"Until *morning?* Such prolonged silence will surely kill me."

My grin turned into a smirk. "Good thing you're already dead."

The offended look on his face was priceless, but he did relent and go silent.

For ten whole minutes.

"This is boring," he whispered, shooting a glare at me.

"Bring a book next time," I whispered back.

He opened his mouth to reply but hesitated and turned slightly to one side. When he narrowed his eyes and tilted his head, I knew he was listening for something.

Uh-oh.

A few seconds later, I heard sniffing from around the corner.

Shit, it's one of the Fauna Demons—

After gesturing for Elvylli, Sathira, and Daryn to wait, I turned to Shade and beckoned him to follow me.

Without a word, he nodded and dissolved into my shadow.

Ideal compensation for his gigantic body's lack of stealth.

Cautiously peeking around the outcrop, I spotted none other than the coachman about twenty feet away. He was still sniffing the air, but, luckily, his back was to me for the moment.

Well, his presence is a good indication Roänach is here.

That was what we wanted, but it just made my nausea worse.

Get it over with.

Taking a deep breath, I left my position of cover and headed right for him. I hoped my false confidence would be convincing.

A moment later, he turned and nearly fell over from the force of his double take. "Athaeÿn?!" The look on his face was priceless. "What the— Where did— How— Why are you here?!"

I shrugged. "Xythe was an asshole, so I left."

"How did you get past the solar shield and make it back without the coach?"

"None of your business."

"I'm on patrol. It is absolutely my business."

"Whatever. I'm sure Roänach will ask the same stupid questions."

"And then some," he scoffed. "Either way, your interrogation will have to wait."

My chest tightened. "What do you mean?"

"He left a few days ago."

"What?!"

The coachman winced and rubbed his ear. "Fucking *relax...* Sheesh…" He shook his head as if dislodging my shriek. "Anyway, the patrol at the time saw the queens of Eidolon fly over, and Roänach got really agitated for some reason when they told him. He left right away as a swarm of bats, so it must've been urgent."

It felt like my organs were about to implode. "Did he say where he was going?"

"Nope."

The lack of confirmation changed nothing. I knew exactly where he went.

This isn't happening—

Before I could say anything else, Shade rematerialized behind me and lightly tapped my shoulder. "Does this mean our plan is useless?"

The coachman took a wary step back and pointed a shaky claw at Shade. "Wh-What the fuck is that?"

"Um, an Arbiter?"

Shade had barely finished speaking when the coachman spun around and fled in the direction of the cave.

There was a moment of silence. "Did he not see my mothers too? I look pretty similar to them…"

As I stood there fuming, multiple sets of footsteps approached from behind.

Sathira's dismayed voice sounded first. "I knew one of us should've stayed in Eidolon."

Nearly immobilized by rage and disgust, it took me a few seconds to forcibly turn myself around. "Roänach has visited the city many times over the centuries. I bet he's been summoning and enthralling Demons right under your noses."

Elvylli's horns glowed red-hot to the point of smoking. "Every missing citizen…" Her fists clenched and trembled at her sides. "How many were killed by him?"

I was going to be sick at any moment.

How did this never occur to me—

It was then I noticed Daryn standing motionless nearby, staring wide-eyed in the direction the coachman went. The look on his face rivaled Shade's horror when Xythe revealed his true nature. I had never seen such a raw expression on him before.

Did I miss something?

I started to worry when he remained frozen. "Daryn?"

He didn't react at all.

"Are you alright?"

When he finally spoke, his voice was a broken whisper. "That was Xiir."

What—

I briefly glanced in the same direction before turning back to him, only to find his eyes brimming with tears.

Oh no…

All of a sudden, his face twisted into a grimace of murderous intent. "Roänach was already fucking dead, but now," a single tear came down his cheek as he bared his fangs, "this just became *personal.*"

Elvylli also looked like she was about to explode. "Tyrran, you stay behind. Roänach will *not* escape the city, but if he somehow does, I need you here to protect Athaeÿn and the other captives. Sathira and I will deal with that bastard ourselves."

"With my help," Daryn hissed.

Shade's eyes widened, but he nodded without protest.

Meanwhile, I was stuck in my own catatonic state of disbelief. By the time I snapped out of it, the queens had taken off with Daryn and were far out of earshot.

Damn it all—

Before I could stop myself, I ran to the containment stones from earlier and reached forward until my hand pressed against an unyielding, invisible wall. I had expected as much, but the confirmation only enraged me further.

Fuck—!

I let out a sharp growl of anger and slammed my fist on the barrier. When I turned back around, it was just in time to see Shade come to a stop in front of me, but I pointed in the direction his mothers went before he could say anything. "Go with them."

His worried expression snapped to confusion. "What? No, they told me to stay here."

"I don't care what they said. They might need your help."

"But I don't want them to get mad at me."

"They're not Xythe!"

He flinched back half a step and averted his gaze.

Shit—

I took a long, shaky breath. "I-I'm sorry, Shade, I didn't mean to yell. I just—" I shook my head and dragged my hands down my face. "We were *so close,* and things took the worst possible turn. Barrier or no barrier, I can't stop Roänach myself," I lowered my hands and looked up at him, "but you can."

When he turned back to me, he still seemed a bit shaken.

"Please, Shade."

He shook his head. "I'm not leaving you here."

"I'll be fine."

"Not if he escapes and comes back."

"If you deal with him in the city, we won't have to worry about that."

"I'm not risking it."

"Shade, we don't have time to argue about this. Every second we waste here is another second he could be using to summon more Demons."

He tensed and looked away again. "My mothers have taken care of Eidolon just fine without my help. They don't need me this time either."

"You don't know that."

"Yeah, well, I don't know how to handle Roänach anyway. We've already established that my darkness would be useless against him, and even if I was standing right in front of him with a wooden stake in my hand, I'm not sure I could bring myself to kill him."

"Then help them protect innocent people! Just something, *anything* other than nothing. Please!"

To my dismay, he shook his head again. "I'm sorry, Athaeÿn, I can't leave you defenseless. I just can't. Not after what Xythe did." There was a long pause. "Besides, I don't even know Eidolon." When he turned back to me, his eyes were glistening with fear. "I know *you.*"

All I could do was stare at him.

But...

His voice crumbled. "Please don't make me choose."

The heartbreak in his tone shattered my aggravation like glass. The frustration lingered, but I could no longer find it in myself to argue.

What am I going to do?

I hung my head and ran my fingers through my hair.

If not for the stupid runes—

My eyes widened.

Wait, that's it!

I looked up at him again. "I need you to get Vernyth."

His gaze turned wary. "For the runes?"

I nodded. "He's the only other living Arch-Vampire I know of," my throat tightened with uncertainty, "and the only one we can trust."

Shade's entire face contorted with unease.

You and I both.

"Listen, I know how this sounds coming from me of all people, but if Callyn trusts him, that's good enough for me." I glanced at the rocks that relentlessly oozed containment magic. "I just need him to deactivate the runes. Nothing more."

Shade remained silent.

I turned back to him and put my hand on his arm. "It's not like I can be turned into a Vampire a second time."

He looked down and used his free hand to press mine against his warm skin. A full minute later, he found my gaze again. "Alright."

Finally…

"Thank you, Shade. Believe me, I'm not thrilled either, but this is the only solution I can think of to the problem *you* handed me," I chided, poking his chest.

Can't say I blame you, though.

A guilty smile tugged his lips. "Sorry…"

I sighed and shook my head. "Sometimes, I think you care about me too much."

"I can't help it."

"Don't worry," I grinned up at him, "it wasn't a real complaint."

He pulled me into a hug. "So, where do I find Vernyth?"

Chapter 28

Athaeÿn

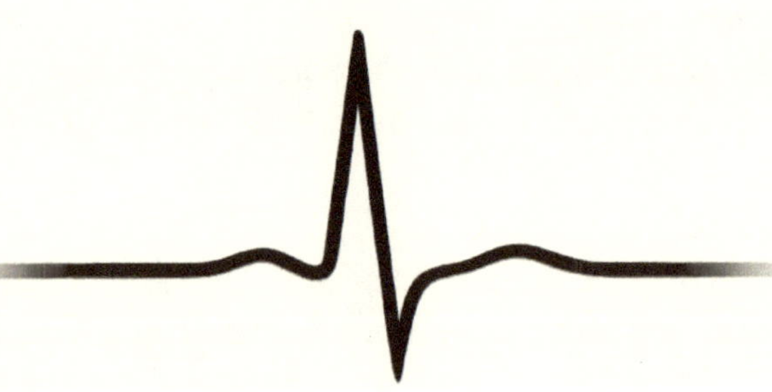

To my surprise, there was no illusion shrouding the cave entrance.
The coachman probably told the others to hide.
My throat tightened.
Xiir…
I still couldn't believe it.
Escapes one Arch-Vampire only to be snatched up by another.
And seeing Daryn so upset just made things infinitely worse.
I promise Xiir will be free.
Shaking my head, I looked around and failed to spot a single Demon. It was an odd sight after three hundred years of the opposite.
Stellar guard work.
Halfway through the glowing gardens, a voice unknown to Shade but all too familiar to me called out from off to one side.

"Athaeÿn!"

When I turned to see Fiella running toward us, my relief seeing her safe and sound was immeasurable.

Thank the gods.

Her eyes were already brimming with tears when she skidded to a stop just a few feet in front of me. It was evident in her fidgeting she could barely contain herself. "Y-You're back!"

Without a word, I smiled and pulled her into a hug. As expected, some anxiety resurfaced, but it was a whisper compared to before I left.

I'm sorry this took so long, Fiella.

She froze and gasped sharply. "A-Athaeÿn, you're hugging me—" After a brief pause, she buried her face in my chest and squeezed me tightly. "You're really hugging me!"

I chuckled at her muffled voice and the sound of her feet pattering excitedly. "Not entirely free of my issues, but more than enough for now."

"I'm so happy for you!" The moment she pulled back and looked up, her eyes widened fearfully. "Wh-Who is that?"

Did she really not notice him until now?

I couldn't help but grin. "Fiella, this is Tyrran. He's my… uhh…" When I glanced at him, he just blinked a few times. "Well, let's just say he's a special friend I met on my trip." I turned back to her with another smile. "It's a long story."

Before she could say anything, another familiar voice sounded.

"Special friend, huh?"

My gaze was met with an infuriating smug grin. "Yes, *Haana.*"

Her smirk was long gone by the time she stopped next to Fiella. She hadn't looked away from me once. "I never thought I'd see you hug anyone ever again."

"Neither did I."

We both smiled and shared our first embrace in centuries.

She gave me a squeeze. "But I always hoped I would," she added softly, leaning her head on mine. "I'm so glad you found yourself again."

Despite lingering unease, her touch was more comforting than anything. "I'm still working on it, but thank you."

Hopefully, this is just the beginning.

Once we released each other, I stepped back so I could see them both. "Alright, Tyrran and I need to grab something from Roänach's study real quick. If you two don't mind waiting, I'd love to catch up afterward."

Fiella's eyes widened again. "You're going to steal from him? I don't think that's a good idea."

I offered a reassuring smile. "I promise it's for a good reason, but I'll explain when we come back out."

Halfway to the fortress, I noticed a distinct lack of footsteps behind me.

Again?

I was less than surprised to glance back and find Shade still in front of Fiella and Haana. Admittedly, the huge smile on his face was adorable.

He extended both hands in greeting. "Hi, nice to meet you."

Haana returned a polite smile and shook one of his hands. "The feeling is mutual."

Meanwhile, Fiella openly gawked at his other hand while gripping it with both of hers. His massive claws dwarfed her fingers. "Whooaaa…" Eventually, she looked up at him with a guilty smile. "Sorry for being afraid of you at first."

His grin never wavered. "It's alright. I doubt you'll be the last."

"At least you're nice. That should help!"

Their meeting was cute, but I had to cut it short. "Tyrran, we have a schedule to keep!"

"Ooo—" He pulled his hands free and waved to them. "We can talk more later. Bye!" Once he caught up, we entered the castle together. "Sorry, I was just introducing myself."

"And that was very polite of you, but we've dawdled too much already," I shook my head a little, "which, to be fair, is mostly my fault."

"To be fairer, it was my fault first when I refused to leave."

"*Fairest* enough." When we arrived at Roänach's study, I stopped and gestured to the closed door. "Mind slipping under and unlocking it for me?"

He just stared at it for a few seconds. "Want me to violently break it down instead?"

I was about to turn down his offer but paused and glanced at the door again. A door I despised with every fiber of my being. "You know what? I think I would enjoy that, actually."

He giggled mischievously and rubbed his hands together before reeling back and obliterating the door with a single, devastating punch. "Ow…" He shook his hand a few times and grinned at me. "Satisfying?"

"Very much so. Thank you." The crunch of wood debris beneath my boots was music to my ears as I entered and pulled a large, annotated map off the wall. When I returned to Shade, I stood so we could both see it. "Let's see, where is… Ah—" I pointed to a landmark on the map that wasn't too far from our current location. "Their hideout was in here, an abandoned mine called the Iron Abyss."

"That's a cool name."

"It is. Callyn described the entrance as an adit in a hillside, and, if I remember correctly, there should be ruins of the adjoining town in the surrounding area. As long as you stay on course, you shouldn't miss it."

He nodded and took the map to study it. "What should I say to convince Vernyth to help?"

"Apparently, Callyn asked him to help look for me a while back, so just mentioning my name would probably be enough."

"And if that doesn't work?"

"Then tell him about Roänach summoning Demons in Eidolon. I know it's just speculation, but I would stake my life on it." I thought for a moment. "Demons or no Demons, many of his fellow vassals probably still live in the capital, so a more characteristic Arch-Vampire like Roänach stalking those streets should help convince him as well, even if he hasn't spoken to said vassals in centuries. After all, they used to be friends."

"Alright. Hopefully, your name will be enough."

I nodded and squeezed past his large frame. "Come on. The sooner you recruit Vernyth, the sooner we get to Eidolon."

And the sooner we kill Roänach…

After exiting the fortress and passing through the glowing gardens, we stopped just shy of the innermost barrier and stood facing each other.

Shade cradled my head with one hand, as the map was rolled up in his other. "The whole point of shutting down the runes was so I didn't have to leave you behind, yet here I am leaving anyway." His face was tense with worry. "Are you sure there's nothing else we can do?"

I smiled and leaned into his touch. "If there were options, do you really think my first choice would be seeking out another Arch-Vampire?"

He exhaled a weak laugh through his nose. "I suppose not…"

"If it makes you feel any better, an efficient trip to and from the Iron Abyss should land you back here before your mothers even reach Eidolon. Meaning, if their arrival spooks Roänach into fleeing, you'll have already returned to protect me."

His tension seemed to ease a little, but he still looked unconvinced.

My hand found his wrist and held it gently. "I'll be fine. The other vassals are my friends, the Demons aren't allowed to touch us, and the only real threat isn't going to show up while you're gone." I caressed his hand with my thumb. "Everything will work out."

"Promise?"

"Promise."

He finally managed another smile as he dropped to one knee and pulled me in for a kiss, which he held for a few seconds before resting his forehead against mine. "You're almost free."

I shivered from the resonance of his deep voice against my lips. "There's only one person in the way."

"He's been in your way for a long time. Too long." He nuzzled my face with his. "No matter what happens, I'll make sure he never hurts you again."

"Promise?"

"Promise."

Despite the dread in my heart, I smiled and hugged his head to mine. "I'll be here."

"And I'll be back."

He kissed me one last time and headed out.

It's just for a couple of hours…

As I stood there with my hand on my chest, Lune's warmth helped soothe my nerves. My heart remained silent, but it wasn't quite as cold and dead anymore. I almost felt alive again.

You'll watch over Shade while he's gone, right?

There was a surge of warmth in my chest.

Thank you, Lune—

"Special friend indeed."

Gods—!

Fiella's voice scared the shit out of me, but my surprise turned to annoyance when I glanced back only to find *two* smirks this time. I felt like a teenager being caught making out. "Wha-uhhhh, y-yeah? So, what?"

Haana put her hands on her hips. "Relax, Athaeÿn."

"Yeah, there's nothing to be embarrassed about," Fiella added with a tiny giggle. "I think you two are really cute together."

"O-Oh. Well, uh, thank you…" I rubbed the back of my neck awkwardly. "I *may* have downplayed how important he was to me…"

Haana's brows went up. *"Noooo—"*

"Shush. You're being a bad influence."

Fiella was practically squinting with smugness. "She had nothing to do with my comment."

"I don't appreciate being ganged up on."

Haana leaned forward a little. "You'll live." She said nothing for a moment. "This may be even more shocking than the hugs."

"Believe me, I'm as surprised as you are. Now then," I waved my hand dismissively, "if you've both had your fill of teasing me, I have some important details to share." My gaze drifted to Fiella. "But first, has the lunelight helped?"

"It has. The three of us sit around it every night before we go to bed."

"The *three* of you?"

Her smile never wavered as she gestured to get someone's attention.

When I looked over, I was surprised to see Lánelli of all people approaching. Her eyes weren't the icy blue I remembered.

Damn, she did go through with it.

She stopped at Fiella's other side. "Athaeÿn, right?"

I was still a bit dumbstruck but managed a nod.

She nodded back. "Glad to see you intact."

"Thank you." I kept any jokes about the contrary to myself so as not to worry Fiella. "I must admit—"

"You're confused."

I opened my mouth but didn't get the chance to reply.

"Understandable, considering how I spoke to you when we first met. I apologize for being so insufferable."

"It's alright. What changed?"

"My entire perception of this place." She shot a disapproving glance at the ceiling. "I knew Roänach would have vassals, but I was under the impression they were loyal followers and lovers who willingly became Vampires." She sighed and thumbed one of her new fangs. "I'm an idiot, I know."

It hurt my heart to hear her say that. "He's a really good liar."

"Maybe. Doesn't change how stupid I feel."

I nodded glumly. "I can relate more than I care to admit."

There was a brief pause before she put her arm around Fiella's shoulders and lightly jostled her. "And to think, I accused this little darling of jealousy."

I couldn't help but smile when Fiella giggled a little. "I'm glad to see you've grown so close."

"It was effortless after Roänach's illusion of grandeur shattered. The first line he crossed was my realization about the other vassals. I thought you were all miserable because he named me his new favorite, but the first time he took the back of his hand to my face, I knew why you were actually miserable. That slap was the second line he crossed. Admittedly, I enjoy men with a dark side, sinister aesthetic, whatever you want to call it, but I don't tolerate abuse.

"Fiella was the first to offer comfort after he slapped me, which was all it took to set aside our differences. She reminds me of my little sister Deänna." Lánelli paused to smile at Fiella but became even more serious when her attention returned to me. "The third and final line Roänach crossed was when he threatened her. That was the end of it. Luckily, he was still obsessed with me, so I took the liberty of keeping him occupied as much as possible."

My brows went up a bit. "Did it work?"

"As far as I can tell. He and I were joined at the hip until a few days ago." She rolled her eyes. "A bit too literally for my liking, but it made my job easier."

I sighed and shook my head. "Then you succeeded where I failed." When I glanced at Fiella, she looked sad instead of confused. "How long have you known?"

Her gaze fell. "I had a vague suspicion after some weird comments you and Haana made, but Lánelli confirmed it after Roänach left."

"Let me guess. He bragged about knowing my motive all along, right?"

Lánelli nodded. "It was sickening to listen to."

"I can imagine." I shook my head and forced a smile. "Anyway, thank you for trying to protect the others while I was gone."

"You're welcome. I've made many mistakes in my life, but none quite this permanent. I really fucked myself this time." She sighed and ran her tongue over her fangs. "Oh well. At least I got the chance to do some good before he left, though I still have no idea where he went."

"That's actually what I was about to discuss before you came over." I refocused on Fiella and Haana. "I sent Tyrran to fetch Vernyth, a neutral Arch-Vampire some of my friends are vassals to. Once he deactivates the containment runes, we're going to Eidolon to kill Roänach."

Fiella's eyes shot wide. "Are you serious?"

Haana looked surprised too, but Lánelli just nodded with approval.

"Yes. He's finally going to answer for everything he's done."

"W-We're going to be free?"

"That's the plan."

Fiella teared up and wrung her hands together. "I'm really going to see my family again? My friends? My boyfriend? Even my cats?"

I smiled and nodded. "Everyone."

As Fiella broke down sobbing, Lánelli pulled her into a tight hug. "I have to introduce you to Deänna. You'll love her."

"O-Only if you both agree to meet Joryn and my cats."

"Cats first."

Fiella giggled through a tiny sob. "Okay."

It was nice to see her hope rekindled, but the mention of her family once again reminded me of my parents.

I need to find them.

With so much time having passed, I couldn't shake the fear of them wanting nothing to do with me.

But I have to at least try, even if it's just for closure.
I hung my head a little.
If they even remember me…

...

As we waited in the glowing gardens, Fiella finally got to teach me how to make flower crowns. The learning curve was steeper than expected. She beamed with pride when I finished one all by myself, then applauded when it stayed intact once set on my head. I likely felt more accomplished than I should have.

Just as I was about to start a second one for Shade, there was an unfamiliar sound behind me. I glanced over my shoulder just in time to see the two primary containment runes on either side of the cave mouth brighten with a loud hum before going dark and silent.

It worked?

Not a second later, Shade flew in and landed next to us. "Found him!"

His cheerful announcement was followed by the sound of rushing wind as a large swarm of bats poured into the cave. The chattering cloud rapidly condensed and transformed into a middle-aged Human with a neatly trimmed silver beard, equally metallic hair tied back in a loose knot, a dark patch over his left eye, and the skin tone of bronzed terracotta. His Arch-Vampire status was confirmed by the black fang markings on his forehead. I had never seen him before, but he was exactly what I expected.

Callyn described him quite accurately.

Vernyth settled next to Shade and glanced down at me. "So, this is where you ended up, eh?"

I nodded. "The worst decision I ever made."

He returned a nod and looked at the ground. "Yeah…"

As I stood to face him better, I couldn't help but note his furrowed brows creasing the symbol on his forehead. "Most of them forgive you."

He shook his head. "I don't deserve it, but my opinion is irrelevant. If they wish to grant me that, I won't argue, even if I disagree." His gaze slowly lifted to meet mine. "Regardless, I didn't come here to sulk. I came to help."

"You already have by deactivating the runes."

"Which is all well and good, but it's not enough." He paused and shook his head again. "When Callyn asked me to look for you, I did nothing. Only when I traveled for myself did I keep a vague eye out, but it would be a stretch to consider what I did actually *looking.*"

His gaze drifted off to the side. "Many years ago, I passed through this area once or twice. I sensed the runes and wondered if you had been snatched up by whatever Arch-Vampire laid claim to the area, but I didn't investigate much further. It was nothing less than shameful. Even if I knew you weren't here, I should have done everything in my power to help anyone else held captive. Instead, I did nothing."

He hung his head miserably. "I damned my friends the moment I drank our master's blood. Because I stay out of their lives, they essentially have the same freedom as any truly liberated Vampire, but it doesn't matter. They're still tied to me and will be as long as I live." It took a few moments for him to look at me again. "I'm sick of wallowing in isolation as a reprehensible coward. Tyrran told me everything, and I wish to help you defeat Roänach. If you'll have me."

At first, all I could do was stare in shock.

No wonder Callyn defended him.

"I accept and appreciate your help, more than you'll ever know." I paused for a moment. "You're truly willing to risk your life for this?"

"I am, but don't give me too much credit. I'm risking nothing of value." He averted his gaze again. "To be clear, Roänach's death is the only one I seek, but if he kills me first, so be it. At least I'll have died trying to do the right thing for once."

I offered a small smile. "Well, whatever happens, thank you."

He just nodded and headed back to the cave mouth to wait.

Once Vernyth was out of earshot, Shade leaned down closer to my ear. "I couldn't get him to smile once," he whispered, sounding bummed.

"Don't blame yourself. He doesn't have much to smile about," I whispered back. "Hopefully, this will be a new beginning for him."

Trying to make up for past mistakes seems like a good start.

All of a sudden, Fiella's voice sounded behind us. "What can we do to help?"

I turned to find her, Haana, and Lánelli now standing. "Stay here and be safe. Please."

Fiella pouted. "That's not helping."

"I know, but Tyrran can't carry all of us." I grinned at him before pulling her into a hug. "I have no idea what to expect, but knowing you're out of harm's way will help put my mind at ease."

She nodded reluctantly and clung to me. "Please be safe too."

"This will all be over soon…" Once we released each other, I took the small portrait out of my boot and handed it to her. "Will you hold on to this for me?"

She clutched it to her chest and blinked away a few tears. "Y-You have to come back for it."

A light chuckle slipped out. "That *is* my intention."

"P-Promise."

Seeing the fear in her eyes, I pulled her into another hug and held the back of her head. "I promise I'll be alright. I came back this time, didn't I?"

After dying horribly…

She sniffled and buried her face in my chest. "Don't let Roänach win."

"He's about to be the biggest loser in all of Terraen." When we separated, I took off my flower crown and set it on her head. "Do you have any idea how hard I worked on that? Now I *really* have to come back."

She cracked a small smile and huddled into Lánelli's arms instead, still clutching the portrait as if her life depended on it.

Meanwhile, Haana offered a tense nod. "Good luck, Athaeÿn."

"Thank you."

We'll need it.

After saying our see-you-laters, we joined Vernyth near the exit.

I stood in front of Shade and patted his arm. "When we reach Eidolon, we'll go straight to the citadel to find out what's happening. That's most likely where your mothers will be."

"Alright, but what if Roänach escapes and comes back here?" He glanced over his shoulder at Fiella, Haana, and Lánelli. "I'm glad I don't have to leave you behind, but now I'm worried about them."

"Just beat him here. You can move faster as a shadow than he can fly as a swarm of bats."

"You think so?"

"I know so, but we'll make sure it doesn't come to that."

He still looked concerned but didn't argue as he turned back around and secured me to his chest. "I don't feel good…"

"I don't either. We'll feel better once this is over."

"I hope you're right."

As Shade flew out of the cave into the cool night air, I was relieved not to be ripped from his arms by an invisible wall.

Wow, it really did work.

Unfortunately, this brief satisfaction was swiftly razed by the two warring factions within me. One wanted nothing more than to confront Roänach. The other wanted to avoid it at all costs. Both used my broken heart as the battlefield.

At least I don't have to kill him myself.

Even if that was an option, I wasn't sure I could do it. Thinking about it was one thing. Doing it was another entirely. It didn't matter how much I hated him.

Please just let this nightmare finally end…

Chapter 29

Athaeÿn

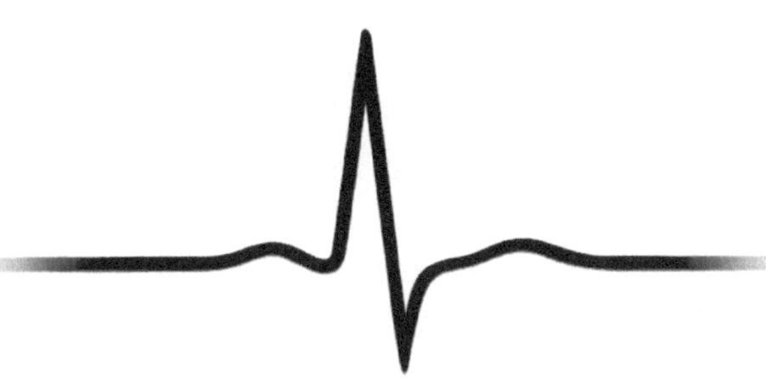

It was still dark when we finally approached Soaring Sanctum, the formidable mountain decorated by the sprawling metropolis of Eidolon. From a distance, there was nothing out of the ordinary, but that meant little when it came to Roänach. He was an expert at hiding in plain sight.

I hope his arrogance finally gets the best of him.

Considering his history of patience and paranoia, he must have seen this as his best or only chance and taken it, especially if he thought Xythe died in that unknown darkness. Even if he hadn't presumed Xythe's death, the queens flying in that direction wouldn't have looked good, regardless of phenomenon to investigate. What mattered was they had left Eidolon vulnerable.

Why are people like Xythe and Roänach never content with what they have?

It was a shame the former was dead. They would've made a perfect creepy couple.

Maybe then they would've been content and left people alone.

I shook my head.

No, they would've just enabled each other even more.

With a tired sigh, I refocused on the task ahead. After pondering for a few seconds, I glanced over at Vernyth's bat swarm. "Are you coming with us to the citadel?"

His voice cut through the chattering. "I doubt the queens would appreciate my presence. No, I'll be more useful looking for Roänach in the city and intervening when and if he shows himself."

"Fair enough."

"Here—" Some of the bats condensed into an outstretched hand clutching a wooden stake. "I know you can't use it yourself, so give it to Tyrran once you land. I have more in my coat's inner pockets."

"Thank you," I took the stake and carefully shoved it into my boot so I wouldn't drop it, "and good luck."

"You as well." Once his hand separated into bats again, his swarm broke away so he could reform elsewhere.

Meanwhile, Shade readjusted his arms around me. "Most Arch-Vampires aren't like Vernyth, right? Could Roänach have been planning with others of their kind?"

"He only mentioned Xythe, but it's possible." My grip tightened. "I certainly hope not."

"Actually, if he came right here after my mothers flew over, then it's probably just him and enthralled Demons. Forget what I said..."

I thought for a moment. "You know, we just assumed he made a break for Eidolon. We don't actually have proof. Maybe he..." My theory ground to a halt. "No, he has to be here. He wouldn't have passed up an opportunity like this, and I don't think other Arch-Vampires would join him anyway."

"Why not?"

"I get the impression they generally prefer keeping to themselves. Xythe wanted revenge but was otherwise content with his own little kingdom, and I think most Arch-Vampires feel the same way. There's not much incentive for them to come here and risk death when they're already sovereign individuals, even if just in secret."

"That's true… So, why does Roänach want Eidolon so badly?"

"He's a self-important prick who thinks he's entitled to whatever he wants, whether it be sex slaves, nameless servants, or excessive real estate. Apparently, an entire castle full of vassals, enthralled Demons, and helpless blood captives isn't enough."

Shade huffed with disgust. "Well, I think it's about time he loses everything."

My throat tightened. "Agreed."

Including his life…

It wasn't long before we reached the mountain and flew into the immense cavern sheltering the interior districts. The first thing I noticed was how sparsely populated the streets were. The sight likely would have worried some, but I was glad to see it.

Should mean less chaos when the time comes.

A couple of guards approached when we landed outside the citadel, one of whom nodded to the entrance. "The queens are in the war room."

Wait—

I narrowed my eyes at him. "Are they expecting someone?"

"According to them, 'an Arbiter carrying a Dark Elf.'"

The other guard raised her hand slightly. "In particular, 'A good-looking Vampire who will refuse to be contained by a bunch of bullshit rocks,' I believe Daryn specified. Oh, 'and a big, red momma's boy who will show up to help even though he was told to stay put, courtesy of his boyfriend's nagging…'" she relayed, averting her gaze awkwardly. "Again, Daryn's words, not mine…"

Oh.

When I peered at Shade, his eyes were wide with embarrassment.

"I, uhhh… I guess I am kind of predictable," he muttered, trying and failing to obscure my view of his intense blush. Not even his giant hand could hide all of it.

I couldn't help but snort an unattractive laugh. It was nice to have a brief moment of levity before everything went to shit. "You and I both, apparently." I patted his arm and headed for the door. "Remind me to smack Daryn later."

The things that man gets away with saying, I swear…

Shade hurried after me and took a deep breath once inside the building. "Phew… I thought there would be more people out there."

"It tends to be less busy at night, but it did look unusually barren. I'm sure your mothers enacted some kind of plan the second they got here."

When we entered the war room, Elvylli, Sathira, and the Captain of the Guard, who was an Inverse Demon, were busy discussing something marked on a giant map of the city painted on the back wall. A moment later, all three turned and stared at us. The queens didn't look happy.

Uh-oh—

Shade paled and pointed a shaky finger at me. "He made me come here."

Gee, thanks.

I glanced at the queens, but their eyes remained locked on him.

His breathing turned shallow. "A-Are you mad at me?"

Elvylli folded her arms. "For what? Wanting to help?"

Before he could say anything, she came over and pulled him into a tight hug, an embrace he returned with a sigh of relief.

Sathira approached as well and rubbed his shoulder. "We knew you wouldn't be able to stay away, sweetheart." Her attention shifted to me. "Desperate times call for desperate measures, hm?"

My chest tightened, but there was no use lying. "I asked Shade to get Vernyth…"

"I know."

At least she seems more open-minded than Daryn.

She tilted her head a little. "You didn't need to endanger yourself like this."

"Until Roänach dies, I'm in danger no matter where he is. Besides, he's *my* scumbag master. I can't just do nothing while others deal with him for me."

"Athaeÿn, no vassal is obligated to clean up their master's mess."

"I know, but I *want* to help… somehow…" I sighed and folded my arms. "What have you done so far? Maybe your efforts will help me think of something."

She smiled. "You may not be able to kill Roänach, but we just so happen to have an idea that will allow you to get involved," her gaze drifted to Shade, "and *you're* the key element."

His eyes widened. "Me?"

Elvylli finally released him from her hug. "We've been working on multiple plans, some of which rely on you, most of which don't. We were prepared to act if you never showed up, but now that you're here," she looked rather pleased, "we have the opportunity to go forward with my favorite plan."

Shade looked anything but pleased. "Does it involve my magic?"

"It does."

He frowned at his hand and balled it up against his chest. "No, it's useless…"

"I think you'll change your mind once you hear us out."

His neck muscles tensed as he stared at the floor. When he looked at his mothers again, his eyes were misty with frustration, and his quiet, shaky voice reflected it. "I *really* want to help."

Sathira smiled and caressed his cheek with her thumb. "Don't worry, sweetheart, we're about to tell you how." She then turned back to the map. "Announcing a citywide lockdown was tempting, but we didn't want to incite panic, especially without knowing Roänach's whereabouts or the extent of his forces. Instead, we tasked the guards with discreetly encouraging people to go home and lock their doors."

Shade looked alarmed. "But, couldn't he just break into people's homes?"

I glanced at him. "Vampires can't enter private residences without direct invitation."

"Oh. That's… interesting."

Sathira nodded. "Normally, we would have people shelter in the citadel, but its protection is meant for danger yet to arrive, danger we can see coming. This threat is already in the city. Flocking here would just draw attention, and we may already be compromised. We can't risk it."

Shade still looked worried. "Alright, but what about his enthralled Demons?" He paused and turned to me. "Is he only using Demons?"

"Probably. Almost everyone wears enchanted clothing and jewelry to protect against enthrallment, so it's easier for him to kill people and use their souls to summon confused and vulnerable Demons. Between their superior strength and magical abilities," my gaze drifted to the Captain of the Guard, who was likely three times stronger than me despite being a foot shorter, "they're way more useful for him to control."

The Captain nodded. "Especially if used to multiply his forces," he removed one of his gauntlets and flourished his claws, "as we're never without the tools necessary for siphoning souls."

I couldn't help but think of Roänach's box of sharpened Demon bones. Having the equivalent on one's hands would indeed be more convenient.

The Captain put his gauntlet back on and looked at Shade. "I hope to minimize such activity. With the ability to reverse enthrallment, my fellow Inverse Demons will do what they can to thin his forces. It will be a relief to do so without violence."

Meanwhile, Elvylli joined her wife at the map. "Even if that wasn't an option, there should be enough guards stationed throughout the city to prevent break-ins, and we've made it clear lethal force is an absolute last resort. After all, Roänach's Demons are victims as well." She said nothing for a moment. "Civilian safety is our top priority, so the goal is to get as many people out of harm's way as possible before confronting Roänach. We have no idea how many enthralled Demons he has." She sighed and shook her head. "He doesn't need even more hostages."

Shade nervously toyed with his hands. "So, what exactly is your plan, and why is it your favorite?"

"It's my favorite because it should minimize altercations from all sides." She turned back around to look at him. "We want you to cloak the entire city in darkness."

His eyes shot wide with horror. "What?!"

Ah, I see where this is going.

I put my hand on his arm. "Shade, please hear them out."

"But—"

"You'll be helping just like you wanted. I promise."

He took a deep breath and looked at his mothers again. "I don't understand. No one will be able to see anything."

Elvylli smiled. "Including the enthralled Demons. Roänach will still be able to see, but so will every Vampire in the city. They've spread the word amongst themselves and are prepared to guide people to safety right under the Demons' noses. With everyone else out of reach and his backup effectively useless, we're hoping he skips to coming after me and Sathira."

My chest tightened. "Will Daryn be waiting to ambush him?"

Sathira grinned. "He may get that opportunity, but we need him for something else first." Her gaze drifted to Shade. "Before I continue, what do you think so far, Tyrran?"

He swallowed hard and looked at his claws again. "I don't have to hurt anyone?"

"Far from it, sweetheart."

Still focused on his hand, he summoned a sphere of darkness on his palm and altered its size a few times, seemingly keeping it under perfect control. As he stared at it, the corner of his mouth pulled into a tentative smile.

I waved my hand through the void to remind him it wasn't inherently harmful. "And, you'll be able to help us bring people indoors."

He briefly glanced at me before expanding the sphere to the edges of the room. When he dismissed it, he looked at his mothers with cautious optimism. "I think I can do it."

Sathira tilted her head slightly. "Are you absolutely sure? We would never force you."

His smile brightened. "If I can really help that many people, then yes, I *want* to."

"Thank you, sweetheart." She beamed with pride for a moment before turning more serious. "In the meantime, Elvylli and I will be here using the vocal rune network to announce important code words. If you hear *blackout*, it means Tyrran should darken the city. If you hear *daylight*, it means the darkness can be retracted, but don't let the term worry you. It should still be nighttime."

I nodded. "Good to know. Any others?"

"Just one, and arguably the most important. If you hear *torrent*, every Vampire needs to get off the ground immediately. I suggest the sturdy walls separating the streets."

I don't like the sound of that.

"Now then," she gestured to the door, "you two should head out and take up good positions. There's no telling when Roänach will strike, and I'd rather you be ready and waiting instead of scrambling."

Shade put a hand on my shoulder. "I want you to come with me."

I looked up at him and shook my head. "You need to go wherever you're needed most, and I won't be able to keep up."

"But, you can't defend yourself against Roänach."

"The other Vampires will have my back." I rested my hand on his. "Shade, I appreciate your concern for my safety, truly, but I don't want to be treated like a fragile doll who can't take care of myself. I need you to have a little more faith in me. Please."

His eyes widened a little, but, instead of arguing, he managed a worried smile. "You're right. I'm sorry."

"Thank you." After gesturing for him to lean down, I gripped his intact horn and pulled him in for a kiss. "Now shoo. I'm sure we'll run into each other during the chaos."

"At least promise me you'll be safe."

"I promise."

He nuzzled my face before smiling at his mothers. "You too."

Sathira smiled back. "Of course, sweetheart. You as well."

Elvylli waved. "You've got this."

He summoned one last sphere of darkness in his hand and stared at it. "I've got this." By the time he dismissed it, he was smiling brightly. "I can do it. I can help everyone!"

As Shade dissolved into a large shadow on the floor and rushed out, Elvylli spoke up behind me. "Good luck, Athaeÿn. Take care of yourself out there."

My gaze was still locked on the threshold. "I'll try."

"Roänach will be dead before sunrise. You have my word."

I nodded tensely. "Thank you."

This is it.

Chapter 30

Athaeÿn

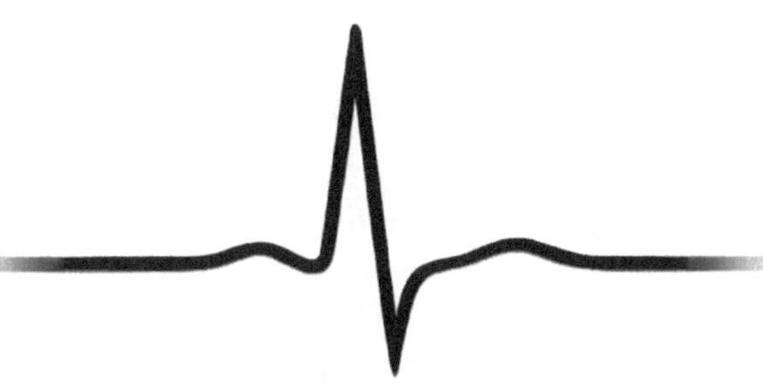

When I left the citadel, even fewer people were out than before.
Looks like the guards have been productive.
Some of said people were Demons, but not as many as I expected.
Maybe most of his forces are hiding.
It was then I spotted Daryn leaning on a wall nearby, seemingly engrossed in a book, the title of which was obscured by a folded piece of paper draped over the cover. I approached to talk to him but took a second to read the handwritten, substitute title neatly penned on the paper.

Reasonable Men and Their Idiot Friends Who Won't
Stop Talking to That Fucking Arch-Vampire

By Disregarded Daryn

I sighed and pinched the bridge of my nose.

And he called Elvylli dramatic…

He didn't look up from the book. "Curious to see you here."

"Is it, though?"

"Hmm," he flipped a page way louder than necessary, "I suppose what's truly curious is your decision to involve a *second* Arch-Vampire in this mess."

"I had to get past the bullshit rocks somehow."

His eyes tensed as he stared at the page. "You're not safe here."

"Better than cowering miles away."

After a long pause, he finally looked at me. "Vernyth is here, isn't he?"

I nodded.

He averted his gaze and shook his head. "If he somehow manages to trip and fall into helping us, perhaps I could be persuaded to at least shake his hand before killing him."

I folded my arms. "I've only known him for a few hours, but I felt his remorse in minutes. *Real* remorse. I truly believe he would never hurt innocents on purpose. More importantly, he's willing to lay down his life fighting Roänach."

"Good, maybe we can get rid of two Arch-Vampires at once."

A huff slipped out. "Will you *please* just give him a chance?"

"I *am* giving him a chance. It's up to him to prove any usefulness outside of death."

I waited for him to look at me. When he didn't, I sighed heavily and averted my gaze as well. "I suppose that's all I can ask…"

"It's all you're getting."

Neither of us said anything for a minute.

Daryn was the one to break the silence. "I'm not angry with you."

"Really? Could've fooled me."

He shook his head. "I'm sorry, Athaeÿn, I can't trust Vernyth. I just can't. I've seen far too much suffering at the hands of Arch-Vampires to give even one a chance that none deserve in the first place. Redeemable or not, none should exist. That's just how it has to be."

The defeat in his tone was all too familiar.

I know, Daryn. I'm tired too.

My gaze dropped to his book. "I'm not asking you to trust him." I plucked the loose paper off the cover and folded it into a bookmark, which I gently placed in the middle of the open pages. "I just want you to see he's not what you think."

After staring at the blank bookmark for at least a minute, he finally looked at me again. "I suppose I wouldn't mind being proven wrong just this once."

I was relieved to see his demeanor soften. "Vernyth or no Vernyth, Roänach is a confirmed threat. I promise we'll get him."

"Pff, how quaint of you to reassure *me* when this is *your* master we're talking about."

"In my defense, he's a danger to everyone. I'll make sure he never hurts anyone again, even if it's the last thing I do."

He shook his head and waggled his finger. "No, no, no. You've already died twice, my friend. You're not allowed to die a third time."

"Shade would agree, so make sure your plan works." I smiled and began walking away. "And he's not a big, red momma's boy!"

"Yes he is!"

I was still grinning to myself as I continued making my way down the streets, but my amusement faded when a guard ran past me toward the citadel.

Uh oh—

I paused to look around and spotted a different guard speaking with a Human teenager. The girl smiled and nodded when bid farewell, but her expression turned eerily blank once the guard's back was to her. Instead of leaving, she just kept standing there.

Why aren't you going home?

As I hesitantly considered approaching, yet another guard came around the corner but stopped dead in her tracks when she noticed the girl. This guard was a Mirage Demon.

Wait—

All of a sudden, a lone firework went off above the exterior districts, drawing both my and the guard's attention.

Shit—

I whipped back around to find the girl charging me, now grinning wildly with manic bloodlust in her eyes. She was wearing shoes, but her footfalls made the distinct sound of claws scraping the ground.

I knew it—

She had yet to reach me when the vocal runes lit up with a loud hum.

"Blackout."

Just one second later, everything went pitch-black.

Good job, Shade.

I switched to thermal vision just in time to see my attacker come to a screeching halt a few feet away. Sure enough, the illusion of a Human girl was betrayed by her heat signature, which revealed the unmistakable form of a Mirage Demon. Fortunately, the darkness had left her looking around blindly and hissing profanities under her breath.

Please just stay there—

A cry rang out nearby. To my dismay, her head snapped toward it, and I was further mortified by the sight of what appeared to be a young couple holding two small children.

Why are they out here?!

I watched the Mirage Demon for a few moments to see what she would do. Luckily, while she did make an attempt to feel her way toward where the sound had come from, she moved incredibly slowly and slightly off course from where the family stood.

Good.

Without further hesitation, I rushed over as quickly but quietly as possible. "Don't panic, the blackout is meant to protect you," I said just loud enough for them to hear, keeping an eye on the Mirage Demon over my shoulder as I carefully herded them toward the closest building. Fortunately, my touch anxiety remained minimal.

As the woman attempted to quiet the toddler in her arms, she kept her voice low as well despite sounding a bit frantic. "What's happening?"

"Arch-Vampire with enthralled Demons. Lock the door and don't let anyone in," I whispered back, gently pushing them inside and closing the door behind them. After some muffled fumbling on the other side, the lock clicked into place.

This might actually work.

I set about ushering every non-Demon civilian I came across into any unlocked building I could find, regardless of private residency or not. At this point, just getting them off the streets was more important. It felt shitty ignoring every Demon in my path, but I genuinely couldn't tell which were enthralled. I couldn't risk anything.

When I reached the gap in the mountainside, a familiar, rapidly approaching presence froze me where I stood. Sure enough, when I looked out over the descending exterior districts, the undulating color spectrum of an aggressive bat swarm was barreling my way.

No—

Just as I was about to panic, a second swarm flew over my head from behind and intercepted Roänach before he could reach the cavern. An immense wave of relief just about knocked me over, and I was left gawking as the two masses clashed in a giant, writhing cloud of screeching chaos.

Thank you, Vernyth.

After taking a moment to collect myself, I headed out to the exterior districts and resumed helping people indoors. Fortunately, the streets were already pretty clear of non-Demon civilians thanks to the head start provided by the guards, but with most of them now unable to see, my fellow Vampires had picked up where they left off.

I kept an eye on the raging bat swarm but was repeatedly distracted by the efforts all around me. Of the many Vampires working tirelessly to get others to safety, the vast majority were just regular civilians. The few who were guards primarily teamed up with Inverse Demons and guided them through the darkness to free any enthralled Demons they could find. I had already seen quite a few instances of success.

The Captain of the Guard will be pleased.

I actually got a bit emotional seeing so many of my kind working together to protect the city from one of our own.

See, Roänach? No one wants you here.

When I turned down the next street, it was entirely clear of living civilians.

Hopefully, that means most of the city is secure by now.

Other than a few living guards who had been placed in front of some doors, the only people out in the open were Vampires, all of whom were watching the screeching tempest high overhead. One of the dark silhouettes was unusually familiar, and I nearly tripped in shock when they spoke to the person next to them.

That voice—

I could barely move. "Callyn?"

The Vampire in question flinched. "What—" They slowly turned until they were facing me. "I-It can't be—"

Time stopped as we stared at each other.

"Athaeÿn?"

Callyn—

We collided in an almost violent embrace before I even realized what was happening. Three centuries of missing my best friend had shoved aside any and all anxiety I may have felt from their touch.

I thought I'd never see them again.

They broke down sobbing into my chest. "I-It's really you—"

"It's me." I struggled to remain composed while cradling the back of their head. "I missed you so much."

"I looked for you so many times. I-I was afraid you were dead."

My throat tightened. "Well—"

"Wait, how did you—" As quickly as they had flung their arms around me, they pulled back and looked me up and down with increasing panic. "No… No, no, *no!*" Their trembling hands gripped my shoulders tightly. "Why do you look like that?!"

Guilt poured from the wound inflicted by their anguish.

"Callyn—"

"What happened?! *Who turned you?!*"

I winced slightly from their enraged shout, but my heart hurt far more than my ears. I had never seen them this angry before.

I'm so sorry, Callyn.

Heavy with shame, I slowly pointed at the warring bats overhead. "Roänach, the Arch-Vampire trying to take over the city… The man I left with all those years ago…"

It never gets easier to admit…

Callyn glared up at the swarms. "If Vernyth doesn't kill him, I'll tear his throat out myself." There was a pause before they looked at me with surprise. "Wait, if you and Vernyth are both here, does that mean he actually took my letter seriously?"

"He *is* the one who deactivated our runes, but he didn't exactly find me. It's a long story."

"I see. Well, I'm just glad he's helping." They paused again to look around. "By the way, do you know who's wielding this darkness?"

"The queens didn't say anything?"

"Not much, just that they found whoever was responsible for the giant void on the horizon and that they might show up to help. I assume the secrecy is a tactical choice, but I'm not really sure what difference it would make. Seems weirdly cryptic for them."

I averted my gaze a bit awkwardly. "I'm pretty sure they're being purposefully cryptic to avoid additional chaos and confusion."

"Sounds like you know their identity."

"I do, but that's an even longer story." I pulled them into another hug. "Speaking of which, I'm heading out to look for this person and to make sure no other civilians were missed."

They hugged me back. "Can I go with you?"

"I appreciate the offer, but you should stay here to help watch over this street."

"Athaeÿn—"

"I'll be alright. Vernyth is keeping Roänach distracted."

"Mm-hmm…" They exhaled heavily. "At least promise you'll stay close to other Vampires so you have backup in case he sees you."

"That's what I've been doing so far."

They nodded and squeezed me tightly. "Please be careful."

"Of course." I pulled back with a grin. "We can't catch up if I'm dead."

"Yeah, *Undead* is bad enough, so don't make it worse."

A bit late for that…

I continued down the road and waved over my shoulder as I rounded the corner, knowing full well Callyn had seen right through my excuses and deflections.

Please forgive me.

As much as I would've loved their company and support, I couldn't risk their safety if Roänach came after me. He was already terrorizing the city. I didn't want him anywhere near my best friend.

Roänach is my responsibility.

Everything seemed fine at first, but I became increasingly unnerved when each street had fewer Vampires than the previous. When I wandered into a market lane and found it completely vacant, my concern elevated to alarm.

Wait, I think I hear voices—

Knowing isolation could be a death sentence, I started running but only got halfway down the street when the vocal runes hummed again.

"Torrent."

I skidded to a stop.

While it's still pitch-black?!

Wasting no time, I clambered onto the four-foot-high wall to my left that lined the outer edge of the street. Once situated, I looked back up the ascending levels and saw two distinct heat signatures fly out of the mountain, one of whom appeared somewhat obscured by a smaller, dark shape. The unobscured figure proceeded to summon an enormous cloud that was nearly black in my thermal vision.

Alright, that's Sathira—

A few moments later, the dark shape partially obscuring Elvylli gestured toward the freezing cloud, prompting her to unleash a blindingly bright and equally massive wave of fire directly at it.

Ah, so that's what they needed Daryn for.

The force of the queens' combined magic resulted in a torrential waterfall cascading down and flooding the streets. I could only assume the water would knock over everything and everyone in its path, especially with the subtle downslope of the roads. When the rapids arrived at my street and rushed past, however, they weren't nearly as aggressive as I expected. The current wasn't even fast enough to mist me.

What exactly is the point of this?

As though answering my question, the sound of crackling ice began echoing down the mountain. When I looked toward the higher end of the road, the lingering flood stopped moving and darkened in my vision as a wave of freezing passed by, leaving the entire street submerged in a layer of ice at least a foot thick. Glancing down at the adjacent street, I saw a handful of Demons and non-Vampire guards stuck in said ice but standing upright and seemingly unharmed.

Oh, that's the point.

With running water no longer a threat, I gingerly slipped off the wall and crouched down to touch the ice with my bare hand. At most, its chill was similar to that of cool stone.

Good. The last thing we need is rampant frostbite.

The rapid flooding aspect of their plan wasn't my favorite, but I appreciated how simple and effective the ice was. Fortunately, it was highly unlikely that any Demons who were still enthralled would be able to free themselves. Demons were strong, but Arbiter magic was stronger.

Now, we just have to deal with Roänach.

As I stood back up, my hand brushed against the wooden stake Vernyth had given me. It was still sticking out of my boot.

Shit.

My stomach plummeted.

I forgot to give it to Shade...

All of a sudden, the screeching bats overhead crashed down and reformed both Arch-Vampires at the end of my street. Vernyth was nearly incapacitated by overwhelming damage, but he did manage to prop himself up on his elbow, albeit with a severely pained groan.

Come on, get up!

Roänach wasn't much better off but, to my dismay, was in good enough shape to crawl over to Vernyth and snatch a spare wooden stake that had fallen out of his overcoat.

No—

He shakily got to his feet and flashed a bloody grin. "Mind if I borrow this?" he sneered, kicking Vernyth in the face hard enough to break his neck before plunging the stake into his heart.

No...

My eyes burned as he went limp.

I'm so sorry, Vernyth...

As Roänach crouched down and sank his fangs into the defeated Arch-Vampire's neck, the vocal runes hummed again.

"Daylight."

The darkness vanished a few seconds later, leaving me and Roänach alone in the icy street.

Oh no—

Locked in wide-eyed terror, I barely noticed my vision switch back to normal all on its own.

Shade, help me—

The ice wasn't cold, but my feet were frozen.

Please—

A painful shudder racked my body when Roänach stood with ease, having fully healed thanks to Vernyth's Arch-Vampire blood resonating with his own.

Anyone—

The dread that consumed my entire being when he slowly turned and looked at me was indescribable. His completely blank expression was the most terrifying thing I had ever seen.

H-Help—

Chapter 31

Athaeÿn

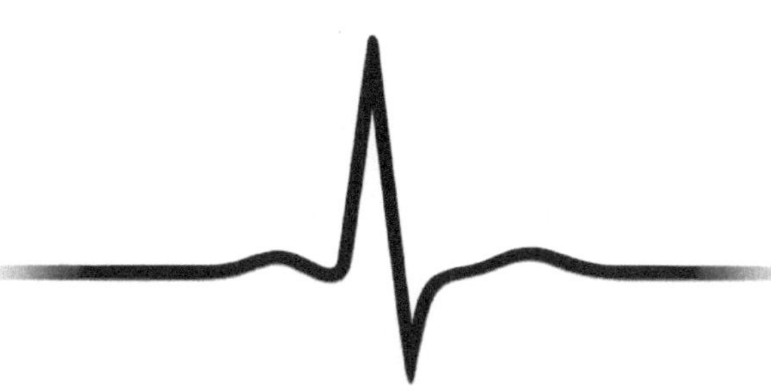

Roänach and just I stared at each other in dead silence. He hadn't moved a single muscle since we made eye contact, but I had never felt more helpless and afraid in my entire life. This stillness was somehow worse than both of my murders.

I should've stayed with Callyn—

My shoulders trembled as my eyes frantically darted across his face, trying to find even the smallest hint of emotion. Anger. Disappointment. Frustration. *Anything.*

There was nothing.

Shade, I need you—

Any rage I had saved for this moment was gone.

Shade, please—

All my determination evaporated, allowing endless, unchecked fear to fill the void. I desperately searched for the gall I had thrown in Roänach's face when refusing to be sent away, but I couldn't find it. My desire for revenge was supposed to be giving me strength. All I had was shot nerves and broken courage.

Shade…

I had reached the breaking point when spurning Roänach in his study. Other than fading memories of loved ones and pathetic attempts to protect the other vassals, I'd had almost nothing to lose at the time. That was no longer the case.

I had been reminded of how much friendship meant to me.

I still had to find my parents.

I had promised Lune to make the most of my life.

There were people waiting to be freed.

Shade and I had devoted ourselves to each other.

But I didn't get to tell him how I truly feel.

I had everything to lose this time.

And I'm about to lose it all.

Roänach finally moved.

Oh no—

In my deteriorating mental state, I instinctively drew the wooden stake from my boot and pointed it right at him, knowing full well the gesture was useless. My entire body was shaking and panicking. There was no doubt in my mind I looked like an imbecile, awkwardly clutching the stake with both hands and holding it at arm's length as if hoping he would just walk into it.

I didn't know what else to do.

Between the slippery ice and the fact he could easily outpace me as a swarm of bats, there was no point in trying to run. If anything, that would just get me killed faster.

At least he's not in a hurry for some reason.

His oddly calm demeanor was still terrifying, but I tried latching onto it instead.

It's not over yet.

I forced myself to take a few deep breaths.

There's still time to turn this around.

As he continued his slow approach, something in me snapped. The closer he got, the more this feeling shifted and fell apart as if nothing more than broken pottery. To my genuine surprise, it was my paralyzing fear. Like a sundered shield, its cracks were further split by a force they could no longer hold back. Everything began seeping through.

The pain and misery.

I trusted him, and he betrayed me.

My dread faded with each step he took.

I loved him, and he killed me.

My shoulders heaved with loathing.

He ruined my life for no reason.

He had sealed his fate long ago.

I hate him.

It hurt to accept.

I hate him so fucking much.

But I had to.

I hate him even more than myself.

And I finally did.

I want him dead.

By the time he reached me, I stood tall and confident with my arms folded defiantly, having slipped the wooden stake back into my boot long before he arrived. Our steadfast eye contact only intensified now that we stood face-to-face with the toes of our boots almost touching.

I've waited so long for this moment.

Shade was undoubtedly scouring the city for me, so it was only a matter of time before he showed up.

I just need to stall.

"Took your sweet time sauntering over here."

Roänach's blank expression turned into a calm smile. "Had you met me halfway, some of those precious minutes of yours could have been salvaged."

"True, but I was also hoping you would slip and fall on your face."

"Charming. Is the anticipation of my suffering your only source of arousal these days?"

"Lighting your funeral pyre is a close second."

His smile faded as he put his hands on his hips. "You know," he shook his head and sighed dramatically, "I dare say I took Polite Athaeÿn for granted." He then pulled the wooden stake from my boot and used it to point over his shoulder at Vernyth's body. "Though it would seem you've maintained at least a speck of common courtesy. Why else accept a gift you can't even use?"

"Who says it was for me?"

He didn't bother looking around to see if we were alone. "Then why do you have it?"

"I forgot to give it to the intended recipient."

His brows went up a little. "Interesting choice of circumstances to prove that centuries of deception haven't robbed you of all integrity."

When I said nothing, he headed over to the wall and peered down at the next street. I could hear the Demons trying and, thankfully, failing to claw through the ice around their feet.

Hopefully, they're not hurting themselves.

After watching for a few seconds, he came back over and stared at me expectantly, but I remained silent.

This time, his voice had a slight edge to it. "I'm waiting."

My arms were still folded. "For what?"

"Do you really think you're in a position to test my patience?"

"You could've just asked how I pulled this off, but you're allergic to rational conversation."

"Tension is more titillating." He shook his head again. "Well, now that the topic has been so eloquently broached, do enlighten me as to how you managed to single-handedly ruin everything."

"I had quite a bit of help ruining everything, actually."

"Is Xythe dead?"

"Yes, but not by my hand."

"That was never my assumption. Your otherwise talented hands are inept when it comes to violence."

"Which is a shame, considering your face is within reach."

His gaze lazily drifted off to the side. "How fortunate for me…" he mumbled, briefly toying with the stake before pausing and narrowing his eyes at my chest.

Shit. He senses you, Lune—

Without warning, he violently gripped my throat with one hand, but I was more startled than surprised. This was nothing new for him. He had strangled me with lethal force many times during sex, so I knew this was different. In fact, I knew exactly what he was doing.

At least I don't have to feign enjoyment anymore.

It had always been difficult to do so. Just because Undead couldn't be choked to death didn't mean it wasn't painful, and this time was no exception. I tried to remain stoic, but a small grunt still slipped out when he dug his thumb as hard as he could into the soft underside of my jaw.

This isn't even a good excuse to touch me.

Fortunately, his attempt at enthrallment didn't work.

Would you please just let go already—

When he finally did, I refused to rub my neck but couldn't stop myself from coughing a few times. It felt like his hand was still there.

Meanwhile, he glared at my chest again. "It almost feels like a soul, but…" He shook his head once more and found my gaze. "What is it?"

"A dear friend."

He scoffed loudly. *"Please.* All of your friends have either died or forgotten you."

I sighed even louder than his scoff. "Look, as much as I would love a typical, romantic evening of being insulted for hours on end, don't you have better things to do?"

A casual grin returned to his face. "Yes, as a matter of fact. All of this admirable effort will have been in vain once I regroup and launch a second invasion." He dragged the tip of the stake down my facial scar. "A *successful* one."

"By adding one more Demon? Yeah, that might do it."

He repositioned the tip of the stake to my throat. "My plans won't concern the dead."

"Killing me and leaving so soon?" I put on a laughably fake pout. "But I've rather enjoyed your insufferable monologuing."

Any day now, Shade—

He tilted his head with an unwavering smile. "If you're going to continue stalling, at least make it a bit less obvious."

"We both know I can't fool you anyway."

"Too true, so why don't we put an end to this charade?" He pressed the tip of the stake harder against my neck, enough to indent my skin but not pierce it. "Once you're dead, I'll have all the time in the world to come up with an improved plan."

I grunted a little from the pressure on my throat. "I wouldn't be so sure of that."

"Your bluffing needs work as well."

"I'm not bluffing."

His smile fractured ever so slightly. "Care to elaborate?"

"I took the queens to Castle Veil on the way here." It was my turn to smugly tilt my head. "I'm afraid you'll have to find a new secret fortress."

The look on his face was priceless.

Worth every second of misery.

His smile was long gone. "You—"

"Rat bastard. Yes, I know." I put on a neutral expression to match my deadpan tone. "Do you need a minute? This must be very upsetting for you."

His hand trembled with rage as he retracted the stake and pointed it at my face. "You… have become *far* more trouble than you're worth."

I didn't break eye contact. "Maybe you should have left me alone from the beginning."

"Maybe I should have." He pressed the weapon to my chest this time. "And yet, it's because of *me* you have any value whatsoever."

"That's not going to work on me, jackass."

"Won't it?" He twisted the stake into my shirt and hissed through his teeth. "You were *nothing* when I found you. Just a lonely, desperate *slut,* willing to throw your whole life away the moment someone pretended to show genuine interest."

I felt Lune's worry but ignored it. There was no backing down now.

I've had it.

And yet, my glare of pure hatred was betrayed by the burn of heartbreak. "That's rich coming from a parasite who turned his castle into a fucking *brothel* so his dick would never dry."

"I just know what I like and take what I can find."

"Like how you took everything from me."

"As if you're free of blame. Unlike innocent, kidnapped Fiella, you eagerly gave yourself away."

"And I've never regretted anything more in my entire *life!*" I leaned forward on the stake and pointed a shaky finger right between his eyes. "You're nothing more than a rapist and a murderer."

"And you're nothing more than a slave and a whore." His words flowed with gut-wrenching ease as he got right in my face. "I never felt a single fucking thing for you. No one ever has."

Tears finally came to my eyes. "Th-That's not true."

"Your history of failure says otherwise." He leaned so close I could taste his breath. "You have never been anything more than a means to an end."

Shut up—

"A tool to be used and discarded."

Stop—

His lips brushed against mine. *"Scraps."*

P-Please—

It was at that moment I realized Shade still hadn't come for me.

Wait—

And just like that, my resolve shattered.

N-No—

Roänach was wrong.

He *had* to be wrong.

He just knows how to get to me—

Shade was different from the others. I was something truly special to him. He had said so himself. He had meant it. I had seen it in his eyes. He was going to show up at any second. He was going to save me.

I won't be abandoned this time—

I was certain of it.

But nothing happened.

I waited.

But he didn't come.

What...?

I started to panic.

Wh-Where is he?

Meanwhile, Roänach silently pulled back and readjusted his grip on the stake.

But... I-I thought...

Seconds away from a complete breakdown, I caught movement in my peripheral vision. When I subtly glanced past Roänach, it was just in time to see a formless void whip around the corner at the end of the street.

Shade!

I barely managed to contain a sob of relief as he raced toward us through the ice. His shadow was the fastest thing I had ever seen.

He came for me—

My tearful gaze drifted back to Roänach. "You wasted too much time."

He almost looked bored as he reeled back with the stake. "The only one wasting my time is you." The moment he moved to strike, he hesitated and squinted down at my feet.

You're too late.

As much as I wanted to hide behind Shade, I stayed put and kept my eyes locked on Roänach. Specifically, the increasing alarm on his face as a towering figure materialized behind me. The more his head tilted back, the paler he became, but when he froze entirely, I knew he had made eye contact with an unfamiliar Arbiter he had no strategy against.

Finally.

In that moment, Shade was death incarnate.

It's over, Roänach.

Knowing I was safe, three hundred years of anger, betrayal, and resentment melted away my fear one last time. Despite the satisfaction of Roänach's pure terror, it was less than a fraction of what he had instilled over the centuries. No amount of retribution would ever be enough, but this would have to suffice.

It's your turn to know fear.

Evidently, he was paralyzed with it.

Shade took the opportunity to reach over my shoulder and grab him by the throat, drawing a deep, guttural rasp as he effortlessly lifted him off the ground until they were eye level. There was a pitiful grunt when his claws dug in. "You made a grave mistake coming here."

I shuddered at his dark tone and the scent of cold blood seeping from Roänach's neck. I had never heard such formidable authority in Shade's voice before.

Before Roänach could snap out of his terrified daze, Shade ripped the wooden stake from his hand and drove it through his heart.

It was over.

All I could do was stand and watch as he twisted and wrenched the stake deeper and deeper.

"I think we've all had enough," he added lowly, using so much force the weapon erupted from Roänach's back with a spray of blood.

At first, Roänach gasped and twitched in his captor's iron grip. Then, he stopped moving entirely.

Despite Roänach's obvious passing, Shade tightened his grip on the dead man's neck until there was a reverberating crunch. "You will never hurt anyone ever again," he hissed in the Arch-Vampire's ashen face before dropping his lifeless body at my feet with an unceremonious thud.

I had no reaction when he hit the ground.

That's it?

My gaze slowly lifted to the cloudy night sky.

Is that really it?

A choked sob clawed its way out of my throat.

It's finally over—

I clenched my eyes shut and sank to my knees. Before I could stop myself, I clutched my chest and let out a bloodcurdling scream.

Three hundred years—

When my lungs gave out, I lost all control and broke down sobbing violently. My body was shaking so badly it hurt. I tried to cover my mouth to stifle the wails of anguish, but my trembling fingers just curled in on themselves and caught tears instead of cries.

Three hundred fucking years—

I heard a shift behind me but barely registered my own movement as something gently pulled me backward. Something strong and unusually warm. There was also a familiar, steady rhythm beating against my arm. It was oddly soothing, but I couldn't figure out what it was. Not in the state I was in.

All I could see was a blur. All I could feel was disappointment.

I'm finally free, but…

I shook my head and sucked in a sharp breath through my teeth.

Why don't I feel happy?

In my disoriented mindset, I angrily slammed my fist on the broad surface next to me but froze when I heard a grunt from the impact.

What was—

I looked up and gasped the moment I found Shade's eyes. All of a sudden, reality came rushing back.

Wait—

I frantically attempted to ground myself.

I'm on Shade's lap.

His arms are around me.

The rhythm was his heartbeat.

I'm leaning on his chest—

My eyes widened with horror when I realized what I had hit.

Oh no—

I could barely see him through my tears. "Shade, I-I'm so sorry."

"It's alright, Athaeÿn—"

"N-No, it's not alright. I didn't realize— I-I didn't mean to—"

"Stop." His tone was soft but firm as he pressed his thumb to my lips. When he lowered his hand, he offered a reassuring smile. "It takes a lot more than that to hurt me."

I just stared at him for a few seconds before closing my eyes and burying my face in his chest. Every unnecessary breath was a struggle for my tormented throat, but at least the trembling in my shoulders faded as he slowly combed his fingers through my hair. *Grateful* was insufficient.

Thank you anyway…

Neither of us said anything for quite a while.

Eventually, I cracked my eyes open and pressed my hand to his chest where I had accidentally hit him. I could barely manage a whisper. "I didn't realize it was you."

"I know."

There was another stretch of silence.

"Why were you so angry?"

The concern in his voice punched me in the gut. "To be clear, I'm not mad at you," I mumbled, sniffling and wiping my eyes.

"Then, what's wrong? I thought you would be relieved."

"I am. It… It's just…" Organizing my muddled thoughts into something more coherent was proving difficult. "I thought his death would be more satisfying, that I would feel better and get back everything he took from me." I shook my head against his chest. "I thought I would finally be free…"

"You *are* free, though, right? Or, at least, no longer a vassal?"

I nodded weakly.

He said nothing for a moment. "Are you still sad he had to die?"

I nodded again.

"You're allowed to be upset."

My throat twinged with frustration. "But I don't *want* to be upset. All his control, all this heartache, *everything* was supposed to die with him… but he's still hanging over me."

Shade quietly ran his fingers through my hair for a few minutes. "You know, rational or not, I thought Xythe was my loving father for a thousand years. Now that he's gone, am I just supposed to act like nothing happened?"

I shook my head while listening to his heartbeat.

"Then give yourself the same grace."

One final tear came down my cheek as I closed my eyes and exhaled deeply.

He's right…

After another minute of silence, he gently lifted my chin so I could see his face, where he had a warm smile waiting for me. "Let's not be harder on ourselves than we need to be."

His amber eyes had never been so comforting.

Eventually, I managed a fragile smile of my own. "I suppose I've already done enough of that."

"Probably too much." His smile softened as he caressed the side of my face. "You've been so patient and understanding with me from the very beginning. You deserve the same."

I leaned into his hand. "You *have* done the same for me."

His smile never wavered as he lightly shook his head. "I meant for yourself."

Oh.

My smile widened as I knelt on his thighs and draped my arms over his shoulders. "I'll try, but for the moments I can't, I know you'll be there for me."

He rested his forehead on mine. "Always."

We both closed our eyes and locked each other in a tight embrace.

I shut out everything else.

Shade was far more than just my friend.

He was my love.

My world.

My everything…

Chapter 32

Athaeÿn

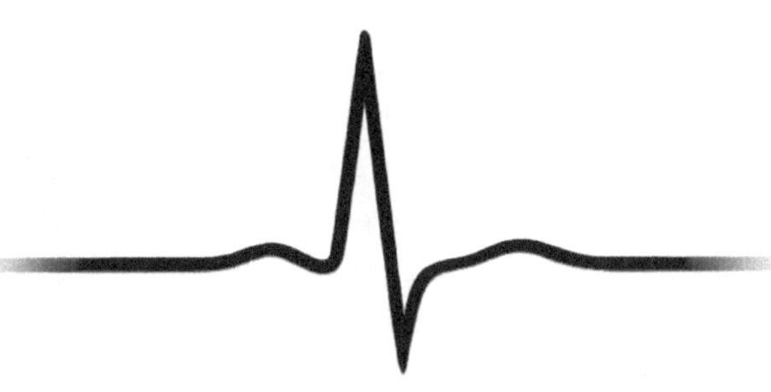

All things considered, the chaos of Roänach's failed invasion and subsequent demise were surprisingly short-lived. There was even enough time for the city's Vampires to reach the interior districts before sunrise. Shade could have shielded them if necessary, but it mattered little since the clouds had yet to break.

As we headed for the mountain, Shade brought Vernyth but left Roänach's body, which Elvylli incinerated as if simply clearing debris. He may as well have been litter. I certainly considered him garbage, but I didn't stay to watch his cremation. I had seen enough.

Once Sathira dismissed her ice, the guards began tending to the newly freed Demons throughout the city, and their unaffected kin eagerly stepped in to help. Some had been enthralled far longer than others, but all retained their memories and regained their true personalities. It was heartbreaking to hear the cries of confusion from those struggling to make sense of everything. Fortunately, there were already vast support systems in place to help them.

It was eventually determined that over a thousand Demons had been dragged into this mess. Quite a few were able to describe the people whose souls had been used to summon them, but discussing murder was difficult at the best of times, let alone under such personal circumstances. For many of them, a bloody corpse was the first thing they saw post-summoning. Sadly, memories like this were common and haunted most forever.

The queens were dismayed to learn a sizable portion of the Demons had been summoned elsewhere and sent to the capital to lie in wait. A number of disappearances from Eidolon were "found" in memories, but many descriptions didn't match anything in the capital's census data. They promptly requested the records of missing people from other cities, towns, and villages to try and identify as many victims as possible.

While specialists organized these investigations, preparations were made to hold a citywide service for everyone lost to Roänach over the centuries. Unidentified and unknown victims would be included as well. In the meantime, Shade requested that his own remembrance, Tyrran's Shrine, be converted into a permanent memorial for the victims. Knowing their son was actually alive and well, the queens were happy to fulfill his wish.

In the hopes of commemorating as many names as possible, they scheduled the primary service for a much later date but gave Vernyth a funeral right away. His death marked true freedom for his vassals, but most had already forgiven him. A few, including Callyn, took turns embracing his body while they still could. Their old friend had come through when it mattered most.

Elvylli personally lit Vernyth's grand funeral pyre, which had been encircled by a surprisingly large crowd of old friends and strangers alike. The most unexpected attendee was Daryn. Not only did he show up to pay his respects, but he went out of his way to publicly acknowledge Vernyth's relentless fight with Roänach and how his honorable sacrifice undoubtedly saved many lives. I could tell Callyn was touched by his sentiment.

...

As soon as Elvylli and Sathira confirmed Eidolon's security and retrieved Daryn, they met up with me and Shade to make a return trip to Castle Veil. To my annoyance, this was when the clouds finally decided to break. Shade, on the other hand, took the opportunity to see if his magic could protect Vampires like I had suggested. It proved incredibly effective when Daryn and I served as test subjects. When shielded by Shade's darkness, we were immune to the sun's light but could still feel its warmth. I had never experienced anything like it. Without thermal vision, it was like standing in the middle of a sunny field with a heavy blindfold on. With thermal vision, it was a bit too blinding for my liking. Shade was thrilled regardless.

Rather than waiting for nighttime, we flew to Castle Veil concealed inside a sphere of his darkness. It probably looked weird and creepy to anyone who didn't know what it was, which Daryn found highly amusing. This kept him in good spirits for quite a while, but he became increasingly anxious the closer we got to our destination. I knew exactly why but kept that to myself.

Upon arrival, there was a triumphant and emotional reunion with Fiella, Haana, and Lánelli, the first of whom was still wearing the flower crown I had given her. We had all felt the arcane bond disappear the moment Roänach died, so they knew of our success long before we got there. They and the other vassals had been tending to the Demons and blood captives to the best of their ability, which the queens thanked them for in addition to promising counseling for all of them.

The blood captives were in the worst shape due to their particularly intense enthrallment, but Daryn had seen many cases of similar aftermath and was certain they could recover with enough time and care. I felt tremendous guilt for never being able to help them, but the ones who were coherent enough to understand the situation didn't blame me, the other vassals, or the Demons. For the most part, they were just relieved to have been liberated like the rest of us.

I forgot what true freedom felt like.

As Shade cheerfully busied himself with Fiella, Haana, and Lánelli, I spotted Roänach's opulent, black coach abandoned at the side of the cavern. Instead of being hitched to it like usual, the two glossy draft horses stood freely nearby with Xiir coddling them affectionately. Next to him was the Fauna Demon Roänach had summoned the day he sent me away.

Hopefully, I can learn her name too.

Before heading over, I got Daryn's attention and gestured for him to follow me. His silent compliance betrayed just how nervous he was, so I made sure to keep him hidden behind me as we approached.

It'll be alright, Daryn.

Meanwhile, Xiir guided the other Fauna Demon's hand across the closest horse's shoulder. "You see? They're just like the nosteryx back in Dominion."

She looked like she was on the verge of tears, but I knew it wasn't because of the horse.

Thank the gods she already has a friend to distract her.

Speaking of which, I was downright floored by Xiir's gentle smile and soft tone of voice. After three hundred years of him being an unwilling jackass, it was almost hard to believe this was the real him.

Xiir turned his head slightly when I stopped a few feet away, but he refocused on his companion before addressing me. "Here, hug Nimbus' face for a bit." He put her arms around the horse's head. "He loves being held like a big baby."

She immediately clung to Nimbus and buried her face in his cheek, a gesture he seemed to enjoy as he snorted happily and leaned into the embrace.

With his companion occupied for the moment, Xiir finally turned to me. "Athaeÿn…" His eyes were heavy with shame. "I'm so sorry for how I treated you all these years."

I shook my head a little. "You don't need to apologize for what wasn't your fault, but if you still want to point fingers at bad behavior, look no further than when I dropped my trunk on your feet." A guilty smile tugged my lips. "That was all me, and I apologize."

He returned a small grin. "That *was* rather painful and unjustified, but I can't say I blame your frustration at the time."

"You had definitely gotten on my nerves, but I was still relieved when Xythe didn't kill you."

"As was I."

It was nice to finally have a real conversation with him. "Anyway, there's someone who'd like to speak with you, Xiir."

"Who— Wait, how do you know my name?"

I just smiled and sidestepped to reveal Daryn, who had seemingly frozen where he stood.

Xiir's eyes widened. "I remember you."

Once Daryn got his feet to cooperate, he approached and stopped right in front of Xiir. "I saw you when you were still enthralled." He shook his head. "I couldn't believe it."

Xiir sighed and nodded. "To this day, I'm not sure why Roänach went after me, but, as was most often the case, he got what he wanted." He paused and tilted his head. "As good as it is to see you, why are you here?"

There were already tears in Daryn's eyes. "I never got to thank you again. You freed us by killing Rialla a second time, but you were gone by the time we found out and searched for you."

"And now you know why."

Daryn extended a trembling hand. "I did everything I could to set things right."

Xiir took it without breaking eye contact. "Did you kill Roänach?"

"No, but I helped the queens during his invasion. We were able to stop his other Demons without losing any."

Xiir didn't hesitate to pull him into a hug. "Thank you."

Daryn's eyes widened before closing tightly, sending tears down his cheeks. "I owe you everything."

"You owe me nothing, Daryn."

They held their embrace for over a minute.

When they separated, Daryn smiled and wiped his eyes. "If you ever move to Eidolon, I think you would be a great Representative for your fellow Demons."

"I've never been one for cities or leadership, but I'll gladly visit you someday."

Daryn nodded. "I understand. Until we meet again, take care."

"You as well." Xiir offered a lighthearted grin. "If I find any more Arch-Vampires, you'll be the first to know."

"I'll hold you to that."

When Xiir turned back to his companion, she was still hugging Nimbus' face. "Xira, why don't you come with me? I hear there's a forest out west overflowing with the most wildlife of any region on the continent. What better place to find other Fauna Demons?" He put his hand on her shoulder. "Besides, I could always use extra help caring for the horses, and Nimbus already likes you."

She let go of the horse in question and turned to him. "You really wouldn't mind?"

"I would be welcoming your company, not tolerating you." He smiled and tilted his head. "Has a nicer ring to it, don't you think?"

She managed a small smile of her own. "Yes, I like that better."

Fiella came over during the lull in their conversation. "I'm so sorry about Xixi. Will she be alright?"

Xira's smile weakened a bit but didn't break as she turned to her. "Yes. We were living with my brother at the time, so he'll have found the sigil my summoning left behind and know what it means. He'll take good care of her for me. I know it."

"Do you think you'll ever see her again?"

She hung her head a little. "I don't know. I pray she's never ripped from Dominion like I was, but Daemir forbid if she *is* summoned one day, I hope she finds me."

Fiella smiled. "I know you'll both be okay."

"Thank you, dear."

After sharing a hug, Fiella and Xira separated so the latter and Xiir could mount the horses.

I waved to them both. "Good luck with everything."

Daryn pointed right at Xiir's face. "You'd better write to me once you're settled down."

"I will. You have my word."

"I look forward to many words."

Meanwhile, Fiella sniffled from where she stood huddled next to me. "Please be safe."

Xira smiled at her. "We promise."

With departing waves, the two Demons rode out of the cavern together.

Once they were gone, I glanced down at Fiella. "Feel better?"

She nodded and wiped her eyes. "I had to know her baby would be okay."

"And now you do."

Her gaze was still locked on the cave mouth. "I went outside a few times after the runes were shut down, but now that the sun's out, it feels like it's taunting me."

As it just so happens—

Before I could say anything, Shade rushed over and stood in front of her so she had to look at him instead. The beaming smile on his face may as well have been her sunlight.

And to think, he was afraid his magic couldn't help anyone.

Fiella just stared ahead as if he wasn't even there. "Hi, Tyrran…"

He dropped to one knee so he was closer to her eye level. "I never mentioned how Daryn and Athaeÿn were able to travel in the middle of a sunny day, did I?"

She shook her head.

His smile widened as he offered his hand. "Let me show you."

Despite the confusion in her eyes, she nodded and took his hand, if a bit warily.

He led her to the farthest point of the cave mouth and paused right at the edge. "Ready?"

She nodded again.

After giving her hand a light squeeze, he formed a small sphere of darkness in the center of his chest and expanded it until they were both swallowed up.

I switched to my thermal vision in time to see Fiella look around for a few seconds before glancing up at Shade, likely having switched visions as well.

"This is your magic?"

"Some of it, but this is all we need." He gently tugged her hand. "Come on."

They were still in the mountain's shadow when they stepped outside. The farther they went, the more Shade expanded his darkness, but just enough to overlap with the cave mouth for a safe retreat if needed.

When they reached the edge of the mountain's shadow, Fiella stopped and nervously eyed the thermally brilliant, sunlit ground in front of her.

Shade lightly waggled her hand. "I promise you'll be okay."

She didn't move at first but eventually nodded and clung to his hand with both of hers.

Meanwhile, Haana, Lánelli, and I watched intently from inside the cave.

You can do it, Fiella.

A moment later, Shade stepped into the sunlight and gently pulled her with him.

She gasped when the sun's warmth embraced her skin for the first time in months. "Is it working? Are we really in sunlight?"

"We are."

A small sob jerked her shoulders as she turned her face toward the sky. There was a long pause before she smiled to herself. "I can feel the sun..."

My thermal vision proved as much as I watched her slowly brighten with warmth.

How it should be for a Light Elf.

All of a sudden, she turned back to Shade and started jumping up and down with his hand still clutched in hers. "I can feel the sun!"

I couldn't help but choke up when she let go and started running around with her arms flung out to the sides, laughing and cheering as she went.

"I can feel the sun!"

Lánelli didn't hesitate to join them, but Haana hung back to share a glance with me. I just smiled and gave an encouraging nod toward the others, which she was hesitant to accept but eventually acquiesced when my feet remained planted.

Thank you, though.

As Haana and Lánelli enjoyed the sun's warmth from the ground, Shade snatched up Fiella and sat her on his shoulders, where she held her arms high above her head and continued cheering as he spun around to celebrate with her.

It wasn't long before the other vassals noticed what was going on and went outside as well. Like me, some of them hadn't felt the sun's warmth on their skin in centuries, but I politely turned them down when they asked if I wanted to join them. I was quite content watching everyone from afar, especially Fiella. Basking in their joy was more than enough for me.

You have no idea how much this means to them, Shade.
I had to dry grateful tears from my eyes.
Thank you.

Chapter 33

Athaeÿn

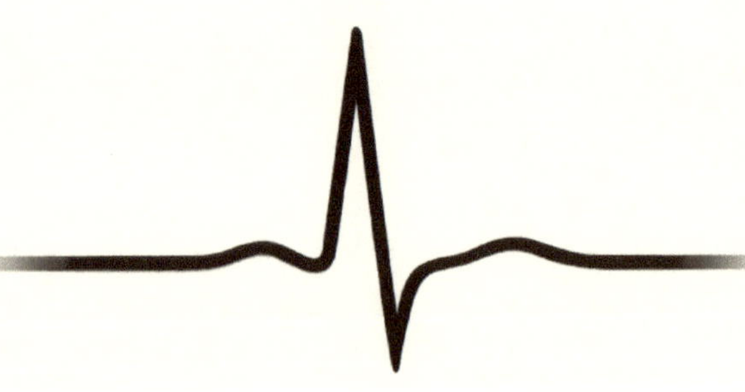

It took Elvylli, Sathira, and Shade numerous trips over multiple days to transport the freed blood captives, other vassals, and remaining Demons to Eidolon. Not all were from the capital, but the queens insisted they get the best help available before going their separate ways.

Daryn and I stayed at Castle Veil while everyone patiently awaited their turns to be whisked away, and he refused to leave until we were the only two left. Even then, I had to convince him I would be fine on my own until Shade came back for me. In the end, reminding him of Roänach's death was a good enough argument.

Meanwhile, the clouds had the nerve to return in full force the same day they had broken, right before nighttime, of course, which I took personal offense to. I wanted Shade to see the stars in their full glory, but the weather was not cooperating all two hundred miles between Mount Umbra and Eidolon. It was infuriating.

Maybe the gods are having family drama or something.

It certainly wouldn't be the first time. Whatever the case, I hoped the clouds would go away for my final night at Castle Veil. Seeing the stars again would be a nice send-off.

. . .

It was early afternoon when Shade arrived one last time. I watched him fly into the cavern from the windowsill of my old room, where I sat playing my zephyr harp I hadn't seen in almost three centuries. Its obvious neglect saddened me, but I planned to have it fully restored in Eidolon.

I was also going to bring my small portrait and lunelight. Fiella had returned the latter after expressing profuse gratitude for letting her borrow it. I had fully intended to let her keep it, but, admittedly, it was nice to have back.

I'm just glad it helped.

I was still playing my harp when Shade appeared on the threshold. "Look what I found."

He smiled and awkwardly crammed himself through the doorway, which had definitely not been built with Arbiters in mind. "Where was it?"

"Stashed away in one of Roänach's many, dusty closets. Frankly, I'm amazed he didn't trash it."

Shade attempted to lounge on my small bed in the corner of the room. It was more of a struggle. "Apparently, no one can resist holding on to your stuff…" By the time he settled, most of his limbs were hanging over the edges with his right wing smushed against the wall and the left covering most of the floor. Unsurprisingly, he scrunched up his nose with annoyance.

I couldn't help but snort a laugh. "Comfortable?"

"No, but it's still nice to lie down after the constant flying back and forth over the past week, or however many days it was."

"Please tell me you made time for regular sleep."

He yawned widely. "I think I took a few naps here and there."

"Shade—"

"It was hard to sleep knowing you and the others were still here!"

I mulled over his excuse for a few seconds. "I suppose that's fair… Well then," a smile came to my face, "since I'm the last one, you're now free to sleep as long as you want."

"But we need to go back to Eidolon…"

"And we will, *after* you've rested up. I'd rather you not pass out mid-flight."

"Mmmnnneehhh…" He repeatedly huffed with aggravation on his futile quest to get comfortable. Eventually, he gave up and sprawled on the floor instead, but there still wasn't enough room for him to fully spread out. "Please tell me a bed exists that can fit my gigantic body."

"Your mothers probably have a huge bed. I'm sure you can get a similar one custom made."

"I don't want to be an inconvenience."

"Shade, there are craftspeople who make furniture for a living. As long as they're paid for their work, you're not inconveniencing anyone."

"But I don't have any money."

"I guarantee your mothers will gladly pay them for you."

"But—"

"But nothing. I promise everything will be properly taken care of."

He anxiously patted the floor a few times before letting out a heavy breath. "Okay…"

"Good, now go to sleep."

"I'm going, I'm going…"

I had stopped playing my harp during our back-and-forth, and it remained silent as I watched him finally close his eyes.

Joining him might be a good way to pass the time…

After weighing my options, I got up and set my harp on the dresser next to a bag I had found in the same closet. The small portrait and lunelight were already stowed in it for the trip.

I should probably find a bag for the harp too.

For now, I hunkered down on Shade's chest with my face buried in his neck. "I'm tired too."

He shook his head and draped one arm over my back. "Just admit you like feeling my muscles."

"I already have."

"You're allowed to admit it twice."

"I refuse."

"So stubborn for no reason…"

"You bring out the best in me."

He sighed and ran his claws through my hair. "Debatable…"

I just smiled and ghosted my fingers across his chest.

You really do, though.

It wasn't long before he passed out from exhaustion. His hand had stopped moving when he fell asleep, but his fingers were still lost in my hair as I lay enjoying his warmth. It felt like he was sharing his heartbeat with me.

I don't need one to feel alive anymore…

…

It was unclear how many hours passed once I fell asleep. When I finally stirred, Shade was seemingly still out cold, so I pressed the top of my head into the underside of his jaw in the hopes of gently waking him.

He grunted after a few seconds and pulled me down his torso. "Excuse me, that's my throat you're squishing."

"Breathing is overrated."

"Maybe for you, but some of us are still alive."

"Wow, okay—" My fake offense was betrayed by a grin as I pushed myself upright with both hands firmly planted on his chest, drawing an even louder grunt this time.

"Rib cage—"

I stood and stretched my arms over my head. "Gods, you're such a baby."

He sat upright and cracked his shoulders. "Aren't people supposed to be nice to babies?"

"I'm the exception."

"Ooo, lucky me."

I snickered and looked out the window to check the time. A glance toward the cave mouth indicated it was nighttime, but my eyes widened when the ground appeared lighter than usual.

Are the clouds finally gone?

I smacked the windowsill and impatiently tugged one of his wings. "Shade, get up!"

"Why? Is something wrong?"

"The exact opposite. Follow me." I practically ran out of the room without waiting up for him. When he caught up to me near the castle's front entrance, I turned to him and pointed at the ground. "Eyes down."

He narrowed them instead. "Why are you acting so weird?"

"I'm not acting weird. I'm excited to show you something."

His eyes widened this time. "Ooo, what is it?"

"You'll see, but you can't look up until I say so."

"Uhhh, okay."

As we traversed the cave, I glanced back now and then to make sure he was still looking at the ground. Luckily, he had the necessary willpower to survive the trek outside.

He was jittering impatiently by the time we stopped in the middle of the grassy field. "Is the secret thing more interesting than your boots?"

"Hopefully, but I'll let you be the judge of that."

This is it—

I exhaled deeply and turned to face him. "Before you look up, do you remember what you could see of the night sky from inside the solar shield?"

His eyes widened. "I… Yes, but it wasn't much of a night sky, at least compared to descriptions I read in books."

"How many stars do you think there are?"

"Well… There were various diagrams showing at least a hundred each, but I could only ever see maybe ten at most in real life. Eventually, I told myself the drawings had to be fake." He halfheartedly twiddled his claws. "I hope there's at least double of what I could see."

I could barely contain myself as I took gentle hold of his hand. "See for yourself."

He hesitated before slowly lifting his head. The moment he saw the stars, he gasped and froze where he stood. "Athaeÿn—" His hand trembled in mine. "I-Is this real?"

I looked up as well and smiled brightly. "This is real."

The sky was anything but dark. Above our heads, the night elegantly wove a shimmering tapestry of glinting pastels across an infinite expanse of amethyst and azurite. From one horizon to the other, a single, violent brushstroke painted a gaping wound of nebulous clouds and even brighter stars. Visually, it was comparable to a worn seam splitting open.

In reality, it was a window to the ever-shifting celestial plane our world called home.

There was no solar shield to obscure our view.

There were no voices to shatter the serenity.

For one ethereal moment, it was just me, Shade, and the heavens.

This was worth the wait.

His voice was weak when he finally spoke again. "A-All of this was right there the whole time?"

My gaze drifted to him. "Is it everything you hoped for?"

He sniffled and used his free hand to wipe tears from his eyes. "Not even my dreams came close to this."

I smiled and gave his arm a light nudge. "Here, let's sit for a while."

Once he sat down, I settled on his lap with my legs on either side of his waist and my arms gently draped around his neck. Without a word, he returned the embrace and leaned his head on mine so we could stargaze in each other's arms. If perfection existed, this was it.

I've wanted this for so long.

Ten blissful minutes of pure serenity came and went.

Why can't life always be this peaceful...

After another minute or so, I smiled and playfully nosed his ear. "So, change your mind about heading back to Eidolon right away?"

"We can stay here a little longer..."

My grin widened for a second but faded when I glanced at the cave. "Is it alright if I bring up Roänach for a second?"

"Do you want to talk about his death?"

"Yes, but for you this time."

"What do you mean?"

I pulled back just enough to look at him. "We both know I was a wreck, but I never asked if you were okay."

"Why wouldn't I be? I'm not the one he relentlessly tormented for three hundred years."

"True, but you had been dreading the confrontation as well and, more importantly, had never killed anyone before him. Are you sure you're alright after that?"

His eyes widened a bit. "Oh. Uhhh, I think so?" He rubbed his temple for a few seconds. "If anything, I'm a bit unnerved by how easy it was. I would never hesitate to save you, but… Shouldn't it be difficult to take a life? Even when it's someone like him?"

"Not to excuse or diminish what happened, but you *are* an Arbiter. By divine intent, one of your instincts is to protect the defenseless in any situation, no matter how extreme. Maybe that helps you do whatever is necessary."

"Maybe…" He glanced off to one side. "I should probably ask my mothers to teach me more Arbiter stuff so I can be a good one."

I smiled and rubbed his shoulders. "I think you're off to a decent start."

His gaze drifted back to me and brought a small smile with it. "I'm just glad I only had to use my magic to help and not hurt."

"That's something else I've been meaning to ask about. You said you were able to uncover some harmful aspects with your mothers' help, right?"

His tentative smile vanished. "It was horrible. The worst part was Elvylli having me practice on her."

"Wha— Did she really?"

He nodded. "She promised that her healing factor would fix any damage, but it was still terrifying."

My brows went up a bit. "I mean… She's probably right, but I would've been scared too." I paused to think for a moment. "If it makes you feel better, she clearly trusts you with her life. That's pretty significant."

The tension in his face somewhat relaxed.

I was glad to ease his mind on that front, but my curiosity wasn't satisfied. "If you don't mind me asking, what were you able to do?"

His face tensed again. "Absorb more than just light." He shook his head a little. "The darkness I made for Fiella is the neutral form, I guess. When Elvylli had me push toward intentional harm, it started… *taking* things from her."

"Like what?"

"Her senses."

Whatever I may have expected him to say, it wasn't that. "Physical or mental?"

"Only physical, according to her. The neutral darkness just hides what people see, but the next level actually takes sight itself. And hearing.

Touch, taste, smell, even spatial orientation… She was only able to tell me what happened after her healing factor restored everything."

Gods…

My fingers stiffened on his shoulders. "Is there a deadly level?"

His face paled a little. "She had me push toward that as well. After taking her senses again, I felt it trying to take her soul." He vehemently shook his head. "That's when I refused to continue."

I gawked at him and the implication of what his magic was capable of. "Well… Now I see why you didn't want to use it for harm."

He shook his head again. "I don't care what situation I find myself in. I will never, *ever,* use my magic to hurt anyone. I'll always find another way."

"Like with Roänach."

"That required a unique approach anyway, but yeah…" His gaze slowly fell. "I hate that such magic exists. I hate that it's part of *my* magic. Even if I never use it, I hate that it's always an option."

I quietly rubbed his shoulders for a few seconds. "You know, I'm glad you have the abilities you do."

"What? Why?"

"Because the neutral one can shroud an entire city from danger and allow Vampires to walk in their own version of sunlight, something that's never been possible before. As for the harmful ones," my hands found and held his face, "I don't know about you, but I'd much rather have such capabilities in your thoughtful claws than the troubled hands of Arbiters like Aëlla or Sae."

His skeptical look softened into relief. "I guess I never thought of it that way."

I smiled and prodded his cheeks with my thumbs. "I know, that's why I did for you."

He finally managed a smile of his own and rested his forehead on mine.

We sat in silence for a few minutes.

"You really did help save a lot of people… Thank you…" I leaned into his embrace. "And thank you for saving me."

He chuckled quietly and threaded his fingers into my hair. "You saved me first, so it was the least I could do." His smile faltered a bit. "I wish I could save your soul like you did mine, but I know yours is gone."

My smile never wavered. "I think I'd rather have Lune anyway."

There was a surge of warmth in my chest.

I love you too, Lune.

Shade's smile warmed more than usual. "Lune loved you right from the start."

And...

My hands slid down his neck and came to rest on his shoulders.

I want him to know.

A few anxious moments later, I pulled back so I could look into his eyes. "Shade, there's something I need to tell you, but I don't want to say it without a heartbeat."

He looked slightly confused but didn't hesitate to offer his hand.

Keeping his wrist steady, I sank my fangs into the usual spot at the base of his thumb and practically inhaled him. It was easy this time.

I swear this is the best he's ever tasted.

With my heart beating once more, I slowly dragged my lips across the already healing puncture wounds and left a soft kiss on his palm. There was an amusing blush darkening his face when I glanced back up.

Still got it.

My hands drifted back to his shoulders. "I'm sure you remember everything I said in the spirit den," an embarrassed smile tugged my lips, "or, rather, everything I sobbed." To my annoyance, I suddenly felt the need to avert my gaze and was unable to stop myself. "My heart has been broken more times than I can count. Anything that reminded me of those failures became terrifying, and that fear became pain when I wanted to feel nothing but still felt everything."

Shade sat perfectly still as he listened. Even his fingers waited patiently where they had woven into my hair.

"But then I found you." Gathering all my courage, I finally met his gaze. "You spoke to me even when you couldn't say anything. You touched my soul even though it's gone..." My chest caught fire when I pressed my hand to his and found a second racing heartbeat. "I've been dead for a long time, but you make me feel *alive.*"

By now, there was a gentle, half-lidded smile on his face, but he still didn't move.

"I… I ended up feeling something for you I never intended."

Just say it already.

My fingers trembled on his chest. "Shade, I-I…"

Dammit—

"Would it help if I said it first?"

My eyes shot wide. All I could manage was a small nod.

He cradled the back of my head and pulled me close. "I've wanted to say this for a while myself…" His lips brushed my cheek. "I love you, Athaeÿn."

An embarrassing gasp escaped my throat.

He said it—

I couldn't move.

H-He really said it—

I could only shiver violently in his warm embrace.

And I know he meant it.

"I love you too, Shade—" I was still saying his name as I grabbed his face and locked him in the most confident kiss I had ever given anyone. Every ounce of adoration, gratitude, and passion I could find went into it. Without question, it was the best kiss of my entire life.

My chest—

All of a sudden, I realized this was our first kiss with two heartbeats. Mine was so out of control it almost hurt, but I loved every second of it.

He truly is my everything.

The stars were ours alone that night.

Never let me go…

He found me

Epilogue

Athaeÿn

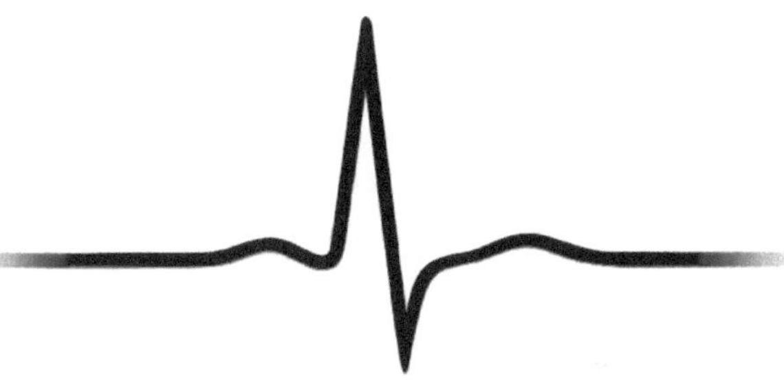

Phew, long day…

That didn't stop me from smiling, if a bit tiredly, as I bid my final client farewell. Once they left, I set about my usual routine of cleaning and organizing my small but cozy massage spa before closing up for the night.

It's relaxing, honestly.

My days as an escort were over, but I had made enough progress to revive my second favorite service and hone my skills to a professional level. Shade was still the only person I could touch entirely without issue. In the meantime, I was grateful to keep an essence of my original career with a level of intimacy I could handle for everyone else.

In the first few months after returning to Eidolon, I had received expert training, earned my license as a massage therapist, and acquired my spa with just enough help from the queens. Shade had contributed as my enthusiastic practice dummy. It was less than surprising when he begged for a daily massage after learning how good it felt, and I was happy to oblige. His gigantic, muscular body certainly gave me a lot of practice.

And sore hands.

My tired smile turned into a giddy grin as I waited for him to arrive. Without fail, he came to the spa at the end of every workday to walk me out, and today was extra special.

I can't wait to give him his present.

He finally knew his real birthday, and there weren't just three Arbiters celebrating. There were five. Galaeÿthe and Haephir had returned to Eidolon to meet the grandson they thought had been murdered. I would never forget the look on Shade's face when he saw them for the first time.

"They're as tall as me!"

Their meeting was one of the cutest things I had ever seen, and it was highly amusing to watch them tussle and fly around like playful, adolescent dragons. From their lively antics, one would never know how ancient Galaeÿthe and Haephir were just by looking at them.

They certainly wear their age well.

My reminiscing was interrupted when I heard the front door open, followed by Shade's distinct footsteps barreling into the waiting room.

There he is—

"Is everyone decent in there?"

I glanced at the closed door separating us. "It's just me!"

"Same question for just you!"

"You know only the clients disrobe. Besides, you see me undressed all the time."

"Oh yeah." He promptly rushed in and made a beeline for me. The moment I was within reach, he snatched me off the ground and squished me against his chest. "I'm so proud of you."

I wheezed in his tight hug. "F-For what?"

"Your spa and all the massage stuff! I was afraid you would change your mind about everything, so I'm relieved you still love it."

"Th-Thanks, but you're crushing me—"

"Oops—" He set me down and smoothed out my clothing. "Sorry about that."

"It's alright—" I coughed a few times as my rib cage expanded back to normal. "I think you tell me how proud you are at least once a week." One final cough ended with a smile. "It's very thoughtful, but you don't have to keep saying it if you don't want to. I know how you feel by now."

"But I like saying it. Also, you may not notice, but you smile every time. There's no way I'm saying it less."

Oh.

I averted my gaze and rubbed the back of my neck. "Well, I wasn't *demanding* you stop…" Eventually, I cleared my throat and looked at him again. "Anyway, did you have a good birthday?"

"Yeah! Galaeÿthe and Haephir know so much about everything. I think we spent a few hours just listening to them tell stories."

"Don't tell Daryn. He'd probably declare anecdote war on them."

"I think my grandfathers would win."

"*Definitely* don't tell him that."

A mischievous grin flashed across his face but left behind a more relaxed smile. "As much fun as I had today, I think I'm even more excited for tomorrow."

"Yeah, it'll be nice to have a day for just you and me."

"Speaking of us, I wasn't late today, was I?"

"No, why?"

"I stopped at Fiella's on the way here."

"Again?"

"Her cats are *so cute!*" He clutched his chest as if in pain. "I am physically incapable of passing her house without stopping to see them." A tiny smirk tugged the corner of his mouth. "Sometimes, I even remember to say hi to her and Joryn."

I just stood there smiling at him.

"What?"

"I think you're going to like your present."

His voice became more air than sound. "You didn't have to get me anything."

"Nonsense. This is the most important birthday I could ever have the honor of celebrating, and I want it to show. Now, close your eyes."

"But—"

"Eyes *closed.*"

He opened his mouth but changed his mind at the last second and did as told.

After waving my hand to make sure he wasn't peeking, I hurried to and from my small office in record time. On the way back, my footsteps were accompanied by a tiny meow.

Shade froze on the spot. "Wh-What was that?"

"See for yourself."

He slowly opened his eyes and looked down at me, where I stood holding a tiny kitten with fluffy white fur and brilliant blue eyes. She looked more like a puffball than anything.

Much to my amusement, Shade covered his mouth with both hands and started pattering his feet like an excited kid. Eventually, he dropped to one knee so he was eye level with me and closer to the kitten. He hadn't looked away from her once.

In a similar vein, I had yet to stop smiling. "Does she remind you of anyone?"

His eyes widened. "She has the same colors as Lune!"

"That's why I chose her." I gently set her on his upturned palms and chuckled over how small she was in his massive hands. "This is Luna."

His smile quivered as he lifted her up to his face. "Hi, Luna." He teared up a little when she meowed again and nudged his nose with her forehead. "I love her so much."

My cheeks were starting to hurt from all the smiling, and a familiar surge of warmth didn't help.

I'm glad you approve, Lune.

As Shade cradled Luna to his chest with one hand, he pulled me in with the other and kissed me deeply. "Thank you."

"You're welcome, love."

All of a sudden, he got even more excited. "I have a present for you too."

I snickered under my breath. "That's not how birthdays work."

"I know, but I think it'll make you really happy, which'll make me really happy. So, uhh, consider it a present from you to me… from me… to you…"

I just stared at him with my hands on my hips.

He added a big, toothy grin.

The corner of my mouth twitched into a half-smile. "Alright, but *only* because it would be rude to argue on your birthday."

"Great, let's go!"

He fled the room with Luna before I could even blink.

Adorable as ever.

My smile widened as I retrieved Luna's bed from my office and followed Shade outside, making sure to lock up on the way out. The sun had yet to sink below the horizon, but my spa was safely tucked away inside the mountain. Unsurprisingly, many of my clients were other Vampires.

When we reached the citadel, he took us to Daryn's office instead of our living quarters.

Okay, now I'm really confused.

Shade gently pulled Luna's bed from my hand and stood aside. "I'm not the only one who should get to spend time with family."

Wait—

My chest tightened. "What?"

He just smiled and nodded to the door.

I couldn't tear my gaze from him for a solid ten seconds. When I finally turned and gripped the handle, my hand was shaking violently.

There's no way—

I stopped breathing and nervously pushed the door open, only to freeze when I spotted two Dark Elves in front of Daryn's desk. On the opposite side was Daryn himself, Elvylli, and Sathira. All were standing and talking.

Those voices—

When Daryn glanced past his guests and smiled at me, they turned to see what he was looking at.

It can't be—

The three of us were statues as we stared at each other from across the room.

It's them—

It took all of my courage to approach.

I-It's really them—

Tears came to the woman's eyes the moment I stopped in front of them.

"Athaeÿn?"

My shoulders trembled as she cradled my face with one hand.

Mother—

I leaned into her comforting touch and shifted my gaze to the man. Tears were already streaming down his face as he held my other cheek.

Father—

Without warning, I broke down sobbing and collapsed into them.

Th-They're here—

I could barely take in enough air to speak. "I-I'm so sorry. Please don't hate me—"

My mother shook her head and hugged me tightly. "My darling moonlight, we could never."

"Y-You really didn't forget me?"

My father kissed my forehead. "Not a day has gone by without thinking of you." He put his arms around both me and my mother. "Love doesn't forget."

All I could do was bury myself in their embrace as if my existence depended on it.

Shade—

Blinded by tears, I managed to glance over my shoulder and discern his silhouette in the open doorway. The moment I could see clearly, I found a loving smile on his face.

Thank you.

Bonus Chapter

Athaeÿn
(contains explicit sexual content)

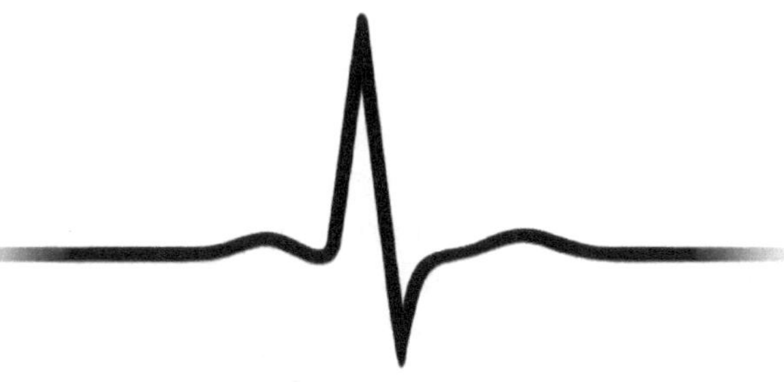

Shade groaned in the hallway outside our living quarters. "I ate too much bread."

A chuckle slipped out as I unlocked the front door. "You can eat an entire deer in less than a day but can't handle ten loaves of bread in one sitting?"

"My stomach prefers meat, but I dream of *bread*. I must consume as much as possible."

Once we entered, I closed and locked the door behind us. "And you make good on that every time we go out to eat. *Every single time*. You never learn."

"Hey, I could only eat bread one month a year for a thousand years. I have a lot of making up to do, especially if butter is involved. Besides, I had an excuse this time."

"Conversing with my parents is not an excuse to shovel bread into your face with reckless abandon."

"Yes it is. Also, the waitress kept bringing more! It would've been rude *not* to eat it."

I sighed and glanced at Luna, who was kneading him like a pincushion where he held her against his chest. "And you even had something to occupy your hands this time…"

"The problem is, I have two hands and only need one to pet Luna."

"Then perhaps we should get a second one to keep both of your hands occupied."

"We can get more?!"

"Fiella has five, does she not? Additionally, there will be times Luna has to stay home, and I bet she would appreciate having a friend to play with."

He lifted her up and nuzzled her face. "Did you hear that? You can have a sibling!"

I smiled and patted his arm. "Alright, she's had a long and over-stimulating day. Time for her to go to bed."

"Can she sleep in our room?"

"Eventually, but we should probably wait until she's a bit older."

"Oh, alright…" He kissed her forehead and gently placed her on her bed in the closet, where she circled a few times before snuggling in to sleep. "Goodnight, Luna. See you in the morning," he whispered, closing the door as quietly as possible. After a moment, he turned back to me and clutched his chest. "She's so *precious.*"

"She really is."

I made my way to our immense master bedroom and sat on the edge of our equally gigantic bed. It looked absolutely ridiculous at twelve-by-twelve feet, but it did a good job supporting Shade's hulking frame and huge wings. I barely took up any space in comparison.

He followed me in and closed the door behind him. "Speaking of precious, did you see the look on your mother's face when she heard you still had the lunelight?"

"I did."

And I'll never forget it.

My smile slowly faded. "If I can be honest for a moment, I almost wish I hadn't let you give your gift until tomorrow."

"What do you mean? You were thrilled to see your parents."

"That's exactly the problem. How can reuniting with them after three hundred years possibly compare to giving you a kitten?"

He blinked at me a few times. "You've seen how much I love her, right?"

"And I'm so glad you do, but it's not the same. No offense to Luna, of course."

"Athaeÿn, it's not—"

"A competition. I know…" I shook my head and frowned at the floor. "But this was supposed to be *your* special day, not mine."

He came over and sat next to me on the edge of the bed. "It can still be my special day without being all about me."

Without looking at him, I nodded a little and hung my head. "I'm sorry, Shade, I'm not trying to sound ungrateful. I just wanted you to be the happiest person in the whole world today, and…" I sighed heavily. "And I also wanted to be the best gift-giver, not the other way around. That probably sounds selfish…"

"Hmm, maybe, but not really. It's not like you sabotaged everyone else so your gift would be the only one. Now *that* would be selfish."

I exhaled sharply with amusement but otherwise remained silent.

"Your happiness is my happiness, so the reunion with your parents just made my birthday that much better." He pulled me into a side hug. "If anything, I'm the one who has to overcompensate."

"Why?"

"Because you sacrificed yourself to save my soul. I don't think I can ever top that," he put on a tiny smirk and shook me a little, "so let me do nice things for you."

I couldn't help but laugh as he jostled me back and forth. When the motion stopped, I was left with a bashful smile. "I guess you have a point."

"I know I do," he kissed the top of my head, "so, no more feeling inadequate, please."

One more chuckle slipped out. "Alright… *but,* since we're on the subject," I let my full body weight lean on him, "is there anything else you wanted? It's still your birthday, after all."

He tensed for a split second and shook his head. "Nope."

How convincing.

I finally glanced up at him. "Are you sure?"

"Yep."

"Absolutely positive?"

"Mm-hmm."

"Shade, you know you can't lie to me for shit."

"I'm not lying."

"Omission still counts."

He tensed again but said nothing this time.

Seems we're finally having this conversation.

I turned slightly to see him better. "Why are you so afraid to talk about this?"

"A-About what?"

"Shade—"

"Alright, alright…" His free hand found mine. "I'm afraid to talk about it for multiple reasons."

"I'm listening."

He averted his gaze. "I'm obviously a bit nervous since I've never… you know… at least with another person… but I'm more worried about you."

"Because of Roänach?"

It took a few moments for him to look at me again. "How could I even bring this up after everything he did?"

I could feel the anxiety in his fidgeting claws. "I see… Are those the only reasons?"

"The main ones, but I also had no intention of asking on a day like this. I didn't want you to feel any obligation or pressure."

At first, I didn't know what to say.

He really is too caring for his own good.

A few more seconds passed before I got my mouth to cooperate. "I appreciate the sentiment, truly, but you shouldn't silence yourself out of fear of upsetting me. As long as you're considerate, asking questions won't hurt me the way Roänach did."

"Maybe, but there's one more reason I never said anything." His gaze fell to our clasped hands. "I love what we already have. Wanting to go further with you is a desire, not a need. Considering how much you've been hurt, I almost feel bad just thinking about it." He shook his head a little. "I was waiting for you to bring this up, but if you never did," he fully enclosed my hand in his and looked into my eyes, "I would have happily let it go."

I was left speechless again.

He was really willing to do that?

A small wave of guilt forced me to look away. "Shhhh*it…*"

"What's wrong?"

"I was actually waiting for you to bring it up first."

"Wha— Really? Why?"

"I figured you were nervous due to inexperience, and I didn't want to scare you by suggesting anything. Turns out, my first assumption was correct, but…" I rubbed the back of my neck and smiled awkwardly. "I guess in our mutual desire to be respectful, we accidentally ended up failing to communicate."

He shook his head and let out a heavy breath. *"Shit—* I'm sorry, Athaeÿn. I didn't mean for this to happen."

"Me neither, so I'm sorry too."

"Ughhhh…" He dragged his hands down his face and flopped backward on the bed. "I'm such an idiot," he groaned into his palms.

I nestled in the crook of his shoulder and rested my head on his chest. "You and I both."

He kept his face covered and shook his head a few more times. Eventually, he let his hands fall away but draped one arm over me. "I know you were trying to be mindful, but if you were open to this the whole time, why not at least mention it in passing so I knew?"

"I could ask you the same thing."

"Could you, though? Our concerns aren't really on equal footing."

"Says who?"

"Common sense."

I turned my head a bit. "What about your claim is common sense?"

"My nervous inexperience doesn't even come close to what you went through."

"And, therefore, your fear doesn't matter?"

"It matters, just way less than what you've actually suffered."

"You hear how absurd that sounds, right?"

"I don't think it sounds absurd."

With a slight grunt of effort, I turned over and propped myself up so I could see his face. "Why are you downplaying the significance of your feelings?"

"Why are you pushing back so much?" His tone was solid, but his expression didn't match. "Look, all I'm saying is your lived experiences carry more weight than my fear of probably nothing. Doesn't that make at least some sense?"

After mulling over his stance, I shook my head at myself. "I'm sorry, *absurd* was a strong word. I understand where you're coming from, but my point is both sides matter equally, even if one seems less important. It's just…" I sighed and shook my head again. "I prioritized the needs of others for so long I nearly forgot about my own. I don't want you falling into the same trap."

His eyes widened a bit, but he kept quiet to listen.

I leaned closer and softened my voice. "Please don't do what I did."

You deserve better.

Eventually, he offered a small smile. "Okay."

"Promise me."

"I overthink too much to promise, but I'll try."

"Hmm… I suppose I can accept such an honest response."

He held the back of my head with one hand. "I'll do my best as long as you promise to do the same."

I returned a half-lidded smile. "Deal."

As we shared a deep kiss, I hummed contentedly when his fingers got lost in my hair. It was one of my favorite things he did.

And I never even have to ask.

I broke the kiss a full minute later. "So, would you like to change your answer to the birthday present question?"

"Only if you want the same thing."

"I do."

He nodded a little. "I'm still nervous."

"For you or me?"

"Yes."

I couldn't help but chuckle. "Let's start with you."

"I'll be alright. Really. My nerves aren't even that bad. It's your feeling of safety I'm worried about."

"You make me feel safe."

He opened his mouth but closed it again without saying anything.

My turn…

I tilted my head and slowly caressed his jawline. "I never thought I'd recover the ability to touch. The spa has helped tremendously, but it all started with you. I want to prove it."

He shivered a little. "You already have."

"Not nearly as much as I'd like."

"What about Roänach?"

"It's possible unwelcome memories of him will surface, but I'm confident your presence will drown them out." I offered a reassuring smile. "We can always stop if something becomes too much, but I'm not worried. Everything about you is my sanctuary."

He failed to say anything, but his pounding heart spoke for him.

I took the opportunity to slowly drag my lips across his cheek and pause at the corner of his mouth. "I want you and only you."

An intense blush darkened his face. "You're really good at this."

"I haven't even done anything yet."

"S-Still."

I smirked and brushed my thumb across his bottom lip. "So… Are we going all the way?"

"I-I think I'd like that."

"Not good enough. I need explicit consent."

He let out a short breath and nodded. "I want to go all the way with you. Please."

Still so adorable.

"The feeling is mutual, my love." I had barely finished speaking when I kissed him even deeper than before. "Is it alright if I take the lead, at least to start?"

"You actually know what you're doing, so please do."

"Thank you. I promise you won't regret it."

"I would never regret any attention from you."

"I know." I left a playful smooch on his nose before wriggling out of his embrace and gesturing toward the headboard. "Lie down with your head on the pillows." As he repositioned himself, I slipped off the bed and pulled a small bottle from the top drawer of my bedside table.

"What's that?"

"Something for later."

"Wha— How long has that been in there?"

"Quite a while." I set it on the table for now and began disrobing. "I wasn't sure we'd ever have this conversation, but I wanted to be prepared just in case."

Everything will be fine…

Once fully nude, I knelt over his thick tail and removed the custom belt that hid the subtle slit on his pelvis. "You don't mind a bite so I can participate equally, right?"

"You know I never mind."

A tiny smirk tugged my lips as I straddled his hips and rested my backside against his bare pelvic shelf. "Do you perhaps secretly enjoy it?"

His lingering blush deepened. "Are you referring to…?"

My grin widened mischievously. "The incident in the cave…"

He gasped and covered his face with both hands. "Noooo, that was so embarrassing!"

"I found it highly amusing."

"That's even worse!"

"It's the opposite of worse." I pulled his hands down so he had to look at me. "The more I know, the better."

As we gazed into each other's eyes, I noted how his rugged good looks were more enticing than ever. He had always been handsome, but it was nice to see recovering symmetry where it had been denied for so long. His stunted horn had caught up to the other, and the rest of his beard had filled in, so evening out his thick mane of raven hair was all that remained. It had already grown a few inches on the previously bare side.

He's striking, regardless.

My fingers rode the waves of his jagged clavicles as I leaned down and nosed his ear. "I want to learn everything that makes you shiver and moan… if you'll let me."

His hips shifted a little. "A-Apparently, your voice is enough."

"And we're just getting started. Speaking of my voice," I pressed a finger to his lips, "let me do the talking for now, but feel free to make as much wordless noise as you want." I kissed the indent at the base of his neck and smiled when he gasped softly. "I've always found it encouraging."

As I slowly kissed a line up his throat, he shifted his hips again and let slip a quiet whimper when I reached the sharp outline of his larynx.

"Let yourself go," I murmured, tilting my head and lightly sucking under the corner of his jaw. When I added my tongue and pressed it firmly against his warm skin, there was a wave of satisfaction when it drew a moan under his breath. "That's it…"

Gods, how I missed enjoying this.

Once I had thoroughly worked that spot, I held his face with one hand and planted the other where his neck met his shoulders. "Beg me to consume you." When his only response was lightheaded panting, I roughly dragged my thumb across his bottom lip. "Say you want it."

"Mmnnn—"

"With words."

"I-I want it—"

Without hesitation, I sank my fangs into the tender area below his jaw and inhaled his intoxicating blood as though I had been starved for weeks, springing my entire body to life with fervor I hadn't felt in centuries. *Invigorating* was an understatement.

As for Shade, the sudden puncturing of his skin drew a small yelp of pain that turned into a moan of pleasure. The apparent ecstasy was so intense that he arched his back off the bed and flexed his knees until both feet were sliding back and forth on the sheets. The chaotic sound of shifting fabric was quite amusing.

And reassuring.

I barely noticed when my thumb hooked itself in the corner of his mouth, but the faint whimper and violent shiver the gesture elicited were hard to miss.

Desire never tasted so good.

After indulging for at least a minute, I unclamped my jaw and let out a deep exhale of gratification while lapping up any stray blood on his skin. By the time I knelt upright, the two small wounds had already healed over.

That was even better than expected.

My racing heart left me feeling breathless, but because the latter was nothing I needed to worry about, I was easily distracted by the yearning pulse at the base of my abdomen.

Speaking of which—

I could feel Shade's arousal pressed against my backside.

Please be something I can manage—

Tucking a stray lock of hair behind my ear, I cranked my head around to see what had emerged. There was a thick, nine inches begging to be touched. It was bigger than most I had tended to, but a rare few had been even larger despite belonging to people much smaller than Shade. Considering his towering stature, I had feared he would be too much to handle. I was elated to discover that wasn't the case.

Perfect.

I turned back around so I could check on him. "Are you alright?"

He nodded and clapped a hand on his heaving chest. *"Phew...* Yeah." His eyes widened a bit. "This is a lot."

"We can slow down or stop if you want."

He smiled and shook his head. "It's a good *a lot.*"

I returned a smile. "I'm glad you're enjoying yourself."

"Are you having fun too?"

"Very much so."

He glanced at my bedside table. "Is it time for the bottle?"

"Not yet." Staying low, I shifted backward to feel his excitement slowly drag between my legs. Teasing him got the blush I wanted. "There's something I want to do first."

"A-Alright."

I lounged prone on his tail so my head was right next to his length. "Anything I should know before I continue?"

"What do you mean?"

"Is there anything you don't want me to do?"

"Oh. Uhh... Nothing comes to mind, so please do whatever you want."

"Gladly."

The moment I started stroking him, he dropped his head onto the pillow with a soft thud and let out a deep, elongated groan.

Off to a good start.

I watched my fingers stutter across his thick skin as it tugged and released from the friction. I made sure to be gentle. "How does it compare so far?"

"It's so much better when someone else is touching it."

"I'll be sure to leave a good impression until the end." Keeping my hand busy, I shifted until my lips hovered right over the tip. After leaving a few kisses, I took him in and pressed my tongue where the head met the shaft. I couldn't decide whose throbs were more enjoyable.

Shade draped one arm over his face as soon as I got to work. The muscles in his tail were already contracting from the stimulation, and it wasn't long before his heavy breathing turned into panting. Writhing hips soon followed.

Using his motion, I lowered my head until he slid down the back of my throat.

He sucked in a sharp breath. "F-Fuck—"

I paused for a moment but picked right back up when he groaned with need. His increasingly frequent gasps and moans were music to my ears, but I chose a pace of leisure to savor every inch of him.

I want him to watch.

There was a desperate throb as I released him and patted his hip. "Look at me."

He didn't seem to hear me at first. When he finally lowered his arm, it looked like he was lost in a haze of bliss and could barely keep his eyes open.

Good.

Our gazes held as I got back into my rhythm, but I could tell he was already getting close. His struggle to contain involuntary hip thrusts made it obvious. What he didn't bother stifling were the groans of pleasure reverberating throughout his entire body.

Don't hold back.

All of a sudden, he shivered and gripped my head with a trembling hand. "A-Athaeÿn, I—" Before he could finish his warning, he choked out an aching moan and was completely overtaken by an orgasm that made his body go rigid but sent the muscles near the base of his tail into a frenzy.

Yes—

I grunted as he pushed my head all the way down without warning, but my shock gave way to satisfaction when my throat received the pulsing flood it had been waiting for. Admittedly, it was handy to remain secured around him as long as I wanted without fear of suffocation.

Seems blood isn't his only good flavor.

Keeping a tight seal with my lips, I slowly lifted my head and only loosened my hold to leave a kiss on the tip.

Not a single drop wasted.

Meanwhile, Shade just lay there in a breathless daze. "Wow…"

I smirked and knelt upright. "So, my mouth versus your hand."

"Y-You win. No competition."

The only correct answer.

Still smiling to myself, I leaned forward a bit and caressed his thighs with both hands. "Should we take a break?"

He shook his head. "I want to make you feel good now."

"Are you sure?"

"Of course." With a slight grunt of effort, he pushed himself into a sitting position and pulled me into a loving embrace. "It's my turn to provide."

My more submissive side had me blushing and wrapping my arms around his neck before he even finished speaking. "I-I guess I can't argue with that."

He teased my hip with one claw and murmured against my cheek. "I need explicit consent from you as well."

Oh gods—

I dug my fingers into his muscular back. "I want you to take me."

P-Please—

He reassured me with a half-lidded smile. "Anything you wish."

I shivered with anticipation as he turned and laid me on my back in his previous spot.

Mmm, the sheets are still warm…

Overwhelmed by lust and driven by instinct, I crossed my arms above my head and bent one knee to obscure my hips. Shade had already seen everything, but I wanted him to unveil me this time.

He hummed with desire as he watched. "You really are stunning."

"You make me feel stunning."

I've never felt so treasured.

The unexpected wave of confidence was exhilarating. "Touch me however you want."

"But, I— Are you sure?"

"Yes. I want to feel how you look at me."

The worry in his eyes faded as a smile came to his face. "Just say the word, and I'll stop."

"Of course. I trust you wholeheartedly."

"Thank you."

I lay perfectly still but felt my heart racing as Shade's attentive gaze slowly drifted across my body. Patience had already given way to a longing ache, and my chest nearly caught fire when he gently pushed my knee aside to study the rest of me.

Using his thighs to spread my legs, he grinned and slowly dragged his claw in deliberately avoidant circles around what wanted to be touched most. His teasing had my knees shaking sooner than I cared to admit.

I need more—

Eventually, he pressed his thumbs into the soft indents along my hips and slid his hands up my sides. The meticulous pace he chose was torture. "You truly are the most beautiful man I've ever seen."

His breathless tone sent another shiver down my spine and left me trembling with need. By the time he eased to a stop under my shoulders and slipped his long fingers behind my back to lock me in place, my heart was threatening to beat out of my chest.

M-More—

As if reading my mind, he drew a soft gasp from my throat the moment his thumbs found and massaged my nipples. The delicate pressure had me quivering and whimpering in his grip, but I outright moaned when he leaned down and sealed his powerful lips over mine. I didn't bother trying to breathe. I didn't need air. I just needed him.

Still not enough—

The only thing more palpable than our shared desire was the heat between us, and his ample supply made up for any my body lacked. I didn't need the sun's warmth. I just needed Shade's arms around me.

Need... everything...

All of a sudden, he knelt upright and lifted me by my thighs until I dangled upside down with my hips just below his chin. I was caught off guard but looked up just in time to see a powerful tongue at least a foot long eagerly slither from his mouth and wrap around its prey like a boa constrictor.

Whoa—

His unique tongue and natural skill with it were news to me, but I certainly wasn't complaining. Quite the opposite, in fact.

G-Gods—

Each increasingly aggressive stroke summoned a moan of equal or greater magnitude. I was already a trembling mess, but when he suddenly took *everything* into his mouth, I nearly cried out in ecstasy.

Yes—!

Without warning, he abandoned my screaming arousal and left me gasping in shock.

Huh? Wait—

He just grinned and laid me back down as if nothing happened. "Bottle time?"

I-I... uhhh...

My head swam as I lay there panting heavily. Putting my hand on my chest did nothing to steady my frantic heartbeat.

Hold on, can't think—

Once I managed to settle down and clear my mind, a slightly unrelated thought occurred.

Actually...

I slowly looked up at him. "Would it be alright if we made a small detour?"

"Is something wrong?"

"No, no. Not at all." My hand drifted to my clavicles. "Can you... Can you touch my neck?"

He stared at me for a few seconds before lowering his gaze to my bite scars.

"You've been avoiding it on purpose, haven't you?"

"N-No. At least, I don't think so..." He blushed and twiddled his claws. "Maybe..."

I couldn't help but smile. "Thank you for being considerate."

He nodded a little and reinstated eye contact. "Are you sure you want me to?"

"I am. Do you not want the same?"

His blush deepened. "I want to touch *all* of you, but only if you're absolutely sure."

"I just said I was."

"I know, but…"

My gaze fell when he didn't finish his reply. "Roänach knew my neck was one of my favorite weaknesses. He did everything in his power to take that from me," I shook my head a little, "and not just with his bite of death."

But that was definitely the worst…

I looked into Shade's eyes with unexpected shyness. "I want to love what was lost, and when I feel vulnerable, when I *want* to feel vulnerable, I don't want to think about his fangs," my voice trembled as my fingers ghosted over the puncture marks, "I want to think about *you.*"

Please do this for me.

After a few seconds of stunned silence, he smiled and pulled me up to his chest.

I was surprised he hadn't just lowered himself onto me, but I gladly clung to him as he shifted into a sitting position and set me on his lap so we were face-to-face. It was difficult not to melt under the warmth of his loving gaze.

His smile lingered as he leaned his forehead against mine. "I know my touch won't erase what he did," he rested his hands on my shoulders and traced my jawline with his thumbs, "but if my love can stay with you in dreams, maybe it can banish nightmares."

I closed my eyes and took a shaky breath, but it wavered with desire rather than dread. There was nothing to fear when tucked away in Shade's arms.

It's the safest place in the whole world.

Eventually, his thumbs dipped lower to massage my delicate neck muscles, but he used the gentle touch of a lover's caress instead of the bruising force I was used to. His seamless movement continued down the front of my neck, across the divot at the base, and back up to my larynx, only to purposefully bypass it so I had to wait for more. The care in his gesture sent my heart reeling.

It's working—

He slipped his hands under my shoulders to mimic his earlier hold, but, this time, it was to lean me back so he had more room to tilt his head down. Before I knew what was happening, his lips found my right clavicle.

O-Oh gods—

My hands instinctively gripped his shoulders as he kissed a line up my throat. I kept it together at first, but when he circled back and finally gave my larynx the attention it craved, a desperate moan slipped out before I could contain it.

Don't stop—

Fortunately, he didn't, but I "thanked" him by accidentally digging my fingers even deeper into his shoulders.

S-Sorry.

As if hearing my silent apology, he reassured me with a quiet hum against my throat.

Good…

To my delight, his powerful tongue joined his lips in their relentless effort to devour me, making his consuming hunger all the more evident in every heaving breath. I couldn't get enough.

Finally, after all this time—

My eyes were still closed as I let flow a steady stream of moans and stuttered gasps. It was the only audible begging I could manage in my haze of rapture.

Keep going—

When I choked out a particularly embarrassing whimper, he pressed his face into the soft underside of my jaw with such fervor my head was forcibly tilted back, drawing a yelp of ecstasy from my already aching throat. It was the best kind of ache.

A-Ahh—

By now, my hips were writhing on his lap. Too much.

W-Wait—

I had gotten so worked up I didn't realize how close I was. Hoping to distract myself, I squeezed his midsection with my thighs and pulled him up into a normal kiss.

N-Not yet—

The delay was successful but left my legs shaking.

Phew…

We were both panting by the time he turned his head to speak. "Everything alright?"

My aching throat tightened. "Better than you could ever know."

Thank you, Shade.

He just smiled and pulled me into another kiss.

And now, I need all of you.

I pressed my hips forward to feel his desire. There was a lot of it. "Okay," I grinned against his lips, "it's finally time for the bottle."

"It *has* been waiting rather patiently."

He laid me back down and poured some of the slippery contents into his hand. It was amusing to watch him gawk at the foreign substance and repeatedly touch his fingers together to make glistening strands.

I probably did the same my first time.

My gaze fell to his arousal. "I look forward to where you take us, but I would appreciate a little more warming up before the main event."

He lowered himself until his face hovered right over mine. "Already on it." After a minute or two of rhythmic pressure, he carefully introduced the tip of his middle claw and slipped his tongue into my mouth to stifle the noise we both knew was coming.

Sure enough, I let out a muffled whimper. There was the occasional grunt as his thick finger slowly worked its way deeper and deeper, but relaxing came more easily when his lips found mine and kept my thoughts occupied. Before I knew it, his knuckle made contact.

Fuck—

"Are you alright?"

I nodded as my hands uselessly fumbled against the headboard for something to hold on to. "Wh-What happened to your nerves?"

"Your presence is soothing," his claw ghosted over an incredibly sensitive area that had me squirming, "and I guess making you feel good is another inherent ability."

"Y-You have no right being this perfect—"

"I can be as perfect as I want," he continued massaging the same spot and smirked when I gasped and started thrashing his sides with my knees, "especially if it means pleasing you."

The only response I could manage was a deep, guttural moan.

Can't wait any longer—

My hips were trembling by the time I flung my arms around his neck. "I need you to fuck me right now."

His grin widened as he slowly withdrew his finger. "Your wish is my command." He retrieved the bottle and applied generous lubrication to both of us. "I'll try to be gentle."

"To start, and then I want you to break me."

He looked a bit surprised but didn't argue as he settled over me again and slowly pressed forward. Our gazes were locked when the first few inches finally sank in, but he hesitated when I grunted softly and closed my eyes. "You okay?"

I nodded and exhaled deeply.

There was a brief pause before his gentle momentum resumed. This time, he didn't bother stifling his groans of pleasure.

My hips continuously writhed from the intrusion, but, despite some minor discomfort, I was able to let him in with relative ease. Still, every inch demanded attention, and my chest was heaving by the time our pelvises met. Other than the occasional shiver of bliss, I lay motionless to revel in his fierce throbbing.

I-It's so much—

Meanwhile, Shade braced himself on his forearms and let out a comically long breath. "Fuck, that feels good…"

I grinned and reopened my eyes. "Everything you hoped for?"

"And then some, but loving you is still the best part."

Shade—

He locked me in a passionate kiss before I could reply.

Gods, I love this.

My legs were already shaking when they wrapped around his waist. The harder his bulk pressed me into the mattress, the deeper I sank into my sea of euphoria, but my mind was swept away when he fell into a slow thrusting rhythm. We moved as one body.

Yesss—

He started panting into my mouth. "Hypocrite."

"Wh-What?"

His head dropped next to mine on the pillow. "You're far more perfect than I am."

I couldn't form a single coherent thought, let alone string together a sentence, so I just leaned my head on his and let the compliment hang in the air. Our hips still had yet to separate.

Don't stop—

My eyes were barely open by the time his pace quickened, but they eventually rolled back when our lovemaking became wild fucking.

P-Please don't stop—

His violent thrusting sent me into a frenzy of moans and sharp gasps. It felt like the world around us had fallen away, and I clung to him so desperately my fingernails nearly drew blood. I swore my entire being was trying to merge with his.

G-Gods y-y-yesss—

It was now my turn to beg. "Sh-Shade, I w-want— I-I want it. Pl-Please—"

"It's yours."

I beat him to it and cried out with an explosive surge of ecstasy, losing all control as my knees spasmed and my body jolted sharply against his chest. The pulsing ache between my legs finally found its long-awaited release.

Shade followed suit with a muffled groan into my neck. Tangling his fingers in my hair, he sank as deep as possible and flooded me with a powerful torrent of heat that left him twitching and whimpering. If he wanted to weigh me down in multiple ways, he had succeeded.

Mmmmmnnnn…

We both went limp at the same time.

That was also worth the wait.

My chest was still heaving when I turned my head and smiled at him. "That was breathtaking, if I do say so myself."

"I second that." He returned a smile and caressed my cheek with his thumb. "I'm glad we finally talked about this."

"Agreed. From now on, please speak up if something's on your mind."

"That goes for you too."

"Of course." I kissed him softly. "I love you, Shade."

"And I love you, Athaeÿn."

End.

Thank you for reading
♡Alden Drake

Author Bio

Alden Drake, whose super real name is totally, one hundred percent on his birth certificate and definitely not a pen name he made up after three hours of googling "A-Z baby names," is a brand-new author in the world of *actually publishing things* instead of just writing gay fanfiction on AO3. (He'll probably still write gay fanfiction on AO3.)

Halfway down the Garden State, Alden spends most of his time writing; drawing; gaming; petting his cats, who act like being held like the babies they are is a personal attack; and trying new recipes (usually messing up, even with very specific directions) in the kitchen with his mom, whom he loves dearly and considers his greatest role model.

Soul of Solace is Alden's debut novel, but he already has ideas for future books. Yes, they will also be gay (primarily, but also just queer in general) fantasy romance. No, he has not strayed far from the gay fanfiction. It always comes back to the gay fanfiction with this guy.

Alden just hopes readers enjoy and/or find meaningful things in his work, as it means a lot to him too. He drew lots of pictures to prove it.